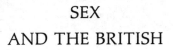

SEX
AND THE BRITISH

SEX
AND THE BRITISH

A Twentieth-Century
History

PAUL FERRIS

MICHAEL JOSEPH
LONDON

MICHAEL JOSEPH LTD

Published by the Penguin Group
Penguin Books Ltd, 27 Wrights Lane, London w8 5tz, England
Penguin Books USA Inc., 375 Hudson Street, New York, New York 10014, USA
Penguin Books Australia Ltd, Ringwood, Victoria, Australia
Penguin Books Canada Ltd, 10 Alcorn Avenue, Toronto, Ontario, Canada m4v 3b2
Penguin Books (NZ) Ltd, 182–190 Wairau Road, Auckland 10, New Zealand

Penguin Books Ltd, Registered Offices: Harmondsworth, Middlesex, England

First published February 1993
Second impression March 1993

Copyright © Paul Ferris 1993

Typeset by Datix International Limited, Bungay, Suffolk
Set in 11½/13½ pt Palatino
Printed in England by Clays Ltd, St Ives plc

A CIP catalogue record for this book is available from the British Library
ISBN 0 7181 3141 X

The moral right of the author has been asserted

In memory of my parents
Frederick and Olga

Contents

❧⊸∘⊱❧

Acknowledgements

THE London Library, Brecon Public Library, the British Library, the Newspaper Library at Colindale, the Public Record Office and Westminster Reference Library were my main suppliers of miscellaneous reading, and I am grateful to their staffs for so much patience and expertise. Also to Bob Jenkins of Arrow Books, Kington, Powys.

I am indebted to many others at libraries and institutions: Mark Jones, BBC Recorded Programmes Library; BBC Written Archives; James Ferman, British Board of Film Classification; Colin Shaw, Broadcasting Standards Council; Nigel Williams and Rob Parsons, Christian Action, Research & Education (CARE); Channel 4 Television; Capts. Gordon Kitney and John Smith, Church Army; Stuart Orr, Crown Prosecution Service; Doreen Massey and Barbara Kenmare, Family Planning Association; Malcolm Wicks and Katherine Kiernan, Family Policy Studies Centre; David Duggan, Fawcett Library, City of London Polytechnic; Lynda Finn, Health Education Authority; Jane Hardy Smith, *Health & Efficiency*; H.M. Customs & Excise; Imperial War Museum; London Brook Advisory Centres; London Metropolitan Police; Ian Franks and Elaine Edwards, London Rubber Industries; Dorothy Sheridan, the Tom Harrisson Mass-Observation Archive, University of Sussex Library; National Council for One Parent Families; Richard Whitfield, National Family Trust; Jeff Care, the *Observer* library; Office of Population Censuses and Surveys; Penny Mansfield, One Plus One; Zelda West-Meads and Renate Olins, Relate; R. Hardy, Royal Commonwealth Society Library; D.W.C. Stewart and Robert Greenwood, Royal Society of Medicine Library; Stranraer Library; Swansea Reference Library; Tavistock Institute; Television History Centre; Terence Higgins Trust; Robin Price and Lesley A. Hall, Wellcome Institute for the History of Medicine.

Others to whom I'm grateful include: Leo Abse, Roger Baker, the late Sir Cyril Black, Sheila Boswell, Anthony Bush, John Calder, William

Camp, Edward Chesser, Martin Cole, Richard Davenport-Hines, Peter Diggory, Udi Eichler, Norman Fairfax, Charlie Geerts, Ted Goodman, Chris Gosselin, Anthony Howard, Lord Hutchinson, Robin Johnson, Ossian Jones, Peter Kay, Lawrence Kershen, Carol Lee, Peter McDougall, John McGarry, Jill Mindham, Brenda Maddox, Pamela Morris, Diane Munday, Tuppy Owens, Freda Parker, Candida Royalle, Julian Reindorp, Geoffrey Robertson, Peter T. Scott, Linda Semple, Alastair Service, John Silverlight, Carl Snitcher, David Sullivan, Liz Swinden, William Thompson, Graham Watson, David Webb, Kaye Wellings, Donald West.

A number of people are not acknowledged at all. They include a magistrate, some police officers and others of impeccable reputation who think it wiser to keep a low profile, and who may be right. I thank all the Anons, especially 'Harry', a special case, who knows how important his diaries have been.

Interviews and conversations going back over many years have been made use of, but there were too many of them, and it was too long ago, to identify more than a few in the Notes. I am grateful to those who talked to me in the past, even if, which is likely, they have forgotten they ever did.

I would like to thank Faber & Faber Ltd for permission to reproduce the following extracts from copyright poetry: 'Whitsun Weddings' from Complete Poems by Philip Larkin, edited by Anthony Thwaite; 'Les Sylphides' from The Collected Poems of Louis MacNeice, edited by E.R. Dodds; 'The Monogamous Union' from Serious Concerns by Wendy Cope.

Copyright Mass-Observation material is quoted by permission of the Trustees of the Mass-Observation Archive, reproduced by permission of Curtis Brown Ltd, London.

If this book were not dedicated to my parents, it would be to Mary, whose advice throughout, together with her indexing and proof-reading, I acknowledge gratefully.

Introduction

❧◦❧

THIS ATTEMPT TO WRITE a narrative of sexual life in Britain since 1900 is as honest as I can make it, which may not be saying much. We are all imprisoned by our personal experiences of sex, about which most of us are understandably reticent in public. If I say that mine are heterosexual and unremarkable, it is as far as most people would want to go, unless we all went in for self-revelation: moralistic Members of Parliament and the editors of tabloid newspapers included.

What I couldn't pretend is that I find the subject of sex anything but enthralling. One encounters among men (less often women) a tone of superiority, no doubt self-protective, towards our sexual antics. It can often be sighted in articles and reviews, when pornography – which has replaced prostitution as the favourite object of distaste – is mentioned. 'Frankly,' the writer will declare, 'I was bored.' But one finds (frankly) that most people, when shown a piece of pornography in private, are curious, amused, alarmed or disgusted, not to mention interested; they are rarely bored. Boredom, however, is the safe response. While saving the writer from any suspicion of prudery, it keeps the material at a distance. Also useful for distancing purposes is an affected ignorance. Lord Snow, C. P. Snow the novelist, once remarked in the House of Lords that to hear his colleagues you would think they had never met any homosexuals, who were apparently 'something strange, like the white rhinoceros.'

Sex has had a good run for its money this century. Furious public debates about morals, censorship and misbehaviour were inevitable, seeing that no society has ever felt free to leave sex alone for individuals to enjoy. Pleasure is too persuasive; it smells of anarchy. But as soon as unthinkable behaviour was discussed, it ceased to be unthinkable. People began to make up their own minds. They won a sort of victory. The censorious society faltered in the sixties. Some pretences were got rid of. Irreversible benefits – one hopes they are irreversible – came from women's control of their fertility. As contraception became acceptable, the laws on abortion and divorce were being re-examined and relaxed. The unmarried came to live together, uncensured. All these changes were driven by people's wishes, against the bias of the State, as they moved falteringly away from sex as sin towards what the poets and the affluent always knew, that sex was a mixture of pleasure and distress.

The British altered their ways, though they had largely ignored the creeds of sexual radicals in the sixties. Feelings about 'taste' and 'decency' still run deep, and the old intolerances are easily aroused. There is an understandable vein of scepticism about sexual progress; for millions of commonplace lives, sex still finds the same raw nerves and hopeless dreams. In theory we have all been liberated by a freedom unthought of fifty years ago. In practice our experience of sex can be as difficult as ever, reminding people how vulnerable they are. Throughout the century authoritarians have been able to hypnotize us with their programmes for confining the so-called beast that lurks in the flesh, and entrepreneurs have been able to make money by doing the opposite and exploiting our desires.

All this has produced lasting conflict among interested parties. Some of it is scandalous, some absurd and hypocritical; most of it has comic potential. This is just as well for ordinary citizens, who might find the system unbearable if they couldn't laugh sometimes at its merchandisers, its moralists, its policemen; and themselves.

Those who want an account of the sexual evils that are supposed to be typical of our time, the rape and sexual abuse that are reported daily, must look elsewhere. Sexual crime is another subject, and I leave it to the criminologists. It is not clear how much of the evil is new, and how much happened in the past but went unreported. In any case, sexual freedom is not, for most people, a licence for wrongdoing. It is their non-violent lives I have tried to address.

As an epigraph for the book I thought to use some lines of Meredith, from his poem 'Love in the Valley'. I didn't, because they are about romantic love rather than sex, and that would be a different book. In an ideal world, or an ideal book, the two might be inextricable. That they are so obviously extricable is one of the problems. The lines are:

> Had I the heart to slide an arm beneath her,
>   Press her parting lips as her waist I gather slow,
>   Waking in amazement she could not but embrace me:
>   Then would she hold me and never let me go?

1

'Intimest Details'

The New Agenda

IN A COUNTRY LIKE Britain where puritan values still hover behind our lives, the sexual past is made to seem bleak and uninviting. The wealthy could indulge themselves; the poor coupled in haste and didn't brood on the erotic side of life, any more than they brooded on the pleasures of food. Perhaps we patronize our ancestors. When it came to sex behind closed doors, there must always have been those who found more in the act than just a moment's pleasure. But only the faintest echoes can now be heard of what 'ordinary people' felt.

Before the 1980s, no one in radio or television was bold enough to coax frank sexual reminiscence from old codgers, and by then it was almost too late to catch living memories from the early years of this century. Written records can be found here and there, the memories usually negative. An osteopath, born 1899:

> My grandfather strongly disapproved of my mother having any female underwear on the airing rack before we lads went to bed. In consequence ladies' undies were, to us, wrapped in a fascinating mystery.

A housewife, born 1897:

> My husband accused me of being 'cold' but little knew the passionate longings I experienced if only he had made love to me instead of using me . . . Now, at fifty-two, I feel that the whole business is nature's great joke, of which we are the victims.

A woman teacher, born 1890, writing when she was forty-nine:

> Our great horror was to be regarded as 'fast'. The 'glad eye' was not funny. Visiting a WC when a male – brother, fiancé or stranger – was about was iniquitous. In 1911 when out with my future husband, I

asked to be excused, and for days after wondered, nay, even inquired, if he 'still respected me'.

Sometimes the reminiscence shows people escaping from the conventions as we assume them to have been. Tabitha John, born into a respectable working-class family in the tinplate town of Llanelli in 1893, was allowed to have a boy-friend before she was fifteen; although to begin with her mother slapped her and said, 'I'll give you boys!' Tom was years older than Tabitha. But his father had been a deacon in the chapel, he was persistent and well-spoken, and their friendship was eventually approved of. When Tabitha was sixteen, Tom got her mother's permission for them to go on holiday to the village of St Clears. It was 1910. Jack, a friend of Tom, was also there, with his own girl, the girls sharing one bedroom at the boarding house, the boys another. For four nights everyone behaved themselves. On the fifth night Tabitha was in her nightie when Jack appeared and told her to join Tom. The other couple had planned it, as Tabitha wrote when she was in her eighties:

> Very shy, I went into Tom's bedroom, Tom looked stupefied, as he expected Jack back from the toilet. I stood behind the door crying, I was so very young. Tom came over to comfort me and said not to make a bother, as I wanted to go downstairs to call the landlady. He said, 'Come to bed, I've promised your mother to look after you, and I'll keep that promise.' He cuddled me just like a child.

She married him a few years later.

Mostly it is reports of mistakes and accidents that survive, not of the demand for pleasure that gave rise to them. The history of sex is written from the point of view of what went wrong, not of how much people enjoyed it. Pleasure has to be glimpsed between the lines: 'Immoral relations before marriage are not unusual and are indulgently regarded' (Charles Booth, 1903, on the London poor), or 'Girls do not seem to suffer in self-respect nor greatly in the esteem of others, if they yield themselves to the lad who is the sweetheart of the time' (James Devon, 1912, on the Glasgow poor). It is the suffering that is spelt out. Letters written to Marie Stopes, the birth-controller and eccentric, survive as reminders:

> What I would like to know is how I can save having any more children as I think that I have done my duty to my country having had 13

children, 9 boys and 4 girls. I have 6 boys alive now and 1 little girl who will be 3 years old in May. I burried a dear little baby girl 3 weeks ago who died from the strain of whooping cough the reason I rite this his I cannot look after the little ones like I would like to as I am getting very stout and cannot bend to bath them and it do jest kill me to carry them in the shawl . . .

She had been married at the age of nineteen, '20 years come next Thursday', and you realize with a shock that when she wrote to Stopes she was still only thirty-nine.

The Christian religion, always dreaming of spiritual perfection at the expense of the flesh, had been on the offensive in Victorian Britain. The great society that was taking shape must soar above materialism. Pleasure was dangerous. Administrators, too, liked the idea that the British were exemplary in matters of sex. Morality suited the rulers' taste for discipline and order, as well as enhancing their sense of Imperial apartness from a world full of loose-living foreigners. The British were different, the conquerors (over the previous century and a half) of an Empire that contained a fifth of the human race.* Perhaps the rulers believed the myth of British pre-eminence; certainly they made the most of it while they could.

But self-satisfaction was being undermined. By the turn of the century, intellectuals were responding to unsettling ideas in psychology, in medicine and in literature, and had begun to look more sceptically at human behaviour. Along with everything else, sex came under scrutiny: at first its deviant, medical or criminal side. The sick could be contained; they were a safer subject than behaviour in ordinary bedrooms. The idea of dwelling in detail on ordinary sexual lives would have seemed outrageous, likely to end in tears. (Ninety years later we have learned to dwell on sex, and take for granted the tears that go with our new-found freedom.)

A foreign bounder, the Viennese psychiatrist Richard Krafft-Ebing (1840–1902), wrote a book on sexual aberration, in its tenth edition by

---

* A *Coronation Guide* for those visiting London in 1901 to see King Edward VII crowned told them that the Empire was 'fifty-three times the size of France, fifty-two times the size of Germany, three-and-a-half times the size of the United States . . .'

1899, which had reached the shores of Britain, though only just. On no account would the publishers sell it to anyone but a doctor or a lawyer; as an additional safeguard, some of it was in Latin, so that an uneducated reader would encounter words like *libido sexualis* and *frigiditas uxoris*. For the first time, sexual eccentricities were described in detail in a few hundred case histories: the engineer who loved slaughter-houses, the cobbler who stole women's clothes, the woman who thought she was a man, the merchant obsessed with self-abuse. All were lumped together as patients in need of treatment. Reviewing it, the *British Medical Journal* was in such a frenzy at the 'nauseous detail', it suggested the book be used as toilet paper ('put to the most ignominious use to which paper can be applied').

Nearer home, and perceived as more dangerous to the state of the nation, were the writings of Havelock Ellis. Ellis, born near London in 1859, was a doctor who made his career as a writer, with sex as his principal subject. Since the 1890s he had been at work on a series of books called *Studies in the Psychology of Sex*. Like many radicals in sexual matters, Ellis' interests were driven by the peculiar clockwork of his own nature. A gentle, rather stately figure, he was attracted to women but for most of his life confined himself to manual lovemaking. His greatest pleasure was to see his lover urinate, a function that he endowed with mystical qualities. When he got married, it was to a woman with strong lesbian characteristics.

From these difficult ingredients Ellis made a satisfactory life, helped by being able to shed his quirks in print among a thousand other stories of 'sexual anomaly', to use his neutral phrase. For many years, only one part of the *Studies*, which eventually ran to seven volumes, was published in Britain, and that was quickly suppressed. It dealt with homosexuality, and had first appeared in Germany, a country with an active – many Englishmen would have said, a disgusting – interest in sex. For publication in Britain, in 1897, Ellis naïvely turned to a Dr Roland de Villiers, one of whose imprints was the University Press of Watford. There was no university at Watford, a trifle that Villiers explained away by saying that the printing plant was there, and the books appealed to universities.

Villiers was an early exponent of the publishing principle that a risky book, when presented as a scientific work, may avoid prosecution, while commanding a good sale because of its riskiness. Ellis' *Sexual Inversion* was a genuine study, but it was worth money to a publisher who could exploit its added value.

This time Villiers came to grief. His timing was wrong: it was only two years since Oscar Wilde had been gaoled. The police prosecuted a bookseller, ostensibly because he was selling *Sexual Inversion*, really because he had anarchist connections that bothered the authorities. Ellis was unable to defend himself in court because he was not the subject of the charge. Villiers absconded, the bookseller pleaded guilty to obscene publication, and the judge described the work as 'a pretence and a sham'. Ellis was driven to publish the rest of the series in America – not that America was any less prudish than Britain, but the medical overtones proved sufficient to protect it there.

As for Villiers, the police caught up with him in 1901, when Inspector Arrow of the Yard, who specialized in pornography, raided a house in Cambridge and seized quantities of forbidden books, among them *Sexual Inversion*. Villiers, who now called himself Roland, was found hiding in the loft. He died an hour later, either of apoplexy or by poison concealed in a ring – there were conflicting stories. His real name was von Weissenfeld; the public was not surprised to learn he was German.

Like Krafft-Ebing, though with more elegance and a wider range, Ellis based his work on tales of the unexpected. It has come to be regarded as a brilliant curiosity, describing the absurd, the sad and the unpleasant with a steady candour that puts the forgotten judge's 'pretence and a sham' to shame. The books became first a revelation and then a monumental reminder that the lives of 'ordinary people' had room for private fantasy and behaviour to a degree unadmitted by most Britons then, and many Britons still. The stories, or rather the habit of candour that they stood for, seeped into the public consciousness over decades – the government official whose first sexual encounter was on a staircase with a woman who had a creaking shoe, so that ever after he sought out women similarly shod; the lecturer who found sexual pleasure from burning his skin with hot wires; the boy of fifteen whose list of things that excited him included flies coupling, reports of girls saved by men from drowning, dresses that buttoned from top to bottom, statues of bare-breasted women, and a woman shot out of a cannon in a circus. The oddity, the sadness, endure. 'I knew a lady who in old age still treasured in her desk, as the one relic of the only man she had ever been attracted to, a fragment of paper he had casually twisted up in a conversation with her half a century before.' Ellis sets it all down with the neatness of a butterfly-collector. 'I am informed by a gentleman who is a recognized authority on goats, that they sometimes take the penis into the mouth and produce actual orgasm, thus practising auto-fellatio.' He never smiles.

None of the sauciness in his anecdotes would have surprised those educated Edwardians who went in for pornography. The acceptable response to indecent material then was to find it 'shocking', rather as today it has to be dismissed as 'boring'. Others quietly enjoyed it; no doubt the categories of shock and enjoyment overlapped. In the second half of the nineteenth century, pornography had flourished with the advent of cheap printing and picture-reproduction. Speeches about the 'rising tide of filth' were already heard in the 1880s. Cab-loads of seized material were taken from erring booksellers. Conrad has such a character in his novel *The Secret Agent* (1907), with a shop in Soho that sells 'books with titles hinting at impropriety' and 'closed yellow paper envelopes, very flimsy . . . marked two and six in heavy black figures.' This is more than five pounds in modern currency, and is unlikely to have been value for money. A Blackpool street-seller was fined in 1902 for selling packets at around the same price. They contained photographs of nude statues.

The real stuff, as collected by gentlemen, is easily identified by the prices charged. There was never any doubt about the willingness to pay for solitary pleasure. Paris was the centre of the trade. English-language catalogues printed there around 1900 offer books by mail order costing more than a workman earned in a week. *Suburban Souls*, 'The Erotic Psychology of a Man and a Maid', is listed at four guineas, not far short of £200 in today's money. Three guineas, cash with order, bought *The Horn Book*, much of it taken up with Postures ('The Ordinary . . . Ordinary with Legs Up . . . The Wheelbarrow'). For two guineas, *Genital Laws* would be on its way across the Channel under plain cover, allegedly a medical study by 'Dr Jacobus X, French Army surgeon', which, in the 'University Press' tradition, declared it was 'not meant for common folk. The man in the street will not understand it'. The mock-heroic language of the brochures was designed, perhaps, to make it all sound a jolly conspiracy: 'I address you, young man, whose tool stands up . . .' All the leading deviations were catered for, notably flagellation; nor was Havelock Ellis' obscurer taste forgotten. One of the books available may even have been written by him, the notorious *Gynecocracy* (1893), a masochist's tale whose author was certainly not 'Julian Robinson, Viscount Ladywood'. The moral reformers who fought pornography paid more attention to the cheap end of the market, the packets and postcards on sale at street corners; they could do little about gentlemen's erotica.

Photographs were available in albums at a pound or so apiece. Translators had done their best: 'The sexes are very apparent and the couplings are admirably obscene. It is the high fife lust, surprised in the moments of sexual depravations.' Or, 'Sexual Parts. This series is realistic without saying. It shows the intimest details of pretty women's paradies where to men like to enter for love or for money. These parts have specially been focused by the operator.' Alone with their purchases, flushed citizens in Clapham and Crewe turned up the gas to examine pretty women's paradieses in peace.

Nor was high society much of a target for reformers in Edwardian Britain. Discreet liaisons were rarely punctured by publicity, apart from a trickle of disclosures, usually via divorce cases. In the late nineteenth century a Member of Parliament's wife ran off with the Marquess of Waterford; Lord Colin Campbell married a Gertrude Blood and gave her syphilis; Sir Charles Dilke and Charles Stewart Parnell, both MPs, were cited as co-respondents in divorce actions (and were politically ruined as a result). Privilege encouraged sexual licence, if the privileged were that way inclined. Period pornography was sprinkled with titles, as in *The Pearl*, the notorious late-Victorian magazine ('At last the Honble. Miss Vavasour stumbled over a prostrate gentleman, who happened to be the young Marquis of Bucktown, who . . .').

The country-house circuit encouraged liaisons. The romantic novelist Elinor Glyn was taken up, as a young married woman, by Frances, Lady Warwick, and saw the discreet goings-on at close quarters. Adultery was the approved activity: sex before marriage, though commonplace among the poor, was an abomination, unless it was sex with a prostitute, which was generally all right. 'In England as in France,' wrote Glyn, 'in the society set every married woman was considered fair game, the assumption being that if the husband did not look after her that was his fault.' She didn't add that two years after her own marriage, she and her husband were among the guests at Warwick Castle when their host, known as 'Brookie', molested her in the rose-garden. (Hoping to make Mr Glyn jealous, she told him about it as they were dressing for dinner. 'Good old Brookie!' he said, and went on tying his tie.) J.B. Priestley wrote about women of the nineteen-hundreds encased in clothes that incited one to take them off, duly lusted after by men 'crammed with all that Edwardian food and inflamed by all its drink' as they advanced on bedroom doors, behind which lurked 'the delicious creature, with heroic bared bosom and those great marmoreal thighs' – 'or so,' Priestley adds, disappointingly, 'I suspect.'

Many well-bred men visited prostitutes as a matter of course. Rosa

Lewis (b. 1867), proprietress of the Cavendish Hotel, and known as 'the Duchess of Jermyn Street', grew famous as an operative on the edge of high society who provided services and kept her mouth shut. An undertaker's daughter from Essex, she got a foot on the ladder through an uncle who knew the chef to a French countess. She became a professional cook to the aristocracy, and in 1893 apparently agreed to an arranged marriage with a butler, so that they could provide a 'front' at a house of convenience that the Prince of Wales used for sexual assignations in Eaton Terrace. Her heyday was in Edwardian London. In 1902 she bought the Cavendish, which flourished because of her character and her connections. Her conversation was said to be 'pungent and spiced with references to tarts, backsides and chamber pots.' Most of the hotel's services were above board, but in the First World War she certainly procured women for officers on leave ('a nice clean tart, dear' was her prescription), and it is reasonable to assume she procured for others as well. She may have had a measure of police protection. She knew Piccadilly prostitutes, one of whom, a madam called Queenie Gerald, tried to use her name when she was in trouble; though without success. There is a persuasive story that in her prime, Lewis used to supply women, doubtless 'nice clean tarts', for the sexual initiation of well-born young men.

Whatever their class, men were beasts. Everyone knew it. Ever since the purity campaigns of the 1880s, the shortcomings of the flesh had been vigorously preached at. The campaigns were still recent events. Who could forget how the journalist W.T. Stead, with the Salvation Army at his side, had used the reputable *Pall Mall Gazette* to expose the trade in child-virgins procured by London madams? The clever Stead was a Congregational minister's son. Fascinated by prostitutes, he perfected the hectoring newspaper exposé that shakes its fist at prurience while ensuring a demand for extra copies. The virgin-trade undoubtedly existed; whether it did so on the scale implied is less certain. The row, in 1885, was tremendous, and made it impossible for Parliament to resist passing an Act, long delayed, that raised the age of sexual consent from thirteen to sixteen, where it has remained. In this and other agitations, advocates of purity organized themselves with offices and news-sheets, and tasted power.

For the clergy it was plain sailing. 'Make the good in you to keep down the beast,' declared the bachelor Bishop of London, Arthur Winnington-Ingram, at a 'Great Purity Meeting' at Clerkenwell, in the winter of 1906. Appointed to the see a few years earlier, when he was forty-three, he was still there, hoping for better things from his diocese, when he was eighty.

It was natural for the Church to exercise authority. In 1904 there were complaints about a play at Wyndham's Theatre by Arthur Pinero, *A Wife Without a Smile*, in which 'a doll suspended from the ceiling was agitated in a suggestive manner.' As chairman of the Public Morality Council, a London group of few members but important connections that drew in Roman Catholics as well as nonconformists, Ingram appealed to the Lord Chamberlain, official censor of the theatre. London, he confided, one Lord to another, must be relieved of 'what many feel to be a degrading spectacle.' The play was withdrawn.

The issue was simple. God must be revered. 'Without reverence,' wrote the Revd J.B.S. Watson, 'the rudder of life is lost.' Watson, the prison chaplain at Brixton, was writing about the formation of character. He quoted Tennyson, late poet laureate: 'Man, if he keep not a reverential look upward, no matter how much he knows and does, is only the subtlest beast of the field.' All this was received wisdom down at the National Vigilance Association, founded 1885, and by the twentieth century immensely influential in the morality business. Christian teaching, still dominant in daily life, held that sex interfered with man's real vocation, which was to seek perfection of the spirit. Rationalist and materialist might argue otherwise; they were only flashes in the pan. The NVA was staffed by practical men and women who had ways of keeping moral delinquents in line.

At its headquarters, eventually in the Strand, the general secretary, William Coote, raised money, processed information and exposed vice. Coote, converted by reading a religious tract at sixteen, was a newspaper compositor, by then in his forties, when he was caught up in the rapturous crusades of 1885. W.T. Stead, who was putting together the NVA, decided that the obscure Coote should run it, which he did successfully for more than thirty years.

It was or should have been a question of keeping down the beast rather than eliminating him. As the Bishop of Stepney told the Pan-Anglican Congress of 1908, 'social purity is the arena in which the Church makes its challenge to the standard of the world. It is the scene of the primary battle between the spirit and the flesh.' The bishop was fighting battles; winning the war would have to wait for Armageddon. Not all were so modest. The Edwardian educated classes were optimists.

With the Fabians peddling their man-made, socialistic solutions to society, Christian morality had to keep its end up. Another bishop, of Rochester, declared that people should not think that immoral tendencies were a permanent feature: 'if that sentiment gets hold of any mind, it is paralysing to the humanizing forces.'

There was no shortage of immoral tendencies to stamp out. Paragraphs in local newspapers add up the wages of sin. Suicide by pregnant girls, often servants cut off from home and friends, was not uncommon. Corpses of new-born babies turned up in drains, ditches, ponds, back lanes, mine-workings, hayricks; sometimes naked, sometimes neatly parcelled. 'Bastardy order' cases, where unmarried women who were bold enough took fathers of children to court to make them pay maintenance, were well reported.

> The rose is red and the violets blue
> Like honey is sweet and so are you;
> And so is he that sends you this,
> And when we meet we'll have a kiss,
> And when we part we'll have another.
> That is the way to love each other

wrote an Aaron Griffiths to a Mary Jane, whose solicitor read the letter in court, to general amusement, when she accused him of giving her a child (1905). Her stepfather 'gave evidence to the effect that he had seen the defendant with his arm round the applicant's neck on several occasions.' She got an order for half a crown a week, about five pounds today.

There was less illegitimacy than fifty years earlier, though how much of this decrease (if any of it) was due to better morals is uncertain. The birth rate was falling fast by 1900, a matter that demographers still argue about. One factor must have been a wider use of birth control, if only of a primitive kind. Contraception, like other good things, was available to the upper classes generations before it reached the poor. A locked despatch case from the muniment room of an English country house was examined in modern times and found to contain condoms, made of animal membranes stitched with cotton, kept in packets of eight, probably dating from the late eighteenth century. By the early twentieth century, small manufacturers and importers of 'rubber goods' were learning there was money in birth control. The middle classes had begun to discover it, the better-educated workers were close behind. Brave spirits among the unmarried would have known where to go, too.

On the darker side of birth control lay the induced miscarriage, attempted each year by unknown numbers of women, married and single, with an unknown degree of success. Abortion was a subject too horrid to mention. A blind eye was turned to self-help among the pregnant, who relied on traditional means (scalding hot baths, if you had a bath, gin, jumping off chairs), together with a range of folk remedies. These included gunpowder mixed with margarine, water in which copper coins had been boiled and purgatives.

Women often made themselves ill. If they were lucky they miscarried as well; if they were unlucky they died. In Sheffield, an outbreak of lead poisoning when the water supply became contaminated was observed to cause pregnant women to abort. This made lead a popular remedy. It could be obtained from a compound, diachylon, found in a plaster used to dress wounds. Soon women were scraping off the diachylon and eating it. Chemists sold diachylon pills for years until eventually (in 1917) it was put on the poison list.

Commercial medicines with time-honoured ingredients like aloes, slippery elm and penny-royal did good business, now that there was a mass readership for advertisements in newspapers. These often purported to come from reliable-sounding women with titles like 'Nurse', 'Madame' and 'Widow'. They spoke of 'irregularities' and 'unusual delays', of relieving 'distressing symptoms' and of achieving the 'desired result'. This was all part of the tradition by which women excused the practices as being designed merely to 'bring on the period'.

Caught between morality and the law on the one hand and unscrupulous operators on the other, women with unwanted pregnancies have always been especially vulnerable; time soon runs out. In a lurid episode at the end of the nineteenth century, three London brothers called Chrimes, who had already duped ten thousand women by selling them useless pink and blue pills for 'female complaints', tried to blackmail them by letter for having attempted to 'commit the fearful crime of abortion'. The brothers were caught and gaoled, but not before nearly three thousand women had replied, some sending the two guineas that was demanded, others pleading for mercy – 'I should not like my missus to know, else I shall lose my situation,' and 'I will promise that I will never do wrong any more, for Christ's sake. Amen.'

Many women, more than the authorities cared to think about or investigate, used the services of semi-professional abortionists – retired midwives and the like who employed douches of soapy water and worse. The medical profession thought these interventions disgraceful, while ignoring the reality of the need that drove women to them. Quacks and abortionists were beyond the pale, with the exception of those members of the profession who did abortions discreetly, using nursing homes and managing not to kill anyone. The price in the late nineteenth century is said to have ranged from three pounds to thirty – a ratio that was maintained as late as the mid-1960s in London, when the going rate in Harley Street was between a hundred and a thousand pounds. The young playwright Harley Granville-Barker (1877–1946) tried to discuss the abortion issue in 1906 with *Waste*, in which a middle-class woman, pregnant after a brief encounter, dies when 'some quack' operates on her. The play was, of course, banned by the Lord Chamberlain. *The Times* summed up the prevailing mood by first praising the play for its 'extraordinary power' in dealing with 'some of the most fundamental facts of human life', then arguing that its very realism made it 'wholly unfit' to be seen by a 'miscellaneous public . . . Questions of art are one thing and questions of public policy and public expediency are another thing.'

In this wicked world the Cootes pressed on vigorously. Cleaning things up became an industry: bedrooms, streets, books, postcards, music halls, minds, hearts. The reformers had no doubt they could win. An MP at the annual meeting of the National Vigilance Association in 1900 denounced the 'luxury and idle wealth' of London, where 'vast numbers of people have no occupation except to amuse themselves.' He feared that it would soon be like the Paris of his youth; he wasn't far wrong. But the usual mood at the NVA was heroic optimism. To wild applause, a clergyman at the same meeting said that he had been the hidden hand behind closing two hundred immoral houses in his part of London, having persuaded police and local authorities to act. Five years later, when the NVA celebrated its twentieth anniversary, Coote asked himself if London was 'becoming morally better,' and answered resoundingly, 'Yes, in every way.' Even electricity was acclaimed for its moral properties. When Sunderland got the new street-lighting, it meant 'the scattering of darkness under cover of which the workers of impurity have been wont to hide.'

The NVA was quick to identify temptations and inform the police. The mutoscope, based on the new moving-pictures principle, was a device that revolved a cylinder of card-based photographs when you turned a handle, flicking them into view to make an animated episode. The viewer paid a halfpenny and peered through an eyepiece. This was the famous what-the-butler-saw machine. Some of the scenes were innocent, but with so short a programme, a touch of naughtiness helped patrons feel they were getting their moneys-worth.

In one of the first prosecutions (1902), the bench at Newcastle, pronouncing on 'The Artist's Model. Special Extra,' said they 'had no objection to the nudity of the figure shown, but they considered that there were obscene suggestions when the handle was turned.' According to the NVA, the five-pound fine was sufficient to sweep away indecent mutoscopes throughout the north-east. As often as not, the defence was vaguely cultural. A man working for Pastimes Ltd in south London told a policeman, 'What you think is hot are works of art.' Two hundred and fifty customers, most of them boys and girls of eleven or twelve, were surrounding thirty machines. The company irritated the justices into fining them twenty-five pounds, by saying they saw nothing improper in 'photographs of girls being undressed or undressing.' Arrow of the Yard, the detective who did for Villiers, was involved in several London cases, including one in the refined district of South Kensington, where the mutoscopes had signs saying 'Very tasty'.

Nudity, whether real or simulated, was always a threat. Nude models in art schools were an abomination: 'In the name of motherhood, in the sacred name of womanhood, we protest,' said the *Vigilance Record*, official organ of the NVA, in 1904. Town councils were urged to ban stage displays of 'living statuary', where women (and sometimes men) appeared naked, discreetly posed behind veils or ferns, often wearing flesh-coloured tights. Once again 'art' was made a defence. In Manchester, the authorities responded by telling music-hall managers to cancel all such contracts.

Dirty books were hotly pursued. These included the works of Balzac and, especially, Zola, who was much hated. The NVA was not alone in this. Tennyson wrote a disgruntled poem about the modern age which contained the lines,

> Set the maiden fancies wallowing in the troughs
> of Zolaism.
> Forward, forward, ay and backward, downward too
> into the abysm.

Their nationality was against French novelists, as it was against anyone from abroad who tried to contaminate the British. The Germans came in for special attention; for a decade before the First World War, Germany was increasingly seen as a political threat to British interests, so it was only natural to keep an eye on the morals of its citizens. As a West End magistrate put it in 1904, in a case of disorderly behaviour, 'This part of London might be kept reasonably decent but for German and other foreign women who come here for the express purpose of making it what it is − a scandal to the eyes of Europe.' The filthy-postcard trade was based in Germany, if the *Vigilance Record* was to be believed, and Berlin was the world's most immoral city.

The English were convinced their morals were better than those of the Continent. The belief had little foundation. Illegitimacy rates were high; prostitution thrived; a decade earlier the VD rate in the Army was among the highest in Europe. But moral discipline was the virtue that a powerful nation wished to assume before those it refused to see as equals. An opposite motivation may have been at work among its next-door neighbours, the Welsh, who, haunted by feelings of political inferiority, found consolation in believing that their strength lay in purity. Rural Wales was supposed to be a heartland of innocence. An identity was invented and believed in, 'Hen Wlad y Menyg Gwynion', the Land of Pure Morals. The illegitimacy figures gave a contrary picture, being remarkably high in country districts. The *Vigilance Record* reported a Welsh boast that 'not a single impure book or pamphlet had been written in the Welsh language.' Even this turned out to be a half-truth: in 1991 a scholar compiled a book from erotic Welsh verse of the Middle Ages, previously ignored or suppressed. But lands of pure morals were an appealing fiction.

Men with non-white skins were easily suspected of being concerned with abduction. Coote reprinted a correspondent's item from the *Pall Mall Gazette* as a warning to readers. A pretty girl who looked like a typist had been seen walking along the Strand one morning:

> A Hindoo in a Panama hat passed her, then took his place at her side, and endeavoured to open up a conversation. I was pleased to see that the white girl, upon looking at his dusky face, received the shock which one would hope every nice English girl would feel at being suddenly addressed in terms of equality by a black man. The lady refused to reply to the intruder, and at Temple Bar she proceeded to

cross the road. The Hindoo at once did the same. I then tapped the native on the shoulder and informed him that if I ever saw him address a white girl again I would give him in charge. A policeman standing near awaiting a case had the desired spontaneous effect, and the native slunk off into the Temple.

It is easy to deride the forgotten moralists of the NVA, but some of their campaigns were more enduring than the skirmishes with mutoscopes and flesh-coloured tights. They saw the need to increase women's wages so they might be less tempted into prostitution. They investigated bogus newspaper advertisements from men seeking 'young women or widows, view to early marriage', which attracted replies from none-too-bright servant girls who were then seduced and abandoned; one man, when arrested, was carrying letters from eighteen innocents and ten photographs.

The NVA demanded that incest be made a crime, a move that met bitter resistance in England; in Scotland it was already punishable. Children and women were still seen as adjuncts. Incest was a repulsive subject, and the less said about it the better: this was the argument put forward in 1903 by an old, authoritarian Lord Chancellor, the Earl of Halsbury, who persuaded the House of Lords to oppose a Bill, drafted by the NVA, which had already passed through the Commons. It was five years before the measure succeeded, and a further fourteen before incest cases could be reported. Until then the courts were cleared of public and press, with the result that men were able to claim that they didn't know they were breaking the law.

To speak about sex was to take lids off forces that might prove ungovernable. In 1903 Halsbury thought an Incest Act would do 'an infinite amount of mischief', and found the supposed need for it a sad reflection on the century that was just beginning.

The old view had always been that silence was the civilized way of dealing with such matters. To be too concerned with any aspect of sex was to risk drawing attention to its pleasures. Men were beasts, perhaps: why not leave it at that? But in the twentieth century, sex was to be on everyone's agenda; women's as well.

2

'Free-Born Fornicators'
The Cultured Classes

THE IDEA OF changing the rules in favour of a wider distribution of sexual freedom was at first distasteful to almost everyone, high and low. This was despite the movement towards social change in Edwardian Britain. 'It was to be the age of democracy, of social justice, of faith in the possibilities of the common man,' wrote the historian R.C.K. Ensor. Sex had nothing to do with this, and was still generally viewed by opinion-makers as a trait to be subdued. Part of the problem was that issues of the day had to be articulated in language that wouldn't give offence – one of the crimes of the Suffragettes, as they began to assert themselves later in the decade, was that the words they used were too raw for genteel ears. Sexual reformers had to be careful.

H.G. Wells (1866–1946), already a famous novelist, caused a stir in 1901 with a book, *Anticipations*, that speculated on how science and a scientific outlook might shape the future. Tucked away in it were condemnations of the old morality ('Our current civilization is a sexual lunatic'), and an optimistic vision of free, or at least freer, love, in the World State that was going to save mankind. The book reprinted eight times in a year, and was read throughout Europe. But it was theoretical and soberly done; no one felt threatened.

Sober books were all over the place. In one of the most influential, August Forel, a Zurich psychiatrist, examined the new territory with a tongs, anxious not to get his hands dirty. His book *The Sexual Question* reached London and New York in 1908, carefully described on the title-page as a study 'for the cultured classes'. To Forel and to most reformers, sex was more than a private matter for individuals to enjoy. It was part of a larger scheme of things. He defined the 'question' in broad terms of human behaviour that embraced Krafft-Ebing and the emerging work of Freud, but took a dim view of the unorthodox.

Unlike Havelock Ellis, still deep in his uncomplaining account of human 'anomaly', Forel looked into the bottomless pit of man's depravity (as it seemed) and told his readers to beware. He did this not on religious but on scientific grounds. Unlike the purity-mongers, he approved of sex under the right conditions. He wrote briskly about its mechanical side, discussing how often married couples should have 'connection', and quoted Luther, who thought two or three times a week was about right for the young married couple, a strike-rate that has remained constant for centuries. Forel even gave advice about contraception, a subject that would have got him into trouble in Britain if offered outside the educated classes. His fancy was for condoms made of animal membranes ('Purchase some vermiform appendices from a butcher; clean them and disinfect . . .').

What disturbed Forel were perversion, pornography, prostitution and over-indulgence. He argued that sexual change must be tightly controlled, lest morals decline and civilization be ruined. There was still life in this ancient cry. It had been heard from Krafft-Ebing, writing that 'the material and moral ruin of the community is readily brought about by debauchery, adultery and luxury.' Forel enlarged on the new capacity for satisfying unwholesome desires:

> Photography and all the perfected methods of reproduction of pictures, the increasing means of travel which facilitate clandestine sexual relations, the industrial art which ornaments our apartments, the increasing luxury and comfort of dwellings, beds etc., are, at the present day, so many factors in the science of erotic voluptuousness.

Feather beds and the motor car would be the death of us. Restraint and a simple life were the answer.

Forel's scientific plans for the future included 'painless narcosis' at birth for monsters, idiots and the congenitally deformed. This view was highly regarded. To discuss, as Forel did, 'the fatal decay of our race', was no more than wise eugenics, though not everyone believed in extermination. Eugenics as a science was invented in the nineteenth century by Sir Francis Galton (1822–1911), a cousin of Darwin, who defined it as the study of controls to 'improve or repair the racial qualities of future generations.' With industrial and military competition between countries at a high pitch, 'the race' was usually interpreted to mean one's own nation. The subject, popular before the First World War, continued to mesmerize people for decades, until Hitler and Nazism discredited it in the 1930s. H.G. Wells aired its ideas in *Anticipations*, envisaging a society of the year 2000 shaped to 'favour the procreation of what is fine and efficient and beautiful in humanity,' while keeping down the supply of 'base and servile types'.

Eugenics also made a handy scientific case for curbing sexual excesses, offering those who wanted it a kind of concealed puritanism, disguised as progress. Casual breeding was not at all scientific. The penis was dignified by calling it 'the racial organ', a name that caught on in some circles; no comparable courtesy was extended to the vagina. There was a scientific case for condemning birth control, since it was largely practised by the educated classes, whose offspring were necessary, rather than by the lower orders, who simply went on breeding more lower orders. The Bishop of Ripon spoke his mind at a public meeting in Leeds in 1904:

> His Lordship said that in London alone, while the marriage rate was increasing, the birth rate was decreasing, and it was estimated that the nation was deprived of 500 children per week. It was among the wealthy and well-to-do that the evil was greatest. Those who could rear families refused to do so, and it was left to the tramp, to the hooligan and the lounger to maintain the population. This was not the way to rear a great Imperial race. (Applause.)

Further complications of the sexual question arose, thanks to women. New roles for them were taking shape, not least because of their usefulness to a society that had good economic reasons for wanting to see more of them at work, since usually they could be paid less than men. Women schoolteachers and clerks had been accepted well before the First World War; the post office lady was a familiar figure. But when it came to sex, women remained uncomfortably enthroned as creatures of grace and purity, the 'angels in the house' of Victorian imagination. Millions were brought up to see their sexual life as ancillary to the man's, to be endured because he liked it and the activity was necessary to make babies. To enjoy sex was to be dirty. However, the domestic angels were not entirely proof against hints that under the skin they had desires. The 'new woman' had invented herself in the late nineteenth century. Direct evidence of sexual behaviour was always hard to come by in reticent times, but disturbing ideas were creeping into fiction. Occasional novels had been written in which heroines jibbed at their conventional roles and referred daringly to sexual matters.

Edith Ellis, the wife of Havelock, who thought herself a creative writer (and rather despised her husband for his pigeonholing of data), wrote a novel just before the end of the century, a 'Cornish idyll' called *Seaweed*, later rechristened *Kit's Woman*. The obliging Villiers alias Weissenfeld had published it at his University Press. Mrs Ellis imagined a young wife who (like Lady Chatterley twenty-five years later) has a husband made impotent by an accident, leaving her vulnerable to temptation. Mrs Ellis' heroine resists, just. But, as in *Lady Chatterley's Lover*, the 'useless husband' becomes a device to set off a discussion of women's sexuality.

At the centre of the book is a dialogue between the stiff-necked parson, Trownson, and the paraplegic Kit, who eventually explains that he wants his wife to have a child by another man, horrifying the clergyman but at the same time defeating him. Before they get that far, Trownson consoles Kit by assuring him that 'women's natures are quite different from ours; indeed it is a kind of profanity to think that could be otherwise ... my good man, you don't suppose for one moment that women have animal passions like ours, that they are radically lawless and savage or even temperately animal as men are, do you?' 'Yes, by God!' says Kit, and goes on about 'the beast i' a woman' till the parson blushes.

In cheap magazines, where vast new readerships were being catered for by proprietors who had realized the potential of universal literacy, the tone was far more cautious, and would remain so for generations. Alfred Harmsworth, Lord Northcliffe, knew all about this market, though in his private life he took a more realistic view of sex. From the 1890s Harmsworth flooded Britain with magazines. One of the most successful was *Forget-me-Not*, designed for women. Beginning lamely in 1891 with articles about music and dressmaking, it had progressed ten years later to the harmless nonsense that paved the way for a century of harmless nonsense, with articles such as 'How to Kiss and When to Kiss' and 'Are Flirts Always Heartless?'

Contemporary observers wondered who they were, these women paying their weekly pennies and twopences: tired shop assistants, perhaps, and sentimental typists, and pale-faced waitresses, speculated the superior sex who ran the *Financial News*. 'Does she make her own ill-fitting blouse? *Home Fashions* will give her the latest Paris model. Has she a taste for fiction? The *Heartsease Library* will dull her senses.'

Harmsworth knew about fiction, too, and made sure the stories were on the side of purity. The new woman was a long time developing; her well-established sister, the domestic angel, was safer. In Harmsworth magazines people wrote things like, 'An oath from a woman's lips is unnatural and incredible. I would as soon expect a bullet from a rosebud';

and this, from a bedroom scene between man and wife, where she has to ask him to put out the light before imparting a secret:

> 'Can't you – can't you guess?'
> 'Can't I guess? Let me see. Oh!' He tried to read her eyes through the darkness. 'Do you mean,' he said solemnly, 'that I may call you little mother?'
> She spoke no word. Yet the angels of God heard her answer.

This may not be as ridiculous as it sounds. When Olga Boulton of South Wales was a grammar-school pupil in 1915, she remembers returning to the house one evening with her mother, who told her not to light the gas in the hall because there was something she had to tell her. Standing in the dark, the girl of sixteen heard her mother say, 'I want you to know that Auntie Agnes is going to have a dear little baby.' Olga had to bite her tongue not to say that her cousins had told her weeks ago. I know the story because Olga was my mother.

There was something between magazine fiction, which reached hundreds of thousands, and a book like Mrs Havelock Ellis', which was read by only a handful of people. A skilful author could skate on the thin ice between decency and indecency, making a fortune in the process. One of the most daring and successful Edwardian novels was *Three Weeks* by Elinor Glyn (1864–1943), published in 1907. Glyn was a romantic, unhappily married, whose heroines all had milk-white skin like hers. On her honeymoon her husband (who soon lost interest) hired the public baths in Brighton for two days so that Elinor could swim naked, trailing her long red hair. In *Three Weeks* the heroine is a mysterious Russian princess who seduces the hero, Paul, a young upper-class Englishman. She is voluptuous but safely foreign. All the goings-on take place across the Channel. Had she been an Englishwoman, seducing him in Bedfordshire, the book might have been more harshly treated. As it was, reviewers were disgusted, or pretended they were. Public schools banned it. Eight years later, when Glyn took legal action against a film company accused of stealing her copyright with a bit of nonsense called *Pimple's Three Weeks (Without the Option)*, the judge dismissed the case on the grounds that those seeking justice must have clean hands, and hers were not; his lordship added a hint that *Three Weeks* ought to be suppressed. No one took any notice, and the book continued to sell in millions.

If *Three Weeks* was willing to show a woman enjoying a sexual affair (even if it was under special conditions, described in carefully circumscribed language), it also hinted at home truths about upper-class Englishmen. Paul, 'a splendid English young animal of the best class', has been sent abroad by his titled father to get over an infatuation with a parson's unsuitable daughter. Father instructs the servant who accompanies him to keep quiet about anything the boy may get up to; he also makes sure that Paul has plenty of money, and tells his querulous wife, 'He's my son, you know, and you can't expect to cure him of one wench unless you provide him with shekels to buy another.' Just before Paul meets the princess, he is sitting morosely in his Grand Hotel in Switzerland. 'The wine now began to fire his senses. Why should he remain alone? He was young and rich and – surely even in Lucerne there must be – and then he felt a beast, and looked out on to the lake.'

Paul was quite right, in Lucerne there surely would have been. In Glyn's kind of story it would have been unthinkable to show the hero stooping to such behaviour, but at least she doesn't dissimulate about the way well-born young men were licensed to behave.

More dangerous than Elinor Glyn, when it came to using fiction to make an intellectual case for sexual liberation, was H.G. Wells. The same Wells who floated his theories in *Anticipations* had a burning personal interest in sex, which, since he believed in social reform and the rights of women, was usefully elevated into behaviour that was novel, responding to the spirit of the times. This came in handy for someone anxious, as Wells was, to have as many attractive women as possible. Birth control was one of his early interests (his own practice of it was erratic; he made three women pregnant out of wedlock between 1906 and 1914). When in 1904 the Bishop of Ripon made his speech deploring the fall in birthrate, and encouraging the British to be fruitful and multiply, Wells wrote an article in Northcliffe's *Daily Mail* asking if the bishop thought rabbits should inherit the earth.

Wells' interest in sex dominated his private life and for a period spilled over into his novels. *In the Days of the Comet* (1906) showed the world transformed when a passing comet brings about a 'Great Change' in human behaviour. The ending seemed to anticipate sexual promiscuity. There were rumblings. The *Daily Express* said that such views were part of a socialist plot. Wells, who was a leading Fabian, replied that it was outrageous to suggest that 'free love' was the goal of socialism. He was even angrier when voters in a Birmingham by-election of 1907 were warned in a pamphlet not to elect the Socialist candidate, who would lead them on Mr Wells' path to promiscuity. The Conservative candidate in whose name (but apparently without whose knowledge) the pamphlet was published was William Joynson-Hicks, later a puritanical Home Secretary. A libel suit was threatened; apologies were made. But Wells was correctly seen as a threat to sexual stability, even if it had nothing to do with politics. He was a dangerously persuasive writer who liked sex for its own sake and was good at extending his preferences into social principles; his views were powerful nails in the old order's coffin.

The following year, 1908, when he was forty-two, he sat down to write a tale that was more dangerous because it was less fanciful. His subject was a New Woman he called Ann Veronica, a student who defies her father and leaves home, falls in love with her teacher, Capes, a married man ten years older, and fights for his affection in a way that ladies didn't:

> 'What do you want?' he asked bluntly.
> 'You!' said Ann Veronica.

Between the lines of the book were two of Wells' own love affairs. The first had been with a student when he was a struggling biology teacher. It ended his first marriage. He and the student, Jane, went to live in sin in north London, and later he married her. The second affair inspired the book and was going on as he wrote it. This was with Amber Reeves, a darkly attractive Young Fabian half his age who called him 'Master' and, like Ann Veronica, made the first move. 'We lay together naked in bed as a sort of betrothal that night,' wrote Wells. They embarked on an intense love affair, their fornication better documented than most. They did it in London apartments, at Southend, in France, under bushes, enjoying 'the faint flavour of sinfulness' in a country church that the sexton kindly opened for them, and in the woods on a copy of *The Times* that contained an article deploring the decline in morality. Amber Reeves was a New Woman. By making her the chief model for Ann Veronica, Wells let her be recognized by many who knew them.

In *Ann Veronica* Wells is not really joining in the debate on the 'sexual question'. Theorists in the book get short shrift, whether they are Fabians or Suffragettes — the heroine herself is not very impressed with her sister-feminists. What she senses, what Wells surrounds her with, is not a system of ideas but 'a big diffused impulse towards change ... a great discontent with and criticism of life as it is lived.' It is less Wells the seer, peering into the future and outlining a brave new world, than Wells the satyr carried away by his own passions, seizing the chance of changing times to get a real world of real sexuality down on paper.

Ann Veronica is twenty-one years old when she leaves home and tries to make a life for herself in London. Lodgings are hard to find for a young single woman. So is work, except sweated labour. Men accost her. 'He wore a silk hat a little tilted, and a morning coat buttoned round a tight, contained figure . . . "Whither away?" he said very distinctly in a curiously wheedling voice.' Unwisely accepting a loan from a City gentleman who knows her father, she finds herself having dinner with him in a private room at a restaurant, where he locks the door and says he means to have her. She escapes by using her fists and threatening to smash the crockery.

In the end she finds happiness with Capes, who was once cited as co-respondent in a divorce case, and now lives apart from his wife. Divorce then was as rare in books as it was in life; in 1906, only 546 divorce decrees were granted in Britain. But it was Wells' own world, and he wrote it all down and frightened the life out of the circulating libraries with this incomprehensible young woman from a middle-class family who was so eager for freedom that she permitted premarital sex, a phrase whose time had nearly come.

To get *Ann Veronica* published at all, Wells was forced to leave the austere house of Macmillan, which shrank from a plot that 'would be exceedingly distasteful to the public which buys books published by our firm,' and go elsewhere. In the book, Ann Veronica's father is made to snarl at 'these damned novels . . . this torrent of misleading, spurious stuff.' Reviewers now snarled at Wells. The novel was 'dangerous to every woman into whose hands it is likely to fall,' said the *Bookman*, because it was 'persuasive against the great human law which bridles passion.' The *Spectator* found it 'a poisonous book' in which 'self-sacrifice is a dream and self-restraint a delusion . . . [Mr Wells'] is a community of scuffling stoats and ferrets, unenlightened by a ray of duty or abnegation.' The *Spectator*'s editor, St Loe Strachy, had puritan leanings, and knew the tales of the amorous Wells that were told in Hampstead.

The big circulating libraries that supplied the middle classes with fiction —W.H. Smith's, Mudie's Select, Boots' Booklovers', *The Times* Book Club — joined forces to fight 'literary filth', or 'the new immorality' as Fleet Street called it. There were important-sounding plans to censor all novels, a task that proved too much for the libraries. 'My personal unpopularity is immense but amusing,' Wells wrote to a friend. 'People listen with blanched faces to the tale of my vices, and go and buy my books.'

Men, more than women, may have seen Wells as an entertaining rascal who got away with things they would have liked to get away with themselves. Still, the prospect of sexual licence also alienated many people who would not have regarded themselves as prudes. It hinted at anarchy. Beatrice Webb, the well-connected socialist, leading light of the Fabian Society with her husband Sidney, admired Wells but became uneasy in 1906 about the arguments for promiscuity in the *Comet* novel. Having a series of intelligent lovers, she wrote in her diary, would certainly enrich a woman's intellectual life, since physical intimacy was the only way to get to know a man thoroughly. But after those emotional upheavals, would she have any brain left to think with?

> I know that I should not − and I fancy that other women would be even worse off in this particular. Moreover, it would mean a great increase in sexual emotion for its own sake and not for the sake of bearing children, and that way madness lies.

Nor was Wells much at ease when it came to disposing of his lovers in *Ann Veronica*. He brought the book to an abrupt end, getting them as far as Switzerland, where they climb mountains and get nicely sunburnt. They have given up everything for love − his job, her home, their reputation. 'One doesn't wait,' murmurs Ann Veronica, and we seem about to leave them in the Alps, facing an uncertain future with brave smiles and glad hearts, left in suspense by the scrupulous novelist.

Instead he cheats with a short final chapter. Four years have passed. Everything is now legal. The lovers are married − with one bound Capes is free of that troublesome wife. He is rich, having turned from teaching biology to writing plays that everyone raves about. His wife's father and aunt are there to dinner. All are reconciled. Only a heavenly choir is missing. And in the last scene, where husband and wife cuddle in the firelight, we learn that Ann Veronica is pregnant.

Wells can hardly have expected the new freedom to be as painless as that. The last pages are a day-dream; reality for the author was inconvenient at the time. In the real world there was Amber Reeves. In the spring of 1909 Wells made her pregnant, apparently at her insistence; the place is on record, a room near Victoria Station. In her role as a New Woman Amber acted as if she didn't want him to leave his wife, Jane (who knew about the affair); in her heart she may have wanted it. As his mistress she was aware that their relationship was becoming untenable. Wells was playing a difficult game. He believed in promiscuity but couldn't say so without offending publishers and, worse, readers. He once told Bertrand Russell that he didn't mean publicly to espouse the cause of free love until he could afford it.

The Amber episode ended lamely, though the friendship survived. Amber's father, who was a friend of Wells, became threatening. A young lawyer called Blanco White was keen to marry her. On a Channel ferry she thought of killing herself, but decided to stay alive and compromise. Wells let her go, and she married Blanco White that summer. There is a story that the new husband then threatened to sue Wells for libelling Amber in *Ann Veronica* unless he promised never to see her again. The child was born soon after the book was published. Wells went on seeing her. The problem of reconciling sexual passion with the rest of one's life, and with other people's feelings, harassed even the high-spirited Wells. There was no such thing as a free fornication.

As far as men were concerned in Edwardian times, the New Women they knew most about were the Suffragettes. It was the militant wing of the movement that attracted popular attention. Violent deeds and words in pursuit of votes for women were seen as unfeminine and sometimes an expression of hatred for men, while critical views of sex, put forward by militants as part of the case against men, seemed — to men, at any rate — the ravings of an alien race. For a few years before 1914, they were telling men they must control their sexual urges in order to preserve civilization. Men found this both ridiculous and terrifying.

The women's suffrage movement had spent thirty years of the nineteenth century clawing at power, before gaining a foothold early in the twentieth, as feminism and feminists (the terms date from the 1890s) began to come into their own. The campaign for the vote, accompanied by increasing violence from 1909, ultimately shifted public opinion in women's favour because the moral case was unanswerable. Violence may have done the cause more harm than good; at the same time it was a way of concentrating women's attention on themselves. The process generated bitter feelings on both sides; not least because the campaign was accompanied by a series of sexual sideshows, as men and their habits came in for feminist attention. Each side was seen in sharper focus by the other, with women denouncing and men defending themselves, or pretending not to hear, on lines that have been familiar ever since.

Prostitution gave feminists ample proof of men's depravity. The issue had arisen in peculiar form fifty years earlier, when anxiety about venereal diseases led to a series of 'Contagious Diseases' Acts in the

1860s that compelled prostitutes and suspected prostitutes in dockyard and garrison towns to register and be medically examined. This was widely regarded as a dirty and demeaning business, introduced from the Continent. The *Pearl* had a poem about it that could have been written by an early feminist (perhaps it was), with its digs at a 'double standard' for men and women:

> . . . And thus began the era of Sexual legislation:
> To man alone the State allows Free-trade in Fornication;
> Diseased or sound — no matter — let him riot fancy free,
> And gaily pox the ladies that the Peelers guarantee;
> Is not Man the Nobler sex, for whom was Woman made?
> And shall harassing Inspections his liberties invade?
> For Man alone, the Bill of Rights, and Magna Carta passed;
> And shall Free-born Fornicators be with dirty Harlots classed?
> The sauce that suits the Goose, o'er the noble Gander pour?
> Or the State restrict the God-like Sex's privilege to whore? . . .

The prostitutes found a champion in Josephine Butler, a schoolmaster's wife. She spent her life denouncing the two-facedness of men who sought to punish the women they were responsible for corrupting. As with many sexual reformers, a personal event is said to have been responsible. She saw her daughter, five years old at the time, killed in a fall. 'Mrs Butler,' wrote the reforming journalist Stead, 'always wanted to save daughters.' Leading the campaign against the Acts, which had been slipped through Parliament with little debate, she was called a 'shrieking sister', an 'indecent maenad'; when she told men they were 'lustful destroyers' of women, a mob smeared her with flour and excrement. The Acts were repealed after nearly two decades, having lasted as long as they did only because so sordid a subject was little publicized. The memory of a feminist on the warpath was a more enduring legacy.

Having surfaced for a while in public debate, prostitution ('the social evil') and VD ('the social disease') sank from view again. They were not nice subjects. VD was widely regarded as a punishment for sin, which did not encourage active treatment. It was only when conscience and curiosity stirred in the years after 1900 that such matters became accessible to inquiry, and were seized on by militant women as propaganda against man the beast.

Prostitution fascinated the Edwardians, their morbid interest provoked by the moralists and suffragettes. Like pornography at the other end of the century, it was too visible and popular to ignore. Edwardian Britain marked the end of a golden era for professional tarts. London before the First World War is unlikely to have had fewer than eight thousand; wild guesses by reformers and journalists put the figure at sixty or even eighty thousand, dismissed by the police as fiction. But women have always drifted in and out of the business, and no one could be sure how many were at work.

Already their trade was being infiltrated by the 'amateur', the girl who took money or gifts but didn't need them to survive; and by early Ann Veronicas, making themselves available out of love. H.G. Wells makes Capes, the married man, confess to Ann Veronica before they become lovers that since he has been separated from his wife, he has succumbed to the 'craving in one's blood . . . Irregularly, in a quite inglorious and unromantic way, you know, I am a vicious man. That's — that's my private life. Until the last few months.' In other words, he was visiting prostitutes until he fell in love with her.

Girl-friends in the modern sense were uncommon, so a prostitute was the decent alternative. Infidelity was different for women. A woman's lapse was more serious. A child that wasn't her husband's might be introduced into the marriage, a cuckoo in the nest, and inherit his property. This was reflected in the divorce law, which until 1923 made it easier for a man to divorce his wife than vice versa.

Men's lapses were merely hygienic interludes. The prostitute's therapeutic role was hinted at in the fantasy played out by street women of Edwardian (and later) times, where they plied for hire dressed as nurses, or wore the uniform for bedroom and bathroom scenes. This was the better-class end of the market, where men paid at least a pound or two. Spurious 'special baths' and 'massage parlours' could be found on the top floors of West End buildings, with fashionable shops trading below. 'Nurses' offered 'special oils' or 'electrical treatment for all muscular ailments.' The madam Queenie Gerald, who said she knew Mrs Lewis of the Cavendish, advertised herself in newspapers as a specialist in the treatment of rheumatism, with hospital-trained nurses in attendance. When police raided her, they were admitted by a uniformed 'Nurse Betty'. Others advertised via 'sandwich men' with boards, parading in Regent Street and Leicester Square.

Cultural disguises were always popular. The Edwardians knew about 'French lessons', or anything with 'French' in it. 'French lady would receive a few paying guests' has done service in its time. 'Elocution lessons' was known to work:

> Madame Osborne Gray has reopened her studio for lessons in elocution and deportment; also classes can be arranged to study the art of fencing. Interviews daily from ten to eight p.m.

Madame Gray, first name Violet, was twenty-six, and kept a brothel above a sweet shop north of Oxford Street before the First World War. A brass plate outside announced 'Ring. Walk up.' There is no way of tracing it now. It is very likely an innocent address, though police say that the same flats are sometimes used by generations of prostitutes. If Violet Gray came back after eighty years, she would find her West End successors still in business, hardly changed. Her girls specialized in flagellation, and demand for this — and other eccentricities often not readily obtainable from wives and lovers even in late-century London — remains brisk. There has not been much new technology.

> Detective Inspector Curry said that he then made a thorough search of the premises, and took possession of two large leather bands, partly lined with wool; several dog whips, 19 canes, some bearing marks of blood; four birches, a mask, three pairs of handcuffs, three padlocks, and 22 books, many of which were of a grossly obscene character. In one room was a large medical leather couch. The prisoner said that was what she lay on, as she suffered from her heart.

This was 1913. In a bedroom the police found two young women and an elderly gentleman, all fully dressed. The elderly gentleman wouldn't give his name. 'You can guess what I came for,' he said. 'I came to have a cup of tea.' Violet Gray explained that the girls were friends of hers. Like the gentleman, they had popped in for cups of tea. One of the women, aged about twenty-two, confirmed that tea was their motive for being there; adding that she was a married woman, and she hoped the officer wouldn't involve her. As for the implements, Violet Gray was indignant. 'If men want to be whipped, and like to pay me for it,' she said, 'I suppose I can do it. I can do as I like in my own house.' But Inspector Curry knew he had a nice little conviction.

Commercial sex in Britain was famous for compromises between police and prostitutes. Prostitution, the act itself, was not a crime. The offence lay in being a 'common prostitute' and in importuning a man; in London it was not even necessary to prove the importuning. This gave the authorities power to clear the streets, though in practice they merely stopped prostitution becoming too blatant. Throughout Britain, about ten thousand cases were brought each year before 1914, many involving the same women on different occasions. Small fines were the usual punishment. Keeping a brothel was a more serious offence, though logically, since the prostitute had to do it somewhere, a room with curtains was presumably preferable to an alley or a park, the usual alternatives.

There was a vague feeling that the Englishman's freedom was involved. Abraham Flexner, an American sent to look at vice in Europe before the First World War, wrote:

> The English urge that personal liberty in this realm can be infringed only to prevent scandal – that is, only when something beyond mere prostitution is involved. 'A woman may become mistress or paramour,' said a high police official to me, 'she may indulge in occasional immorality as she pleases – why not in prostitution? She is only using her personal freedom.'

Across the Channel, too, they compromised over vice, but more regulations and paperwork were involved. Several countries, including France and Germany, went in for 'registered' prostitutes, an idea that had died in Britain with the Contagious Diseases Acts. Formally to recognize prostitutes would not have been at all British; in any case, the system on the Continent was riddled with loopholes, and medical examination to see if women were infected – the object of the exercise – was inadequate. Flexner wrote a pained account of a session he attended in Paris, where harlots received a ten-to-fifteen-second examination; the doctors used soiled towels, didn't change their rubber gloves, and indulged in 'unseemly jocularity'.

London was also distinguished by having more religious and moral organizations at work, trying to save prostitutes, than any other European capital. William Coote of the Vigilance Association wouldn't use the word 'prostitute'. His rescue missions roamed the streets looking for 'unfortunate women'. The Salvation Army and Church Army spoke of 'poor, lost sisters'. The *Church Army Review* (February 1909) saw its workers comb 'the streets and alleys of our great, wicked city . . . Their little Receiving Homes [where prostitutes were taken in] are like our block-houses in the Boer War, isolated, lonely, yet doing splendid work in keeping back the enemy.' No doubt there was a proportion of successes, especially among those who were sick or ageing, but the pool of servants, shopgirls and barmaids was continually renewed. Ann

Veronica found she could legitimately earn 'from fifteen to two-and-twenty shillings a week – for drudgery.'

It was no wonder that magistrates had been known to request the press not to publish evidence of how much a prostitute was paid. One of the girls in the Queenie Gerald case, aged seventeen, had previously earned two shillings and sixpence a week as a dressmaker's apprentice. Newspapers obligingly kept quiet about how much she made from sin. What did emerge was a boast by Gerald that the brothel once received a hundred and seventy pounds in a week. A hundredth of that sum in wages would have been riches for a shopgirl or a skivvy.

Most prostitutes had no wish to be saved. The National Vigilance Association employed fifty paid workers to patrol railway stations and ports where 'foreign unfortunate women' were likely to be found, arriving from the Continent. This was both a work of charity and a means of keeping the immigrant prostitute at bay. 'These aliens,' said a Vigilance worker, 'are worse and bolder women, more deeply learned in all the arts of vice, than English women of the same class generally' (The clients might have been more enthusiastic about the 'arts of vice'). A potentially corruptible girl with a suitcase had only to hesitate, and a worker with an armband inscribed 'International Guild of Service for Women' would be ready with advice and safe addresses.

Four volunteers from the West London Mission spent three weeks on patrol. It was winter, raining continually. 'Plenty of evidence was obtained, but after speaking to hundreds of girls (foreigners), offering to repatriate them . . . not one accepted our offer of help, but smilingly announced their intention of staying here until they are turned out.'

Coote had no illusions about the attractions of vice. A presentable working-class girl, temporarily persuaded off the street by Vigilance workers, would be taken to him for an interview. He would tell her she must change her ways and become a decent member of society. 'Why should I?' she would reply. 'I am having a good time. I am receiving large sums of money weekly. I do as I like. I have fine clothes and plenty of amusements. What can you give me equal to that?' As Coote said, the best he could suggest was twenty pounds a year in domestic service. They were hard hearts to melt. A friend told him of a young middle-class woman, attractive, well-educated, a linguist, who had fallen into error. She and Coote met by appointment.

I put before her the anxiety of my friend that she should give up the life she was leading, and try a more excellent way. Then she said, 'Yes, I would gladly do so. But what can you or your friends offer me in exchange? I have a very fine suite of furnished rooms, there is nothing I want I cannot have. I need deny myself nothing. I am not a street walker, I go twice or three times a week to a place of public resort, which answers better the same purpose. I have money in the bank, and you ask me to give all this up — for what?'

Unlike some of the reformers (among them George Bernard Shaw), Coote didn't believe better wages for women were the whole answer. He quoted examples to show that the market-place could never compete on equal terms with vice. His arguments were moral. But whether the arguments came from Fabians or moralists, they were irrelevant to the carnal trade.

Perhaps Forel was right, and Europe was threatened by a new decadence. Ferry steamers shuttled to and fro, the telegraph could book rooms and make assignations, liquor was cheap, silk underclothes and soft beds were in the shops, and a man who was daunted by the prospect of buying the appendix of a cow to make himself a condom could now find retailers selling such marvels as 'The Newest Sheath. Silk Finish. Never Rip' and 'The Most Reliable Sheath Ever Produced . . . rolled up and placed in small square envelopes'; there was even 'W. George's Apparatus for Re-rolling Elastic Sheaths,' complete with French chalk. An industry was beginning. Dark visions of the future would have to consider the effects of cheap and easy contraception. W. George's literature was prefaced by the magic words, 'N.B. — PRIVATE. This List is printed for and supplied only to the Married,' but that was purely a precaution in case English police and puritans came meddling. 'Business Hours,' it said, '10 a.m. to 12 p.m.,' an unusually long day. Furthermore, 'Ladies can communicate with the Manageress.' One assumes that some of the ladies were prostitutes.

Like Forel, Abraham Flexner saw signs of a deplorable new licentiousness. The 'fascination and the curse of the great city' were inextricable.

> With this local pride to be a great city through forcing the sensual pace, modern Europe is fairly mad. Berlin and Vienna are rich and gay; the idle and curious throng thither from all quarters of the world. Smaller towns like Geneva, smitten with envy, struggle to imitate the licence of those great capitals.

The sensual pace may not have been forced quite so energetically in Britain. Were the British truly different, or did they conceal their real nature with hypocritical skill? The question is hard to answer satisfactorily except in terms of one's own prejudices.

Flexner said what was perhaps true, that demand for prostitutes by continental males was 'practically universal', since 'male continence has not been required by either tradition or experience.' In England, he added, pausing uncertainly in a footnote, family and religious life were so differently organized as to create a strong presumption that 'correct living is in certain strata of society distinctly more probable than on the Continent.' But 'as to the extent to which continence prevails I have been unable to form a conception.'

One of the bright spots, according to Flexner, was that the difficult task of making nations continent was being faced by a 'small but earnest band of men and women bent upon the purification of the sexual life.' There was, too, the rise of a women's movement that was willing to confront 'masculine irregularities'.

In an age that was beginning, however tentatively, to question the rightness of its assumptions about behaviour and progress, who could tell what would emerge? After the bicycle, one might have expected the super-bicycle; the technology in H.G. Wells' *The Time Machine* (1895) seems to be based on the push-bike. Instead there came the automobile. By 1910 Havelock Ellis was writing optimistically (but few in Britain were yet reading) that women would come to control their own sexual lives. This would undoubtedly make prostitution ('in many respects a most excellent arrangement,' as proved by its flourishing history) seem inappropriate. 'It is possible,' added Ellis, 'that women may begin to realize this fact earlier than men.'

Feminists were already fishing in these waters. A pamphlet of 1909 (written by Lady McLaren, a minor figure) said that the horror with which 'open immorality' was discussed by statesmen and thinkers was equalled only by their lack of activity in ending it. A 'strong commission of women' should be given the authority and finance to clean the streets and suppress the brothels. But in practice, 'as long as womanhood is not represented either in England's legislative nor on its administrative power . . . so long will the sex-supremacy of man achieve the degradation of women.'

More would be heard of this. In the early part of the century, and again towards its end, feminists and moralists have found common ground in condemning aspects of men's sex lives. If the fight for women's suffrage before 1914 was a 'war of the sexes', then men's lust and its consequences were essential ammunition.

3

'Bromide in the Tea'
Maiden Warriors

BEFORE THE First World War, political pressure to improve men's sexual behaviour came in two varieties. One was orthodox, the work of assorted moralists who believed that prostitution in general, and in particular a wicked underworld known as 'the White Slave Traffic', must be curbed. The other was unorthodox, a byproduct of the Suffragette movement, whose militants had political reasons for castigating men as part of the business of getting the vote, and who came to believe that men had to cure themselves — or be cured — of lust, if prostitution and its attendant scourge of venereal disease was to be ended. In neither case was there a suggestion of any defect in women's sexual behaviour. Women were flawless, unless they were prostitutes, in which case men had made them into their playthings. For public purposes, women had to be either pure or a-sexual. The idea that they might even enjoy sex rarely occurred outside pornography, where they had been allowed to have multiple orgasms for years. Men could not excuse their lust by arguing that women experienced it, too. Lust was a male preserve.

To some extent the two groups, moralists and Suffragettes, overlapped, although in spirit they were far apart. The Suffragettes had sprung from obscurity, a crew of women, many of them young, who quarrelled among themselves, demanded the vote, and in 1909 moved from protest to violence — at least if they were followers of Mrs Pankhurst and her three fearful daughters, especially her fearful eldest daughter, Christabel.

They were fair game, these unnatural sisters or wailing kittens, as jovial politicians called them. In God's good time they might be given a measure of suffrage if they behaved themselves. In 1910 they even called off militant action before a general election, anticipating a 'Conciliation Bill' that would have given the vote to about a million women who owned a house or even a room (as someone pointed out, this would have enfranchised successful prostitutes). It was an unsatisfactory Bill, which didn't succeed, and by the end of the year there was more violence. When Suffragettes demonstrated in public, heckling politicians or trying to force their way into the precincts of Parliament, men who got their hands on them sometimes roughed them up in a sexual way: clothes were ripped, breasts seized, legs pinched under skirts. Over the next four years, as the militants turned to extreme violence with bombs and fire-raising, so the rhetoric acquired a sexual edge.

The moralists, on the other hand, were part of the British tradition, and few politicians would have cared to be impolite about them in public. They made a fuss about White Slaves, who were popularly supposed to be the young women of one country, lured away into sexual bondage in another. It could be an English girl in a Brussels *maison*, though more colourfully it was a European girl entrapped in South America.

The trade in young hopefuls, typically from poor rural districts, seduced in cities by men who promise love and security, but are really offering sex and prostitution, was nothing new. In the nineteenth century it grew with cities and rail networks. Writing of Warsaw before 1914, Isaac Bashevis Singer said his sister thought the city was full of men who 'seduce girls, take them to Buenos Aires, and sell them as slaves.' W.T. Stead and his exposés of 1885 were directed at the London end of the trade. Its worst excesses were supposed to take place on the Continent. Girls would be recruited in backward areas of Poland or Hungary, and sent to their doom by train, or, if they were destined for other countries, steamer.

The line between 'white slaves' and 'common prostitutes' was indefinable, and, for British moralists, not important. 'White slaves' sounded exciting. From 1899 international conferences were held regularly to monitor the trade. The National Vigilance Association was the prime mover, and any court case where a prostitute was seen to be managed by a foreign pimp was automatically labelled 'White Slave Traffic'. A meeting in 1905 was told that Germans, Belgians and French were heavily involved in London, together with 'low Russian Jews'.

Seedy episodes were presented as part of a pattern, in which the dirtiest deeds were those done by foreigners. It was true that they did much of the procuring. London was an attractive place for prostitution. In Continental cities where the brothels were legal and the business came under municipal control, the police bureaucracy was oppressive. The Berlin prostitute regulations for 1911, a formidable document, made women subject to the Morals Police, even listing the streets where they could walk. London attracted foreign prostitutes and pimps because it was more tolerant. Everyone rubbed along, and if the newcomers behaved themselves, they were generally left alone. This, and the fact that immigrants to London found themselves at the bottom of the social heap, and so were willing to try anything, helped ensure that men with non-Anglo-Saxon names often appeared in court.

A Max Lewis and a Hyman Levy went to prison after enticing a girl of fifteen, Bessie Yamovitch, away from her elderly father, a Russian Jew who had fled to Britain from a nineteenth-century pogrom. They said they would make Bessie rich; locked her up for a week; got her drunk; introduced her to men. This was in 1903, one of many cases. In another, two Frenchmen were gaoled after enticing a girl from Paris and installing her in a brothel in Great Portland Street. The prosecuting police officer said that one of them had sold French girls 'like cattle' in Egypt. The judge wanted to know why more wasn't done to stop such men. The police replied that it was difficult getting women to give evidence against pimps. (Police still take this for granted. Women may fear their pimps, but they need them as minders, and often are in love with them.)

For years William Coote and the Vigilance Association kept up their campaign, lobbying MPs, preparing parliamentary Bills that would make life harder for pimps, and printing any item that might help the cause:

> Dear Sir,
> Contrary to my habitude, I was tempted last night by a friend to visit
> an Alexandria music hall (so-called) . . . I was horrified to hear behind
> me certain questions asked in Arabic that are too absolutely disgusting to
> put on paper. Turning round, I saw a young English girl, aged, I should
> say, 14, in the company of two extremely well-dressed men of the Effendi
> class, both of whom talked English . . . [these two satyrs] gloated in their
> accustomed indecent manner over the unwitting child . . . Surely, Sir, our
> Consul, if this letter comes to his notice, will see his way to informing the
> Home Office, with a view to their circularising the theatrical agencies at
> home respecting the way English artistes are treated out here . . .

Nice English girls were always at risk. The *Vigilance Record* reported a case where a Miss Annie Danks, stage name Mamie Stuart, sued a theatrical agent who got her a booking in Buenos Aires that went wrong. Mamie had gone off in 1907 to what she thought was a 'leading vaudeville theatre' at twelve guineas a week. On arrival she found it was 'a casino'. When she sang one of her songs for the manager, he complained it was not suggestive enough. So she tried him with 'A Little Pink Pettie from Peter', in which she raised her skirt to show her petticoat. The manager wanted her to remove the skirt altogether, but this was too much, and her South American career came to an end. The implication was that foreign devils were ever ready to pounce on English roses. The Lord Chief Justice, who heard the case himself, took to Mamie, advising the jury that 'in spite of the fact that scenes occur in music halls which you would hardly allow in your own houses, artistes' testimony is none the less trustworthy.' Mamie was awarded substantial damages of two hundred and fifty pounds. With the White Slave Trade in people's minds, no South American music hall stood much chance against an English rose, even an actress. *

In 1909 Coote and his friends had hopes of a Criminal Law Amendment (White Slave Traffic) Bill which would have permitted the police to arrest anyone on suspicion of procuring, without a warrant. The measure was introduced but made no progress in Parliament in 1910 or again in 1911. The Liberal Government was too busy orchestrating its social reforms to find the time. One Liberal critic of the Coote initiative remarked that Lloyd George's National Insurance Bill, by helping domestic servants in time of sickness, would 'do a thousand times more to prevent immorality and prostitution.' This was probably true. But the moralists wanted something more exciting. Had not NVA workers warned '17,000 girls and women' in Britain of their wicked ways? 'Some, at least,' added the Association, showing admirable modesty, had been 'in many ways saved.' By 1912 the White Slave lobby, led by the National Vigilance Association, backed by the Jewish Board of Deputies and the Bishop of London's Public Morality Council, was becoming vociferous. It was not only the White Slave Trade they were fighting but a Yellow Slave Trade as well, since the Orient was involved. International legislation was being demanded. In the meantime it was time for Britain to put its own house in order. Early in 1912 an influential MP took on the Bill as a Private Member's measure, again without success, although the Liberal Home Secretary, Reginald McKenna, claimed to be in favour of it. Governments

---

* Mamie Stuart later married a marine surveyor — who was already married, as it turned out — then vanished in 1919. During the search for her there were hints that she was not quite the innocent English rose. She was not found for more than forty years, when (her husband having died in the meantime) her dismembered skeleton was found in a cave near the house in South Wales where they had been living.

prefer not to be seen giving a lead in matters of sex and morals; they find it safer to present themselves as mere agents, bowing to public opinion. The moralists now gave them something to bow to.

The cause was helped by the death of W.T. Stead. He was among the passengers drowned when the *Titanic* sank in April, and it made useful propaganda to see the Bill as a memorial to the dead hero of morality. In June the government took responsibility for the measure. More than one MP had doubts. The proposed powers of arrest on suspicion were thought dangerous. The idea of London as the centre of some fearful world traffic in women's bodies was derided. But the doubters were in a minority. The *Vigilance Record* said that 'the voice of the people' had spoken.

Eager suggestions were made that flogging be used as a punishment for pimps. Many MPs, and many of their constituents, thought corporal punishment an excellent idea. At the time it was extensively used (in the form of whipcord applied to the shoulders) to punish prisoners who attacked warders, and (as a birch applied to the buttocks) on erring juveniles. After the Oscar Wilde case the punishment was extended to include homosexual men, and by 1912 birchings were being handed out to them, too. These could be savage enough for a pornographic novel. In one case of many, four men were sentenced as 'incorrigible rogues or vagabonds', the useful form of words applied. A shop assistant of seventeen was found to possess 'a golden-haired wig, the long tresses of which were tied back with a long black bow.' A valet of twenty-nine was described as 'a shameless and dangerous character frequenting the West End, with face rouged and powdered and eyebrows pencilled.' Both were sent to prison for nine months' hard labour, with twenty-five strokes of the birch. The other two, a clerk and a sailor, were similarly dealt with. Such men were moral outlaws in a society that liked to think it had a conscience.

Pimps could be regarded in the same light. When a prostitute called Eva Davies, who preferred to be known as Dulcia Torriani, was charged with murdering her pimp, the court took a lenient view. The *News of the World*, already an old hand at reporting sex as if it were doing a duty to society, carried the headline, 'SLEW HER TORMENTOR. MERCIFUL SENTENCE ON WHITE SLAVE VICTIM. SIX WEEKS' IMPRISONMENT FOR MANSLAUGHTER.' Davies was twenty years old. A coachman's daughter from Rotherham, she was brought to London at the age of sixteen (by, typically, a person whose name 'need not be mentioned'), and was deserted after three months. This was a real-life version of events several rungs down the social ladder from H.G. Wells' Ann Veronica, who only glimpsed the abyss. Eva Davies was taken up by the man she later stabbed. His name was Herman Weinberg, another of those Germans. She lived with him and worked as a prostitute in the Leicester Square district, but he beat her so badly that she left him. This happened more than once. She reported him to the police, but, as the court heard, 'with the strange characteristic of a woman, she repented and refused to charge him.' Finally he told her to pack her jewellery, said he was taking her to Hamburg, and then went off with another woman. One day she met him in Leicester Square and stabbed him with a dagger. Even then she told police she was sorry the 'poor devil' was dead. Her sentence was six weeks in prison. 'Many people in court', said the News of the World, 'were moved to tears.'

Fleet Street kept the pot boiling with investigations. The News of the World, again, announced, 'GIRLS SOLD TO INFAMY. LONDON AS CENTRE OF HIDEOUS TRAFFIC.' This was based on an interview with a Mr F.S. Bullock, an assistant commissioner of police, who said that hundreds of girls were recruited each year by foreign 'impresarios' for theatrical troupes or dancing companies abroad. Often they were 'domestics of merry disposition' or shop assistants. Mainly, said the policeman, they were 'of the simple, simpering class, smitten with a love of the stage.' Most, he added, came to a 'disastrous finish', and London was 'the great clearing house for this terrible traffic.'

It was November before the Bill was disposed of by the House of Commons. Much of the argument now was about whether to include flogging as a punishment. The Asquith Government was against it, but on a free vote there was a small majority for 'the lash', as newspapers liked to call it. Asked who among them would be willing to cast the first stroke, a Tory colonel offered his services. The Daily Mail, populist and successful, wrote scornfully on 2 November of humanitarians who opposed corporal punishment, adding that 'bishops and many prominent social workers' saw it as the only punishment for the crime. The Bishop of London, Winnington-Ingram, obliged a few days later by telling a meeting at Crewe that what white slave traffickers feared was the whip on 'their own beastly skins'.

The House of Commons continued to debate and the Daily Mail to deplore. On 12 November it attacked the 'so-called humanitarians' who threatened to remove a punishment that was 'absolutely necessary, as it is the only means of clearing this unsavoury class out of the country.'

The same day, as it happened, a Royal Commission on Divorce had reported, and the *Daily Mail*, like the rest of the press, gave it extensive treatment. The report proposed to make divorce simpler and fairer. But there was a minority report, signed by the Archbishop of York, Cosmo Lang, which warned that any slackening in the rule of lifelong monogamy would be ruinous to the nation; and with this argument the *Mail* fervently agreed.

So while one of its leading articles that Tuesday morning advocated the lash for miscreants in the prostitution business, another rejected a measure that might, in the end, release a few more people from dismal marriages whose existence was helping to create more clients for the prostitutes. This was not a connection that would have gone down well in 1912. And in warning readers to beware of 'strong tendencies against the continuous union of man and wife,' the *Daily Mail* had read the public mood correctly. The Royal Commission's liberalizing report was shelved and forgotten.*

Flogging, too, was the popular choice. It was included in the Bill, though not for a first conviction, to the disappointment of many. By the end of the year the new law was in force, and moralists were convinced that the 'inhuman traffickers' were on the run. But life and the prostitution business seem to have gone on as before. White Slave fever took time to die down. Colourful stories filled the papers in January 1913. From Bath came reports of a 'dastardly plot to trap a girl'; offered half a crown by a stranger to take a sealed envelope to a house, she showed it to her father, who opened it and found a message that said, 'Chloroform the bearer if necessary.' At London telephone exchanges women operators were warned by the management to beware of mysterious strangers. Drugged chocolates were being offered to girls on trains. There was no end to the fiendish cunning.

The later stages of the White Slave agitation had attracted indirect support from the more extreme Suffragettes. Others in the movement thought the agitation was nonsense, likely to do the feminist cause more harm than good. The most vocal of these was Teresa Billington-Greig (1877–1964), a schoolteacher who had been recruited by Mrs Pankhurst. Her maiden name was Billington. When she married a man called Greig

---

* Lord Northcliffe, the *Daily Mail's* proprietor, had the lifelong marriage that his papers preached about, but it was childless. Instead he fathered three children by his mistress, Kathleen Wrohan, in 1910, 1912 and 1914.

in 1906 they adopted a joint surname. The first of the militants to be imprisoned (for slapping a policeman's face), she was three years older than Christabel Pankhurst, and was regarded as the leading young Turk or Turkess of the Suffragettes before the title went to Christabel. This may have coloured her view of the Pankhursts.

An article she wrote for the *English Review*, 'The Truth about White Slavery' (June 1913), did a robust demolition job. A search for evidence that girls had been trapped – 'carried off in broad daylight by force, drugs or false messages' – failed to find a verifiable example. The Bath case ('Chloroform the bearer if necessary') had been investigated by the police. All they could find was a newspaper report by a woman of being chloroformed while walking in the street; she was now in a mental institution. The same ingredients recurred – mysterious motor cars (from its inception the car had something immoral about it), strange events at railway stations. Billington-Greig wrote:

> The hospital nurse of one tale became the Sister of Mercy or the Rescue Worker of its fellow. The fainting lady fainted in front of three separate West End establishments. The tales of drugged handkerchiefs, sweets and flowers had so many variants as to create the impression that the homes of the country must be decimated of their daughters by drugging.

She even made contact with Assistant Commissioner Bullock, who had told the *News of the World* about girls going abroad as actresses, but he was unable to recall an authenticated case, using Billington-Greig's definition of entrapment, in the previous ten years. 'Most of the stories,' he added, 'are the result of hysteria or nerves.' As for the White Slave measure, which had become law six months earlier, none of the police forces she wrote to could report that it had had any effect.

Billington-Greig's conclusion was that the outcry had been created by 'neuropaths and prudes', who had 'slandered men only to slander women with the backward swing of the same blow. They have discredited themselves.' Then she put the knife into her colleagues:

> That this exhibition has been possible is due in no small measure to the Pankhurst domination. It prepared the soil; it unbalanced the judgment; it set women on the rampage against evils they knew nothing of, for remedies they knew nothing about. It fed on flattery the silly notion of

the perfection of woman and the dangerous fellow notion of the indescribable imperfection of man.

It was no wonder they never forgave her.

The well-adjusted Mrs Billington-Greig was undoubtedly right about White Slaves and the effect of militant propaganda, but her cool appraisal was swept aside. The illogical currents of ideology were cutting new channels. It is the Pankhursts who are remembered, not the Billington-Greigs.

Man the Beast needed curbing as much as ever. Forty years earlier Josephine Butler thought male sexual desire an error that could be controlled, like alcohol. Nor was this enthusiasm for purging the flesh confined to feminists. Flexner in his 1914 book on European prostitution wrote that 'continence is, in general, increasingly regarded as both feasible and wholesome.' Even the hard-headed Forel suggested that mankind should reproduce itself in an elevated fashion. In Britain the public-school ideal of manly self-control was wished upon a wider circle by Robert Baden-Powell (1857–1941), whose moral injunctions coloured the Boy Scout movement and especially its senior division, the Rovers ('Behave like a man. Play fair and square with the girl and remember your future son whose germ is in your keeping').

But arguments that men should restrain themselves as a kind of moral hygiene were not at all the same as the insults flung at them by aggressive women. Mrs Emmeline Pankhurst (1858–1928), the widow who led the Suffragette extremists, used the evils of sex as a theme in a major speech she made on 17 October 1912. There had been nasty incidents with sexual undertones in the summer, when militants – who were pursuing one of their prime targets, David Lloyd George, Chancellor of the Exchequer, around the country – were attacked at events on his home ground, in Wales. Dresses and blouses were torn from women, who were thrown over hedges and had to be rescued from crowds. On one occasion the Chancellor incited violence; on another he jumped on a table and tried to restore order by singing the Welsh national anthem.

In her speech Mrs Pankhurst referred to these 'outrages', saying that 'until we can establish an equal moral code, women will be fair game for the vicious section of the population, inside Parliament as well as out of it.' She turned to prostitution and VD:

> When I began this militant campaign I was a Poor Law Guardian and it

was my duty to go through a workhouse infirmary. Never shall I forget seeing a little girl of thirteen lying in bed playing with a doll. On the eve of becoming a mother, she was infected with a loathsome disease and on the point of bringing, no doubt, a diseased child into the world. Was that not enough to make me a militant Suffragette?

The 'White Slave' Act, passed soon after this, appeared ludicrous to Billington-Greig, but to the extremists it was merely inadequate. In the spring of 1913, following months of violence in which acid was poured on golf-course greens, telegraph wires cut, and empty buildings attacked – among them a house in Surrey that a newspaper proprietor was building for Lloyd George – Mrs Pankhurst was arrested, tried in April and sent to prison. At her trial she managed to smite 'the abominable trade of ministering to the vicious pleasures of rich men,' remarking that those who administered the law were themselves depraved. Her husband (a radical lawyer from Manchester, who had died fifteen years earlier) had apparently told her of a senior judge who was found dead in a brothel. Mrs Pankhurst treated the court to this reminiscence, of a kind often heard though difficult to pin down. The Old Bailey judge, complaining of a 'shameful want of decorum', gaoled her for three years.

Perhaps to help deflect attention from the crimes of women to the crimes of men, the *Suffragette*, the militants' newspaper, now began to attack male shortcomings with a skilful vehemence that was not to be seen again until modern American feminists got under way in the nineteen-seventies. The principal author was Mrs Pankhurst's daughter Christabel (1880–1958), who had taken a degree in law seven years earlier, and became the goad and polemicist of the movement. It was never certain whether she or her mother was the more militant; they complemented one another in wrath. As the 'Maiden Warrior' Christabel inspired a generation of young feminists. To men who saw her in action, the rounded, well-brought-up face and slim figure made her behaviour seem all the more pernicious.

As chief organizer and a leading activist herself, she was gaoled a number of times, until in March 1912, after inciting window-smashing raids on London shops ('We will terrorize the lot of you!' she shouted at a meeting), she thought it prudent to leave the country, and set up her headquarters in Paris, where she continued to direct events. The first of her articles about sex and men for the *Suffragette*, edited from France, appeared the day after her mother was sent to prison. It attacked politicians for continuing to tolerate prostitution. Soon, in a series that ran until September 1913, she was particularizing about men's sexual habits and how to deal with them. Prison doctors, she said, prescribed medicine for convicts to keep their sexual desires in check (forty years later, new recruits to National Service were still having their legs pulled by old soldiers who said there was bromide in the tea). It was an easy step from the convict to the libertine. 'If prostitution can thus be abolished in prisons, it can be so in the world of free men. Self-control for men who can exert it! Medical aid for those who cannot! At all costs prostitution must go and the race be saved.'

The material was made into a book, *The Great Scourge and How to End It*. The scourge of course was VD. Citing the wildest guesses she could find, Christabel told her readers that between 75 and 80 per cent of all men had gonorrhoea, and a 'considerable percentage' were infected with the deadlier syphilis. The cure, 'briefly stated', was 'Votes for Women and Chastity for Men', the idea being that the former would lead to the latter. In best evangelical style she dismissed any idea that syphilis was curable once you caught it.

> Always [men] want to sin and escape the consequences ... they proclaim that they have found at last the cure for which they have been seeking through the centuries. A cure for sexual disease, which is of all diseases the most incurable! — as though Nature had not willed that there should be no way of escape from this scourge except one, and that one way the way of purity.

This was the New Woman restating the Old Morality, as described in the satirical verse:

> There was a young lady so wild
> Who kept herself pure, undefiled,
> By thinking of Jesus,
> Venereal diseases,
> And the danger of having a child.

What upset Christabel (as it upset many moralists) was that a German biochemist, Paul Ehrlich, had just discovered a compound that could cure syphilis. He and his colleagues had tested hundreds of substances, searching for one that would work with the disease. Number 606 in the series was discarded at the time, in 1907, but retested a year later by a

Japanese colleague and found to be effective. By 1910, '606' (later Salvarsan) was famous, the laboratories in Frankfurt had to be guarded, and the wealthy were anxious to try it. Northcliffe, the press lord, was said to have had syphilis and to have been treated in Germany, though there was never any proof. Because it was both secretive and sordid, the disease was often attributed to the famous on flimsy evidence.

The idea that men might now be in a position to manipulate the organism and buy their way out of trouble was unwelcome. Christabel announced that Salvarsan was not a cure at all and that it was killing people — it was true there were deaths at the beginning, though improved methods of administering it soon diminished the risk. But she was not writing a medical textbook. She was denigrating maleness and men. They were nasty creatures.

> They crave for intercourse with women whom they feel no obligation to respect. They want to resort to practices which a wife would not tolerate . . . Marriage does not 'satisfy' them. They fly to women who will not resent foul words and acts and will even permit unnatural abuse of the sex function . . .

As with many pieces of sexual writing, in the long years when sex had ceased to be unmentionable but explicitness was still far away, exactly what Christabel meant by 'practices' and 'unnatural abuse' was not revealed. She was on safer ground with aspects of male physiology, this being an area with a literature of its own, much of it concerned with the power of men's vital fluids. She quoted with approval a doctor who wrote about how 'The proper subjugation of the sexual impulses and the conservation of the complex seminal fluid, with its wonderfully invigorating influence, develop all that is best and noblest in men.' Semen had sacred overtones.

The effects of chastity on the penis were not overlooked. There was no need to fear, as some men apparently did, that their manhood would rust away. Was it out of conviction or devilment that Christabel quoted one of the King's physicians, Sir Dyce Duckworth? 'The sexual organs can lie dormant for years, can be left alone, out of consideration, and forgotten, so to speak, till the time comes for matrimony.' Also enlisted on the chastity front was 'the late William Acton M.R.C.S.,' a nineteenth-century doctor later famous for the dottiness of his views. Christabel quoted him as saying it was quite wrong to fear the atrophy of the organs. The problem was 'early abuse', when 'the organs become worn out, and hence atrophy arises.' However, 'every year of voluntary chastity renders the task easier by the mere force of habit.'

Acton was influential in his day, fifty years before Christabel's. His chief contribution to the literature was a mid-nineteenth-century book on *Functions and Disorders of the Reproductive Organs in Youth, in Adult Age and in Advanced Life*, where he announced that most women had little interest in sex. The book conceded that occasional women, as the divorce courts showed, had 'sexual desires so strong that they surpass those of men.' These, however, were untypical:

> I am ready to maintain that there are many females who never feel any sexual excitement whatever . . . Many of the best mothers, wives, and managers of households, know little of or are careless about sexual indulgences . . . [a modest woman] submits to her husband's embraces, but principally to gratify him; and, were it not for the desire of maternity, would far rather be relieved from his attentions.

If we had a better idea of what Christabel thought about Acton and his views on women's sexuality, we might learn what views she held herself. Her 'Great Scourge' tirade was an attack on the enemy but said little (apart from 'Beware!') about how women should conduct their sexual relationships, even in the Utopian society she believed that Votes for Women would create.

A prurient but all-too-natural interest in what the Suffragettes were like in the bedroom hovers behind any account of them. Half-hearted attempts have been made to show there was a streak of lesbianism in the movement. But female homosexuality at the time was too esoteric to have had a high profile, or any profile at all. Few writers had come to terms with it. Forel had recently written with disdain about lesbians, adding that such habits as the oral sex practised between women were 'aberrations of the sexual appetite, and it is needless to say that every human being should refrain from them out of self-respect.' Later on, in the nineteen-twenties, when lesbianism emerged tentatively as another sexual novelty for people to shudder at, it was possible to look back and blame the Suffragettes for having invented it. The *New Statesman* magazine, reviewing a derisive novel about lesbians, could suggest (1928) that 'now it is a comparatively widespread social phenomenon, having its original roots no doubt in the professional man-hating of the Pankhurst Suffragette movement.'

Christabel's pronouncements about diseased men and the state of their organs used a language that would have been impossible a few years earlier. Susan Kingsley Kent, a historian of the movement, says that feminist pioneers 'rarely spoke *publicly* of the sexual nature of their motives and aims . . . Suffrage memoirs, however, suggest that in private the theme of sexual problems dominated feminist discussions. Meikle [Wilma Meikle, a much-quoted figure] recalled in 1916 that "very frequent discussions with older suffragists of the more sordid problems of sex" took place in suffrage meetings, deputations and lectures.'

How far individual women of those times went in accepting their own desires, heterosexual or otherwise, is a mystery. Some of them doubtless behaved as Dr Acton said they should, though the pure doctrine of Actonism itself was dismissed even by some of his contemporaries. Some must have displayed the appetites that would be thought unexceptional today, but evidence tends to be about unusual women, since otherwise it wouldn't have survived. Olive Schreiner (1855–1920), a South African writer who came to Britain in the 1880s and had a botched love affair with the unusual Havelock Ellis, was so highly sexed that (like Christabel's convicts) she took bromide, prescribed by Ellis, in an effort to calm her frustration. Sexual abstinence, she claimed, was worse for women than for men. When staying on the Isle of Wight, she is said to have fallen in love with a sadistic headmaster, and to have enjoyed submitting to him, while hating herself for such behaviour. To Havelock Ellis, who wrote her case history, she spoke of wanting the sadist 'to tread on me and stamp me fine into powder.' Acton would have had one of his classifications ready for her: 'Nymphomania, a form of insanity which those accustomed to visit lunatic asylums must be fully conversant with.' But how many Olive Schreiners were there? How many Christabels?

Christabel's private life seems to have been spotless, but there must have been elements in her nature that drove her to go on about men as she did; unless her sexism was merely an effort of the will, contrived in cold blood for the greater good of the cause. But it doesn't read like that. When it was all over, her own life dwindled. A decade later, in her forties, she wrote 'Confessions of Christabel' for a newspaper, saying that she had never married because no man she met ever came up to her standards. If her own statistics were to be believed, it would have been difficult to find a man it was safe to marry. Nevertheless, you see what she meant. An entire future world seems to wait in her dark contemptuous eyes and disturbed adjectives. Her followers, as she said, would have felt betrayed by her marriage. This didn't apply to followers like Teresa

Billington-Greig, who, even before she married Mr Greig, was heard to talk about the pleasures of fornication that they were already enjoying. But Mrs Greig was too normal to be a heroine on Christabel's scale.

According to David Mitchell, Christabel's biographer, by 1913 more than 60 per cent of subscribers to the Women's Social and Political Union, the Pankhurst organization, were unmarried; so were all its twenty-three organizers. As the campaign continued with great fury, through 1913 and into 1914, the core of the militants consisted of young, single women. In the war they would drive ambulances, learn shorthand and typing, and (sometimes) make love to young men who were on their way to the battlefields. They had played their part; after the war (in which all militant action was suspended) they would get the vote.

There were other implications. What the movement had done was to provoke large numbers of the middle-class women who made up the majority of the Suffragettes into thoughts about their status, about sex and even about how to regard men. Precisely what they would make of these thoughts in the years to come was another matter. But it was the beginning of an education.

Behind the rise of political feminism was something more personal, women's slow-dawning perception that sex was theirs to enjoy as much as men's. To make this bold move, from being 'angels in the house' to sexual creatures who were in that respect no more and no less 'beasts' than men, meant taking a more realistic (and thus more ruthless) view of their own natures. They would need all the help they could get from technology, in particular from contraception. The process would take the rest of the century, and still be incomplete by its last decade.

The Queenie Gerald Affair

Queenie Gerald was a young prostitute who ran a brothel at the top of Haymarket, near Piccadilly Circus Underground station, in the years before the First World War. Perhaps she had been an actress of sorts; her name was assumed. The police raided her in June 1913, she pleaded guilty, there was a short prison sentence. But the case aroused interest, with questions in the House and articles in the papers. It was taken up by

Christabel Pankhurst, who wrote about it in her 'Great Scourge' series, alleging, as others did, that important names were being concealed, and attempts made to hush things up. There was no real evidence of this; only hints and one or two odd features.

No names were disclosed, but there was nothing unusual about that: the names of prostitutes' clients never were, and never are, except when men are charged with the modern offence of kerb-crawling. Conservative newspapers ran stories suggesting that Liberal Cabinet Ministers had been involved. Christabel took for fact what others read as gossip. The affair may have been no more than that.

Police led by Detective Inspector Curry went to the flat at 6.30 one evening. There was no secret about the brothel's existence. Later a letter appeared in a newspaper (signed 'An Englishman') to say that 'on several occasions for about a year, when I have myself been returning from theatre and supper to my club – the place having been pointed out to me – girls have been at the windows, apparently in night attire, for one purpose, and this under the eyes of the police. Why did the authorities delay prosecution?'

The flat was decorated with arum lilies, displayed in vases visible from the street. When the police knocked, a woman calling herself a 'mental nurse' came to the door. Queenie was in the bathroom with two girls, aged seventeen and eighteen, who were 'almost nude'. 'This *is* a surprise,' she said, adding that she was 'only giving the girls a bath.' The flat consisted of sitting room, bedroom, bathroom and lavatory; it was short of furniture, and Queenie didn't live there. She was twenty-six, attractive and well-dressed. Police took away one whip, one cane, one revolver, a penny copy of the 'White Slave' Act and twenty-one improper photographs, together with cash totalling two hundred and two pounds and eighteen shillings, nearly nine thousand pounds today. About half this was in gold sovereigns, the rest in ten and five-pound notes, which meant a wealthy clientele. But no men were on the premises, only a few of their letters.

The first hearing of the case was at Marlborough Street in June. Queenie, dressed in 'a stylish straw hat with a large drooping black feather, a dark boa, close-fitting black costume and patent boots,' pleaded guilty to living on immoral earnings. The magistrate, Frederick Mead, had a sharp tongue, no patience with women, and a conviction that things were changing for the worse (in 1929, by which time he was eighty-two, but still running Marlborough Street, he deported a Japanese, saying, 'You have come to this country to work in competition with Englishmen. I consider this objectionable').

In 1913 he was in his mid-sixties. He heard the evidence, cleared the public gallery – but allowed the press to stay – forbade any mention of Queenie Gerald's real name, although it emerged that she was a married woman, and adjourned the case. When it came up next, the police mentioned the letters they had found. Mead said he didn't think such correspondence was material, and sent the case to the London Sessions for trial, where it was heard on 10 July by the deputy chairman, Allan Lawrie. Gerald pleaded guilty and was sent to prison for three months.

Rumours spread and questions were asked. The Pankhursts were on to it at once. So was the *Globe*, a Tory newspaper, and Keir Hardie, the Labour MP. Hardie busied himself pursuing the Liberal Home Secretary, Reginald McKenna, with questions, and followed up with a penny pamphlet, *The Queenie Gerald Case. A Public Scandal. White Slavers in a Piccadilly Flat. An exposure.*

The whispers said that Queenie could have been charged with procuring, the implication being that she was procuring under-age virgins destined for special clients. If evidence of this had been produced, the clients themselves would have been guilty of a criminal offence, and they would have been in the dock with Queenie. Instead the system had let her off with a trivial sentence, while brazen lechers continued to offer gold for innocent girls.

A hint of fire could be detected through the smoke. Prosecuting counsel, as reported by reliable newspapers, had told the court that 'letters found on the premises made it clear that the accused was carrying on the trade of a procuress.' When passing sentence the judge mentioned that there was 'some evidence' of this. There is no doubt that Queenie's trade was supplying sexual services, that a procuress is what she was. This didn't have to mean procuring virgins or respectable women; procuring prostitutes was the usual interpretation. But was someone afraid that if a specific charge about procuring was framed, it would lead in awkward directions? Or was it simply that after so much disinformation in the past year about the White Slave traffic, even a lawyer could be momentarily confused about the interpretation of 'procuring'?

This was McKenna's line when he was questioned in the Commons. Wriggling a little, he said that counsel had been speaking 'in the colloquial sense', and meant 'a person who keeps an immoral house.' The judge had been 'incorrect on the facts of the case'. The rest of what

McKenna had to say was straightforward enough. The flat had been raided because of a statement made to the police by a prostitute who had worked there, presumably someone with a grudge. The girls had all been 'on the streets' before Queenie employed them; this remark implied that she had not enticed any woman, whatever her age, into prostitution. A ledger had been found recording hundreds of payments, in some cases with a name alongside the amount, but in no case was it the name of a Member of Parliament, let alone a Cabinet Minister. The letters found in the flat, which were supposed to contain evidence of girls (perhaps virgins) being procured, were unsigned except in one case – this was a man called Morris, who found clients for Queenie. There was no evidence that she had procured anyone who was not already a prostitute.

As for improper intervention with the process of law, no one had sought to influence Mead or Lawrie. McKenna said that when he was told about the case, 'my instructions were that the prosecution should be pressed to the full.' Comforting words for Queenie's clients rounded off the statement: 'Every man, so far as I am concerned, may rest at ease that I would not disclose his name unless I had better evidence ... than a mere entry in the handwriting of a brothel keeper.'

None of this deterred Keir Hardie. 'A huge conspiracy is afoot to defeat the ends of justice,' he wrote, an extravagant evangelist who had convinced himself that a third of a million fallen women walked the streets of Britain. He saw it as propaganda in a good cause, an appeal to the puritan conscience, that mysterious constituency, part noble (as it seems now, looking back), part daft: 'Let temperance societies and kindred organizations speak out. Purity is an integral part of temperance. Let the nation speak out.'

Titbits included in the prosecution's case were winkled out as evidence of unspeakable vileness. Hardie said that Morris, the tout, 'haunted fashionable hotels to bait idle rich guests into allowing Madame Queenie Gerald to provide nice sweet virgin morsels.' She had written Morris a letter that said, 'Your friend wishing to meet a few Society ladies, I can arrange for three on Sunday. They are the real thing and frightfully expensive. Will you ask the Prince what he is prepared to give.' Keir Hardie added sarcastically, 'foreigner, of course.' There was nothing about virgins in the Morris letter; though the prosecution did intimate that a cadet at Sandhurst, the military college, had written to Queenie asking for one.

Hardie refused to believe that 'three or four soiled girls' (two of whom were reported to have been heavily pregnant at the time of the raid) were the source of Queenie's affluence. 'Is it a likely tale?' asked the Nonconformist Conscience. 'Was it for such that the flat was decked with sixteen dozen Arum lilies, that the hot-scented baths were prepared, that the whips and lashes, reminiscent of Oriental orgies, were provided?'

But no one was able to take the story further. A single Public Record Office file about Queenie Gerald survives, composed of material from a series of original Home Office files, most of which have been destroyed. There need be nothing sinister about this: only a tiny percentage of Civil Service paper on any topic is preserved. Having decided to keep Queenie Gerald, it seems a pity that the official did away with papers that may have dealt with such matters as the decision to prosecute and the controversy about names and letters. But he left a few clues.

A handwritten note survives from Frederick Mead, the Marlborough Street magistrate, to say that he sometimes stopped the press reporting 'unnatural offences' and 'other cases where the facts to be disclosed are of an excessively obscene nature.' In the Gerald case, he didn't want the facts heard in open court, but relied on the discretion of reporters. Names were not suppressed as part of this arrangement, but because both defence and prosecution counsel requested it.

Mead's note sounds as if it was written to order. So does a note that Allan Lawrie, the trial judge, addressed to a Home Office official on 5 August. This said there was no evidence to support a charge of procuring, and that no evidence given in court was suppressed, except that 'I requested that the considerable sums of money earned by the women in the flat should not be reported.'

Also in the file is a police list of property to be returned to Queenie Gerald. This identifies some of the correspondence:

> Letter undated 'I brought a friend Prince.' Letter undated 'Will you get me a virgin' signed Somerset. Sheet of paper 'Another little girl here now' etc. Letter undated signed 'The American.' Memo 'Please ring up Ritz.' Letter signed 'Harry J. Fitzroy.'

At the back of the Home Office file, a pocket contains a letter, undated but headed 'Monday', to Queenie. It covers one sheet of writing paper. The printed address is 'Corsemalzie, Whauphill, Wigtownshire, N.B.' – i.e. North Briton, meaning Scotland. There is no indication of why the letter was left in the file.

Dear Miss Gerald,
I shall be up on Thursday and should be glad if I could meet
your auburn friend early in the afternoon as I shall want to leave
Waterloo by the 4.12.
Will call in the morning Thursday.
Yours ever, [illegible – it might be Jackshire, Yorkshire or Jackson]

The paper has a crest, the silhouette of a man bearing a club on his shoulder, and the motto 'Dread God'. The device is said to have been used by a family called Macaffie, possibly a branch of the Gordons, who lived at Corsemalzie. The house is now a hotel, where the crest can be seen on a wall.

The Queenie Gerald case leaves questions unanswered, but so do many criminal prosecutions. Complicated matters are reduced to sufficient order for some kind of justice to be done, and the debris cleared away to make room for more. No one pays to have every loose end tidied up. One can only speculate – on, for instance, McKenna's statement that 'my instructions were that the prosecution should be pressed to the full,' when the case was brought to his attention. Why was it brought to his attention in the first place? Home Secretaries are not usually consulted about routine police matters.

There is also the matter of McKenna's response when Keir Hardie asked him about the letters. Was there, asked Hardie, 'no signature of any kind – no means of identification?' McKenna replied, 'None whatever,' adding that none of the letters was written on 'ordinary writing paper' that might have identified it. Given the existence of the letter asking about 'your auburn friend', McKenna's answer wasn't true; though the honest answer might have been no more than the worldly retort that the authorities had better things to do than track down prostitutes' clients in the hope of finding that someone, somewhere, had broken the law.

The Record Office file continues into the 1920s, when the unreliable magazine *John Bull* repeated allegations of a cover-up in 1913, and said that Queenie was still in business. What she called 'persecution' by journalists was making her paranoiac. It was at this time that she cited Rosa Lewis of the Cavendish Hotel as a friend. She now called herself the Hon. Geraldine Q.C. Gaynor, which conceivably contained part of her real name, and lived at various West End addresses. A letter to the Home Office in 1922 came from an address in Maddox Street, in the West End, with four telephone numbers on the writing paper; prostitution had to move with the times. At different periods she was in Long Acre, in Jermyn Street, in Half Moon Street, abode of gentlemen and abortionists. On one occasion she was awarded a farthing damages for an assault in Brighton. She began writing letters of complaint to the Home Office. 'Doubtless', began one, 'you are well acquainted with my name and with the circumstances of the theft of my furs.' Another said that in 1913 she had been mistaken for somebody else. She wanted a gun licence so she could have a revolver.

In 1927 she was in a flat off Oxford Street, writing to the Home Secretary, now the pious Joynson-Hicks. She told him of a man outside her flat who kept annoying her, and a persistent scuffling on the stairs. By this time there was no headed notepaper. Keir Hardie would have seen the decline as her just deserts, as would William Coote and Christabel Pankhurst, those students of self-satisfaction that the tight cords of morality drew together. But by then, the 'social evil' was no longer causing such delicious shudders of horror.

The uneasy rumours that surrounded Queenie Gerald sprang from a bad conscience, and the dread that great men might be caught with their trousers down. For the Edwardians, as for the Victorians, the prostitute was a private necessity who had to be seen as a public sinner. By 1914, the slow processes that would both diminish her role, and make hypocrisy a shade less iniquitous, were under way.

4

'Interfering Toads'

The Nation at War

WELL BEFORE 1914, many people resented what they saw as the decline of the old sexual order, whether this was measured by the themes of advanced novels, by the gradual spread of contraception, by middle-class women's new awareness, or simply by a general willingness to discuss subjects that were formerly forbidden. Thousands of little battles would help determine the outcome.

In April 1912, Bradford city council held the line on mixed bathing at the municipal swimming baths. The baths committee wanted six hours every Thursday set aside for 'mixed and family bathing' at one location, but the full council shook its head. A Councillor Varley, who led the resistance, objected to being called a prude, though he didn't object to 'puritanical' and 'grandmotherly', and suggested that some on the council would be better men if *they* had listened to their grandmothers. What the council had to consider, he said, were the moral weaklings who might not be able to resist the temptations of mixed bathing. 'Society has gone far enough on the lines which make for liberty and licence. It is time for the State and the municipality to cry Halt!'

Time was not on Bradford's side. Men and women, safely covered from throat to knee, already swam side by side at baths in Scotland, in the north of England and in London. The London borough of Willesden was still holding out. One councillor had argued that bathers in the water might be able to look through chinks in the doors and see ladies' naked feet and ankles. 'At this sally,' reported the *News of the World*, 'everyone smiled, from the sober mayor down to the uniformed attendants.' By 1912 it was already a bit too much.

The war two years later affected sexual morals, as wars usually did. From the start, the shifts and separations in people's lives began to accelerate the drift towards 'laxity', British newspapers were full of stories about 'khaki fever', which led girls to make immodest advances to men in uniform. Stories were told from all over Europe of promiscuity. A doctor in Paris said that 'numerous French women' patriotically gave themselves to soldiers on their way to the fighting that summer. Expecting the worst in Britain, social workers egged on by journalists were talking about the 'War Babies' crisis even before 4 May 1915, when the nine months from 4 August 1914 were up.

Attempts were made to excuse the War Babies by representing them as 'children of our dead heroes', the men who 'fought at the Marne and Mons' in the early days of the German advance. A *Times* correspondent (April 1915) dismissed this slander against the Regular Army: 'Most of the men responsible for the miserable position of these girls and women belong either to the Territorials or the new armies. A large proportion of them have not up till now fought anywhere.' The same correspondent was doubtful about proposals to legitimize children born out of wedlock if the parents subsequently married; these would 'strike at the basis of our present laws of inheritance.'

A campaign to make better social provision for illegitimate children and their mothers was stamped on by the churches, on the grounds that it was a fuss about nothing. A clergyman wrote to *The Times* from Nottingham to say that he thought the illegitimacy rate (about forty thousand per million births) would go down in the war, not up. His argument, widely heard in a country that was still trying to run itself on Christian principles, was that 'the discipline and solemnity of war will have purged our manhood, and our women and girls, in all cases except that of the youngest, are learning much.' They learned other lessons. As the war went on, illegitimate births rose above sixty thousand per million. But in 1915 it was still early days.

Speaking on 26 April, the chilly Archbishop of York, Cosmo Lang, said the figures had been exaggerated, and that in any case, it was no use being sentimental about immorality. We couldn't sustain our fighting spirit, suggested Lang, if we saw moral decline ahead of us. Throughout the war this view was respected by politicians, who went along with the British clergy's belief that what 'moral decline' meant was sexual promiscuity. Perhaps it was true that in the earlier, more innocent days of the war, the prospect of laxer sexual morals would have been enough to lower national morale; perhaps not. It was Lang's job to have no doubts about such matters; and to have no time for undue sympathy with unmarried mothers, either.

Church organizations already made provision for bad girls — some with criminal records, some unemployable because they were undisciplined or 'immoral', some pregnant. When secularists criticized the methods as harsh and unsympathetic, the *Vigilance Record* responded angrily. In 'hundreds of cases', girls had been shown Christian love, and their feet 'firmly set once more on the path of rectitude.' However, warned the writer, 'It is certainly not the province of such Institutions to make heroines of these poor girls, or to condone the steps which led to their trouble.'

The Church Army, an evangelical offshoot of the Church of England, had been running Homes since before the war. Photographs of inmates show them clustered in laundries and sewing-rooms, or posed in rows outside a wooden fence and bay windows. All wear the domestic servant's uniform, with a cap perched on the head. Their faces look guarded, as if they are waiting for an order. Of those who were pregnant, some would have been in service when it happened; others had been ejected by poor families or had no families at all. Either way the object was to turn them into penitents who would do what they were told and become satisfactory housemaids for middle-class homes. If possible the mother kept her child; if not it was adopted. At the time it seemed an adequate regime for sinners. The Church Army was even criticized by stern Christians for being too sympathetic.

A newspaper article, reprinted with approval by the Church Army, described the Frances Owen Home in Cheltenham, a 'dumping ground for incorrigible girls. They enter disorderly; they come out at the end of twelve months as prim as West-end table maids.' 'Before-and-after' photographs show 'Two Rough Diamonds' — drab children in shabby domestics' garb — followed by 'One of the above Rough Diamonds after polishing, i.e. training for service' — now in immaculate uniform, with embroidered bodice, resting an arm on the back of someone else's dining chair, and looking about forty years old.

The girls arrived 'all covered with the mud of sin, for which a low standard of parental duty, giddy companionships, love of gaudy dress, the jewellery canvasser etc., are largely responsible.' One, according to the housewife who had employed her, was 'Negligent, addicted to novelette reading, her one desire is to roam about the streets — what am I to do with her?' Another was said to have 'a temper like a tiger'; her employer advised the horse-whip, prison or a reformatory. Never mind, the Church Army ensured that most of them were 'real treasures in a household when they leave us.' In the nineteen-eighties Steve

Humphries* recorded the memories of some former Church Army inmates, now elderly women. What they remembered was the air of punishment, the poor food, the coarse clothes, the heavy clogs that rubbed the ankles raw.

The fact that in rural districts, and sometimes in towns as well, a community often expected pregnancies out of wedlock — and sustained the mothers if men failed to do the decent thing and marry them — didn't alter the punitive way a society brought up on 'Christian morals' behaved when it had a woman at its mercy. When the British Army adopted a sensible policy of paying allowances to soldiers' common-law wives, as though they were legally married, churchmen were furious and called it 'an outrageous insult to respectable and self-respecting womanhood.' The Archbishop of Canterbury said that the distinction between married and unmarried mothers was 'vital to our country's well-being.'

Among wartime novelties was the employment of women, some of them former Suffragettes, as a genteel morals police. These came in two varieties. One was the Women Police Volunteers (later 'Service'), set up soon after the war began by Miss Damer Dawson, whose firm chin and steel-rimmed spectacles would have seen off most burglars. Dawson, who was a mountaineer and drove a car, was meeting Belgian refugees as they arrived in London in August 1914. At a railway station she watched a woman who had 'changed her dress and the colour of her hair three times in the same night,' and caught her trying to spirit away two women refugees. This convinced Dawson that she had stumbled on one of the White Slave Traders, and gave her the idea of using women police to combat them. The authorities were persuaded, though not of the need to catch White Slavers. The police volunteers could be, and indeed were, useful auxiliaries. They also had a middle-class presence that was respected, or at least deferred to, by the lower orders.

Dawson designed a blue uniform with a felt hat, and presently she and two colleagues arrived in Grantham, where there was a large military population, and began improving standards. The Army general commanding the district gave them the right of access to any building within a six-mile radius. 'This,' said Dawson with satisfaction, 'gave us power to go into the women's houses to see if the girls were in bed.' Khaki fever was raging. Dawson claimed to have ejected 'hundreds of soldiers and girls'. Soldiers' wives convicted of drunkenness or immorality (which meant

* *A Secret World of Sex.*

prostitution) could lose their Army allowance, so that informal intervention by social workers, which was the Police Volunteers' role, was arguably saving errant women from something worse. The Home Office advised police to be tactful when dealing with wives who fell into error, and to remember that they had been 'deprived of the company and guidance of their husbands.'

It was an England of sexual busybodies. Dawson's second-in-command, Mary Allen, a former Suffragette with a sense of humour — when made to stitch men's shirts in prison, she embroidered 'Votes for Women' on the tails — described how she spoke to a young officer who was talking with 'two girls of known bad reputation.' He said they were his cousins. 'Very well,' said Allen. 'You are an officer and a gentleman. Naturally I must accept your word.' Five minutes later he did the decent thing, admitted he had been lying and chastely returned to camp. It was an England of codes of conduct, too.

The other force of women, rarely mentioned in the memoirs of Damer Dawson's brigade, was the Women's Patrols, also formed soon after the outbreak of war. Two weeks before the war a deputation had gone to the Home Office, proposing that women be used in police work against such immorality as men soliciting women (not the other way round) and 'nuisances complained of in parks etc.' This idea owed something to the White Slave scares, but even more to middle-class women's new interest in sexual matters. Although expressed as a concern with the moral welfare of girls, behind it was curiosity and the desire to explore a forbidden subject.

A bishop's widow proposed the Women's Patrols. She was Louise Creighton, whose husband was the Bishop of London when he died in 1901, an ecclesiastical historian with an interest in 'social hygiene' — a vogueish term that embraced health and morality, and offered a polite way of approaching sexual problems. Mrs Creighton was a social hygienist, too. Her interests included the National Vigilance Association and the National Union of Women Workers (NUWW), a society of philanthropic workers of which she was the president. The intention of the patrols was to be 'neither police nor rescue workers, but true friends of the girls, in the deepest and holiest sense of the word.' The authorities gave their blessing, and the patrols, organized via the NUWW offices, were ready by October 1914.

Their authority consisted of armbands and a card. They had to be 'women of tact and experience between thirty and fifty years of age,' and they worked in pairs. Some police forces disliked the idea. The chief constable of Bradford said he was thinking only of the women's own good – they risked being insulted by 'indecent loafers' (perhaps the 'moral weaklings' they had to be careful of in the Bradford swimming baths), or even being attacked. A Lancashire vicar said the patrols were un-English and it would be better for mothers to guard their daughters.

Most of the work was done in London, or in the vicinity of Army camps and depots. More than two thousand patrols were deployed. A soldier's wife said they were called 'interfering toads' at first, but now were 'rather wonderful'. Where camp followers hung around billets on the old pretence that they were washer-women, the patrollers set up prostitute-free laundries. Where dark alleys and lovers' lanes threatened goings-on, patrollers conducted searches and where necessary sent for a constable. 'We have several open grass patches which are very dangerous,' said one report, 'as the young couples lie there in the dark, and even in daylight such things are seen that we have been obliged to call the attention of the police.' A couple, both civilians, were found behind a bush 'in a disgraceful position,' and told to move on. Later the patrol returned to the bush. Several couples were lying on the damp grass. This time they were in 'decorous attitudes'.

Virtue was being brought to the children of the poor whether they liked it or not. Small though the scale of the exercise must have been, in a nation where tens of thousands availed themselves nightly of damp grass and bushes, as their forefathers had done, the patrolwomen were a potent symbol of high-mindedness coming to the rescue, determined to save pleasure-seekers from themselves. A seaside patrol reported that at their instigation, 'a seat on the front, which was used by couples, has been boarded up.' In another town, patrols were so short-staffed that they concentrated their energies on Sunday night, the worst time of the week, when 'there are only men, soldiers, boys and flappers* in the streets after the evening services.' The good news was that 'patrolling among these giddy girls somehow has a sobering effect.' Elsewhere, woods had been patrolled every Sunday evening throughout November 1915. Couples were seen behaving indecently; the patrols used lanterns to have a good look. Eventually, said the report, the patrollers were recognized as official persons by the 'numerous groups of lads and girls',

---

* Before 1914 an immoral young woman, the meaning later softened to 'flighty' or 'indecorous', though still with a sexual undertone.

after which they 'did not meet with so many rude remarks.' Not surprisingly, someone at Women's Patrols HQ voiced the fear that certain workers were 'inclined to dwell too much upon the seamy side.'

The police were touchy about amateur investigators on their ground. After a newspaper praised the work of patrols in London, the authorities asked a local police commander for his comments. He said that six patrolwomen had been seen nightly, walking behind prostitutes and standing as close as possible whenever one of them solicited a man. They would then 'by their ostentatious action and persistent gaze compel the parties to occasionally separate or move away.' Far from closing down brothels, he said, they had ruined police observation of a house in a side street, when a patrolwoman followed a couple to the front door, and let herself be seen writing in a notebook.

London parks, another traditional venue for fornication and worse, were a popular target. Parks at Norwood and Blackheath were patrolled at dusk; the reports sound disheartened at the lack of activity. Hyde Park, used both for paying and non-paying sex, offered more scope. A Miss Salisbury and a Miss Peebles were in the park with a male constable on an August evening when all three observed a corporal in the London Regiment having sexual intercourse with a lady clerk from Harrods. Miss Salisbury and her friend declined to appear in court; not that this mattered much, since the couple pleaded guilty, the corporal being fined ten shillings and sixpence, while the clerk was told not to do it again. But the patrols' activity may have had some effect on behaviour. Police pointed out wearily that couples were now starting to have sexual intercourse in dark corners of Park Lane, alongside Hyde Park, a greater nuisance than if they had been allowed to get on with it under the trees.

In a case involving 'gross indecency' between two men, police said the patrolwomen who witnessed the act were 'not only willing but anxious to give evidence.' The act was described circumspectly in a police memo: 'Two male persons are in Hyde Park; a youth of 17 years is seen lying on his back and a man of 42 years had the younger man's person in his mouth.' The significance of the women's evidence, according to a senior police officer, was that charges involving indecency between men were usually referred to the central criminal court, where juries returned a 'not guilty' verdict in three-quarters of the cases; the reason being that 'it is extremely difficult to convince twelve jurymen that men exist capable of committing such filthy acts.' But the men pleaded guilty, so the patrolwomen were not needed. It was this willingness to expose themselves to the horrors of sex that dismayed many men, among them Mr Mead the Marlborough Street magistrate, who once lectured five patrolwomen (after a case involving a prostitute who had told a policeman to 'fuck off') about how disgraceful it was for them to listen to such filth.

The call of duty even took some of them to the cinema, widely suspected, because of its darkness and cheapness, as a hotbed of indecency. A new Home Secretary, Herbert Samuel, perceived the cinema as a deadly threat, much as righteous politicians came to see television later in the century. Samuel was anxious to 'know what really does take place at these Entertainments', and saw the Women Patrols as an economical way of being seen to do something. The patrols in turn were 'very keen and pleased' to be asked, especially since they were getting six shillings plus expenses for an eight-hour day.

Twelve women, five of them married, were sent off to investigate central London and the suburbs. Boxes, in those days found at cinemas as well as theatres, were stared at from all angles, especially if they had curtains. 'Angry voices' were heard from a box at a cinema in Great Windmill Street. A woman's voice said, 'I shall see the manager.' A door banged and there were footsteps. Nothing else happened, except that when the film ended, the patrolwoman observed that a couple of girls hung about, saying 'Where shall we have tea?' in loud voices. But no one took them up. In a cinema off the Strand, it was noted that pillars could be used to conceal indecency. None was in progress. A gallery was improperly lit at Clapham. At the Palladium, Brixton Hill, a couple in a box were spoken to twice by the manager. Men spat on the floors and babies crawled about. There was a general feeling that films depicting crimes ought to be censored (they were already), and one observer thought that Charlie Chaplin's films were vulgar and 'suggestive of evil'.

The final count was sixty-six cases where it was too dark to see if any indecency was taking place, and another thirty-nine where the geography made indecency possible. Hard as the patrolwomen worked, no wickedness came to light. It was even more discouraging than damp grass.

Harsher issues were in the air. The debate about sex that had gone on for the past decade was cloaked in high-minded language. Even the supposedly blunt home truths of the White Slave Trade were kept at a safe distance: it was mainly foreigners (with perhaps a few wicked Englishmen) who were up to no good. Now the circumstances of war were directing attention to the everyday behaviour of the British. The emotions of war and separation had led to more sexual indulgence. The fact was quickly recognized, and the indulgence reported on, attacked and occasionally defended; but always given publicity. Sexual behaviour in general (unless it was homosexual) thus began to receive more attention than would otherwise have been possible in so short a time. The attention in turn affected the behaviour.

Venereal disease had become a matter of public interest before the war, notably with the setting up in 1913 of a royal commission to investigate the problem. Events then made VD into a wartime problem, endangering tens of thousands of men who might have led less irregular lives if they hadn't been tempted to sample the delights of brothels in France and elsewhere. Pleasure and entertainment also came under scrutiny. Eventually a fifth of a million troops slept in London every night, most of them in transit to and from the inferno. What indulgences, if any, were our brave boys entitled to?

Max Pemberton, one of Northcliffe's men, wrote in 1917 about life for soldiers on leave now that 'the prude on the prowl has ruined London.' Dancing was difficult, said Pemberton, because so many dance-halls had been closed. The music hall offered scraggy chorus girls and red-nosed comedians. Hyde Park was dangerous because of the patrols. 'To kiss a girl in Hyde Park is an offence against the law for which a soldier is often fined the whole of the money he has in his pocket. The lightest demonstration of a man's affection can thus be twisted into a criminal offence by these prying women.' It was not clear if Pemberton meant his words to be taken literally, or if 'kissing' was a euphemism for stronger deeds. He quoted an officer:

> At night we used to dine at the Savoy and afterwards have a jolly little dance in the rooms off the Palm Court. You can't do that now — it's become wicked. But I tell you what you can do. You can settle up about midnight and go to a house in a by-street not three hundred yards from the Criterion Theatre — and if you've got the entree, you can open the door up on the first floor, find yourself among a dozen couples who haven't troubled the tailor or the costumier; you can dance and drink with them till the cows come home, and see an orgy which would have made Cleopatra blush. And that's the only kind of amusement you seem able to provide for us.

Between the lines is some personal disquiet that never quite gets spoken. It is there again in a moralizing open letter to 'The Flappers' that a woman wrote in the same newspaper soon after, warning girls of what harm they were doing to their future happiness by cheapening themselves. It was headed 'SPORTING' GIRLS AND THE RISKS THEY RUN. The word 'sporting' had heavy implications. The writer had been shocked to see 'quite a young girl, obviously of good bringing-up', select a table in a teashop where a young officer was sitting, and start talking to him. What impression of English girlhood would 'those boys who are fighting and bleeding and dying for England' take back to 'their dreary trenches and dug-outs?' One day real love would come along. 'How will you wish *then* that you had not given your "Flapper" kisses so lightly and so easily? How shamed you will feel when real love's first holy kiss is laid on your lips!'

Flapperish thoughts abounded. They could be found in *Cupid's Messenger*, a sixpenny magazine that began publication in 1915:

> 'Don't touch my hand,' said Dorothy,
> 'I've burned my finger-tips.
> But never mind, there's nothing much
> The matter with my lips.'

The *Messenger* claimed to be the first periodical devoted to love, staking its claim on vague grounds of public need — the thousands of men and girls ('girls particularly') who led 'lonely, uninteresting lives, simply and solely because they are unable to find, unaided, companions of their own or the opposite sex.' The pages radiate cheap respectability and a hint of something else. The illustration at the masthead shows a young man with an oiled-down scalp, facing a young woman with piled-up hair, across a Cupid holding an arrow bigger than himself. Articles include 'HOW TO GET MARRIED', 'BREACH OF PROMISE LAWS' and 'HOW TO TREAT A BROKEN ENGAGEMENT' ('Do not discuss it with even your intimate friends or permit them to mention it to you'). But the cream of the *Messenger* was a section of free personal advertisements. The editor trod carefully. He had no time, he said firmly, for evilly-disposed persons, adding that 'the bigamist will not find my columns a safe or happy hunting ground.' He was merely offering a social service. Thus, 'Lonely Typist' of Birmingham, twenty-one, sought a gentleman not over twenty-eight, who was on government work or unfit for service. 'Business Girl', also of Birmingham, twenty-nine, 'refined, jolly, broad-minded', wanted pen friends or a chum. In the early numbers, some or all of the ads may have been invented, though later on, when the editor found himself in deeper waters than he expected, they were certainly genuine. What kind of chums and gentlemen did girls think they were going to find? What did they mean to do when they found them?

> *Shy One (Catford)*, 23, small, wishes to meet a man 'pal,' not necessarily with a view to marriage. Is very lonely and would like a friend.

Responsible folk naturally had no time for such dangerous rubbish. The romantic novelist Marie Corelli, by now getting on a bit but still widely read, appealed to women to 'give up your foolish sensualities' and take to 'sturdy, sensible Work. Even you "toy-women" who dance half nude o' nights at restaurants and in basement saloons of "fashionable" hotels, wreaking a sly vengeance on men by poisonous lure and seduction, even YOU can be brave and helpful if you will!' All were told to wash the paint from their cheeks (make-up was no longer confined to harlots) and buckle to. 'Men want the women! – not for pleasure . . . but for work!'

Many were confident that the difficulties would pass. The more signs of impurity were detected, the more talk there was of purity. Mrs Creighton, the bishop's widow, told a conference in 1917, called to discuss 'the moral condition of the streets of London,' that whatever the present shortcomings of Britain, the future would be better. 'The virile men are going to begin by ruling themselves,' she said, giving a more temperate version of the Christabel Pankhurst message. Winnington-Ingram told the same conference that in the previous month he had addressed sixteen thousand troops at Aldershot and was sure it had done heaps of good.

General Sir Horace Smith-Dorrien was another optimist of the day. A field commander on the Western Front, he sought to withdraw troops from the Ypres Salient in 1915 because of heavy losses, and was at once removed from his command. In Britain he kicked his heels for a couple of years before he was sent off to be Governor of Gibraltar, meanwhile campaigning against immoral music halls. He was troubled by his frequent visits, usually spoiled by 'a lot of wriggling girls with extremely few clothes on,' and saddened by theatre advertisements like the one for a quadruple bill: 'Nellie, the Beautiful Cloak Model. The Unmarried Mother. A Man with Three Wives. She Slipped. (Soldiers half price).' The general refused to believe that the men wanted such dubious entertainment, insisting that in their hearts they would prefer shows that 'appealed to the best side of their patriotic natures.'

General F.P. Crozier would not have agreed. Crozier, also a staff officer who served in France, wrote a book of unusual insight about the war, *A Brass Hat in No Man's Land*. He noted that fornication by soldiers serving overseas traditionally went unnoticed, 'but in our England, somehow, the idea didn't go down quite so smoothly.' If so, that was unfortunate, but everything had to change. 'In 1914,' wrote Crozier, 'England changed her soul, otherwise she would have lost.'

As the killing went on, the mood grew harsher. The slaughter on the Somme in 1916, halfway through the war, was the climacteric. In *London Nights* Stephen Graham recalled New Year's Eve at the end of that year, outside St Paul's cathedral. 'Down below there was a wild mixture of khaki and women. They passed bottles to and fro; they cursed the passing year. "To hell with 1916!" was the cry.'

The behaviour of servicemen was a delicate subject. War was meant to purge the nation, bringing home (wrote the *Vigilance Record*) the 'absolute necessity of subjugating the material to the spiritual.' Clergymen were always saying it, and the secular authorities thought it expedient to agree. The reality of being a soldier was different. One social-purity group claimed, on the basis of undisclosed evidence, that a fifth of soldiers were so righteous that nothing would tempt them, and another fifth so vicious that nothing would save them; the remainder were open to influence (The US Army used the same rule-of-thumb ratios in the Second World War).

General Crozier, writing at a safe distance after the war, described the temptations, at least for officers, when living in billets with French families behind the line. His own quarters were once in a house with a woman and her daughter of twenty. The daughter brought a hot-water bottle to his bedroom, wearing her nightdress, long hair over her shoulders. Next night she came again, asking 'personal questions'. The general resisted the flesh, 'on the principle that it is a dirty bird which fouls its own nest', but knew that others were saying, 'Why not? The war is long, life is short.' Crozier had an eye for impropriety. He described a mock kit inspection he carried out on two officers who were late arriving for a train. Their luggage was opened.

> The result is astounding! Two pairs of girls' garters and an odd one. Two pairs of silk stockings and a chemise, one nightdress and a string of beads. A pot of vaseline, a candle, two boxes of matches and an envelope full of astonishing picture postcards, completes the list. 'Souvenirs,' says one rascal.

If respectable Englishmen might be tempted, so might respectable Englishwomen who were in France as nurses, civilians in government jobs, and members of the auxiliary forces. Crozier met the married daughter of a friend at Boulogne, where there were base camps and other military establishments. She told him that girls had become 'war-mad and sex-mad'. There were always rooms to go to, she said; immorality in Boulogne was as common as death at the front. Gossip of this kind was fiercely resisted at official level, without much effect. The WAACs, the Women's Army Auxiliary Corps, were a long-suffering target. 'Would you', asked the caption to a *Sporting Times* cartoon, 'rather have a slap in the eye or a WAAC on the knee?' Nurses were especially vulnerable. The German Magnus Hirschfeld's *Sexual History of the World War* devoted a chapter to the 'Eroticism of Nurses'. This suggested an 'erotic coloration' to their military work, especially among volunteers recruited from educated circles. There was a 'cult of the wounded'. A Red Cross nurse (in an apocryphal story) was washing the face of a simple Bavarian infantryman with vinegar and water. She asked if there was anything else she could do. The simple Bavarian couldn't contain himself. 'I don't want to interrupt your pleasure,' he said 'but so far you're the sixteenth who has washed my face today.'

The subject has always been in bad taste, and irresistible. Compton Mackenzie in a novel of the 1920s makes someone say of wartime nurses, 'Sure, they're splendid. They dress the wounded and undress themselves with equal devotion.' In the same period, the London magistrate who condemned Radclyffe Hall's lesbian novel, *The Well of Loneliness*, claimed to find in it a suggestion that women ambulance drivers in France were addicted to 'this vice', and was suitably disgusted.

What no one in authority could ignore was the soldier's habit of catching a disease. VD is said to have incapacitated, at one time or another, a quarter of all the armies engaged in the war; though statistics about sexual diseases were the despair of epidemiologists. The Army had had fairly accurate pre-war figures because it needed them for its own efficiency and was dealing with a controlled community. The British Army in India, in particular, took a practical view of its responsibilities. Minding its own business in the 1880s, it tried to ensure that Indian women in the 'regimental bazaars' attached to military depots were clean, attractive and properly housed. But an order to that effect sent to Army commanders was rescinded when moralists in Britain heard of it and complained.

VD rates in the British Army were high, up to two hundred and seventy-five cases per thousand in the late nineteenth century, probably the worst in Europe. By 1913 the figure had come down to fifty per thousand. Treatment was improving, and in theory the way was open for practical measures to further reduce the figures, despite the war. In practice the authorities were torpid, worrying what the neighbours would think. The Secretary for War, Lord Kitchener, hero of battles, was a bachelor, not at ease with sex. His signature appeared on a leaflet that men of the British Expeditionary Force took to France in 1914, their only prophylactic:

> Your duty cannot be done unless your health is sound. So keep constantly on your guard against any excesses. In this new experience you may find temptations both in wine and women. You must entirely resist both temptations, and, while treating all women with perfect courtesy, you should avoid any intimacy. Do your duty bravely. Fear God, honour the King.

The problem was the same as it had been with the regimental bazaars, that to take visible action aimed at making sexual intercourse safer was to risk appearing to condone the act.

The same dilemma affected the royal commission on VD, which reported in 1916, three years after it was set up. In some ways the report was far-sighted, calling for (and obtaining) a free national treatment service, thus irrevocably changing the way the disease was regarded. But although the commission thought that as many as a tenth of the inhabitants of large cities might be suffering from VD, it could not bring itself to talk about prevention. Among the commissioners were clergy, moralists (including Mrs Creighton) and medical conservatives. With one voice they spoke of raising moral standards and exercising self-control as the preferred means of prevention, thumping an imaginary pulpit as they declared that VD was 'intimately connected with vicious habits.' Calomel ointment and antiseptic were effective if used immediately after intercourse. Condoms (or 'preventives', the more usual word) were marketed as a safeguard against VD as well as against pregnancy. But it was difficult to speak of such matters. Dr Mary Scharlieb (b. 1845) a high-minded gynaecological surgeon who was another of the commissioners, wrote later, 'It was thought that the offer to make unchastity safe [would be] a blow to the country's morals.'

This triumph of principle over need was nowhere more apparent than in the Army. In the early part of the war, the government did little. It was reluctant to take direct action against prostitutes (who were assumed to be the prime source of infection) for fear of stirring up the feminists. The Home Office may have encouraged the women's patrols in the hope that they would save a few troops from infection. Then, in 1916, the year of the royal commission, the military finally decided to approve some kind of preventive treatment. But the order authorizing it was not clear and was variously interpreted; the Army Council itself was confused, since it felt it had to say that it rejected any form of prophylaxis that might 'afford opportunities for unrestrained vice.'

What were described as 'venereal ablution rooms' were set up, equipped with pots of calomel cream (which contained mercury) and pails brimming with permanganate of potash. These medicaments were expected to stop infection. How much use was made of the facilities depended on local commanders and medical officers. Instruction given to the men was often vague, if it was given at all.

The following year, 1917, an 'Imperial War Conference' in London heard behind closed doors from General B.E.W. Childs of the War Office that prophylactic advice could still not be given officially, 'because that would be immediately followed by a question in the House of Commons which it would be impossible to answer.' The Dominion governments, especially those of Canada and New Zealand, were infuriated by the apparent indifference of the British to the ravages of VD. Childs seemed inclined to agree with them. 'I know this country well,' he said, and muttered about 'grandmotherly legislation.' He also quoted his political boss, the War Minister, by then Lord Derby, as having said that 'the suggestion of a preventive being given to the soldier by the hand of his commanding officer is but preliminary to the establishment by the State of organized vice.' It was not always clear, at the conference or anywhere else, whether 'prophylaxis', another popular euphemism, could mean condoms as well as calomel ointment; the subject was too awkward to be gone into.

Condoms were never authorized for the British Army, though they may have been available with the connivance of officers. General Crozier, who said he arranged with a medical officer that his men should have access to treatment after sex (he doesn't say how long after, a crucial matter), noted that French civilians who had troops billeted on them often kept a stock of 'preventives', for mutual safety and for profit. Many officers must have gone in for condoms, manufactured in America and perhaps even in Germany. British output at the time was small. The

London Rubber Company was set up in Aldersgate in 1915, but for years imported most of its goods. Its main suppliers through the 1920s were in Germany, Europe's sexual engine.

The Navy went its own way with medical treatment. The reliable calomel-ointment method of stopping infection with syphilis, if applied soon enough, was first proposed in 1905. The Royal Navy adopted it, as did many Continental armed forces. Perhaps the popular idea of sailors ('a wife in every port') made it seem less reprehensible to protect jolly Jack Tars. Perhaps the Navy kept a lower profile.

No one in high places was disposed to turn a blind eye to what soldiers did. Half-hearted prophylaxis went ahead, slowed down by moral misgivings. The Army's VD rate was admittedly a shade lower than it had been in 1913, at forty-eight cases per thousand (the cases including some men who presented more than once). But the size of the new armies meant that the totals were alarming. In the first three years of the war, more than a hundred thousand British soldiers with VD were admitted or readmitted to hospitals in the UK, and a quarter of a million to British hospitals in France. There were unseemly differences between the home authorities and the Army as to whether the prostitutes of London or France were principally responsible; each blamed the other's territory.

An alternative approach was to suggest that professional prostitutes were no longer the real problem. The age of the 'amateur' had dawned. The idea that bands of irregulars (whether flappers or adulterous wives) were making themselves available was a novelty, perhaps exaggerated. But police found evidence of the tendency, not least at the big depots and training camps in the south of England. Women swarmed to Folkestone and other coastal towns. Colonial (often styled 'Imperial') troops were especially attractive. Australians and Canadians had no homes to go to when they were on leave, and fell more easily into the arms of strangers. One Australian general (Sir Neville Howse) hinted that Australians were at greater risk than the British because they had 'more virility'. In Liverpool, prostitutes with ladders tried to get at New Zealand troops in their barracks. It was widely alleged that some women offered a guaranteed dose of VD as an extra benefit, charged for at a higher rate, to men who would do anything to escape the front line for a month.

Rates of infection among Colonial troops rose to two or three times the British level, despite better prophylactic policies, including the use of condoms. (Early in the war the New Zealand commander, General Godley, wrote approvingly that a German officer was found to be carrying 'a little khaki bag containing a white flag with a loop on it by which it could be hoisted on the top of his sword, and a french letter'; despite his precautions he was dead.) The Imperial governments kept demanding more action to protect their soldiers. W.F. Massey, New Zealand's Prime Minister, saw hundreds of prostitutes at work in the Strand on an April evening, and said that the parents of soldiers who wrote to him, asking that their sons be forbidden to visit wicked Paris when they went on leave, didn't realize that London was worse. Sir Robert Borden, the Canadian Prime Minister, said that if the same 'horrible outrage' were threatened in a future war, he would refuse to send Canadians overseas.

For all the complaints, the government did little, as though stubbornly convinced that the streets of London were broad enough to bear the old compromise between decency and immorality. There was something to be said for this. The kind of action sought by Imperial spokesmen would probably have failed to keep soldiers and whores apart. As it was, plans for Defence of the Realm Act provisions that would curb or outlaw sex between servicemen and prostitutes were shuffled around Whitehall for a year or two before the War Cabinet approved them in March 1918. They were then largely ignored.

One further issue affecting servicemen's morals arose in acute form during the last year of the war, the business of the French brothels. Armies have habitually used or countenanced paid women to keep the troops happy. During the First World War, a combination of purity movements and fears about VD had a mild deterrent effect. In 1914 there were demands in Germany that the entire army in the field be chaste, perhaps in expectation of a swift victory, the achievement of which would act as an incentive. But as the war settled into stalemate, the Germans set up military brothels in cities behind the lines. Magnus Hirschfeld, who advertised for reminiscences to use in his sexual history of the war, heard from a German soldier who spent three weeks in one of these brothels, working as a 'sanitary official'. Six girls were employed, and on the quietest day they entertained fifty-five men between four and nine p.m., the usual business hours. One evening the most popular girl managed thirty-two men herself. Clients were given treatment before and after they had intercourse, and a note was made of each man's partner.

Nothing so explicit would have been acceptable to the British. There were doctors who spent their time addressing soldiers, telling them, in the words of a Dr E.B. Turner, 'how much better they would be employed pumping lead into the Hun than lying in hospital and having "606" pumped into them,' and reporting that the troops responded with 'acclamation and enthusiasm'.

Voices seeking and indeed expecting continence from men in general and soldiers in particular continued to be heard throughout the fighting. Four Army chaplains wrote a book at the end of the war that demanded chastity as loudly as Christabel Pankhurst had been demanding it before fighting began. The chaplains had spent much of the war distributing 'pledge cards' for men to sign, bearing such messages as, 'I resolve by God's grace always to be able to look my mother or sister, my wife or my sweetheart, in the face and to have in my memory no dark night that I would hide from her.'

But if exhortation didn't always have the effect that the chaplains would have liked, at least there were no British brothels to tempt the troops behind the lines. This was the saving grace, that the brothels belonged to the French, not to us, thus solving half the problem. The French were well known for that sort of thing. Even the official name for the dens of vice was safely foreign, *maisons tolérées*, which sounded less contaminated than the 'disorderly houses' of English common law. It was French tarts who staffed them and French doctors who did the medical examinations to make sure they were free from disease. All the British Army did was let soldiers avail themselves of the facilities.

These were provided at bases, rest camps and ports. Many must have offered the bleakest pleasures. In James Hanley's banned story *The German Prisoner* a soldier reminds his comrade of a brothel at Fricourt — 'Remember young Dollan mounting that old woman? Looked like a bloody witch. I still remember her nearly bald head.' Officers expected something better. This is not a well-documented area, and we are fortunate to have Philip Ziegler's account of the future King Edward VIII (and Duke of Windsor) with fellow officers at a brothel in Calais in May 1916, watching but not touching naked prostitutes as they struck erotic poses (H.R.H., aged twenty-one, found it 'a perfectly filthy and revolting sight, but interesting for me as it was my first insight into these things!!'). Later that year his equerries handed him over to a skilful French tart called Paulette in Amiens, where he lost his virginity amid a haze of alcohol.

The availability of French brothels made many uneasy, especially after

1916, when compulsory military service was introduced. The picture of innocent boys dragged from farms and factories and exposed to vice was easily exploited. But no one chose to make the brothels a major public issue until *The Shield*, the magazine of the Association for Moral and Social Hygiene — which had its roots in Josephine Butler's campaigns of the previous century — published an article at the end of 1917. It described a fifteen-woman brothel at Cayeux-sur-mer, on the coast near Abbeville, serving a convalescent depot for British soldiers. An average of three hundred and sixty men a day were said to use the brothel, in the former Hotel Bellevue. Queues formed along the pavements. There were no blinds on the windows. The townspeople said it was disgraceful.

Since the previous year the Association had been protesting to the War Minister about brothels at Rouen, Le Havre and other centres. Now, with little Cayeux-sur-mer cast as an innocent seaside town invaded by sin, the protest seemed more significant. There was a call for public meetings — resolutions to be sent to the Archbishop of Canterbury and the Prime Minister — and MPs raised the matter in Parliament.

Evasiveness was called for. When a French general said that the brothel had been supplied at British request, the British colonel at the convalescent camp said it was a French responsibility; the Commander-in Chief, Sir Douglas Haig, backed him up. Facilities at Le Havre were brought into the row. Clergymen got to hear of a street where brothels were supposedly under British medical supervision, and soldiers were given leave passes helpfully inscribed in red, 'The Rue de Gallion is not out of bounds between two and eight p.m.' Haig's staff, in touch with the Bishop of London, denied the supervision and the red ink, though not the two-till-eight dispensation.

Lord Salisbury, an elder statesman, was bombarded with letters. He wrote to the War Minister, Lord Derby, in January 1918 — after hearing from the Roman Catholic Archbishop of Westminster and the Mothers' Union — using the argument that moral deficiencies harmed our will to win:

> Everything depends now upon keeping the people keen about the war but if the notion which has already taken root is allowed to spread that instead of being in a sacred cause the war is a vehicle of vice and demoralization there will arise an uneasiness among the soundest part of the people — that is the backbone on which you have to rely — that the war is under a curse. It is impossible to exaggerate the danger of such a sentiment.

The row about prophylactics was still simmering. Sir George Riddell, who owned the *News of the World*, thought that more should be done to protect soldiers. He had been lobbied by a New Zealand feminist, Ettie Rout, who was better informed about VD and the allied armies than were most medical officers. Riddell in turn lobbied Derby, a man who liked to please people. 'Personally, I may tell you,' Derby wrote back, 'my views coincide with your own.' Would Riddell, he asked, be responsible for 'calming the Nonconformist conscience on this subject, because that is the greatest obstacle to my taking action.'

When the Archbishop of Canterbury sent Derby a bishops' resolution calling for 'drastic steps' over the brothels, the Minister said there was nothing to be done except prohibit men from waiting outside the houses. Then, turning to prophylaxis, he put on his Christian hat and said the opposite of what he had said to Riddell, declaring that he had been much impressed with private arguments from the Church against 'the irregular issue of such a thing' to the troops. 'Would you think,' Derby asked nervously,

> that it in any way promoted immorality if we let the men have the lectures as to the dangers of venereal disease, but, sub rosa, let it be known that if they did go with a woman they should at once use some disinfectant . . .?

The moralists could still embarrass the politicians; calomel cream remained a matter of deep significance. Even the brothels had to go, or at least be made unavailable. This became inevitable by March, when the clamour from the churches led the Archbishop to threaten a debate in the House of Lords, and more questions were pending in the Commons. Faced with a memo from Derby about the 'unsavoury and malodorous discussion' that would arise if nothing was done, on 18 March the War Cabinet put the *maisons tolérées* out of bounds to British troops.

Haig and his staff were furious, pointing out that the *maisons* were not the principal source of VD; though brothels were soon the least of the worries at GHQ, since on 21 March the Germans launched the offensive that was meant to win them the war. It was June before Haig had time to write acknowledging the order. He then attacked 'certain sections of public opinion whose main interest in the Army consists in the reduction of fornication on the part of its members,' and suggested that the only result would be more intercourse with women who were diseased, unlike those under supervision in the brothels. It would also mean using up to four hundred military police to enforce the order. The War Office was on

Haig's side, viewing what had happened as 'the surrender of the government to the clamour of religious sentimentalists.' The Cabinet was
unmoved and the order remained in force. It is unlikely, though, that
from then until November, when the war ended, British troops fornicated
less than they did before.

Wives were expected to behave better, and in general they probably
did; or if they didn't, usually went undetected. Betrayed soldiers came
into the news from time to time. A returning soldier murdered his wife in
1918 because, he said, she had infected him with VD; he received a light
sentence. Annual divorce figures crept up, passing the one-thousand mark
for the first time in 1918. Among them was a sprinkling of 'ordinary
people', almost unknown in divorce courts before the war.

A rifleman heard from his Louise that she was pregnant ('I am going to
bed in September' was how she put it). 'It's heartbreaking without you,'
she wrote, 'and in the event of your stopping the allowance I shall be
forced to live with the man.' The soldier got his divorce and a hundred
pounds damages. A former postman, now a machine-gunner, heard from
the co-respondent who stole his Lil. 'We were guilty, but were tempted
and fell,' said the letter, rambling on, 'nobody is infallible, and neither can
one battle against fate, which is inevitable, strive as one may against it.'
The mass market in infidelity was yet to come; lovers' reasons were still
worth printing in a newspaper.

The day the war ended, Monday 11 November, people were saying
that the occasion was too solemn for high-jinks. In the Mall that
afternoon, a noisy crowd fell silent when an ambulance appeared, bearing
a coffin covered in the Union flag. Some munition girls who had been
shouting from the back of an Army lorry began to sing, 'Now the
labourer's task is over, Now the battle-day is past.' But excitement soon
asserted itself. Reporters roamed the West End.

> There is kissing in the streets – open, unashamed kissing between
> people whom one suspects of having first met five minutes ago or
> perhaps not so long. All the taxis in town have been commandeered as
> travelling theatres for hordes of absurd young officers with their
> absurd young lady friends.

Heavy rain fell in the late afternoon. Most lights were still blacked out.
People noticed a strangeness. On the muddy streets off Leicester Square,
girls wearing black trench coats danced reels. 'Their white teeth and
shining eyes gleam through the murk with a suggestion of some savage,

alluring ritual. Here and there a flaring arc lamp, seen for the first time these many months, cuts the gloom into black and white futurist patterns.' And behind everything, 'a perpetual roar let out by many throats strikes the same barbaric note.'

It became famous as the night when strangers copulated in doorways and alleys. Within a day or two, newspapers would be writing stiffly that while exuberance was one thing, it was now time to stop the horseplay; which duly stopped. But since 1914, something in people's expectations had changed.

'Sweet Communion in the Dusk'

Love Among the Rubber Goods

SEXUALLY SPEAKING, the new order in Britain was not going to be like the old order. But in the same breath as they acknowledged change, most people were cautious. Some were hostile. Anyone over the age of thirty had been brought up as a Victorian. The machinery of morals and 'decent behaviour' was still in place. One could argue that all the war had done was to cheapen sex and make it vulgar. Since it was widely accepted that the war had been an aberration, which had taught mankind an unforgettable lesson — 'the war to end all wars' — it was not unreasonable to regard the immorality that accompanied it as part of the same mistake.

There was a market for books like *Manhood* (1919) by Charles Thompson, which picked up where the moral hygienists had left off in 1914, arguing that purity and good health went hand in hand. Eugenics was as popular as ever. 'Sex is not so much individual as it is racial,' wrote Thompson. 'A man is not his own, he belongs to the universe, and is here to fulfil the needs of the universe.' Thompson was the editor of *Health and Efficiency* magazine. Thousands wrote to him for advice about sex, and were told to read the poets, avoid unclean fiction, make sure 'the gas-clouds of suggestiveness' didn't penetrate 'the mask of purity', be aware that only degenerates went in for the mere gratification of desire, and buy dumb-bells and a *Health and Efficiency* chest-developer.

Similarly Sir Robert Baden-Powell of the Scouts was stressing the need for young men to help preserve the race by keeping healthy in mind and body; though Baden-Powell's style was blunter. A man of conviction, he believed he could deduce character from the way people walked, 'e.g. toes turned out imply a liar.' The Chief Scout concluded that 'about 46 per cent of women are very adventurous with one leg and hesitant on the other, i.e. liable to act on impulse.' He once saw a young woman outside Knightsbridge Barracks, whose walk showed the rare combination of adventurousness and honesty. Two years later, en route to the West

Indies, he recognized her by her gait on board ship, and married her. His views on sex were as uncompromising as they were on walks. In *Rovering to Success* (1922) he identified a 'rutting stage' in 'young fellows' which normally passed off 'in a few weeks or months', but if not watched could lead to 'the habit of immorality with women or self-abuse with himself.' Among Baden-Powell's racial remedies was 'keeping the organ clean and bathed in cold water.' The book was in print for years.

There was an element of patriotism in exhortations to Britons to remain pure. What an American writer called 'the respectable, bristlingly proud self that London (and the English) presented in those days' had to be preserved from the taint of ordinary, common-or-garden sexual weakness. Foreigners, especially if non-white, were regarded as scornfully as ever. A young courtesan who had married a playboy shot him dead at the Savoy Hotel in 1923, stood trial for murder, and was acquitted. She was French but he was Egyptian. The defence characterized him as a greasy Oriental with perverted sexual interests, which meant sodomy, and the *Sunday Express*, its moral trumpet as brazen as ever, said that the verdict was 'a vindication of womanhood against the vices that destroyed Rome.'

The criminal courts were busy maintaining standards in humbler cases. The magazine of introductions that began life in 1915 as *Cupid's Messenger*, now renamed *The Link*, came to the attention of the authorities, with unfortunate results. It was all right for the press to be used for discreet signals —

Murfin. Return or communicate. Your distracted wife and children

and

Sorry foiled. Too close watch

didn't worry *The Times* in the early 1920s.

Refined widow lady, aged 55 years, wishes to correspond with captain, view to marriage

in the *South Wales Daily Post* was on the right side of propriety. But in *The Link*,

Bit of fluff (London, SE), 19, very lonely, invites dark sporty Adam to write her

was asking for trouble, as was the cryptic but all too familiar message that

Widow (London, W), interested in discipline question would like to meet others either sex similarly interested.

The Link was established as 'a monthly social medium for lonely people.' Its proprietor and editor, Alfred Barrett (b. 1869), was well known in Fleet Street. He had written more than twenty humorous books under the name of 'R. Andom'; he belonged to a gentleman's club, the National Liberal, and had an entry in Who's Who. Barrett maintained he was providing a public service. He derided newspapers for refusing to carry his advertisements for the magazine. 'To some narrow, prurient and intolerant minds', he wrote, 'we are dubious, if not disreputable, and our purpose is fraught with suspicion to which they hesitate to give a name.' But the world was changing. Men and women were beginning to revolt against being treated as children. He, Barrett, had read Krafft-Ebing and Havelock Ellis, 'and there is not much I do not know on subjects which do not usually form a course in theological classes.' However, 'The Link is intended for decent people.'

Behind this intellectual armour, Barrett let youth and others have their fling, whether it was the educated young lady who sought a dancing partner, the sporty widow (Baron's Court) in search of nice gentleman friend, or 'fair-haired Pinkie from the North looking for tall, sincere boy, Ex Officer preferred.' Men were in short supply after 1918. The ads featured 'bachelor girls' and 'business girls'; the phrase 'broad-minded' often occurred. The enlightened Barrett was even willing to defend ads that mentioned 'discipline', suggesting that 'a man has just as good a right to be interested in corporal punishment as you have to be interested in capital punishment.' The West London widow continued to advertise.

Inevitably, someone laid a complaint against The Link. Barrett was arrested at his club and charged with conspiring to corrupt public morals, along with three other men. The case was lost from the start. The Old Bailey judge began by criticizing a group of men who insisted on staying in the public gallery to hear the 'filthy evidence', saying he could 'hardly distinguish them from those that are guilty' – adding quickly, 'whoever they may be.' Improper literature, 'mainly French', had been found in Barrett's bedroom. There were pornographic letters, some of them from women offering themselves to all comers. It was no use Barrett insisting that The Link's readers included colonels, clergymen and lawyers; the news may have been counter-productive, given the enduring folk-belief that judges, as dispensers of punishment, are not unknown as the clients of middle-aged women offering 'discipline'. Barrett got two years with hard labour, resigned from his club and was expunged from the pages of *Who's Who*; a pioneer of sorts, though ill-advised.

When it came to subverting the sexual order without being prosecuted for it, there was one voice that predominated after the war, that of Marie Stopes. Stopes in popular legend is the birth-control woman, with her clinic and diaphragms, but the facts of contraception were only part of her message, and if they had not been conveyed by an imperious romantic, the impact would have been far less.

Stopes regarded herself as a poet. In photographs she looks misleadingly dreamy. She may have yearned for other worlds, but in the world she occupied she was brutally self-sufficient. She was, perhaps, not quite sane. The language she used at the start of her career in sex has been much smiled at, as when she advises the young husband not to forget the virtues of 'kissing his bride's fingers and coming to her for sweet communion in the dusk.' But her instinct to use such language was right. It was no use suddenly telling people that the angel in the house was really a sexual machine, just like a man. In any case, Stopes believed nothing as crude as that. Sex was a mystery; true love was its key. At the same time, one had to be practical. Her achievement was to be explicit about sex while making it sound a beautiful experience within the grasp of hard-pressed, puzzled readers. No one had come near to doing this before.

Born into a middle-class family in Edinburgh in 1880, Stopes became a scientist, studying prehistoric botany, and later emerging as an authority on the composition of coal. She had some odd affairs with men, behaving unkindly, but at the age of thirty found herself still single and a virgin. She then met and quickly married (in 1911) a gentle Canadian called Ruggles Gates, who is unfortunately remembered for not consummating the marriage. Five years later his wife was at the divorce court, having the marriage annulled, being asked, 'With regard to your husband's parts, did they ever get rigid at all?' and replying, 'I only remember three occasions on which it was partially rigid, and then it was never effectively rigid.'

Perhaps her natural aggressiveness helped make Gates impotent; her second marriage, to Humphrey Verdon-Roe, though it produced two sons and lasted longer, eventually squashed the life out of him, too. Everything about Stopes' private life is odd, but she was a woman who attracted the unusual. She said it was a year or two before it dawned on her that there was anything wrong with her marriage to Gates. Ruth

Hall's biography (1977) has evidence of Stopes' insistence on her ignorance. But she may have known more about the mechanics of sex than she admitted, and been mortified by her failure to arouse Gates, or by her mistake in marrying him in the first place. Her interest in sex was keen. In 1918, two years after getting rid of her first husband, she launched a new career with her book *Married Love*. She was then aged thirty-seven, still a virgin. But the book had been in the making for years, and as early as 1911, before Ruggles Gates' non-rigid parts became a problem, a manuscript was in circulation; though it was later rewritten in response to what she read, rather late in the day, about the facts of life.

Somehow her life to date and her passionate nature combined to produce a book of freshness and authority, short enough to read in a few hours. Although Forel and Havelock Ellis were among the authorities she had read, *Married Love* shrank from sexual abnormality, and concentrated on the everyday. Announcing grandly that the knowledge she had gained at such a terrible price in her marriage should be placed at the service of humanity, she wrote her book on the simple principle that 'Every heart desires a mate.' She then proceeded to discuss the mechanics of erection, the beauty of nakedness, the importance of the clitoris and the need for simultaneous orgasm. Only the prudish or careless husband, she wrote, failed to realize that 'lips upon her breast melt a wife to tenderness.' When a woman was pregnant and unwilling to have sex ('feels that she cannot allow her husband to enter the portals of her body'), she could masturbate him ('will readily find some means of giving him that physical relief which his nature needs').

Not all her advice was well-founded. She wrote of 'rhythms' and 'sex tides' which came and went every fortnight in women, stating it (with charts) as 'my law of Periodicity of Recurrence of desire.' Entranced with this fiction, she used it to make a case for having 'repeated unions' over a period of three or four days, separated by ten days of abstinence. But the principle of considering the woman was relevant enough, especially at a time when pregnancy was a threat and 'excessive demands' by men were always being complained of.

Another of her convictions was that 'the highly stimulating secretions which accompany man's semen' are beneficial when absorbed by the woman. The idea was floated in *Married Love* and elaborated in later books, and is one reason why Stopes disliked condoms as contraceptives. Lovers were advised not to separate after the act but to fall asleep as they were, to give absorption a chance. The man, too, was supposed to be absorbing from the woman. Stopes knew of many cases, like that of Mr O (reported by her in 1928) who would lie without moving for an hour. It was a complicated procedure — 'with the very small movement of his elbow and shoulder necessary to give the leverage, he turns a little on one side so that his head and shoulders can just rest on a second pillow placed there beforehand.' But results were guaranteed. In the morning Mr O was 'observed to whistle and sing on his way to the bathroom.'

The 'absorption' theory had other supporters, though none as vocal as Stopes. Tablets containing the vital fluids were being made by an enterprising pharmacist in Chicago before 1918, and by the twenties at least one Harley Street doctor was developing the market, prescribing the 'male secretion' treatment for wives whose husbands used condoms. The Stopes theory as such seems to have no modern backers. But perhaps there were fringe benefits here as well. Under her quasi-scientific talk about 'complex molecular substances found in the accessory glands of the male' she was signalling in her odd way the need for 'nearness' and 'togetherness'.

Married Love was published in March. By the end of 1918 there had been five editions, and seventeen thousand copies were in print. An Army captain wrote to her from the battlefront in August to say that 'your book is being very largely read and discussed by married officers in France just now.' It went on to sell more than half a million by the mid-1920s, by which time she had written another twelve books, including plays and a work on coal. Most significantly, she had become Britain's leading popular authority on contraception, having published, eight months after *Married Love* (and a week after the war ended), a 'practical sequel' called *Wise Parenthood*. She said it was written in response to those who had read the first book and sought 'wholesome information' on the subject, although Ruth Hall found evidence that the tireless Stopes had already completed this second book before the first one was published.

Wise Parenthood, which was very short, caused trouble, frightening the booksellers and offending both the medical profession and the Roman Catholic Church. Objections to birth control ran deep. To the religious, and those who accepted orthodox moral authority, it meant at the very least indulging in sex for pleasure at the expense of Christian duty, and at the worst murdering the unborn. In addition, the slaughter of the war had predisposed many people towards the eugenicists and their call to rebuild the race. A shattered Europe with millions of men dead provided a new excuse for finding birth control a perversion. The French were panicked into a law in 1920 that made it illegal for anyone to explain or advocate contraception (the result was more abortion but not more births).

Anticipating trouble, much of *Wise Parenthood* was taken up with justifications of birth control; the technical stuff came later in the book. The idea, said Stopes, was not to deprive the race of children but to ensure that those who were born had the best chance of health and beauty. Bravely, she declared that sex was a good thing in itself, not merely an act of procreation, as the churches suggested. She enveloped the statement in high-sounding prose, describing the sex act as 'the restrained sacramental and rhythmic performance of the marriage rite of physical union.' Still, whatever the language, its messages were clear. Stopes had to concede that unmarried as well as married might read the book. But even if they did, she said, would it not reduce the 'racial dangers' of illicit love? – presumably unwanted children and VD, though she didn't go into details.

As for the technical advice, this consisted of a few dozen pages about female physiology, together with arguments and instructions for using the small rubber cap (she called it a 'check pessary') that she advocated, and a general account of other methods, including condoms, that she didn't favour. One of her comments, that the woman could insert the cap whenever convenient, 'preferably when dressing in the evening and some hours before going to bed,' has been derided. But at that point she was writing, as she said, for 'the educated classes', the only ones likely to read such a book. It was only later, when her fame spread as a result of newspaper articles and a notorious libel case which she lost, that her message began to percolate into the regions of the poor and deprived; and even then it was a long time percolating. Middle-class reformers saw the wives of the underprivileged as a race apart, harassed and fearful of male attentions. There was some truth in this. In 1914 a long-married wife was heard consoling a young woman whose husband had gone to the war: 'You don't know what you're up agen yet. But you wait till you've been to bed over three thousand nights with the same man, like me, and had to put up with everything, then you'd be bloomin' glad the old Kaiser went potty.'

Stopes was an optimist; it was the secret of her appeal. Everything she wrote promised a better life and encouraged her readers to strike off their chains. Desire had to be treated in a matter-of-fact way, but it was none the less desire, something to revel in, not be ashamed of. The result of a man's failing to understand a woman's natural rhythms, of using her as a passive instrument for his need, 'has been, in effect, to make her that and nothing more.' Only understand, and all would be well. Her good news was ostensibly scientific, the periodicity of passion, the commingling of fluids, even 'electrical or magnetic currents characterizing each sex and mutually affecting them.' She was careful always to be referred to as 'Dr' Stopes, infuriating those doctors of medicine who wanted to distance themselves from the abominable woman.

But her real authority was not scientific at all. It stemmed from her own character. She believed what it suited her to believe. One of her articles of faith was that true lovers were moral by nature, not because they feared the consequences. This was a useful argument in the nineteen-twenties, since the opponents of birth control held that a man with a pocketful of condoms (or a woman with a check pessary in the bathroom cupboard) was free to be promiscuous. A few brave souls might say publicly, 'So what?', but not someone who wished to remain credible. The safest defence was to say that virtue was a constant factor, unaffected by the absence or presence of rubber goods.

Havelock Ellis had argued in Volume 6 of his *Studies* (1909) that Christianity, with its cult of chastity and virginity, was wrong to assume that without a system of inhibitions man's licentious urges would triumph. In fact, he said, man was subject to restraints in his own nature. Norman Haire, an eccentric young doctor from Australia who joined the thin ranks of sex reformers in London after the war, scorned 'religionists' who took a low view of human nature, always expecting the worst. As for Stopes, she lost no opportunity to state her case, as in her unsuccessful action for libel, brought against a doctor, Halliday Sutherland. Sutherland, a convert to Catholicism, had said in print that her pioneering birth control clinic in north London, opened in 1921, took advantage of the poor and subjected them to harmful experiments. During cross-examination Stopes was asked by counsel in cumbersome language if she had considered 'whether the apprehension of the responsibility of parenthood might be a deterrent to acts of impropriety?' She replied crisply that his question was 'insulting to womanhood . . . we are not moral because we are afraid, we are moral because it is right and intrinsic in our nature to be moral.' *

---

* Stopes finally lost her case in the House of Lords, learned judges having used words like 'revolting', 'detestable' and 'deplorable' in discussing her work.

Honestly to believe this, if (as seems likely) she did, was optimism of the highest order. But sexual reformers had no alternative but to see the reforms, contraception for example, as ennobling. Uncluttered by the false fears and moralities of the past, it was said, people would be able to breathe again. There was much truth in this, but not the kind of absolute, cure-all truth that was implied. It was like sex-education of the advanced kind, another panacea, though it was the nineteen-thirties before this was in full bloom. Walter Gallichan, an author described (by himself, in his *Who's Who* entry) as 'a pioneer of sex education in England', wrote in 1918 about the unhappy past, where parents counselled chastity, but left their children to learn about sex from 'poisoned wells'. Education would cure all this, producing 'minds unassailed by prudery or salacity.'

Such optimism demanded a view of sex as something neater and tidier than it was ever likely to be. Love was not always true love; lust was a reality; people had odd tastes and peculiar habits. Stopes' repugnance for 'perversion' drew a line around what she regarded as 'normal', but the line was arbitrary, as it always has to be. Male homosexuality she had no patience with; she found lesbianism corrupt.

Sometimes her broad-mindedness did extend to forbidden territory. Sex involving oral contact was regarded by many as a filthy practice, well into the second half of the century. Stopes was presumably referring to it in one of her later books, *Enduring Passion* (1928), when she quoted with approval an American writer's injunction to kiss a wife's lips, tongue and neck, 'and, as Shakespeare says: "If these founts be dry, stray lower where the pleasant fountains lie!"' She may have seen the Dutch gynaecologist Van de Velde's book, *Ideal Marriage*, destined to become as famous as hers, which first appeared in 1926, where 'the kiss of genital stimulation' was daringly endorsed; and decided not to be outdone. However, seven years earlier, in 1921, replying to a doctor about a patient of his, she wrote that 'two of the acts you mention . . . are really disgusting and cruel, namely oral and rectal coitus . . . even the attempt to use [them] are acts of such gross indecency that they undoubtedly amount to cruelty mentally to any refined or sensitive woman.' Perhaps she had revised her opinions by 1928; or perhaps straying lower was more acceptable by a man than by a woman.

In *Enduring Passion* she attacked 'Lord X', an acquaintance, who saw woman merely as 'the housekeeper, the breeder', while visiting prostitutes who would 'play with him in any filthy manner that his debased taste craves.' As for the 'anomalies' catalogued by the unshockable Havelock Ellis, she said that reading his books was 'like breathing a bag of soot.' Her optimism lay in believing that everything would remain orthodox, only better and nicer. Pre-marital sex was not on her agenda. She told a titled correspondent how sad it was that 'young people should eat forbidden fruit, for the consequences are so terrible.' Marriage, she once said, was 'a greater national bulwark than many battleships.'

Over the years tens of thousands wrote to her for advice. Mainly they were married. For the first time in Britain, during the early nineteen-twenties, a mass of 'ordinary people' were opening their hearts about sex. As well as the basic questions about birth control and pregnancy, they asked about the frigidity of wives, the indelicacy of condoms, the correct number of sex acts per week, the longevity of sperm. They wanted simultaneous orgasms and infallible contraceptives. A clergyman wrote that he longed for the poetry of love as depicted in her books, but when he asked his wife to come into his arms she said, 'I don't like your breath in my face.'

Most of the letters received only a printed acknowledgement, directing the writer to one of her books. Sometimes Stopes would write a personal letter or add a postscript, her tone always positive. It was impossible to do more, even with a staff of secretaries; one series of articles that she wrote for *John Bull* magazine brought twenty thousand letters within three months from women who wanted abortions – not that she could do anything about them.

Many problems that were blurted out to Stopes the oracle are still with us, although now they sound smarter and raunchier in the hands of media sexologists, and are even employed (or invented) in sleazy newspapers as mild pornography. Some of the 1920s problems are too remote to mean much today. Many women dreaded pregnancy, explaining apologetically that they already had several children, that the health visitor said birth control was disgusting, that their husbands were forced to abuse themselves because intercourse was too dangerous. They asked if it was true that every box of contraceptives contained a dud. They begged to know the sexual positions. They worried about their husbands seeing them nude.

Men, as troubled as women, made up nearly half the correspondents. Lesley A. Hall, who studied the letters they wrote to Stopes, drew a picture in her *Hidden Anxieties* (1991) of men far removed from the received notion of uncaring arrogance. Instead they appear as both compassionate and uncertain of themselves, worried about impotence and hasty ejaculation, keen to have 'topping children', asking if it is 'too indecent to the nicely minded woman' to use a finger to fondle her.

All this frank interest in sex was progress: unless it was a calamity. The rising popularity of birth control was visible evidence. It was where changing morality could be monitored. The change lay in the spread of devices and habits (such as the ever-popular 'withdrawal') to more people. As usual with anything that made life easier, the better-off had been doing it for years. Lady Constance Lytton, a former Suffragette, who was one of Stopes' backers at her clinic, said in a letter to her that birth control had been 'practised in our family and by their numerous friends for generations.' By the nineteen-twenties it was a cliché of debate to produce figures showing how the birthrate of the professional and educated classes had fallen. Even before the war, families of lawyers, doctors and clergymen — professions that provided much of the fire-power for denunciations of contraception — had an annual birthrate less than a quarter that of labourers.

Contraceptives were as old as human records, even if some of the ancient charms (left testicle of weasel, heart of salamander) have come to sound like male gambits to aid seduction; there is a scurrilous story that the poet Dylan Thomas, visiting Prague in 1949, persuaded a Czech woman that toothpaste could be relied on. Every modern form of contraceptive except the Pill was known and available well before the end of the nineteenth century. As with prostitution in Britain, the thing itself has never been illegal. But there were ways of bringing prosecutions. Before the First World War, families who advertised births in London newspapers were liable to receive sales literature from the manufacturers of 'Malthusian devices', as the police called them; the Cardinal Manufacturing Co. and others were successfully prosecuted by the Post Office for sending leaflets through the mail. A shopkeeper in Villiers Street, near Charing Cross, a thoroughfare that had seedy overtones for decades, was sent to prison for exhibiting a Malthusian device in his window; the police got him under the Vagrancy Act.

By the eighteen-nineties barbers' shops and 'surgical stores' selling condoms were well-established in cities, the latter also offering aphrodisiacs and drugs to cause abortion. Few towns lacked a dubious chemist or a herbalist. A 'Professor Deaking' of Swansea was advertising in local newspapers in 1904, just as the last major religious revival in Britain was beginning in the adjacent Welsh countryside:

French novelties 6d each, 3 for 1/-, or a dozen for 3s and 6d; postage extra. On sale weekly at the Saddler's shop at the back of Llanelly market every Thursday.

Once it became obvious that there was money in birth control, commercial pressures got to work, making the business seem wickeder than ever to its opponents. Gradually it crept out from under its stone. At the end of the nineteenth century a London rubber-goods firm, involved in litigation when the Strand was being redeveloped, successfully claimed more compensation than the authorities were offering, on the grounds that its shop in a side street was especially valuable to customers, among them (it was said) judges and clergymen, who could slip in unobserved. A court ruled that the firm must be fairly compensated for the loss of its business, 'however unpleasant might be its character.' The first contraceptive advertisement appeared in the *Chemist and Druggist* in 1910. By 1918 Stopes was publishing diagrams of rubber caps and giving details of how to insert them, while admitting that the procedure might sound 'a little sordid'.

Most things to do with contraception ran the risk of being not quite nice. They conjured up the wrong images. The idea of inserting objects in places that mustn't be referred to was disturbing. Similar taboos have survived to the present. Softish porn magazines on sale by respectable newsagents think nothing of publishing pictures of open-legged sirens, but the hint of an object in the vicinity puts them into the hard-porn category and brings a policeman running (on the same principle, a limp penis is in order, an erect one forbidden). In 1923, copies of a pamphlet called *Family Limitation* by Mrs Margaret Sanger (1883–1966), the less fanciful American counterpart of Marie Stopes, were seized by police from a shop in Shepherd's Bush, west London. The booksellers were charged with selling an obscene publication. What caused the trouble was almost certainly a drawing of the female genitalia, showing a female finger inserted to locate the cervix. 'Would you put such a book in the hands of a boy or girl of sixteen?' asked the magistrate. The booksellers were fined and the pamphlet destroyed; later editions, without the drawing, were unmolested and sold in large numbers.

The subject of birth control had always bred illogicality and extremism. Early feminists, who might have been expected to welcome contraception, were more inclined to see it as another male trick to allow them easier access to women's bodies; the same thing was to happen with modern feminists and the Pill. The churches were slow to make concessions, using their authority to condemn contraception. Winnington-Ingram, who grew busier by the year as Bishop of London, wanted to stop chemists selling rubber goods. Anglican bishops at the 1920 Lambeth Conference called for an end to 'unnatural' methods, despite receiving a printed address from Marie Stopes on behalf of God, communicated to her while she was sitting under a yew tree, and clearly stating that husbands and wives were to 'use the means which God now sends through Science to raise the race.'

Doctors were fond of using technical arguments to show why contraception was useless, harmful or wrong on moral grounds. Cancer and insanity were both alleged as consequences. Between the lines they sound annoyed that unqualified strangers should presume to interfere with the workings of nature, the doctor's department. Lady Florence Barrett, a well-known gynaecologist at the Royal Free Hospital (and wife of a leading spiritualist), wrote a book in 1922 which said that a little moderation between married couples was all they needed to limit the size of their families. 'The beauty of the higher side of love,' she added, 'is apt to lose its delicate bloom by over accentuation of the physical in marriage.'

When sex *was* necessary, contraceptives produced disease. She approved of using the 'safe period' to limit fertility, but, like all doctors at the time, didn't know how to calculate it accurately (in as much as it can be calculated at all), although she thought she did; Herman Knaus didn't publish the first competent studies until the nineteen-thirties. The middle-aged Barrett could be heard laying down the law at the Medical Women's Federation, along with the surgeon Mary Scharlieb, also of the Royal Free, who thought mankind already oversexed. Birth control, she declared, would merely remove the fear of consequences from the husband, and leave the wife at the mercy of his 'unbridled sex passions'; the wife's fear of consequences was not mentioned. In a letter to the *British Medical Journal* she asked whether one could 'imagine a more terrible state of society than that which is bound to evolve from the indulgence of unbridled sexual passions.' Prosperous women doctors showed little sympathy with the burden that child-bearing imposed on working-class wives.

Many lesser doctors aligned themselves with the Barretts and Scharliebs. 'Every medical practitioner,' wrote a woman GP in Dundee to the *BMJ*, 'has experience of the hearty strong mother of sixteen children.'

Halliday Sutherland, who was later sued by Marie Stopes, wrote that no ordinary man or woman could begin to practise birth control 'without experiencing at first an unpleasant feeling of repugnance and shame.' The profession had its liberals, in medical journals and outside them. The jolly Sir William Arbuthnot Lane was a respected surgeon who said mischievously that doctors were either ignorant of contraception or antagonistic to it. He went to court as a defence witness in the Sanger pamphlet case, and told the magistrate that every young person about to be married should have a copy.

Lane, however, was famous for his unorthodox views. It may have been from him that Stopes got her 'mingling of fluids' idea. He also had obsessive theories about the intestines, and is to blame for convincing generations of the constipated that what they needed to put them right was regular spoonfuls of oily liquid paraffin. A safer rallying-point for the liberals was the recently ennobled Lord Dawson of Penn (1864–1945), a leading hospital consultant at the height of his career, politically concerned, who had helped set up a Ministry of Health after the war. His ideas were already turning towards a national health service, two or three decades too soon. Birth control had interested him since he was a student, when he helped write a tract called *Few in the Family, Happiness at Home.* On top of this he was a physician to the King. From this well-fortified position Dawson agreed to speak at the Church Congress in Birmingham in October 1921, taking 'Sexual Relationships' as his subject.

What he said was unheard of from someone of his standing. He spoke of sex as an unstoppable force – 'suppress it you cannot,' he said, adding that 'sex love outside marriage' should be controlled, but 'in practice self-control has a breaking point.' The previous year's Lambeth Conference, said Dawson, had condemned 'sex love' unless it was used to produce children. But that sort of love was 'an invertebrate, joyless thing – not worth the having. Fortunately it is in contrast to the real thing as practised by clergy and laity.' The Church, he said, had to be more in touch with reality. He insisted that romance and deliberate self-control didn't go well together; that for the young, 'a touch of madness to begin with' did no harm; that 'if sexual union is a gift of God it is worth learning how to use it.' If it was not entirely clear what kind of a society Dawson hoped to see, it was unlikely to be one where husbands and wives knelt down to pray before intercourse, as the truly pious were said to do.

Dawson's speech moved on to birth control. He ruled out abstention ('ineffective, or, if effective, impractical and harmful'), said that constant pregnancy wore out women, and thought that most parents' reasons for limiting children were understandable. Using contraceptives, he admitted, could be harmful if used to 'render unions childless or inadequately fruitful,' but he found little evidence of this. Anyway, birth control was here to stay: 'no denunciations will abolish it.'

Much of the press welcomed the speech, and Marie Stopes wrote gleefully to *The Times* to say she was glad that her views were now receiving cordial support in its columns, 'even if, in order to get this attention, they have to be echoed by Lord Dawson'; the newspaper declined her letter, as it declined a paid-for announcement of her son Harry's birth three years later, Stopes not being a suitable name to grace its pages. The Roman Catholics were upset by Dawson, as were many clergymen of all colours. So, in varying degree, was a wider constituency that could not bring itself to look into the abyss as casually as the King's physician, and which took comfort from the *Express* group of newspapers, whose proprietor, Lord Beaverbrook, was a public Christian as well as a private womanizer.

The *Daily Express* got off to a bad start by ignoring the Dawson speech altogether in favour of one by another doctor at the Church Congress, under the headline '"GOOD TIME" GIRL DENOUNCED. MOTORCARS AND FURS NOT THE "END-ALL" OF EXISTENCE'. The doctor was E.B. Turner, 'the eminent London specialist' who had lectured the troops about pumping lead into the Hun. Turner attacked divorce and women's (not men's) morals. Earlier he had had occasion to write to the *BMJ* about the way morality among young women was declining since the advent of birth control. Now he had a bigger audience:

> To be 'found out' is considered by many girls the only sin. Some women have indeed 'got out of hand,' and in dress, manners and morals leave much to be desired. Many mothers and some daughters must realize that furs, jewels, motors and, lower in the social scale, chocolates and pictures [meaning cinemas], are not 'the be-all and end-all' of matrimony.

That was on a Wednesday. By Friday the *Express* had caught up with Dawson. Bishops made cautious comments for the reporter's notebook. The Bishop of Birmingham, who was the congress president, spoke impenetrably about the spiritual side of physical union and how it should 'spring from the perfect oneness, and that perfect oneness is not only a spiritual oneness, it is a oneness also in the expression of a pure passion, which is quite distinct from sensuality.' The message seemed to be that passion *of the right kind* was in order. Momentarily it looked as if the paper had been converted. A leading article said the Church must discuss sex frankly, and accept that where birth control was concerned, 'for better or for worse we now live in an industrial civilization.'

But things changed over the weekend. James Douglas (b. 1867), a brilliant bigot who edited the *Sunday Express*, decided the paper should denounce Dawson. 'LORD DAWSON MUST GO', it said, demanding the palace get rid of him and his 'abominable gospel', which it insisted on calling 'Malthusianism'. To Douglas it was the 'furtive cult' that had 'never dared to show itself openly and shamelessly in the light of day. Now for the first time in our national life it appears, of all places in the world, at the Church Congress!' His peroration was in the best Beaverbrook tradition, declaring that after losing nearly a million men in the war, 'the British Empire and all its traditions will decline and fall if the motherland is faithless to motherhood. We cannot risk it. We are too close to the sound of the guns!'

This was followed up by the *Daily Express* on Monday, making it more than likely that the proprietor had been on the telephone. Reputable newspapers, muttered a leading article, had long refused to publish 'Malthusian advertisements'. Was not the human race exhorted in Genesis to be fruitful, and multiply? How amazing, then, that the King's Physician should advocate 'flat repudiation of God's law.'

The attitudes struck by the opponents of birth control like Beaverbrook and Scharlieb were influential. It is true that from the nineteen-twenties, birth-control information and appliances were easily available. Ten shillings (ten or fifteen pounds in today's money) would have bought a book by Stopes, a good-quality diaphragm and a dozen condoms, or 'french letters', as people would have said then. But this was more than the labourer or even the clerk cared to spend, and in any case, for all the wise words of the pioneers, there were formidable barriers of habit and culture to surmount. The gap between what was theoretically available, and what the humble majority could bring themselves to buy and take home, was large. Dark words about God and cancer and Malthus and Empire carried weight.

It was no use expecting politicians to act. They believed that such matters were too controversial for them to touch. A few minor figures on the Left spoke out, to no purpose. During the first Labour Government's brief tenure in 1924, a deputation to the Ministry of Health, seeking to have birth-control instruction offered at the new maternity and child welfare centres, came away disappointed; the Minister happened to be a Roman Catholic, but the result would have been the same whatever his religion. A Labour MP tried unsuccessfully to introduce a Bill on similar lines the following year. In 1926 there was an instructive row at the Labour Party conference, when an attempt was made by Dora Russell to push the conference into committing the party to a more radical policy. It showed signs of succeeding, so by the following year the Party had done some fixing, and birth control was safely off the agenda. Nineteenth-century socialists had seen contraception as a work of the devil, fearing that birth-control theories were self-interested, favouring the individual at the expense of the community. Prejudice persisted, absorbed into the determined anti-feminism of the working man. As for civil servants at the Ministry of Health, they could be relied on (like their counterparts at the Home Office) to remain a decade or two behind public opinion.

The arguments about birth control, then and for years to come, were complicated by the amount of hedging and downright lying that went on. The truth was that contraception, presented correctly as the boon of harassed mothers, could also double up as the boon of unmarried lovers. Declarations that rubber goods were sold only to the married fooled nobody, but the distinction had to be made if the birth-control lobby was to remain respectable by the standards of the time. The need to distinguish absolutely between 'married' and 'unmarried' became a plank of the birth controllers' faith, causing farcical problems up to and through the nineteen-sixties, the decade of so-called revolution.

Lord Dawson implied in his Church Congress speech that without birth control, people would marry later (because if a family couldn't be postponed, higher earnings were needed at once). 'Absence of birth control means late marriages, and these carry with them irregular unions and all the baneful consequences.' Dawson thus made contraception appear an instrument of virtue, an ingenious defence. What he didn't try to do was defend irregular unions. Birth control was supposed to be a judicious instrument for parents to use in spacing children; a total of four was Dawson's ideal.

The brighter and better-off among the unmarried must have been using contraception on some scale. In the nineteen-fifties Dr Eustace Chesser, a Harley Street doctor, published a statistical survey of six thousand women's sexual histories, based on questionnaires. One in five of the women born before 1904 had slept with a man while still unmarried. For women born between 1904 and 1914, who reached sexual maturity in the nineteen-twenties, it was one in three. This suggests that hundreds of thousands more single women were doing it after about 1920. Since the illegitimacy figures show no noticeable increase, they or their men friends are likely to have been using contraceptives.

This is no more than moralists were saying at the time. Those who did the roaring in the 'roaring twenties' were a cosmopolitan minority whose behaviour got into newspapers and novels, influencing others, though leaving large areas of the population unaware of or indifferent to what was going on. 'Petting parties' were said to be the rage, the term 'petting' probably imported from America, what the British more bluntly call 'feeling'. Feeling a breast was a sort of petting; the business could develop up to but not including intercourse.

Among cocktails on offer in 1921 was Bosom Caresser. Freak parties (in pyjamas, or at swimming baths, or inhaling chloroform) came into the moralists' sights. The motor car was sin on wheels. Short skirts and skimpy dresses brightened the lives of those who wore them, also of those who envied them or said they were disgusting. James Douglas in the *Sunday Express* went on about 'the riot of nudity'. Bradford, reliable Bradford, insisted that shops modify their window displays of ladies' underwear.

A dancing craze went on for years. It was supposed to be an outlet for the pent-up emotions of war; was very likely people tasting pleasure for pleasure's sake. Thousands hopped and wriggled in the Twinkle, the Vampire and the Camel Walk, presently followed by the shimmy craze, followed by the Charleston craze. If Oxford undergraduates were caught dancing in public, the men were fined, the women sent down. 'Jazzmania' was the word. 'Youths dressed in bathing-drawers and kimonos,' reported the *Daily Mail*. 'Matrons moving about lumpily and breathing hard. Bald, obese man perspiring a million pores ... It is the jazz.' A doctor said there was evil in the dance hall.

Night clubs flourished, offering dubious hostesses and drinks at all hours. Winnington-Ingram smote them in speeches ('a hunting ground of sharks and loose women') and led deputations to Ministers. The Cursitor nominally offered 'Bohemia tea, concert and dance' for a shilling ticket, but was really an unlicensed drinking house; raided by the police, customers in fancy dress who were carted off to Bow Street in motor lorries posed for press photographers. Some clubs had a series of locked doors, with bells to give warning so that drinks could be disposed of. But they were not short of respectable customers. Thirty peers were said to be members of the Kit Kat. The Prince of Wales, who had never looked back after his night with Paulette of Amiens, though he now concentrated on married women, was a regular visitor.

Prostitutes were busy in the West End; when had they not been? Stephen Graham, a writer with a sharp eye who complained of immorality but loved to write about it, walked down post-war Piccadilly looking at the electric signs reflected in men's silk hats — the elegant still wore silk hats — and visiting cafés where

> hot-blooded men carouse with women of the carmined lip and hennaed hair ... The men chatter across tables. The women go from man to man:
> 'What sort of a life is your wife leading you now?'
> 'Heard anything more of your Freda?'

Divorce was an important topic in any twenties discussion of sexual behaviour. The figures crept up yearly — 1,600 decrees in 1919, 3,500 in 1921, then a decline, perhaps after wartime infidelities had worked their way through the system, then an upward surge to 4,000 later in the decade. These figures, still tiny, caused comment and anxiety. The *Methodist Times* saw them as 'a symptom of the spirit which throws over conventional standards when the maintaining of them means hardship and sacrifice.'

The British got much of their salacious reading from divorce cases. Thanks to an odd leniency in the law (changed in 1926), newspapers were allowed to publish the evidence given in proceedings, and often did so, however prurient. Few novels and plays poked about on the seedier side of infidelity as newspapers did, especially the *News of the World* on Sundays. Its three million circulation reached homes at every level. Middle-class households kept it from the children, or slipped their copy under a cushion in the sitting room when visitors came.

Some cases have an air of comic opera. An ex-Army officer married to a princess, the daughter of a maharajah, but living apart from her, hears that she is leading 'an irregular life'. He takes a friend to her flat in Knightsbridge at 3 a.m. They climb on the railings and look through a lighted window. The princess and an income tax clerk are lying naked on the bed. A policeman is found, and he climbs on the railings, too. The husband calls to his wife, using her pet name, 'Pratty, what are you doing there?', at which the clerk comes to the window, still naked, and says, 'I say, this is a bit thick!' The hearing is inconclusive; the judge calls it 'a cock and bull story.'

Other cases had fewer jokes. The wife of a family doctor in the Midlands claimed in 1920 that he had committed adultery with the maid, who slept in a room between the separate bedrooms of doctor and wife, and that he was also guilty of cruelty. Under the law as it then was, he had to be guilty of both for a divorce to be granted, though if it was the other way round, her adultery alone would have been sufficient.

The wife claimed that once, when she entered his room in the dark, he called from the bed, 'Is that you? Come along, dear.' 'It is I,' she replied. 'Oh, it's you, is it,' he said. 'Well, get out.' She had them followed by a private detective in London, where they stayed at the same address.

The doctor had a simple answer. The maid was suffering from syphilis, acquired in 1918. She was engaged to be married, and he kindly took her to London to be treated, warning her sternly not to kiss anyone. It was true that she had come back to the friend's flat that he was borrowing, but only because she was afraid to be on her own. He had slept on a camp bed; misconduct would have been the act of a madman.

The jury in its wisdom concluded there had been no adultery, but found cruelty. The misery of the marriage was thus insufficient for a divorce. The wife had to be content with a 'judicial separation', a twilight condition that prevented either of them from remarrying. It wasn't for another three years that women were at last put on an equal footing with men, with no need to prove desertion or cruelty as well as adultery; it had taken eleven years since the royal commission's pre-war proposal. Not that the change would have helped the doctor's wife, who would have needed to wait a further fourteen years, until 1937, before 'cruelty' by itself might have detached her from her husband.

For all the difficulties, the optimists of the twenties had no doubt that better times were coming, or had come. Sex educators, a few enlightened doctors, a very few enlightened clergymen, Marie Stopes and (in their way) the rubber-goods manufacturers, were trying hard to make things better for married couples, and trying equally hard not to be seen to be doing anything at all for those not in the married state. By the latter part of the decade a certain disillusion had overcome Stopes, who said unkind things about men in *Enduring Passion* (1928), grumbling about pathetic figures in middle-age who became over-sexed as a result (she said) of prostate trouble, which was curable ('quietly but firmly take him to an experienced surgeon'), unless of course it transpired that he had 'perverted and somewhat abnormal appetites.' She rather harped on the frailties of men over thirty-five, like a Mr B, who went 'frantic with desire' if he caught sight of his wife's 'silk-clad calves', demanding union 'at any time of the day', but who happily died and set his widow free. By this time Stopes' second marriage had gone awry; her private discontents seeped into her writing. Even then she could still strike a chord. 'Man and woman *in love*,' she wrote, 'should lastingly enrich, not rend and torment and defraud each other.'

A more extreme optimism than hers was establishing itself. Organizations dedicated to a new sexual order took shape. Dr Magnus Hirschfeld, the German who wrote a sexual history of the world war, was quickly off the mark in 1919 with his Institute of Sexual Science in Berlin. Hirschfeld (1868–1935) was a physician whose interest in sex stemmed from his own homosexuality. He was a Jew; young Nazis beat him up in the street and threw stink-bombs at his meetings in the early twenties. Thousands of case histories accumulated at the institute, which supported research, education and therapy. A Latin inscription above the entrance said, 'Sacred to Love and to Sorrow.' Christopher Isherwood lodged next door in the nineteen-thirties, looking over a park. He described the institute's museum:

> Here were whips and chains and torture instruments designed for the practitioners of pleasure-pain; high-heeled, intricately decorated boots for the fetishists; lacy female undies which had been worn by ferociously masculine Prussian officers beneath their uniforms. Here were the lower halves of trouser-legs with elastic bands to hold them in position between knee and ankle. In these and nothing else but an overcoat and a pair of shoes, you could walk the streets and seem fully clothed, giving a camera-quick exposure whenever a suitable viewer appeared.

If Marie Stopes had ever gone there, as Margaret Sanger did, she would have written it off as another bag-of-soot experience. Hirschfeld himself, with walrus moustache and gleaming spectacles, was humanitarian and learned, but his assiduous tolerance was strong meat; he had dirty fingernails and was said to wear no underclothes.

Dora Russell and Norman Haire visited him in Berlin in 1926, and between them concocted a plan for a 'World League for Sexual Reform'. This brought in other distinguished names. August Forel was conscripted.

Havelock Ellis became an honorary president. Writers like H.G. Wells and Aldous Huxley sent telegrams of support. But it had an eccentric air. Russell, whose views were strongly socialist, tried without success to make the league more political.

Its chairman was the burly Haire, the Australian enthusiast. Not only had he helped start a birth-control clinic in 1921, a few months after Stopes', where he would fit single girls with a diaphragm if they were about to get married; he did abortions in his private practice, working on the edge of legality. In the nineteen-thirties he put his name, as editor, to an odd book, Dr A. Costler's *Encyclopaedia of Sexual Knowledge*, a pseudo-scientific work published by a Hungarian in London, Francis Aldor. Dr A. Costler was really Arthur Koestler, the writer, down on his luck and earning himself sixty pounds, for which sum he sold the copyright. The book was sturdy, anatomical, and titillating enough for those days to become a best-seller. Haire commended it for its 'enlightenment' and collected his fee.

The league had impeccable objects, appealing, among other things, for equality between the sexes; birth control; reformed divorce, marriage and abortion laws, and a more sympathetic attitude towards 'abnormality'. At its second meeting, at Copenhagen in 1928, Haire said there was 'probably no country in the world where there is so much hypocrisy concerning sexual matters, and consequently so much sexual unhappiness, as in England.' This may have been true, though the United States took some beating when it came to restrictive policies on birth control. The question was how to convince the nation of its shortcomings.

The next year's meeting was in London. Famous speakers took the platform. George Bernard Shaw gave a whimsical address whose point seemed to be that for ordinary people, as opposed to intellectuals, sexual reform held no attraction. Bertrand Russell, advocating more and better sex education, concluded that sexual nastiness in children was the result of prudery in adults. One can almost hear the applause inside the Wigmore Hall, and the silence outside it. A New York doctor spoke about 'The Pre-Marital Consultation', which, he believed, was inseparable from 'marriage hygiene'. Among suggested procedures, the bridegroom's penis should be measured and the bride's hymen dilated ('the operation itself is comparatively simple'). Each should be instructed in the necessary anatomy, using charts, diagrams and clay models.

Yet despite some odd speeches, the nation's indifference and the absence of any agreed idea within the league itself as to how reforms could be brought about, the *Proceedings* had a glint of fire that remains. The new voices were unromantic and less inclined to prevaricate – like that of the progressive writer Naomi Mitchison (b. 1897), who spoke of birth control almost casually, as something that 'two people burning for one another' should use as circumstance dictated – or, if newly married, might dispense with altogether, preferring the risk to 'letting their lovers have them for the first time with their lovely and thrilling nakedness spoiled by a french letter.' Mrs Mitchison thought the need for contraception would in any case dwindle as standards of living rose – for did not truly feminist women desire 'masses of children by the men they love'?

A new age was coming and all was well.

6

⊸⊰∘⊱⊸

'Unmitigated Filth'

Up to No Good in the Twenties

THE BOOKS PEOPLE READ, and the naughty worlds of imagination that some of them suggested, exercised the authorities in the years after the war. A rot needed to be stopped. The 'educated classes' could no longer be trusted; there were more of them, and they lacked restraint.

In 1926 the critic F.R. Leavis, whose academic career at Cambridge was just beginning, asked a local bookshop, Galloway & Porter, if they could find him a copy of James Joyce's novel *Ulysses* to use for his course on 'Modern Problems in Criticism'. The book had been published in Paris four years earlier, but the British Customs, who had (and still have) an absolute right to decide whether text and pictures are too indecent to import, confiscated every copy that came to their notice. Galloway & Porter thought it their duty to inform the chief constable of Cambridge what Mr Leavis was up to. The chief constable informed the Home Office.

The little wheels of censorship started turning. A senior official at the Home Office who specialized in indecent publications and related matters, S.W. Harris, wrote a minute about this 'amazing proposition', suggesting that 'a lecturer at Cambridge who proposes to make this book a textbook for a mixed class of undergraduates must be a dangerous crank. Permission must of course be refused.' The matter was passed to the Director of Public Prosecutions, Sir Archibald Bodkin.

Bodkin was a safe pair of hands in matters of morals. When he was at the criminal bar his private views had commended him to the National Vigilance Association, and he used to appear for them in immorality cases. He was a leading advocate in Suffragette prosecutions. Bodkin had first heard of *Ulysses* in December 1922, ten months after it was published, when he received a copy via Harris that Customs had detained at Croydon Aerodrome. The importer told them it was a work of art that was being 'seriously discussed in higher and literary circles.' Customs were uncertain whether to return the book or seize it. Bodkin read it over Christmas, or at least, lacking (he said) the time or inclination to read it all, he got through pages 690 to 732. This was the last chapter, where Molly Bloom, wife of the comic hero Leopold, lets life and love stream through her memory in the longest unpunctuated sentence in literature. It is the chapter that schoolboys would turn to years later, divining by some prurient magic that here were the obviously dirty bits. Bodkin was there first.

The pages he read puzzled him. There was no story. It was written 'as if composed by a more or less illiterate vulgar woman.' He was on safer ground when it came to finding 'unmitigated filth and obscenity'. His opinion was that Customs were justified in refusing to return *Ulysses*. If anyone questioned the decision, 'the answer will be that it is filthy, and filthy books are not allowed to be imported into this country.' The Home Secretary concurred. Formal letters went to Customs and Post Office to say the book was deemed obscene.

And now, four years later, here was this fellow Leavis wanting to use it to corrupt undergraduates. It was so outrageous, Bodkin thought it was a hoax. He wanted to know more about Leavis. The Cambridge police said it was definitely not a hoax, adding that other booksellers in the town had been warned. Bodkin was given Leavis' address. A correspondence followed between Bodkin and the Vice-Chancellor of the University, A.C. Seward, who assured the DPP that Leavis said he would never think of recommending his students to buy the book. This was not good enough for Bodkin. He was concerned, he told Seward, to stop knowledge of it spreading at the University, and if he heard that any undergraduate had a copy,

> I shall take every step which the law permits to deal with the matter, and I cannot avoid remarking that if I have to take any such steps, inevitably the source from which knowledge of the book arose will be known, and the publicity will hardly tend to increase the reputation of the University.

Leavis said later that the episode had harmed him.

Possession of an obscene book is not an offence, even if it has been successfully prosecuted. The decision to label *Ulysses* obscene was merely a matter of the personal tastes of S.W. Harris, Bodkin and the Home Secretary, Sir William Joynson-Hicks. But Bodkin's bullying was adequate.

The eagles of the law continued to hover over *Ulysses*. Later in 1926 the Town Clerk of Stepney, east London, told the Home Office that the public library had received a reader's request for the book, and asked if it was banned. The answer, evasive but sufficient, was that all copies imported had been destroyed by Customs (among them were five hundred copies intercepted at Folkestone in 1923). Police inquiries were made about the would-be reader. He lived in Salmon Street, Mile End. Nothing was known about him in connection with indecency. S.W. Harris, however, remained suspicious. 'He may write to France for the book,' he minuted, and so the Post Office was asked to examine correspondence going to Salmon Street. These were the games the authorities played. They acted because they sensed danger. Unlike sexual reformers who clung to high principles, reckless writers embraced the sordid and disreputable, drawing attention to dark sides of life that were surely best ignored; or so the nation's Bodkins must have thought.

Popular sexual reformers who spent their time looking on the bright side were hardly a threat at all, writers like Walter Gallichan who declared (1918), *'we cannot too often repeat that science has the key to purity of thought and behaviour,'* at the same time reminding his readers that *'young men must guard against any thought, desire or action that is likely to cause loss of semen either by day or night.'* Even the powerful, the likes of Stopes and Dawson, could be tolerated, because they knew where to draw the line. In the sexual world they envisaged, married couples would do loving but wholesome things in a regular sort of birth-controlled way. Molly Bloom's memories, however, were rank with sex of a kind associated with pornography. It was plainly not pornography of the variety that was smuggled in from the Continent, but undeniably it dealt with forbidden thoughts:

> I made him blush a little when I got over him that way when I unbuttoned him and took his out and drew back the skin it had a kind of eye in it theyre all Buttons men down the middle on the wrong side of them Molly darling he called me what was his name Jack Joe Harry Mulvey was it yes I think a lieutenant he was rather fair . . .

There was nothing morally uplifting, merely suggestions that those coarse animal passions that the preachers said were on the way out were, on the contrary, on the way in again, or had never been absent. The traditional way to deal with someone of Molly Bloom's stamp was to say that she was abnormal, perverted, degenerate. She was a case history for the pages of Krafft-Ebing or a freak for Havelock Ellis. The alternative was to assume that 'degeneracy' lurked in us all, that a nature like hers could be a proper cause for celebration, as she lies in bed and thinks (against a background of bodily functions) about love and lust, about men and their organs, about masturbation and anal sex, foot and underwear fetishes, indecent exposure, infidelity and, in the end, happiness. Unless they were very daring, even sexual reformers could hardly be expected to welcome *Ulysses*, considering the good work they were putting in to ensure that tomorrow's sex would be clean, decent and well-behaved. It was just as well that no one ever saw the potent love-and-sex letters that James Joyce had written years earlier to his common-law wife Nora Barnacle, which were not published until long after his death. 'Are you offended by my horrible shameless writing, dear?' he wrote, aged twenty-seven, when they were apart and he was inventing fantasies to masturbate with.*

The authorities – in this case Home Office, police and Customs – made little distinction between 'pornography' and 'art'. It was difficult for them: none of the legal definitions was adequate. They knew they could be made fools of. Over the years 'serious literature' had been successfully prosecuted, but sometimes it got away. Balzac's books were frequently seized, when magistrates would make remarks like those of the Manchester Stipendiary in 1905, 'Balzac is rather famous for publishing stories not to be read.' The war came and went, and he was still suspected of impropriety, though there had been no prosecution since 1910. In 1924 the Post Office intercepted a set of printers' proofs of Balzac's *The Old Gadabout* on its way from Holland to a backstreet publishing company in London. When police visited the premises, the company refused to cancel the print order. It published cheap paper-bound editions of classics with naughty reputations, such as Boccaccio's *Decameron* and the works of Aristotle and Balzac. These were then sold through respectable outlets, largely, no doubt, to people looking (hopelessly, by today's standards) for smut. At the same time they were classics. It was enough to make a high-minded civil servant grind his teeth.

---

* It is a nice irony that Joyce's erotic letters are now subject to a posthumous censorship, exercised not by directors of public prosecutions but by his own literary estate. Having allowed Richard Ellmann to publish them in the *Selected Letters* (1975), the trustees defer to the wishes of his grandson, Stephen Joyce, and make it difficult for them to be published anywhere else.

The DPP's office, pointing out that the book might be permissible with a limited circulation but not as 'a cheap book available to all classes', was in favour of prosecuting; so was S.W. Harris. But his seniors concluded it would do more harm than good. Britain was now cooperating with the French in containing pornography, and a Home Office minute argued that 'a great deal depends on our keeping the minds of the foreign authorities free from the notion that we are unduly prudish' — as though anyone would have thought such a thing. So there was no prosecution; although the Post Office was advised, rather meanly, not to let the publishers have their proofs back.

Measures to stop people being sexually contaminated by what they read and saw, found in most societies in one form or another, were pursued with unusual vigour in Britain. Pornography has been opposed not merely on religious grounds, as a stimulus to sin, but because it amounts to a satire at the expense of a society built on stable family values, and is thus liable to destabilize it. It mocks human nature without trying to improve it. It shows people 'behaving like animals', promiscuous, addicted to degrading behaviour, and worst of all deriving such intense pleasure from what they are doing that they corrupt the innocent observer by suggesting to him that he, too, can taste these delights. Many think the fears exaggerated. People are what they are. Lust can coexist with kindness. Even if some of the malign powers of sexual text and images do exist, there is little to be done in an information-rich society. The State's supervisory system has always been inefficient, though since the nineteen-eighties it has been trying to frighten us all again. In the twenties it clanked and whirred menacingly.

The cinema, offering nothing (apart from a few underground films) that could be described as pornography, had been closely watched from the beginning. It was cheap, popular, often vulgar and just the vehicle for indecency if the authorities took their eyes off it. The unofficial British Board of Film Censors was set up by the industry in 1912 for fear of something worse, with no powers except to advise local authorities on whether films were fit to exhibit; its first president was a man from the Lord Chamberlain's office, which censored stage plays. In 1916 there were plans to replace it with a Government-approved Board of Censors — the Home Secretary was Herbert Samuel, the man who sent the women patrols to look for sin at picture palaces. The new board would have had absolute powers to ban films. But plans were dropped at the last minute, and the BBFC stayed in business. Soon an imposing range of sights was being given the black spot. These included men and women in bed together, bathing scenes that passed the limits of propriety, very passionate love scenes, the drugging and ruining of girls (the White Slave Traffic), and anything that brought the institution of marriage into contempt. The 'betrayal of young women' was a delicate matter. The BBFC found that in practice it couldn't be avoided, but the treatment (it said in 1920) mustn't suggest that a woman was 'morally justified in succumbing to temptation in order to escape sordid surroundings or uncongenial work.'

Despite these rigorous safeguards, sex crept in. By the late twenties, five and a half million people in Britain were visiting the cinema each week, and the cheapest, most reliable way of pleasing them was with 'romance'. The sexual-fantasy industry was under way. The censors went on issuing edicts. Bare nipples were forbidden. Men's bare chests were allowed only if demanded by the plot, as in a fight scene or life on a desert island. In finding one film unacceptable, the BBFC said it was not its policy 'to show a scene so repugnant to the English conscience as a married man accepting the advances of a prostitute in the street.' Snails copulating had to be taken out of a popular-science short. But the nature of film made it easy to imply things without stating them. A reviewer complained:

> Adultery is one of the most constant of the prohibited activities, and yet a modern film producer, by the dexterous manipulation of semi-roseate light, warm shade, sweeping movement and a picturesque background, can put up an overwhelmingly attractive defence for his hero or heroine's moral delinquency.

Films were seen as corrupting in a mild sort of way. Books, however, continued for a long time to be the principal threat to the nation's moral health. A few 'serious' authors were deeply distrusted. D.H. Lawrence, like James Joyce, was regarded by the authorities as a crank who used his talents to write dirty books. A thousand copies of his novel *The Rainbow* were seized during the war from Methuen, who had just published it, and a court had them destroyed; Methuen said they were sorry to have handled such a work. Lawrence was in trouble again in 1929, near the end of his life, first with poems and then paintings. The poems, intended for a volume to be called *Pansies*, were intercepted en route from Florence, where he was living, to his literary agents in London. They were released with a recommendation that fourteen of the poems be omitted; which they were when the volume appeared later that year.

Then police raided an exhibition of his paintings, and half of them were seized with a view to having them burnt. Lawrence said that the police — 'these dainty policemen', he called them — had removed 'every picture where the smallest bit of the sex organ of either man or woman showed.' Pubic hair was enough to make a prima facie case for obscenity. (Years previously there had been arguments between the French and British police about Parisian catalogues being sent to London, which showed photographs of naked women. Pubic hair was visible. To Scotland Yard, who wanted the French to cooperate, this meant the pictures were automatically obscene. The French couldn't see this.) The defence lawyers had painters and critics ready to give evidence, among them Augustus John, but the magistrate at Marlborough Street, now a very ancient Frederick Mead, said that art had nothing to do with it — 'the most splendidly painted picture in the universe might be obscene.' Eventually the paintings were returned, on condition the exhibition closed down.

The previous year, 1928, Lawrence's novel *Lady Chatterley's Lover* had appeared in Florence, his confused and confusing testament about 'fucking with a warm heart', an activity that was supposed to revitalize the human race. It was more than thirty years before it was published in Britain, although some copies came in, enabling the press to condemn it as cesspool and sewer, and its author as perverted and evil. By 1930 Lawrence was dead. The only surviving Home Office file about his books concerns a publisher's proposal of that year to reissue *The Rainbow* in a cheap edition. S.W. Harris was all for action, but nothing was done. Harris' last word on the subject was a minute expressing his admiration for an obituary item in the *Daily Telegraph*, inserted in the file, that said Lawrence was a lost soul of literature, a failed genius who had a 'kink in the brain' and 'came to write with one hand always in the slime.'

Such views were unexceptional. The idea that novels containing candid views of sex and sexual behaviour might foreshadow changes in British life was unpalatable; better to see them as aberrations. Perhaps magistrates and officials sensed these changes, which made their opposition all the more frantic. For some reason they decided in 1929 to prosecute Norah C. James' *Sleeveless Errand*, brought out by a small firm, the Scholartis Press. It was a first novel by a young woman who worked in publishing, the story of a young woman-about-town called Paula. Having decided to kill herself after being deserted by her lover, Paula meets a man called Bill whose wife has betrayed him. They pass a day and night doing nothing but talk, at the end of which Bill has failed to dissuade her, and she drives her car over a cliff, as promised.

Paula spends the time belittling her own generation, its women 'rotten to the core' because of the war. Her strictures on England's 'moral mire' would have gladdened the London Morality Council, and they led Arnold Bennett to call the book 'an absolutely merciless exposure of neurotics and decadents.' On the other hand, Paula uses words like 'bloody' and 'balls', and recalls (in the book's one slightly erotic sentence) how she would never again feel her lover's weight on her 'eager limbs', or 'his lips moving from her mouth to her breast.'

Police sought an order from the Bow Street magistrate to destroy the edition of five hundred copies. The prosecution said the story was 'in the form of conversation by persons entirely devoid of decency and morality . . . who not only tolerate but even advocate adultery and promiscuous fornication.' Those who appreciated 'the beauties of English literature' were said to be looking to 'the strong arm of the law' to stop the publishing of 'such foul stuff as this.' The magistrate agreed; the book would suggest impure thoughts to the young, or even to the old.

Ludicrous as this can be made to sound, the decision had a grain of logic. One reason for wanting to ban pornography, or what passed for it, was rarely acknowledged: that it was a 'one-handed book', suitable as fantasy material for masturbation. Whether masturbation did, in fact, damage one's moral and physical health — whether it mattered at all except in terms of private pleasure — was a different question. But at a period when erotic words and pictures were far less common than today, a sentence was more likely to set off a fantasy. Thus a few words about eager limbs and lips on breasts (especially if they were on page two, as in this case) might lead to self-abuse, which — by the rules of the world in which middle-class, middle-aged Englishmen had grown up — was corruption. That, one assumes, was the magistrate's thinking. But no one ever referred to these details.

Sleeveless Errand ceased to exist, at least in England. In France a mysterious character called Jack Kahane, who came from a family of cotton merchants in Manchester and had settled in Paris on a private income, published the book almost at once, with a preface by Edward Garnett deriding the prudes. Kahane went on to found the Obelisk Press, which became famous for publishing both avant-garde writing and erotica, again blurring the distinction between the naughty and the literary. Norah C. James went on to be a prolific writer of novels, though not novels in which lovers went about resting their weight on eager limbs.

If *Sleeveless Errand* was thought likely to lead men into bad habits, *The Well of Loneliness*, which provoked the most notorious literary prosecution of the decade, was suspected of corrupting women, and in even worse ways. Its subject was lesbianism. The author, Radclyffe Hall, was a lesbian, whose sexual inclinations had been publicized in a libel action eight years earlier. The novel, which was long and earnest, had no hint of indecency, except that in 1928 the subject itself was indecent.

Unlike homosexuality between men, which the police pursued as relentlessly after the war as they did before it, the female variety had never been illegal. As with unisex lavatories on railway trains, this was a quirk of the system. Lesbianism is supposed to have been omitted from a statute of 1885, which revised the penalties for homosexuality, because it would have been impossible to convince Queen Victoria that such a thing existed, but this seems to be a joke; it was men who preferred not to know. An MP tried to get some legislation going on the matter in 1913, but the Home Secretary refused to consider it. In 1921 a 'lesbian' clause was floated by another MP, when the House of Commons was discussing a new criminal Bill, to make 'any act of gross indecency between female persons' a misdemeanour. There was a short discussion on an August afternoon about the debauching of young girls and the threat to society, but the general feeling was that such a beastly subject should not be allowed to pollute Parliament. Lesbians went on being tolerated by default.

Marguerite Radclyffe Hall (1880?–1943) inherited wealth as a young woman, wrote and published verse before she became a novelist, and within a small fashionable circle made no secret of her sexual nature. She liked to wear men's clothes, and when her white-blonde hair was coiled up and covered by a man's hat, she looked masculine and handsome. Affairs with other young women came her way. In 1907 she began a long affair with an older woman, Mabel Batten, the wife of a wealthy diplomat. As that affair was wearing out, Radclyffe Hall (who now liked to be known as 'John') found a new lover, Una Troubridge. This was in the middle of the war. Una, small and delicate-looking, was married to an admiral, by all accounts a cheerful and uncomplicated man, who had encouraged his wife to seek treatment for trouble with her 'nerves'. The fashionable doctor she saw prescribed psychoanalysis, with the result that Mrs Troubridge realized she was homosexual. Her affair with Radclyffe Hall (which was to be permanent) followed, and ended her unhappy marriage. The admiral's career had already collapsed, not helped by domestic friction, although they gave him a knighthood in 1919. Lady Troubridge later told friends that he had syphilis; Radclyffe Hall's (male) biographer thinks she made this up to excuse herself for having left him.

Hall's private life was complicated. She joined the Society for Psychical Research and attended seances, hoping to meet the spirit of her former lover, Mrs Batten, who had suffered a fatal stroke while they were quarrelling about Una. When she sought election to the society's governing body, a council member called Fox-Pitt, a friend of the admiral, tried to block her nomination, telling people that she was an immoral woman who had wrecked the Troubridge home. She sued for libel.

The case, heard in 1920, was a treat for newspapers. Fox-Pitt tried to wriggle out of it by saying he had used the word 'immoral' in relation to a book of spiritualist revelations that Hall and Troubridge had written; the book contained passages about bathing in heaven and riding on spirit horses which caused hilarity in court. But there was no shortage of dirty linen. Ugly scenes with the admiral were described; Mrs Batten's morals were referred to; denials were made which only drew attention to what was being denied. When Fox-Pitt, conducting his own defence, asked Radclyffe Hall what was meant by 'unnatural vice', the judge intervened to say the jury were men of the world, and Fox-Pitt couldn't put such an indelicate question to a woman. Radclyffe Hall was awarded five hundred pounds' damages. But when an appeal by Fox-Pitt was allowed on a technicality, she didn't reopen the case, perhaps realizing that enough harm had been done already.

An alternative view is possible: she may have brought the action with every intention of publicizing her sexual views, an aim that had now been achieved. She saw nothing immoral about her behaviour, and it was not illegal. Her social manner was that of her set, tending towards the flashy. Cloaked and dinner-jacketed, they puffed at little cigars, stuck monocles in their eyes and clutched large whiskies, self-sufficient and proud of it.

Six years later Hall began work on a book that was first called *Stephen*, after its lesbian heroine, but had become *The Well of Loneliness* by 1928, when it was completed. Much of it is autobiographical and all of it is a brave statement of the homosexual woman's struggle to find happiness in an alien society. But there is no flashy socializing. Stephen, whose early years are described at length, eventually becomes aware of her nature. As a clandestine satire about the case, 'The Sink of Solitude', put it,

> She kicks, she thrives, she grows to man's estate,
> For trousers love she feels, for knickers hate.

After various adventures she finds the love of her life is a girl she meets when they are both in France as ambulance drivers during the war. But the affair is doomed. The only physical activity mentioned is kissing; a love scene ends with the words, 'And that night they were not divided.' The book concludes with Stephen asking the Almighty to help the cause:

> 'God,' she gasped, 'we believe; we have told You we believe ... We have not denied You, then rise up and defend us. Acknowledge us, oh God, before the whole world. Give us also the right to our existence!'

It was Radclyffe Hall's fifth novel. The fourth had won two literary prizes, and Cassell sold twenty-seven thousand copies of it in six months. But they declined the new book because of its theme, as did three other firms, and it went to Jonathan Cape, who made it look austere with black binding and a plain wrapper, and priced it at fifteen shillings, twice as much as most novels cost. The more a publisher charged for a book, the less chance there was of prosecution. Cape published in the summer and the novel was well received. Even the D.H. Lawrence-bashing *Daily Telegraph* had kind words for Hall's frankness and sincerity. But in mid-August James Douglas of the *Sunday Express* gave another of his performances, declaring that 'I would rather give a healthy boy or a healthy girl a phial of prussic acid than this novel. Poison kills the body, but moral poison kills the soul.' He called on the Home Secretary to set the law in motion, saying that literature should keep its house in order.

Angered by this, Cape unwisely sent a copy round to the Minister. Sir William Joynson-Hicks settled down to read it or perhaps had seen it already, since S.W. Harris at the Home Office had been quick to draw his superiors' attention to the book. Hicks (1865–1932) was a devout Anglican who liked to make life difficult for a wide range of those who offended his conscience, among them Communists, night-club owners and publishers of filth. Hicks consulted Bodkin, the DPP, together with Douglas Hogg, who had just been made Lord Chancellor and ennobled to become the first Lord Hailsham. The chief magistrate at Bow Street, Sir Chartres Biron, was also asked informally for his opinion. The State's legal apparatus was now at full stretch, dealing with a novel. Within a few days Hicks was writing to Cape to say that *The Well of Loneliness* was obscene — more private opinions writ large — and that if it wasn't withdrawn immediately he would have it prosecuted.

Cape did as they were told. More than four thousand copies had been sold in a short time, so they were not doing badly. They now used some low cunning and sent the type moulds to Paris, where they arranged with an English-language publisher, Pegasus Press, to prepare a new edition. But for the moment the Home Office thought they had won, and turned to other matters, among them a book just out from the novelist Compton Mackenzie called *Extraordinary Women*, costing a reasonably safe one guinea.

This book was not unrelated to *The Well of Loneliness*. It was set on the Mediterranean island of Sirene, a thin disguise for Capri, and poked fun at a set of lesbians who spend most of the story being malevolent about one another. Naturally they stare through monocles and smoke cigars. It is said to be possible to identify caricatures of Radclyffe Hall, Una Troubridge and others. The authorities were uneasy. Why was this forbidden subject suddenly in vogue? *Extraordinary Women* was worse, or at least it was more vulgar. Now and then it lurched towards indecency, as when one woman undresses in front of another. There were male witticisms. A mannish woman wears a dinner jacket but can't manage a stiff-fronted shirt because of 'the inconsiderate femininity of her bust.' The Home Office file* has a puzzled air, as if wondering what the world was coming to.

Joynson-Hicks had received a letter early in September from James Hope MP, a friend and fellow-Christian, who urged action against Mackenzie, 'this pornographer', adding, 'At this rate we shall have stories about bestiality next.' The left-wing weekly *New Statesman* had printed a review under the heading 'The Vulgarity of Lesbianism', suggesting a cheap edition at three shillings and sixpence and saying that 'it seems unlikely that Sir Archibald Bodkin will, in this case, venture to interfere.' The anonymous socialist reviewer, as puritanical about lesbians as the Labour Party remained about birth control, welcomed Mackenzie's book as having performed a public service by exposing this 'social disease', adding that

> He forces one to realize that Sapphic love besides being 'abnormal' must lead to situations far more intolerable than any which could be created by the least admirable kind of 'normal' sex relations. The social

---

* This is an *Extraordinary Women* file. No Home Office file survives for *The Well of Loneliness*. See Note to page 109.

behaviour of his women is horrible, disgusting, humiliating – and yet fundamentally inevitable . . . If [the book] does not prove, it at any rate suggests, that women cannot fall in love with women and remain sane and decent human beings.

Bodkin gritted his teeth and read it, as he had read *Ulysses*, finding it 'nauseous'. The danger, he wrote, was that 'women who have not healthy home surroundings are apt to be curious about this disgusting subject, and curiosity might lead to practice.' S.W. Harris was in his element. He had spotted *The Well of Loneliness* a fortnight before James Douglas' attack, and had skimmed both books, looking for questionable material. Radclyffe Hall's, he realized, was the more dangerous because of its advocacy of a cause ('little more than an apologia for sex perversion among women'). *Extraordinary Women* was undoubtedly indecent, but would action do more harm than good? Both books indicated 'a wider spread of the disease than would have been thought possible not many years ago.'

Sidney West Harris was the dedicated public servant who can't help but be an enemy of progress. Born in 1876, he had a wife and five children, lived in Wimbledon, was a regular churchgoer, belonged to the Reform Club, and had been in the Home Office since 1903, serving as private secretary to half a dozen Home Secretaries before he found his niche as an assistant secretary, among the top half-dozen officials, with indecent publications among his specialties. He was still there, long past retirement age because of the Second World War, in 1946, when they gave him a knighthood and sent him off to be president of the British Board of Film Censors. Sir Sidney went in to the board every day, till he was in his eighties, highly regarded as a gent of the old school, still keeping a Victorian eye on indecency.

At the time of *Extraordinary Women*, Harris' superior, John Anderson, perhaps less expert than Harris in the intricacies of filth, favoured prosecution, arguing that if a distinguished author like Compton Mackenzie went unscathed, 'we shall be unable to stop the influx of French books of the same kind, of which there are many.'

But when Hailsham, the Lord Chancellor, was consulted again, he advised that an action would be unlikely to succeed, since the book didn't seek to justify unnatural vice. Like others in authority who read it, he had to be seen to be keeping his distance, telling Joynson-Hicks that 'I spent a miserable afternoon reading your vile book' (S.W. Harris read 'as much ... as I have had time or stomach to tackle'). For good measure Bodkin had another little chat with the Bow Street magistrate, Sir Chartres Biron, who said he had read *Extraordinary Women* twice and found it detestable, but had difficulty in deciding whether an application for forfeiture would succeed. Since Biron would hear the case himself, and his word was law in his court, he was in effect advising Bodkin not to proceed. No doubt his reasoning was the same as Harris' and Hailsham's: Radclyffe Hall defended lesbians, Compton Mackenzie merely sneered at them.

By this time it was October, and the Pegasus Press had printed a new edition of *The Well of Loneliness* in Paris. Cape had decided at last to be brave. Copies were imported into Britain. Customs and Post Office stopped them whenever they could; police seized twenty-five copies in London, and a forfeiture order was applied for. In November the case went to Bow Street, whose chief magistrate must already have indicated, when the DPP approached him in the summer, that he would be likely to find against the book. The law empowered him to make a destruction order if he found it obscene. 'Obscenity' was that which tended to deprave and corrupt. In this fog of subjective criteria, magistrates could do much as they pleased.

The defence fell apart at once. Forty writers, booksellers, clergymen, doctors, biologists, teachers and social workers had been assembled to speak out; among them E.M. Forster, Julian Huxley and Virginia Woolf. Biron, who used a quill pen in court and fancied himself as a literary man (he had compiled a Dr Johnson anthology), refused to allow their evidence. Art and obscenity were two different things. 'There is a room at Naples,' he explained, 'to which visitors are not admitted as a rule, which contains fine bronzes and statues, all admirable works of art, all grossly obscene.' He adjourned the case.

His judgment a week later referred twenty times to 'horrible', 'vile', 'unnatural' and 'filthy' practices. The book, he said, contained not a single word that suggested its tendencies should be resisted; those in the story who objected to such vices were mocked for their prejudice. To the legal establishment, and no doubt to many good citizens, this was all wrong. Biron may have remembered reading about the admiral whose marriage was wrecked. He perceived a slur against women at the battlefront, 'where, according to the writer of this book, a number of women of position and admirable character, who were engaged in driving ambulances in the course of the war, were addicted to this vice.' This was too much for Radclyffe Hall, who was sitting at her solicitor's table, dressed in leather coat and wide-brimmed hat. She stood up and said, 'I protest. I am that writer.' She and Biron had a sharp exchange, which ended with her saying 'It is a shame!' and sitting down again.

The Well of Loneliness says nothing about homosexual practices on the battlefield; but for Biron it didn't need actually to use the words. Stephen, when she joins the London Ambulance Column, recognizes 'unmistakable figures' among her comrades, and realizes that 'many a one who was even as Stephen, had crept out of her hole and come into the daylight.' It is all very oblique, but we are told that they are women who have 'found themselves'. Mary, the girl Stephen falls in love with, is herself an ambulance driver. There is no suggestion that anything of a sexual nature happens while they are still in France. But as far as Biron was concerned, the passage was an insult to heroic women. It must have seemed to the authorities that the book was an insult to womanhood – the mythical English womanhood that everyone spoke of, that had been slipping away since the war. The magistrate made an order for forfeiture. It was twenty-one years before *The Well of Loneliness* was republished in Britain.

When popular reformers envisaged their bright new world of sexual happiness, few of them included homosexuals, male or female, in the blueprint; or if they did, they kept quiet about it. Marie Stopes was so upset by *The Well of Loneliness* that she tried to interest her publisher in an attack that would give 'accurate, clear scientific reasons why, how and where the book is corrupt.' In the climate of 1928, many thought that both sides had made fools of themselves. It was only women playing games with monocles and cigars, after all. As 'The Sink of Solitude' put it,

> But does an Aeropagitic cry
> To this dull morbid episode apply?
> Did SAPPHO sing, did SHAKESPEARE write for us
> Beauty obscenely sweetly amorous,
> That DOUGLAS might be born, and JOYNSON HICKS,
> And RADCLYFFE HALL put CAPE into a fix?

The Secret Sin

The popular reformers who were at work after the First World War, presenting sex as something hygienic and beneficial to the nation which nice people could approve of, were doing their best in difficult times. To acknowledge that sex might include dirt, danger, lust, promiscuity and unnatural behaviour was to ruin the case for cautious progress. Books like *Ulysses* and *The Well of Loneliness* hinted at this darker world, where more was dreamt of than sober birth controllers and mutually satisfying marital acts.

Something else lurked in the undergrowth and had to be confronted, though not too often and always with care. This was masturbation, itself often connected with books and pictures that might stimulate the imagination. Presumably even the fiercest opponent of pornography knew that the secret sinner needed no more than a locked door and imagination. But it was not done to be casual about self-abuse, the threatening phrase that was generally used. It is a statement of the obvious to say it has always been prevalent, but the statement would have been difficult to make publicly in the twenties, or the thirties and forties for that matter. A conspiracy of abhorrence had to be maintained.

Self-abuse was evil because it offered pleasure for pleasure's sake. An accusation regularly levelled at birth control during the nineteenth century, and well into the twentieth, was that those who used it were practising a form of masturbation. They were doing it because they liked it, not in order to have a baby. The *Lancet* declared (1869) that for a man there was nothing to choose between masturbation and having intercourse while using a preventive. Dr Mary Scharlieb, who would say anything to devalue contraception, said (1921) that it made sex into 'masturbation à deux' and would lead to degeneracy. Dr Halliday Sutherland, the anti-birth controller, quoted George Bernard Shaw (1921) as comparing it to mutual masturbation.

The Christian church had had unkind things to say about the habit for centuries. Medieval church codes, laying down penalties for every kind of sexual misdeed, devoted much time to it. St Thomas Aquinas thought self-abuse a greater sin than fornication, presumably because it was so available and so easily concealed. If the Church's idea was to control people's lives for the greater purposes of religion, which were concerned with spiritual values and not earthly pleasures, then uncontrolled masturbation wouldn't do at all.

As a sin, however, it doesn't seem to have weighed heavily on western civilization until more recent times, when a sinister work called *Onania, or the Heinous Sin of Self-pollution and all its Frightful Consequences* was published anonymously in London in the eighteenth century. The author may have been a clergyman who became a quack doctor, out to line his pocket at a period when quackery was thriving – the book advertised his 'Strengthening Tincture' at half a guinea a bottle. He coined 'onanism', which became the standard term for masturbation, by a creative reading of Genesis 38, verses 9 and 10, where Onan is slain by the Lord for a religious misdemeanour that sounds as if it might be self-abuse but is not. The book is strong on masturbation as sin but also lists serious bodily consequences. It went into many editions; its ideas influenced writers, among them Voltaire and the Swiss physician Tissot, who was an adviser to the Pope.

Like the author of *Onania*, the medical profession saw the potential of a little weakness in the human race that needed treating. By the nineteenth century, reputations were being made by European doctors for their skill in establishing that masturbation could cause, among other things, tuberculosis, fits, indigestion, impotence, blindness, headaches, acne, rings around the eyes, pallor, warts, red noses and a range of mental conditions including insanity. Flippancies like 'You'll go blind' and 'It'll drive you mad' echo once-credible diagnoses.

The new industrial society was interested in scientific method but anxious to retain its conscience. Perhaps a medical condition that threatened hell-fire enabled doctors to feel they could cure body and soul at one stroke. Mental disorders, too, were becoming a major field for study, and so masturbation's mental consequences fitted nicely into the imprecise theories of the 'alienists'. Medicine's response to masturbation had its finest flowering in the creation of 'masturbatory insanity' as a fearful disease that lay in wait for young (and sometimes not so young) men with pale cheeks and hollow eyes. Women could catch it, too, but not so often.

An array of treatments was provided in the nineteenth century. The fortunate were prescribed cold baths, fresh air and plain diet. Others had applications of camphor or potassium bromide inflicted on them. For difficult cases in the bedroom, little cages with spikes could be fitted, or a state-of-the-art gadget attached which rang an electric bell in the parents' quarters should the organ stir. It is hard to believe that many of these devices were made or used, but the fact that they were described in serious books suggests the force of the obsession. A London surgeon, Isaac Baker Brown, performed hideous operations on women in the eighteen-sixties to excise the clitoris – clitoridectomy – as a means of curing hysteria and epilepsy, caused, of course, by masturbation. There is no doubt that he did them, because he published the results of forty-eight such cases; long afterwards a colleague said in extenuation that poor Brown had softening of the brain, which affected his judgment.

There were few operators on Brown's scale, but countless popular authors who passed on warnings in little books. Sylvanus Stall, a retired American clergyman, influenced a generation, and had many readers in Britain. *What a Young Boy Ought to Know* (1897) said that masturbation injured the reproductive powers and led to idiocy or even death. A boy who indulged could be spotted by his shifty glance and the way he 'pulls his cap down so as to hide his eyes.'

By the early years of the twentieth century, the worst of the masturbatory obsession was over. But it was to have a long twilight. Even without the efforts of doctors and priests, there is an inherent streak of shame for an act that seems to advertise loneliness or lack of relationship; no one aspires to a life of masturbation. Decades of assault on self-abuse, coming from two directions, medical and moral, had convinced the public that it was a major threat. The charges had been so extreme that post-Victorian writers could ignore the wilder exaggerations of the past and still have ammunition. A. Dennison Light, editor of *Health and Vim* magazine, and devoted to fitness – he said the best time to conceive a child was between eleven and twelve in the morning, when people felt at their best – declared that self-abuse had always been 'the root sin of the human race', causing more pain, shame and sorrow than all the others put together:

> It is indeed very doubtful whether the fairest boy or the most winsome girl you ever saw are totally free from the taint of this poison. High and low, strong and weak, rich and poor, children of the peer and offspring of the peasant – all, all are there in that great vast crowd of soiled and sinful souls.

Havelock Ellis, working his way patiently through libraries, reported that bears did it, sheep did it, even elephants in zoos did it. People did it all the time, or found it happening to them, women sitting on swings or operating sewing machines with their feet, men sliding down poles or merely going somewhere by train ('the vibratory motion ... frequently produces a certain degree of sexual excitement, especially when sitting forward'). But even the permissive Ellis was unwilling to say that masturbation was entirely harmless.

The fantasies that accompany masturbation were deep inside forbidden territory, seen as essentially pornographic. The Revd Leslie Weatherhead, a Methodist minister who was writing about sex in the nineteen-thirties, said it was not the masturbation that was sinful but the imagined scenes that went with it, since this was what Christ condemned when he said that to look on a woman with intent to seduce her was tantamount to adultery. The idea that ordinary citizens would one day publicize their secret desires in books and newspapers would have been too outrageous to consider. No doubt the average fantasy, like the average diet, has grown richer; it has had more material to work on, more time for indulgence. But it was always there, flickering behind the eyelids.

Glimpses can be caught of the fantasies enjoyed by people who grew up early in the century. Havelock Ellis quoted an account of five years at a boys' boarding school. Having been seduced by a servant-girl when he was fourteen, the boy took to embracing a bolster, which he pretended was a woman — 'He said that the enjoyment of the act was greatly increased during the holidays, when he was able to spread a pair of his sister's drawers upon the pillow, and so intensify the illusion.' Mass-Observation, the social-research organization, included questions about erotic day-dreams and masturbation in a questionnaire of 1949 that it sent to its panel of (largely middle-class) 'observers'. These often caused embarrassment and produced curt replies or none at all, especially among older respondents. A minority were more revealing:

Woman, born 1897, married. She last masturbated two or three years previously. She 'tried to imagine someone I liked, but failed.' Her last sexual day-dream was when 'seeing dogs mounting from a bathroom window.'

Man, born 1909, married. Last masturbated two years previously. Last erotic day-dream two days ago: 'Girls I had known. Nymphs and satyrs over the fields.'

Man, born 1910, married. Last masturbated 'yesterday.' His fantasies were of 'sexual intercourse with some girl I have seen who attracted me, usually connected with sadistic tendencies (whips).' When filling in the questionnaire he omitted his index number, by which he would be identified to Mass-Observation, because of 'the part about masturbation and abnormality.'

Man, born 1911, married. Last masturbated 'this morning in bed,' fantasy of 'pretty girls dressed in voluminous frocks, frills, corsets, lacy underwear etc.'

Most of the writing on the subject, which was extensive, continued in the early part of the century to see self-abuse as a problem of the young; whether this was because the mature were thought not to do it, or because they were regarded as corrupt and beyond salvation if they did, is not clear. Norah March's *Towards Racial Health* (1916) was written as a handbook for parents and teachers. They were warned to watch out for hands in trouser pockets or children 'sitting cross-legged and swaying rhythmically,' and the usual hygiene was recommended, the light diets and cold baths. But punishment was deplored. The idea of forces at work below the surface was gaining ground – the 'unconscious sexual life, the existence of which Freud is leading us to appreciate.'

New thinking lay uneasily alongside old circumlocutions. The book includes a sample lecture by parent to son.

> Parent: How old are you today?
> Son: Twelve.
> Parent: You are getting on, quite a big fellow. Going to be a man soon! By the way, I ought to tell you something about being a man . . .

Erection is described by talking about 'the tube'. 'When the racial organs wake up and begin to produce sperms, this tube swells and projects.' But be warned, says Father (or Mother), wasting the semen exhausts the nervous system, so a fellow must never handle the racial organ in ways which excite him, not if he wants to 'come out top of the tree.'

Two years later, in *A Text-book of Sex Education*, Walter Gallichan was heralding scientific knowledge as the guarantor of virtue, at the same time offering not very scientific knowledge about the sperm, that rare species in danger of extinction. The pseudo-science of eugenics was still in full flood, with its dangerous taste for racial perfection. 'A waste of this fluid,' declared Gallichan, 'causes a dull mind and languid body . . . *It is plain, therefore, that the seed is veritably the life of the individual, as well as of the whole race.*' It followed that masturbation must be avoided. Take care, he warned, to reject stimulating foods, tight clothing and heavy bed coverings. Girls should avoid the early wearing of corsets, which might cause 'precocious sexuality'. A connection existed between tight lacing and heightened feeling, said Gallichan, adding, 'It is known that a degenerate cult of tight corset-wearers exists in England, with a journal devoted to their cause.' Gallichan wanted a sharp eye kept on the imagination, which was 'wont to exercise itself upon bizarre forms of sexual pleasure.' Somehow one has the feeling he was interested in corsets.

Marie Stopes found few kind words for masturbation. The old warnings against it were untrue, she wrote (1928), but the modern tendency among some men, 'particularly schoolmasters', to condone it was equally misplaced. The idea that 'such a perversion' was an almost universal habit constituted 'an abominable libel on the majority of decent young Englishmen and the mothers who brought them up.' The men who wrote to her must have confirmed her prejudices, since their letters are riddled with guilt for having done 'this beastly thing', being 'a weak and miserable rotter' and having *utterly loathsome cravings.*' One correspondent strayed into Gallichan's territory by describing 'onanism committed with a lady's corset wrapped around a pillow.' A vicar (who seems to have masturbated without a care in the world) sent her a chronology of his sexual life over five months in the war, 'for purposes of your work.' He slept with his wife six times, had four 'nocturnal emissions' and masturbated fifteen times.

All this would have confirmed the worst fears of D.H. Lawrence, who, though abominated by the powers-that-be for the indecent things they thought he wrote and painted, took a harsh and puritanical view of self-abuse. In finding it 'perhaps the deepest and most dangerous cancer of our civilization,' he stood shoulder to shoulder with A. Dennison Light of *Health and Vim.* Lawrence, however, cursed masturbation for being the wrong kind of sex. Writing in a pamphlet of 1929, *Pornography and Obscenity,* after his poems had been censored and his exhibition closed down, he called it the 'dirty little secret'. Sex had to go somewhere, especially in young people. 'So, in our glorious civilization, it goes in masturbation.' Because people's natural instincts (for open, explicit sexual intercourse) were repressed, they turned to masturbation, encouraged by popular novels, films and plays, the 'permissible pornography' that was supposed to be harmless, but wasn't. 'The most obscene painting on a Greek vase — *Thou still unravished bride of quietness* — is not as pornographical as the close-up kisses on the film, which excite men and women to secret and separate masturbation.'

Lawrence's scorn for prudery and censorship foreshadowed things to come. As for his theory that masturbation is a product of civilization gone wrong, it had few backers sixty years later. Eroticism has become respectable, yet auto-eroticism does not appear to have dwindled as a result. On the contrary, self-abuse (a term rarely heard today, though the popular 'wanking' still sounds derogatory) has merely been added to the long list of acceptable practices. Lawrence would say that the 'warm-hearted fucking' he approved of continues to elude us. But few would follow him into his mystical cul-de-sac.

In the twenties and thirties, all one could say of the secret sin was that it had survived attempts to eradicate it, and, if its social effects were indeed subversive, that they continued to subvert. For years to come backstreet museums and chambers of horrors, featuring models and dubious remains in jars, recorded (along with miracles, abnormal foetuses, the ravages of syphilis and other delights) the effects of masturbation on the organs of generation. 'Onanism', with its Old Testament ring, was the word they liked to use. At Blackpool the summer visitor could have seen

> Exhibit 106. Face of an old bachelor; a confirmed onanist. He became idiotic and rapidly sank into second childhood. (What a fearful account he will have to give of himself at the Judgment Day.)

The crowds paid their sixpences and giggled, and passed on.

'Labyrinths of Eros'

Making the Most of the Thirties

BRITAIN IN THE nineteen-thirties was drifting away from the ideals of continence and chastity. The ideals had never been more than declarations of intent. All the Cootes and policemen and bishops had not succeeded in changing human nature. Nevertheless the existence of a harsh code of sexual behaviour imposed psychological and sometimes legal disciplines that worked their way into every corner of daily living. The code's weakness had always been apparent to those who upheld it: if it became the subject of popular debate, its authority would be diluted. Once the silence was broken, nothing would be safe. The previous decade had already seen pleasure through sex become a desirable accomplishment that one talked about, at least in smart circles. An uninhibited sex-life was fashionable for this small minority. One had to obey one's urges. 'Such' (wrote Robert Graves and Alan Hodge in *The Long Weekend*) 'was the Freudian gospel as it filtered down into people's minds, through translations, interpretations, glosses, popularizations and general loose discussion.'

Throughout the thirties a popular discourse gathered strength. A range of cheap women's magazines had begun to offer advice on sexual problems, along with beauty tips, recipes, knitting patterns and romantic fiction. The letters sat there on the page waiting to share their secrets. A farmer's wife could write (*Woman's Own*, 1934) that her husband, 'a good man except for his weakness for girls', had had affairs with four young maidservants in four years. (Advice: 'Get a good middle-aged woman to live in.') Only a small proportion of letters were so explicit, but they gave the agony columns an extra dimension. They made misconduct seem more ordinary. And oversexed children could find in them a grain of excitement for the imagination to work on.

'Harry', born 1928, an only child of lower-middle-class parents, remembers a letter similar to the one from the farmer's wife, about a husband who 'had relations' with the maid. At this time a family in a semi-detached house, getting by on four or five hundred pounds a year, could afford a full-time maidservant for ten shillings a week. Harry thinks it was 1938 or 1939, by which time he was already attracted to agony columns without quite understanding them. The phrase about 'relations' bothered him. 'I was at home one Saturday, waiting for Ma to return from shopping. I was going downstairs. At the halfway mark was a small round window like a porthole with coloured glass in, looking down into the sitting room. I could see Pa in the armchair, with Hetty, the maid, on his lap. She looked pretty uncomfortable and her legs were open somewhat. The glass prevented my seeing all that much. But I knew it was something I was not supposed to see. When I read that letter I thought perchance that that was what having relations was, sitting squashed up in the same chair.'*

The agony columns and the advice they gave were still timid. It was important that they were doing it at all, but the codes remained in force. The moral conscience of *Woman's Life* in 1930 signed herself 'Your sincere friend Margaret', and when answering one of the key questions, 'How much love-making should a girl permit?', said she must 'STAND FIRM!' In a genteel way Aunt Margaret was saying that men were beasts. 'It is not a bit of good blaming them for it,' she wrote; 'a girl should concentrate rather on making any real liberties impossible.' A girl did this by not doing more than kiss. The slightest weakness in anything undesirable – not specified by Margaret, but any pure-minded girl would recognize what was happening even if it had never happened before – was dangerous. 'MORE WILL BE ASKED', and 'whatever it is beyond kissing, it means only one thing. It is just a step nearer the end nature had in mind when she made men and women.'

At the other end of the decade, in March 1939, the *Daily Mirror*, then unmatched as a daring popular newspaper, devoted a Woman's Page

---

* From an unpublished 'sex diary' kept by the pseudonymous Harry. His father was a printer. Harry is a lecturer, now retired. Both his parents, who were divorced in the 1940s, are dead. He is twice married, twice divorced, and (he says) is 'tired of women'. I met him when we were teenagers in the RAF, doing national service after the Second World War. Since then we have kept up a desultory friendship, mainly by letter. Three years ago, when he heard I was writing this book, he offered me parts – not all – of typescript notes and diary entries that he had been making for much of his life. I use them occasionally from this point in the book.

feature to the same problem. Nothing much had changed. Posed photographs of a dark-haired young woman and a sad chap in glasses spelt out the dangers of 'leading him on'. They are new acquaintances. In one illustration he is kneeling and doing something to her waist with outstretched arms. The text says that it

> shows her getting him to help her finish her dressing when he calls for her. She's late, and it will save time if he does up her frock.
>
> But it is the kind of thing you only ask a man to do if you have known him a long time and are very good friends. There's a certain intimacy about it . . . and intimacy doesn't go with a new friendship.
>
> *What is he going to think?*
>
> *I'll tell you. He's going to think – EASY GAME.*

Kissing was all right, and enjoyed a special status as a permissible act that involved physical closeness and was symbolic of the impermissible act. The same issue of the *Daily Mirror* had an advertisement that said,

> After the sweet thrill of a kiss, will he say 'Kiss me again?' He *will* say it if your lips hold the allure and charm that make men long for kisses. *You* can make him say it by spending a shilling on the wonderful Kissproof *Automatic* Lipstick that the stars of Hollywood use.

For the young and spirited in Britain who had the nerve, progress along the lines of trying to inch beyond kissing was too slow. Some of the avant-garde looked abroad for their sexual models. The French, tradition-ally relaxed about such matters, were less attractive after the First World War, which left them jaded and reactionary. Germany, on the other hand, which had a long history of sexual innovation, offered a more tolerant attitude within the highly organized democracy of the Weimar Republic that was created from the ruins of the wartime State. Stephen Spender's novel *The Temple*, written in 1929 but unpublished until nearly sixty years later, has characters who declare that 'Germany's the only place for sex', and, rather woodenly, 'I want to leave this country where censors ban James Joyce and the police raid the gallery where D.H. Lawrence pictures are on show.' Spender had made for Hamburg. Christopher Isherwood wrote about Berlin, where he found sexual freedom and homosexual lovers. Berlin was the place for bizarre and unorthodox behaviour, offering (Isherwood wrote long afterwards) 'dens of pseudo-vice catering to heterosexual tourists.' Isherwood wondered if Berlin's famous 'decadence' wasn't a trick – 'Paris had long since cornered the straight-girl market, so what was left for Berlin to offer its visitors but a masquerade of perversions?'

The bars and cabarets were real enough. So was Dr Hirschfeld's Institute of Sexual Science. No one had such a collection of erotic material — pictures, documents, even slides of brain tissue from the sexually unstable.

Nudists found a happy home in Germany. The British were prudishly uneasy about organized nakedness for health purposes; the cult had an earnestness, too, that it was hard to take seriously. Introduced to Britain about 1922, it was first called 'gymnosophy', after an Eastern sect of naked vegetarian mystics. The inspiration came from the Continent, and especially Germany, and the British pioneers were not well received. The founder of the Sun Ray Club was fined for using insulting words when he advocated nudity from a soapbox at Speakers' Corner in 1926, the *Vigilance Record* regretting that 'a wave of "culture of the nude" is passing over Europe at present.' Soon newspapers had it in their sights as cranky and indecent. Nudist-colony jokes have been current ever since. An ingenious seaside postcard of the thirties showed a bearded, hook-nosed nudist, his lower quarters concealed by greenery, with the caption:

> The girls all took him for a Jew,
> This saucy old Barbarian,
> But since he joined the Nudist club
> They see that he's an 'Airy 'un.

The Germans saw the healthy outdoor life as part of race-improvement, having found sunlight useful in helping children overcome vitamin deficiencies in diet during wartime food shortages. Nudism was officially encouraged, and by 1930 Germany was said to have three million practising nudists who marched through forests, danced by moonlight and had their minds and bodies purified by nakedness.

The Weimar Republic was not altogether a haven of tolerance. On the surface there was much sexual activity. Homosexuals were not driven deep underground, as in Britain; pornography flourished; sexual matters were widely discussed. In that sense it was a more open society than Britain's was at the time. Yet Germany was riddled with doubts, its sexual behaviour under attack from within. Arthur Koestler, then a young journalist in Berlin, visited Hirschfeld's institute in 1932 and was dismayed at the evidence of 'sexual mass-misery'. He wrote a series of articles about sex in the Weimar Republic which were too unflattering to be published. One and a half million homosexuals, said Koestler, lived in permanent conflict with the law; there were more illegal abortions than live births; it was illegal to offer contraceptive appliances for sale, but ninety million of them were sold in a year. Koestler suggested that theirs was an age of bogus enlightenment. The old sexual taboos had been broken, to be replaced by 'half-baked slogans and catch-phrases. And the lonely wanderer in the labyrinth of Eros is lonelier than ever.'

The ailment was not confined to Germany. Koestler wrote:

> The sexual chaos of the [post-1918] world, has shaken mankind . . . but it has failed to answer the problem of millions, how to satisfy their instincts, how to resolve the tragic dilemma between artificially over-stimulated desire and the stern limitations of custom and law.

The British had lower expectations, about sex and about pleasure in general, and were less ready to be deluded by visions. Aldous Huxley's satire *Brave New World* (1932) expressed humanitarian doubts about a future world State (then still being dreamt of and written about by H.G. Wells), which Huxley caricatured as a society where pleasure is boundless, sex unlimited and promiscuous, the family an obscene concept and babies are born from bottles. Birth control and biological science between them have achieved the ultimate end of separating sex and procreation. Huxley leaves no nerve untwitched in his picture of the horrors of such soft, disconnected living. The book was immediately enjoyed and understood.

The British way was to let things drift, an approach that has a lot to be said for it. All absolute solutions are suspect because absolute promises must be fraudulent. Sexual solutions were no exception. British radicals were not too radical; British reactionaries grumbled but compromised. In Germany the reactionaries swept to power, in the shape of the Nazi Party, and, as one element in their programme to build a new State, redesigned sex as a patriotic activity to produce children.

Hitler was ruling the country within a year of Koestler's cheerless survey. With the Nazis insisting they were not prudes, the lid came down on the sexual excesses of the Weimar Republic, many of which were of course attributed to Jews. Hirschfeld's institute was high on the list, though he himself had left the country already. In May 1933 the Gestapo paid visits and took papers. Then lorry-loads of students arrived early one morning, accompanied by a brass band that played threatening tunes outside. They broke in and sacked the place, and a few days later all the books were burnt in front of the Opera House.

Hitler raged against the iniquity of urban culture, the impurity of cinemas and literature. This crusade against 'filth' helped endear him to some in Britain. Pornography, homosexuality and prostitution were all curbed in Germany. So, curiously, was nudism. Birth control was frowned on, with four children per family established as the Party minimum. Vending machines for contraceptives were banned, Goering ordering police to oppose their installation. Exactly the same distaste for having condoms available by slot-machine was apparent in Britain; there, too, the authorities tried to stop the practice.

As for the embryonic feminism of the day, it was even less popular under the Nazis than it had been under their predecessors. They were there to produce little Germans of Nordic stock, and under those circumstances illegitimate children were no disgrace. The *Lebensborn* ('Well of Life') programme set up luxurious but unpublicized hostels where 'perfect women', usually unmarried, lived out their pregnancies; handicapped babies were disposed of. Breeding was women's real work. Otherwise only 'feminine' jobs such as domestic service, nursing and teaching were approved of. One of Hitler's cronies used the very words that made emancipated women cringe, 'Women belong at home, in the kitchen and bedroom.' Here, too, Nazi policy found supporters outside Germany.

In Britain gentility was more the style. The playwright Peter Nichols (b. 1927) has written of 'the dreary years between the wars' when a rising generation made a new life in nice homes equipped with mahogany gramophones and wireless sets, 'a careful class, achieving security by turning their backs on the drunken excesses of the Victorian poor.' Nichols was writing about the bawdy comedian Max Miller, whom he saw on the stage as a child, and how the response of the audience amazed him, respectable smut-hating folk enthralled and excited by Miller's outrageous act.

Harry, too, remembered Max Miller from childhood, though he never saw him, and assumes that his father, who was busy distancing himself from *his* father (a fifteen-stone workman in an iron foundry who reportedly came home drunk every Saturday night demanding sex from his small Scottish wife), wouldn't have risked being tainted by association. Miller was famous by repute. The BBC had banned him, in Harry's memory because he made an unspeakable joke on the air.

Harry wrote:

> *Smutty jokes.* I used to like them before I can honestly say I understood

them. What I liked I think was the pretending to know about something I knew was there to be known about, that I would know about presently. The first dirty joke I can remember hearing that I understood properly was when I was aged about seventeen. I was told that Max Miller had made it on the wireless before they could cut him off: 'I was walking along a narrow path around a mountain when I met a beautiful blonde without a stitch on. There we were, navel to navel. Blimey, I didn't know whether to toss myself off or block her passage.'* I felt extremely manly, hearing that. It made a deep impression on me. Else why should I remember it? One heard so few sexual references then. One was starved. Ma and Pa had a *Home Doctor* book that was kept atop the wardrobe in their bedroom. That was much earlier, before I was ten. I cannot remember for the life of me how I knew it was there. It contained a photograph of a babe sucking a woman's bare breast. Also a coloured drawing of the intestinal tract that I found disturbing. The first sexual *frisson* I experienced, as I realized many years later, was at the age of four or five, when I saw a picture of a man who was punished by having to walk about wearing a barrel, under which he was naked. The excitement was connected with his humiliation because women were looking at him.

Mass-Observation's archives have some fragments of sexual autobiography from the thirties, notably in replies to a questionnaire of 1939, about differences between respondents and their parents, with sex as one of the suggested topics. They are the perceptions of a literate middle class, generations who were the first to enjoy the new freedoms, their caution diminishing as their year of birth gets later. A married engineer of forty-five said promiscuity was prevalent, and he and his contemporaries didn't think it right. However, they believed in making the most of it. An osteopath of forty wrote, 'In my boyhood days we lads used to stand at tram stops in the hope of seeing a bit of ankle as the girls boarded. Today girls walk about in shorts and brassieres and there's scarcely anything left for the boys to be inquisitive about!!'

A former major of forty-two, now in insurance, dismissed his parents' attitude to sex ('It simply didn't exist. No mention was ever allowed of

---

* 'Tossing off' as a euphemism for masturbation was the universal term in those days. 'Wanking' was rare. Miller's biographer, John M. East, says the story of the BBC ban because of the joke is true. BBC files have no trace of it.

any bodily things') and got on to his description of the last time he took a girl out:

i.   Collected the lassie in a Taxi and conveyed to a big Hotel.
ii. An excellent Dinner and a liqueur afterwards.
iii. A top-hole Dance.
iv. A drive round the park in a Taxi.
v.   Deposited the lassie at her house at 12.40 a.m.

   Except that many people would have kept the girl out later (if she had wanted to be kept out), I doubt if there is any abnormal feature in the proceedings. The cost of the outing was in the neighbourhood of 35 shillings.

A housewife aged thirty-seven said she had tried discussing sex with her mother, 'but she thinks me unduly sensual. I think that if she were to read Havelock Ellis it would shock her so much she would have an illness.' A woman of thirty-four, a bookkeeper, wrote that her ideas about sex coincided with her mother's. 'I don't think either of us are particularly interested. I assumed that one just married and lived together, but, frankly, the world of sex interest depicted in films, plays and certain novels is beyond our ken . . . A friend of mine (female, aged 45) informed me that I am not normal on this subject.'

   A casual manner creeps into the younger reflections. An engineer aboard HMS *Maidstone*, aged twenty-three, said he was frankly not interested in girls who came under the heading *She'll make someone a good wife*. 'I'm afraid,' he wrote, 'the thought of Ginger Rogers with a tin opener excites my interest much more than Mrs Chamberlain surrounded by roast duck.' A single woman of twenty-one, a clerk, described an incident to show how prudish her parents were. She and her boyfriend Robert had walked all day at Easter, arriving at his home in time for tea, and were left there by themselves when his mother had to go out unexpectedly.

> In spite of the fact that, remembering my parents' prejudice, I dragged Robert to the cinema when all we wanted to do was rest in front of the fire, when I told my mother that Mrs S. had left us to have tea, hoping that example would modify her opinion, she told me that I had behaved in a most cheap and brazen manner, and actually suggested that we should have left the house when we realised we should be alone, travelled three miles by bus and then walked up the hill to my house where I would be adequately protected. Tripe!!!

Kate, twenty, stenographer, said that she and Sid attached not the slightest importance to the wedding ceremony (though she and Sid were married). Two or three decades before her time, Kate was writing that 'those men who don't easily centre their libido for any length of time on one girl should be careful not to fuck one of the clinging type who would be miserable when left.' Clearly Kate wasn't a clinging type. Her parents were appraised through narrowed eyes. 'Dad ... notices and remarks on the breasts of his niece (14). Wanted to keep me in (Oedipus situation). Mum says a woman who lets her husband wash her back is vulgar.' How many Kates and Sids were there in 1939? 'Sid and I haven't got any repressions left, I don't think. Not when we're alone, anyway. We share our dirty jokes ...' Officially, though, Kate and Sid hadn't yet been invented.

The formal order to which millions conformed through the decade can be seen drawing its wobbly lines of demarcation in the early sex-guides. Textbooks about sex were a thriving market. If they stressed caution and the need to contain sex within marriage, as most of them did, they were sure to sell a few thousand. The more descriptions and details they gave, the more copies they were likely to sell, but the greater the risk of police action. A reputable publisher would be unlikely to produce a serious textbook with the intention of selling it as pornography, but with a good conscience he could put himself in the way of profiting from sober descriptive passages that readers might (and who could stop them?) interpret as spicy bits. The distinction is more blurred even than that, since the bits were spicy only because there was a dearth of sex information in general, so that dwelling on sentences about limbs and lubrication was, or could be seen as, part of the business of educating the nation.

A Dutchman, Theodoor Van de Velde, born 1873, invented the modern sex manual with his earnest, opinionated *Ideal Marriage. Its Physiology and Technique.* First published in Holland and Germany in 1926 (the Nazis later suppressed it), a translation reached Britain two years later, where eventually it sold more than a million copies. At one time it was the prop of Heinemann Medical Books, who still had it in print in recent times. Van de Velde was a gynaecologist who had an unhappy marriage before going off with a patient, whom he eventually married. The book (which he followed with many others, none as successful) grew out of his life. It describes everything about the sexual apparatus and how to make it work. There is how to use lips and tongue, the nibbling with teeth, the where to touch and when, the importance of smell – Van de Velde was fascinated by smell – the positions, the honeymoon, the hygiene. In the original German edition some passages about coitus were in Latin, but Heinemann had these translated.

At first the sale or even loan of the book was restricted to the medical profession, some of whom must have been surprised to see one of their kind recommending 'what I prefer to term the *kiss of genital stimulation*, or *genital kiss.*' It was not all that many years since the Swiss psychiatrist Forel had said that oral sex, or certainly cunnilingus, was abhorrent. Van de Velde's only injunction was to begin gently and remember that a thin line divided beauty from ugliness. Nothing happened; the police left it alone. The author's stern warnings against perversion of any kind probably helped, even if they left undefined what perversion was (historically, oral sex would have been). 'It is our intention,' he wrote, 'to keep the Hell-gate of the Realm of Sexual Perversions firmly closed.' But reading about the 'vaginal clasp' which 'in its pillowy softness and delicacy, its warmth, is in itself a delight' was all right for medical men and married couples, and in the end for everyone. A former employee of Heinemann Medical once said to me 'Ah, "Nothing is more reassuring than the gentle touch of the lover's hand on a thigh" – years ago when I worked in a medical bookshop, I used to secrete Van de Velde from the shelf and try to educate myself.'

Most books emphasized the husband's need to be considerate to the wife, whose knowledge, it was assumed, would be less than his. Van de Velde said she 'must be *taught*, not only how to behave in coitus, but, above all, how and what to feel in this unique act!' Isabel Hutton's *The Hygiene of Marriage* (1923 and many later editions into the 1940s; another Heinemann Medical book) said that it was normal for a woman 'not to experience in any way the feelings of sexual excitement, even towards the man she loves, till some time after marriage has been consummated.' She suggested separate beds to begin with to make things easier. Forebodings about male anatomy no doubt reflected the reality of bridal innocence – 'It is largely this heaviness and evident strength of the erected penis for which most brides are quite unprepared, and which makes them apprehensive and fearful,' a comment that is unrevised in a 1940 edition. Hutton advises the bridegroom not to reveal any former indiscretions, and says the wise bride won't ask.

Hutton, too, was a doctor; it was safer. The notorious *Encyclopaedia of Sexual Knowledge* that Arthur Koestler ghosted in 1934 as 'Dr Costler' was brought out as soft pornography in disguise by a wily publisher who invented its medical author, 'Dr A. Costler'. Despite the work's commercial intent, Koestler/Costler had gutted enough text books (including *Ideal Marriage*), and was a good enough writer, to produce a fat volume that may have provided a crutch of sorts for the bewildered, though not a very reliable one. The *Encyclopaedia*, which was involved in prosecutions, is still easily found in second-hand bookshops. The first copy I saw had been abandoned in a Wimbledon telephone box in 1953, along with a book on weight-lifting that featured half-nude men.

Sex guides had to take the subject seriously without saying too much about the essential randiness of human nature. Rennie Macandrew, whose books like *The Red Light* and *Life Long Love* sold for a shilling or two from seedy outlets, packed in all the detail he could ('every woman,' he said helpfully, 'has about twenty square feet of skin surface'), but his publishers were able to use recommendations from a distinguished Christian of the day, Maude Royden, in the blurbs. Royden (1876–1956), a Doctor of Divinity and Companion of Honour, praised Macandrew (said to be a medical man using a pseudonym) for combining 'practical advice . . . with a perfectly clear warning as to the danger of erring.' That was the important bit, that the twenty square feet should not be unmarried skin.

The Methodist Leslie Weatherhead, a respected psychologist as well as a minister, wrote his own book, not a sex guide but a remarkably frank assessment of the Christian dilemma. *The Mastery of Sex* (1931, in print throughout the decade) was written in the aftermath of the 1930 Lambeth Conference, when the Anglican bishops, learning from Lord Dawson, had at last shifted a few inches from the fundamentalism of 1920. The sex act was allowed to be a 'noble and creative function.' Any 'illicit intercourse' was condemned, but birth control was now permitted, as long as the reason for using it was not 'selfishness, luxury or mere convenience.'

Weatherhead gave honest examples of the difficulties that Christians could find themselves in, but the solutions had to be ethically correct, and he found it hard to exercise a compassionate modern ministry in the murky waters of sexual reality. A 'Christian worker of some eminence', a single woman of thirty-three with no knowledge of sex who had a brief encounter with a married man on a Continental holiday, had been left with 'uncontrollable feelings of sexual desire . . . Masturbation becomes a habit. It is hard to blame her.' But the only remedy was to tell her to forget and go back to God. In the long term Weatherhead wanted better education to dispel ignorance, raising sex from the level of 'grimy embarrassments and furtive practice.' Many good men like Weatherhead trudged towards this mirage.

The State itself had little interest in sexual enlightenment. The most practical way in which governments could have helped would have been to do something about contraception. Here there was an ignorance among the poor (as well as an inability to pay for the appliances) that could have been diminished by official action. The means were available, the maternal and child-welfare centres operated by local authorities.

Before 1930 these were under orders from the Ministry of Health not to help women 'contemplating the application of contraceptive methods.' In 'exceptional cases' where there were medical grounds for avoiding pregnancy, the woman had to be referred to her GP or a hospital.

In 1930 the policy was modified, not without misgivings. The Labour Government's Health Minister, Arthur Greenwood, concurred with his civil servants' view that it was a delicate political issue, and that 'birth control is associated in many minds with a definite admission that the nation is starting on the road to decadence.' The words 'Yes I agree' and his initials appear beside the phrase about 'decadence', in a minute of 13.5.30. In July the Ministry managed to issue a memorandum which said that although it was not the function of centres to give contraceptive advice, it could now be provided on medical grounds. The catch was that advice must be 'limited to *cases where further pregnancy would be detrimental to health.*' It was better than nothing. But even this small change of heart was poorly publicized, as if the authorities hoped no one would notice.

Having made its miserable concession, the Ministry continued to snipe at the hated business of birth control, as the British Social Hygiene Council found to its cost. This dignified body, founded under another name in 1914 to fight venereal disease, decided in the 1930s to widen its scope. The days of VD as the great scourge were over. The disease was less emotive; effective treatment was well-established, and prostitution, diminished by the rise of non-commercial sex, was no longer seen as breathing infection over the land. So the Council began to interest itself in sex education and marriage guidance.

Because the Council was funded by government and local authority grants, it was not really independent. In 1937 its 'marriage committee' planned to publish a pamphlet, *To Those about to Marry*, which alarmed the Ministry. In fact the pamphlet was typical of its time, making the necessary nods to orthodoxy — 'Marriage . . . is a union of body, mind and spirit, and its only true foundation is real love and mutual respect.

Love is much more than mere physical attraction,' and so on. But it dared to make practical suggestions. The Ministry's file copy has survived, with annotations that show what the objections were. Where the pamphlet advises seeing a doctor before marriage, someone has underlined the words *to learn how sexual intercourse can be happily and healthily managed.* Also underlined is *love is like a fire* and *the woman needs satisfaction as much as the man.*

The Council was quickly brought into line. Its president, the Conservative MP Leo Amery, a former Colonial Secretary, was summoned to see the Minister of Health, Sir Kingsley Wood. There had been talk of the Council getting royal patronage, thus becoming the Royal Social Hygiene Council. The Minister warned Amery that the 'offending publication' jeopardized any such move. A few weeks later the Council changed its policy. The marriage committee was dissolved and the pamphlet forgotten. Nor did the royal patronage ever materialize.

Meanwhile the nation was adopting birth control by stealth. The birthrate, twenty-eight per thousand population at the start of the century, was below fifteen and still falling. There had never been so few births. Contraceptive knowledge had reached the lower middle class, the clerks and commercial travellers and small shopkeepers, and families of one or two children were common.

The poor were less well informed. G.D.H. Cole, the left-wing economist, wrote a verse to the tune of 'Hark the herald angels':

> The middle classes, me and you,
> Already know a thing or two.
> But oh, the poor they breed like rabbits!
> They have the most distressing habits!

It was not only the Ministry of Health that shrank from the diabolical work of contraception. The moral guardians were busy at the Home Office; S.W. Harris was still in place. In 1931 a contraceptive dealer with a private postal franking machine began overprinting his letters 'ASK YOUR CHEMIST FOR VERIBEST DOUBLE 99 QUININE PESSARIES FOR BIRTH CONTROL.' The Post Office got this changed to 'ASK YOUR CHEMIST FOR VERIBEST SURGICAL RUBBER GOODS,' but it was still too strong for the Home Office, which begged its postal colleagues to do more. 'Rubber' was the unclean word, and at last 'ASK YOUR CHEMIST FOR VERIBEST SURGICAL GOODS' was achieved.

More serious were the slot-machines. Not long before Goering was banning them in Germany, S.W. Harris was minuting, with reference to a shop in Leeds, 'I do not like this development at all.' The chief constable of the city had found a chemist with a machine saying 'Surgical Rubberware. Finest Quality. Guaranteed.' For a shilling you got one french letter in an aluminium container, no doubt for emergency use at that price, about £1.50 today. The law offered no redress. Harris suggested the police interview the chemist. When they did, he stood his ground. Complaints from other parts of the country continued to arrive at the Home Office. Police counted sixteen machines in London at the end of 1934. There was nothing to be done.

Older generations found these things hard to accept. Mrs Bramwell Booth's voice was one of many. Mrs Booth (1861–1957) was the widow of General Bramwell Booth of the Salvation Army, and had been a close friend of Josephine Butler. In 1937 newspapers said she was resigning from the Association for Moral and Social Hygiene because in her eyes it had a duty to oppose 'the commercial exploitation of vice', yet stood idly by while 'appliances for contraception' were being advertised. The creation of a 'powerful vested interest', enriching manufacturers by their encouragement of lust, seemed as wicked to her as it seemed inevitable to those who thought a contraceptive industry a good idea.

Mrs Booth's name still carried weight. Her protests took her via the Home Office to the Ministry of Health, where she had an unsatisfactory meeting with two of Kingsley Wood's underlings, following this up with a long letter to the Minister, in which she complained that the 1930 memorandum on contraception had been a terrible mistake: 'The Welfare Services are *not* intended for birth prevention. Motherhood is a natural and healthy condition.' She thought that contraception was sacrificing women's bodies for the gratification of men, just as the discriminatory laws on prostitution that Josephine Butler fought against had sacrificed their bodies long ago. She was incensed at the state of country lanes around Barnet and Potters Bar – where she lived, as it happened. They were 'infested with motor-cars drawn up by the roadside . . . virtually brothels on wheels.' Decent folk couldn't go there.

It was the same complaint that was heard in Edwardian London about the promenades of music halls and the pavements of the Haymarket: sex was rearing its head in public. But it was no longer contained in traditional districts. Vice was abroad in leafy Hertfordshire.

Either 'immorality' had multiplied, or the increase had been modest but was made to seem greater because a minority were more brazen. Writers deplored what they called 'sex mania'. Ivor Brown (b. 1891), drama critic of the *Observer* (and later its editor for six years), wrote scathingly about modern audiences who cared nothing for the issues of power and wealth that fascinated the Elizabethans. They were the 'villa myriads' of the twentieth century, their horizons bounded by home and office.

'Sex,' thundered Brown, 'is their adventure and their dream. Now, for the first time in the world's history, there is a huge machinery of entertainment for this class, employing the camera and the printing press to catch their small change.' The cinema in particular disturbed him – 'The film-stories are mere frames for sexual pursuit; the titles drip with desire.'

A stronger objection might have been that sugary innuendoes were all that the censors would allow. The reality of sexual behaviour was something else, but no one was allowed to be honest about it. Instead there was the 'permissible pornography' that D.H. Lawrence objected to.

Outside the conventions that dictated what could be seen and read, there were glimpses of a more honest vulgarity, the Max Millers, the naughty postcards, the seaside frolics. There is a glimpse of the sinful British, late-nineteen-thirties style, in a Mass-Observation study of Blackpool, where twenty-three Observers were busy with notebooks at different times. Blackpool was one of Britain's two traditional naughty seaside towns. The other was Brighton, where middle-class Londoners went for extra-marital weekends. Blackpool was the proletarian playground, the sands at night popularly supposed to be a heaving mass of mill girls and their lads. This turned out to be not quite true.

Peripheral, smutty-joke naughtiness was undeniably catered for. The Fun House, entry one shilling, where puffs of air blew up women's clothes as they entered, was well patronized. A notebook recorded

> Woman whose knickers show when skirt blows up. Yells of applause.
> Boy calls, 'That was a good one!'
> Very fat woman. Screams of applause. Shouts of 'Mother.'
> Elderly woman cheats by climbing through rails.
> Cries of 'Go back' etc. She laughs, goes on.

Ancient 'what-the-butler-saw' machines, the mutoscopes that shocked Edwardian policemen, were still to be seen in hundreds, with titles like 'Scenes from Paris' and 'Beauty in the Bath'. Breasts and underwear were as far as the clapped-out pictures went. All you saw in 'First Night' was a woman in her undies, legs open, reading a book called 'First Night'.

Real people did a certain amount of picking-up, two-thirds of it initiated by the girls, according to Observers. A female Observer, 'blonde, thirty-five, wife of an Oxford don and Labour Party activist,' received five propositions as she stood at the foot of the Blackpool Tower, including one from a middle-aged man in a bowler hat − 'Will yer come to bed with me, love? 'ave yer done it before?' − and one from a tall well-dressed man − 'Are you all alone, sweetie? Come along with me and I'll give you a real good time.'

The back streets of Blackpool were unfavourably compared, in respect of sightings of serious sexual activity, with similar locations in Bolton, disguised at the time as 'Worktown'. When surprised by Mass Observation headlights, seven couples in Bolton were necking in one street, five in another. After 11.15, when the lights went out, every Worktown back street apparently had one or two couples enjoying a 'knee-trembler', sexual intercourse against a wall, summer and winter. What of Blackpool after dark? Observers, one is told, 'combed the sands at all hours', on all fours where necessary, pretending to be drunk, falling on top of couples to discover exactly what they were doing; fortunately no cases of assault on them were reported. A helpful check-list of one night's survey shows 120 couples embracing as they sat, 46 embracing and lying down, 42 embracing standing up, 25 kissing sitting down, 9 necking in cars, and 7 girls sitting on a man's knee. None of them were actually copulating. 'What we found,' says the Observers' account as published in 1990, 'was petting and feeling', though the original typescript spelt this out a little and said 'petting, feeling and masturbating one another.' In one season, probably 1937, only four cases of copulation were noted, one of them by an Observer who was doing the copulating, with a married woman on holiday by herself; this took place against a wall and was not entirely satisfactory ('No, no more, Jack. I'm afraid').

Very likely, as Mass-Observation concluded, the holiday situation was all right for petting but not for the serious business of intercourse, which implied familiarity with a man and the idea of marriage: 'The girl who will go with any man on first acquaintance is "bad" in the Worktown moral code.'

Slowly, all the codes were changing. Fiction that was and wasn't published in the thirties offers more evidence of that meandering demarcation line. Often it seemed that nothing had changed. *Boy*, a short novel by James Hanley (1901−1985), came out in a subscribers' edition of fewer than a hundred and fifty copies in 1931, dedicated to Nancy Cunard, who had given him a typewriter. The 'boy' is Arthur, an innocent who stows away on a tramp steamer to escape his bullying father, only to find worse harassment at the hands of the crew. At Alexandria he loses his virginity to a pretty young whore, contracts syphilis, and is killed out of pity by the captain. Hanley, who never made much money out of writing (his obituaries called him a 'neglected genius'), is said to have produced *Boy* in ten days. His publishers were Boriswood, a small firm that began as a bookshop in London. To them, Hanley was a down-and-out writer of promise, but they hardly helped him by following the subscribed edition with an ordinary commercial printing that attempted to clean up the text in case the police came round. This was done by leaving blank spaces or inserting asterisks. The result was uncomfortable:

> 'Turn over this way. Now that. Stretch. *** *** ***. No. Not that way. Kneel up now. Turn over. Lie still. Swing *** ***. Now *** *** ***. Oh God! *** *** *** *** *** ***. Yes ***. No. Not that way . . .'

What Hanley wrote was:

> 'Turn over this way. Now that. Stretch. Lift this leg. No. Not that way. Kneel up now. Turn over. Lie still. Swing that breast. Now let it hang. Oh God! Let me place my hand there. Yes there. No. Not that way . . .'

Whole paragraphs disappeared. Sometimes the reader was tempted to insert ruder words than Hanley had intended. When a sailor speaks of a Can-Can dancer who, for a wager, 'had placed a lighted cigarette ** ** ****** ****,' it turns out that what Hanley wrote was 'in her philosophic centre'.

Having half wrecked the book to make it harmless, the publishers brought out a fourth edition in 1934 with a provocative jacket showing a flimsily clad girl. Police in Manchester, living up to their reputation, decided to prosecute under the common law for 'obscene libel', a more serious matter than the usual application for a destruction order, since a prison sentence was possible. The Boriswood directors shivered but got off with fines. They had further trouble with other Hanley titles, and also a reputable textbook, Edward Charles' *The Sexual Impulse*. An application by the London police to destroy it was resisted, the defence calling Julian Huxley and Maude Royden as witnesses, without success. The magistrate thought the book not 'fit and decent for people of the working class to read.'

Heinemann, a larger firm, were also in trouble in 1935 for an American novel of some merit about life in a Chicago brothel, Wallace Smith's *Bessie Cotter*. This, too, was made the subject of a full prosecution for obscenity. The story was circumspectly told, with nothing stronger than such passages as

> [Bessie] slipped from under the crazy-quilt and stood, naked except for her stockings, before she wrapped the kimono around her.
>
> 'Another of those guys that like the stockings on?' asked Maggie.
>
> 'No,' replied Bessie. 'Just one of those girls too lazy to take 'em off.'

The Attorney-General, Sir Thomas Inskip, who did the prosecuting in person, said that the book dealt with 'what everybody will recognize as an unsavoury subject – gratification of sexual appetite.' The publishers pleaded guilty. Someone may have taken them aside and pointed out what they had presumably failed to notice, that the book used a forbidden English word that in North America was slang for a young woman. ' "That fresh quim," muttered Joe. "Thinks she's smart." ' This, and one or two other sentences using the same word, may have spoiled their chances.

In general, the authorities were becoming more cautious. Novels by Erskine Caldwell (*God's Little Acre*), Malcolm Muggeridge and Maurice Richardson were among those complained of to the Home Office in the early thirties, but left alone. Officials knew that the publishers of a prosecuted novel would not necessarily hang their heads in shame. If the prosecution failed, they might make capital from the book's supposed indecency.

The most significant change of heart concerned *Ulysses*. In America a New York district court had decided in December 1933 that the novel was not obscene. A month later T.S. Eliot, a director of the publishers Faber & Faber, was thought grand enough to be received at the Home Office, and the possibilities of an English edition were discussed. Eliot backed out. In the end it was Allen Lane at the Bodley Head who took the chance, persuading nervous fellow-directors to publish a limited edition of a thousand copies in October 1936. A new Attorney-General, Donald Somervell, had replaced Inskip earlier in the year. Somervell had liberal tendencies. In November he and the Director of Public Prosecutions decided to leave *Ulysses* alone, Somervell taking the view that the standard definition of obscenity (that which might deprave and corrupt) was inadequate, and that 'the question of intention has to be taken into account as in criminal law generally' – a casual reversal of principle by a law officer that took more than twenty years to find its way into statute law.

Few people read *Ulysses*. A more popular breakthrough was a magazine that appeared at the end of 1935, *Men Only*, which cost a shilling and contained spicy illustrations. Long afterwards the title was taken over by Paul Raymond and turned into a full-frontal sex magazine. In the thirties it was a pocket-sized affair trying to be affably masculine, interested in humour, sport, motor cars and, in a healthy sort of way, women. Its novelty lay in being frankly if cautiously sensual, while remaining respectable. 'Studio Peeps No. 1' was a full-page drawing of a naked red-haired girl, using her elbows and a green umbrella to cover vital areas. Editorial nervousness is suggested by a self-congratulatory article in the second issue —'Everybody laughed, and no one thought we had overstepped the line.' By Studio Peeps No. 4 the model was revealing distinct signs of breast and bottom. One of the cartoons showed a man looking at magazines on display in a shop — 'Girl Models', 'Saucy Bits', 'Secrets of Nudism' — while the shopkeeper says, 'What d'you mean, you just wanna browse?'

Eighteen months later a second small-format magazine came on the market called *Lilliput*. This was a glossier product, with literary pretensions and clever photographs, edited and owned by Stefan Lorant, a Hungarian journalist of thirty-six who had been locked up by the Nazis for six months before coming to Britain. Lorant started *Lilliput* on a borrowed twelve hundred pounds and sold it a year later to the Hulton Press for twenty times as much. The sex was discreet but persistent, with one or two women in bathing costumes, or naked except for shadows.

In 1938 Hultons let Lorant launch the incomparable *Picture Post*, which became a frame for pictorial journalism about Britain of an uninhibited kind not seen before. Again, the sexual element was incidental. But, like the magazine's eye for ordinary lives and faces, it was part of a new and wittier introspection. Women in their underclothes cropped up quite often. Somebody, probably Lorant, stoked up a correspondence in the summer of 1939 about the wisdom or otherwise of caning teenage girls. This was a traditional English topic. In the nineteenth century more than one respectable magazine ran series of letters on the subject, their impact only marginally weakened by the fact that some of the racier ones kept reappearing with small variants and different signatures.

Flagellation has many aspects, some of them bloodthirsty, but the politer, more domesticated British version has strong echoes of childhood and a controlled discipline that never goes too far. The *Picture Post* letters were invented as a way into that fantasy world.*

---

* The private 'Longford Report' on pornography in 1972 heard evidence from an ex-prisoner who rather improbably blamed his downfall (through theft) on a taste for indecent literature that began when he read the *Picture Post* letters and became obsessed with corporal punishment.

The series began with a letter saying it was 'a mistake for lady cyclists to wear shorts.' A man replied to say this was nonsense, since shorts were less revealing than skirts for athletic girls, and to object to them was 'just one more result of the general idiocy of our self-appointed moral uplifters.' The correspondence lurched towards flagellation. A woman wrote to say that it was only conceited young women who wore 'scanty shorts', and 'it would give me great pleasure to apply a good pliable cane to the seats of some of those tight-fitting shorts.'

Letters poured in. Girls were punished for being rude at holiday camps, for staying out late, for speaking without permission, for posing nude for photographs, and of course for wearing shorts. A few letters may have recorded real situations; most read like fantasies; some were written from streets that didn't exist. It is unlikely that so much schoolgirl flagellation had ever been offered to a mass readership in Britain. There were no feminist sensibilities to consider. In the last summer of peace, a little sadism was part of the fun.

At *Men Only* they sprang into action with the pin-up. By now the magazine had black-and-white nude photographs, quite seemly. It began a series of coloured drawings, 'Ladies Out of Uniform', showing busty women bare from the waist up. A reader was rebuked for complaining – 'He thinks they are *all wrong*. He is shocked and surprised that [the magazine] should so lower itself as to pander to the base desires of those unfortunate creatures who *like this sort of thing*. He can't think why we are doing it.'

The magazine pointed out sarcastically that 'during the past few months, a number of single young gentlemen have set up housekeeping on their own account.' They were in military quarters, and liked to stick pictures torn from magazines on the walls. 'Sometimes (dare we admit it?) their fancy turned to an artist's model wearing nothing much in front – and rather less than half of that behind. They started writing to us, asking for original drawings . . .' *Men Only* obliged by offering to send free enlargements of its half-naked ladies to 'a friend serving at home or abroad.' The British pin-up girl had been invented, though the phrase came from America.

The girls grew more suggestive as the war went on; so did the cartoons. A man in an air-raid shelter leers at a woman. 'We're forty feet underground, it's bomb proof, splinter proof, fire proof and sound proof, but you still seem a little uneasy, Miss Bagnold.' An air-raid warden wrote to the magazine to say that his colleagues at the wardens' post were shocked by the illustrations. A retired policeman had told him, 'We don't want any of your obscene literature here. This post is becoming contaminated.' The warden added that the policeman had spent twenty minutes reading a copy.

The war made it easier to be relaxed or even brazen. Harry wrote (1952),

> I see some policeman has seen fit to take out a prosecution against *A Basinful of Fun*. I had forgotten its existence. It was more of a comic than anything else. S. had an older brother who had copies in the war. They were popular at school (but not up to *Men Only* standard). S. showed me a copy for the first time on the school bus. I recall one item only. It was a drawing of a night sky above a town pierced with anti-aircraft searchlights. One spoke at that period of the searchlights being 'up.' A voice emerged from a darkened building: 'That's better, Colonel, I feel much safer when they're up.' The double meaning was exciting. What is very strange is that the *memory* of the excitement experienced from a small smutty joke about women's underwear at the age of fourteen retains the power sexually to excite in one's so-called maturity.

A Basinful of Fun was a cruder product. The early *Men Only* was designed not to be a magazine that men hid. It published a letter that asked, 'What sort of men admire the sort of stuff you print? What sort of men appreciate naked women and dirty jokes? I shall buy your next copy for the pleasure of burning it. If I see a copy in our canteen I always tear out the extremely unpleasant pictures or confiscate the entire copy.' An editorial note said, 'So that's where they go!'

It would not have occurred to men in 1940 that women might be offended by nude drawings of their sisters. Nor would it have occurred to most women to take offence. In restrospect one might think that the pin-up was a way of reinforcing men's images of women as sexual objects. But the language for such perceptions had not been invented by the Second World War. A rude picture might be regarded in the forties as an ungentlemanly thing to show in mixed company. Yet it was rather as a man with a foul pipe might be expected not to get smoke in a lady's eye. What he did when he was in other company was his own business. There were beastly things men did that wise women didn't notice. The sexes conspired to live within their stereotypes. The pin-ups in *Men Only* were still innocent.

8

◄➤◦⊂►

'All Very Enjoyable'
In the Steps of Dr Kinsey

THE SECOND WORLD WAR was less shocking in its sexual aspects than the first, not because the shifting patterns of casual love and commercial sex were any less intense, but because people were less easily shocked. The 'serious' war-fiction that appeared in *Penguin New Writing* and other pocket magazines was inclined to deal matter-of-factly with wartime relationships when they were set against the background of world conflict. Even going to bed with a lover under those circumstances could be made to seem natural, even sensible; prurience had nothing to do with it.

The humble condom, sheath or french letter, most despised of requisites, came into its own in the war, though lovers in fiction were never seen to use one. Perhaps dim memories of the 1914–18 fiasco over 'prophylactics' prompted wiser counsels among the military. Condoms were still in the shadows, an embarrassment, like sanitary towels, but indispensable to many; now they were issued free to servicemen overseas, who used them for cigarettes and matches in wet weather, or to waterproof the muzzles of rifles, as well as for the intended purpose. Large-scale government demand for the condom gave it a kind of blessing, as well as securing the future of the London Rubber Company.

Set up in a grimy part of London during the previous war, LRC originally imported most of the goods from countries like Germany where they were less inhibited about their manufacture. In the 1930s, the rubber industry was revolutionized. Latex, the product of the rubber tree, coagulated like blood and had to be made into a crude form of rubber on the spot. Once the industry learned how to stop it coagulating, liquid latex could be moved in bulk. For the french-letter business, this meant a thinner and safer article.

At first LRC made the new condoms in a backstreet shed, dipping racks loaded with porcelain formers, penis-shaped but larger than life, into troughs of latex. By the war they had put in mechanized production lines bearing ghostly glass penises, while rows of women did the checking and packing at the far end. The trade name 'Durex', which in Britain became a generic term for a condom, is said to have been invented on a train journey by the founder, a Mr Jackson, who meant it to signify Durable, Reliable and Excellent. Few who worked at the Durex factory went out of their way to tell people what they did. The embarrassment lingered for years. A London Rubber salesman said that when he joined the firm in the sixties, he took his company car home to show his wife, and proudly laid out the samples on the dining-room table. She drew the curtains in case the neighbours saw.

It was not as though the product was used by only a few reprobates. In 1939 London Rubber was making nearly four million a year. By government directive the company became the principal manufacturer for the duration, and was soon making 120 million. Even allowing for rifles and matches, this represented a fair amount of sex.

As in the First World War, anxiety about morals was widespread. Lord Clarendon, the Lord Chamberlain, called a conference at St James's Palace in April 1940 where police, Home Office, local authorities and the entertainment business agreed that something ought to be done. What needed curbing was 'the greater tendency which has become evident since the war of greater displays of nudity and more impropriety of gesture and speech.' This was vague enough for the theatres and music halls to endorse.

The scandalous whispers of the first war about nurses and ambulance drivers became rumours about the way women in the armed services, soon numbered in tens of thousands, were carrying on with men. The 'Wrens', members of the Women's Royal Naval Service, were popularly supposed to be more upper-class and thus randier than their counterparts in the Army and Air Force. This canard was resented and seen as beneath contempt, but was never quite killed off. The travellers' tales about servicewomen in general, suggesting an epidemic of pregnancies and distressing to their families, was investigated by an official committee in 1942. It found that unmarried servicewomen had fewer pregnancies than unmarried civilian women, and blamed the rumours on the younger generation's 'bravado' and 'shock tactics against the shibboleths and conventions of their elders.'

One indisputable gauge for Britain as a whole was the illegitimacy rate. At the beginning of the war, about 26,000 babies a year were born 'out of wedlock', roughly 4 per cent of the 650,000 births. By the end of the war this had risen to more than 63,000 illegitimate babies, over 9 per cent of a slightly larger number of births. Single mothers and their children were entitled to more official compassion than in the past, but a voluntary body, the National Council for the Unmarried Mother and Her Child, bore the burden of getting them provided for. Much of its energy went on looking after middle-class girls in the forces; the council's figureheads included the wives of Winston Churchill and the Archbishop of Canterbury; the 'unmarried mother' was still defined in everyone's mind as someone who had not yet achieved the status of a married mother, and the sense of completeness implied by 'one-parent family' would have seemed offensive, had the phrase been invented.

Venereal diseases were no longer a nightmare but remained a nuisance, their consequences medical rather than moral. At a public meeting in London, which attracted eight or nine hundred people in February 1943, moralistic remarks by the Archbishop of Canterbury, Dr Temple, were not well received; but neither were suggestions that all should carry prophylactics. The feeling of the meeting was towards compromise – that preventing VD was a moral matter, but treating it was a matter for doctors, and no one should be deterred from seeking medical help.

Official campaigning against VD had begun in 1942, the year that American troops began to arrive in Britain. The Central Council for Health Education, a body sponsored by the Ministry of Health, was responsible for VD propaganda. One of its early productions, *What are the Venereal Diseases?*, printed on pages so tiny that it might have been designed to conceal inside the palm of a hand, announced that self-control was not easy in wartime, made a genuflexion towards 'the fineness and the lasting happiness of the right kind of sexual relationships,' and returned to self-control as the only reliable way to avoid catching VD. Advertisements were placed in newspapers, though not before the proprietors had persuaded the Ministry of Health to remove explicit detail that was regarded as offensive to readers. Thus the information that the first sign of syphilis was an ulcer was permissible, but not the fact that it appeared 'on or near the sex organs.'

The campaign had continually to guard its rear against attack by clergy and moralists. The Archbishop of Canterbury resented the realistic assumption behind public policy, that health measures were necessary because large numbers of people were likely to fornicate; clergy in America felt much the same. But the churches' capacity to wound was reduced since the First World War, and government ministers no longer trembled at the thought of what they might do. Pure hearts had ceased to be necessary to win wars. All that the ecclesiastical critics could do was make a nuisance of themselves. Radio broadcasts were included in the government propaganda, together with films, exhibitions and a hundred and sixty thousand posters. No public-health campaign on this scale had been attempted in Britain before.

Folk-tales about VD still in circulation, suggested that education had some way to go. One popular belief was that intercourse with a virgin would cure a man, or, in a more general sense, that you could rid yourself of the disease by passing it on to someone else. The need to find excuses for having VD meant that lavatory seats were regularly blamed; no one was ever able entirely to rule out the possibility that a lavatory might be responsible. Women blamed clothes bought from second-hand shops, or even laundries, saying the washing must have got mixed up. A woman who had worked for the British Social Hygiene Council claimed to have heard the most original excuse of all. A clergyman said he caught it from the wheel of a cart that splashed him. He was standing nearby, relieving himself, when 'the cart moved unexpectedly and *voilà.*'

Perhaps the most widespread myth among men was that only an association with a professional prostitute could cause VD. This was an unwise thing to believe in wartime Britain, where numbers of young (and not so young) women were willing to sleep with casual partners, especially in uniform, because they liked sex for its own sake and because dating strangers had exciting associations. American troops were the core of this problem, if it was a problem, and the US authorities certainly believed that very little of the VD that their men caught in Britain came from prostitutes. Whatever their nationality, men who were so inclined had little difficulty in finding sexual companionship.

The Mass-Observation reports from a 'Sex and Morality' survey of 1944 may amount to no more than superior anecdotage, but they catch the atmosphere of the time, when many women were not only without their husbands, but often lived away from their own towns. 'Evacuation', where women and children were moved (or moved themselves) out of cities to avoid air raids, was assumed to encourage casual sex.

The headmistress of a school that had gone from South London to the countryside reported to M-O that of the forty mothers she knew personally, thirty-nine were 'going the pace in this little village with soldiers.' Mrs A, aged thirty, known in Camberwell as a 'nice respectable woman who never looked at a man,' had become 'a flagrant wanton'. Mrs B, twenty-six, was on her third man. Mrs C, thirty, had lived with three Canadian soldiers in the last two years. The catalogue is daunting; perhaps a headmistress who found so many 'flagrant wantons' had problems of her own. But her pages of neat writing sound flat and matter-of-fact. She had discussed it with the school nurse, who said, 'You're telling me, every week we have a policeman searching our pre-natal records to see if they can discover who abandoned a new-born baby in a ditch or in a pond, or tried to dispose of the effects of an abortion.'

At its worst, this was the world turned upside down. 'Our "virgins" hang around camps and balloon sites or fling themselves into the arms of Yankee soldiers and cuddle them in shop doorways,' wrote Mass-Observation's Mr A, a clerk, thirty-six. Mr C, a commercial traveller, thirty-five, reported that Leamington Spa was littered with french letters every morning. Before the war the town had had a few well-patronized prostitutes, but they were all gone now. One of them told him before she left, 'There are too many gifted bloody amateurs here for a decent pro to get a living.' A soldier stationed in Huddersfield described how to find women: you went to pick-up pubs, pick-up cafés and pick-up fish and chip shops. After dark the park's remoter corners were occupied by 'embracing couples'. About half the men there were in the armed forces, but most of the women were civilians.

Women, more than men, were re-examining their lives. A young widow, arguing about morality with her mother, told her, 'You can't talk. You never had the chance or the temptation.' A single woman of forty-eight, a clerk, thought that promiscuous intercourse was bad for the children, yet 'puts women on a higher plane. It gives an unmarried woman as much right to have children as her married sister, as long as she is in a position to support them.' Rather sadly, she doubted if she could ever be promiscuous. But 'my "chastity" may merely be that my sex instincts have never developed properly, or I have been afraid of sex, afraid of God, afraid of life, afraid of death . . .'

An Observer reported a woman shopkeeper of sixty as having said she was 'fair disgusted' by a recent radio programme. 'Did you hear it? The Radio Doctor was there, and they said it was *right* to have intercourse before marriage. Such young things!'

The programme title was *Learning about Sex*. A recording has survived in the BBC archives. A group of young people aged from sixteen to nineteen, some still in school, talked with Charles Hill, then a minor but anonymous celebrity, 'the Radio Doctor', later Lord Hill, a figure in television. The discussion has a cautious air; sex was not a BBC subject. There are signs that it was scripted, or at least well rehearsed. Hill's question, 'Do you think it's desirable to wait till you're married?', was greeted with loud affirmation. Hill spoke about 'self-control' and the consequences of having none, such as pregnancy. Then a boy suggested that things had changed – people no longer said 'Aren't you wicked!', they said 'Aren't you a silly fool!'

The Radio Doctor steered them back to orthodoxy: the fear of pregnancy, the need for happy homes. And were there not moral reasons, too, for continence? But a girl broke in to say (with others murmuring agreement), 'Sexual intercourse before marriage would be wrong if it's just anyone. If it's the chap you're going to marry, that's different. It isn't quite right, but it isn't exactly wrong.' This was the remark that stuck in the shopkeeper's throat, and no doubt in other throats as well. What was the world coming to?

In public people continued to speak a mock-modest language about sex. Later generations would mourn the loss of this reticence, perceiving that what was concealed had less chance of spreading its influence. But the sentiments expressed in the process were unconvincing. Commercial pop-songs of the time said one thing and meant another. Harry wrote that the lyrics of about fifty songs invoking moons and nightingales stuck in his head, but he could never reconcile them with the girls he fancied.

From Harry's diary, Saturday 7 September 1944. He was sixteen, still at school:

> To a party near the ferry, a dame by the name of Jean, the same gang as that of August 5. I had an invitation more as a stop-gap than anything else I imagine. I went with Nick. He left at 10.30 but I stayed on for another hour. The quantity of cider supplied helped things along. Her Dad and Mum were there but I didn't see them at all. It was all very enjoyable, not the least attraction being the game of 'improvements' we played from 10.30 to 11.30. I started on a chair with Jean, with my hand inside her blouse. She had small squashy breasts and wore a brassiere that undid. My last 'improvement' was with a dame I wanted to avoid, a thin piece from Southsea with a squint. I had my hand inside her panties but she kept her legs tight shut.
>
> *Wednesday September 11.* The thin piece, name of Thelma, is wizard,

and my rather chagrined mood of the late summer has ceased to exist.
I had a date with her tonight and we went on the sandhills. Yours truly
kissed her silly for an hour and to cut a long story short she was more
cooperative and I have now FELT A WOMAN!!!!! If I'd had a Frenchie
[i.e. a french letter] anything might have happened. (Actually, I don't
think she would have let me.)*

In 1945 when the war ended the British were a tired nation. Austerity
and rationing continued to afflict them. Illicit pleasures were not in
fashion. Families reminded themselves of their importance. There was a
lot of forgiving and forgetting; or, where this proved impossible, of
making fresh starts. Divorces rose to the unprecedented figure of sixty
thousand in 1947, then fell sharply. The illegitimacy rate sank back
towards pre-war levels.

In 1948 there were murmurings from America, where Dr Alfred
Kinsey published his report on Sexual Behaviour in the Human Male.
Whatever its deficiencies, this was the world's first serious study on a
scale sufficient to give it authority. Behaviour traditionally regarded as
'unorthodox' and 'unacceptable' was shown to be widespread. Some of
its findings, for example the extent to which teenagers 'necked' and
'petted', were attacked by conservatives because they might foster
immorality, and at the same time were disregarded by cynics who said
they were common knowledge. But hearsay was less authoritative than
statistical tables. Other Kinsey findings, especially in relation to
homosexuality, were seen as deeply subversive. Forty years later moral
zealots were still trying to dislodge him, on the grounds that he was
fraudulent, evil or both.

Kinsey (1894–1956) was a biologist whose first career was studying
the gall wasp. Beneath a prickly, tightly-controlled exterior he incubated
a passion for sexual knowledge. When young he was sickly and religious,
brought up in the era when the American clergyman Sylvanus Stall was
on the prowl, seeing self-abusers in every boy who went by with his cap
pulled down. One might guess that Kinsey's ruthlessness as a sexual
researcher later in life, as he ploughed his way through five hundred-
question interviews or watched people having sex as if they were wasps

---

* Most of the Harry material I have seen was written when he was an adult. Some of
the typescripts recording sexual experiences when he was a teenager are (he says)
copied from diaries he kept at the time. I have not seen the diaries themselves.

in a bottle, stemmed from the emotions he had learned to suppress long before.

In 1938, when Kinsey had been on the staff of Indiana University for eighteen years, his employers devised a 'marriage course', to be taught by professors from various faculties. As though he had been waiting for the opportunity, Kinsey (himself married with three children) began taking sexual histories from his students, as an adjunct to the course. There were complaints about him from clergymen in Bloomington, the University town. It was rumoured, and was true, that among the questions he asked women students was one about the length of their clitorises. Kinsey would ask anybody anything. In 1940 he left the marriage course, said goodbye to the wasps, and, with university backing, devoted himself to sexual behaviour.

It would be hard to think of anything like this happening in Britain. Obstacles would be anticipated before the idea had time to mature. Kinsey acquired influential backing, with money from the Rockefeller Foundation that paid for a staff, whom he liked to be white, the men clean-shaven and wearing a tie. By 1945 he had more than seven thousand sexual histories, all confidential and coded, and his plans stretched ahead for twenty years and a hundred thousand histories.

The *Human Male* volume was the first fruit. A book of more than eight hundred pages, its tone is defined by Kinsey's concluding comment that, while there were many ways of measuring the social values of human behaviour, he and his colleagues were concerned only with 'the record of what we have found the human male doing sexually.' Kinsey was not interested in noble prose or even in humorous touches. What they had found the human male doing was taking his sexual pleasure as best he could. Two-thirds of those with higher education, and virtually all those with lower, had intercourse before they married. Sixty-nine per cent of men had some experience of prostitutes. Virtually all of them masturbated when young, often when old; at the age of fifty-five, college-bred males derived 19 per cent of their orgasms, or 'outlets', as Kinsey liked to put it, from 'the dream world which accompanies masturbation or nocturnal emissions.' The same category found only 62 per cent of their outlets in intercourse with their wives. Before marriage the average American man had one thousand five hundred and twenty-three orgasms, against the average American woman's two hundred and twenty-three.

It was the air of laboratory studies with rats that made people squirm.

Kinsey, for his part, squirmed when newspapers took material out of context. He complained about a syndication service's headline, '50 PER CENT OF MARRIED MEN UNFAITHFUL,' which provoked angry editorials across the United States. His objection was not that the statement itself was untrue, but that it looked as if all that the Rockefeller Foundation had done was waste its money on meddling with private lives.

It was naïve of Kinsey to suppose that the world would do anything with the report but use it for its own purposes, including entertainment. For some years his book joined the select company of respectable titles, from E. Dingwall on chastity belts to G.R. Scott on corporal punishment, that vanish from the most reputable libraries. Its ultimate value lay in the general perception it gave people, few of whom have ever read the book, that oral sex and sex before marriage and infidelity and masturbation and sado-masochistic practices and homosexuality were all common states and habits. Like a mathematical Havelock Ellis, Kinsey produced evidence that challenged orthodox definitions of what was 'normal' and 'abnormal'. The fact that most of his sample was white, aged thirty and below, and lived in the north-eastern part of the United States affected the results but didn't invalidate them.

After the *Human Male* Kinsey proceeded at top speed towards the *Human Female*, which he was ready to publish by 1953. He now had eighteen thousand histories, a collection of books, pictures and films, and considerable experience of watching others engage in sexual activity. There is a description of him moving 'quietly around the room' where a group of gay men were having communal sex, 'occasionally whispering a direction' to the cameraman who was filming; also of him paying a prostitute in Indianapolis to let him take her history, and then, learning she had a two-inch clitoris, paying her an extra dollar to let him have a look.

Sexual Behaviour in the Human Female put paid to Kinsey. The previous volume had been unbearable enough to those of a religious or prudish (perhaps even romantic) frame of mind. *Reader's Digest* had clarified the issue for many people, asking in 1948 if fidelity and chastity were now supposed to be sentimental nonsense, if 'practices long held in abhorrence must now be regarded as acceptable.' The new book was worse because it put woman firmly in the same frame of uneasy lustfulness as man. It outraged the moralists to hear about female masturbation; even more to hear of evidence suggesting that experience of it when she was single might help her have orgasms when she was married. Pre-marital petting was almost universal; pre-marital intercourse was admitted by half the women, adultery by a quarter of married women who had reached forty. Kinsey reported a 'not inconsiderable' group of cases where husbands encouraged their wives to sleep with other men, thus heralding the fashion for wife-and-husband-swapping.

All this helped make Kinsey a monster to traditionalists. His defence was that he was merely a biologist who drew attention to the facts, whatever their awkwardness. Discussing marital infidelity, he wrote that the data emphasized how

> the reconciliation of the married individual's desire for coitus with a variety of sexual partners, and the maintenance of a stable marriage, presents a problem which has not been satisfactorily resolved in our culture. It is not likely to be resolved until man moves more completely away from his mammalian ancestry.

Kinsey knew the power contained in his 'facts'. By accumulating so much evidence of how conventional behaviour was already being challenged, Kinsey became part of the challenge. The 'facts' of private morality would force reassessments of public morality, as the extent of the gap between how people were supposed to behave and what they really did in private was demonstrated with new vigour.

Even in periods of sexual repression and inhibition, the young felt randy, prostitutes were busy, many husbands and some wives were unfaithful, pornography and masturbation flourished, homosexuals took their calculated risks. The moralists tried to make all this seem marginal, deviant and shameful, and authority conspired with them. An earlier researcher would have found some of the same evidence as Kinsey; the gap between public and private was always there. But he would not have been licensed to ask the questions, and it might have been difficult to publish the answers. By the forties the old morality was a shell, and Kinsey, driven perhaps by some long-felt need for revenge, took his chance to describe the new world.

For this he had to be punished. Clergymen as various as the evangelist Billy Graham and the theologian Reinhold Niebuhr denounced him. The anthropologist Margaret Mead deplored 'the sudden removal of a previously guaranteed reticence.' Politicians became active. The Rockefeller Foundation withdrew its support, and the twenty-year plan was never carried out, though the Institute of Sex Research at Bloomington remains. Three years after the *Human Female* appeared, Kinsey died, aged sixty-two.

In Britain Kinsey took longer to seep into the general consciousness. A mixture of disdain and ribaldry had greeted the 1948 report. A peculiar professor with a bow-tie in a far-off country had spent years digging up noxious details about sex. The shock-absorbers of society, the popular press, made the report into mildly prurient reading of no relevance to dear old Britain. It was a familiar response. In two years the *Human Male* volume managed to sell ten thousand copies; in America it sold two hundred thousand in the first two months. The *British Medical Journal* simply listed it under 'Books Received'. The *Lancet* gave it four inches of review-space, praising it as a handbook for those interested in sexual behaviour and deviations.

But the idea of doing a modest survey in Britain occurred to Mass-Observation, which sold the idea of a 'report on British morality' to the *Sunday Pictorial*, then edited by Hugh Cudlipp. As originally planned, this was to include accounts of public love-making, necking parties, dance halls, dirty book shops and low life ('eg. Soho, Tiger Bay'). There would be special interviewing of clergymen, teachers, MPs, film stars and policemen, as well as reports from M-O's regular panel. That grand design was never achieved. It would have cost too much – as it was, Cudlipp paid twelve hundred pounds – and might have caused trouble. An assurance had to be obtained from solicitors that the questionnaire for use by field-workers was legal.

A handful of doctors, clergymen and marriage counsellors were appointed as assessors. A clergyman asked earnestly that one piece of material be deleted. This was the autobiographical account of a waitress in Middlesbrough, collected by an informant. Aged nineteen, she had resisted soldiers and occasional boy-friends until she met Jack, with whom she 'lay on the settee' in his parents' house and 'it just happened'. A year later came Ted, a merchant seaman and 'perfect gentleman', who used to take her back to a hotel, where it 'just happened' again, quite often. The clergyman who objected to this pathetic tale wrote that 'while it has value for Observers and experts, it has none for the ordinary reader.'

Probably for space reasons, only fragments of direct quotation from interviews went into the articles, which was a pity. No one read the middle-aged man defining abnormality as 'doing what you shouldn't in intercourse,' or the housewife of thirty, a labourer's wife, declaring that intercourse was not right, really, not even if you were married:

Sex ain't very nice, to a woman it's not very nice, it is sort of unpleasant to a girl, it ain't very nice at all . . . Yes, it can be harmful, it can ruin a woman's insides as easy as pie, ruins any girl's innards, intercourse can.

The five *Sunday Pictorial* articles ('The Private Life of John Bull') were a cut above the usual Fleet Street method of dealing with sex, which was to present prurient material in a moralistic way, as though performing a duty. Cudlipp, with no holier-than-thou proprietor at his elbow, at least attempted to show his readers a snapshot of themselves, having sex before marriage (half the men, two-fifths of the women), being unfaithful after it (a quarter of husbands, a fifth of wives), enjoying erotic day-dreams, masturbating (80 per cent) and having had some homosexual experience (12 per cent). It was only a faint echo of Kinsey, but it carried a similar message.

By the time *Sexual Behaviour in the Human Female* followed in August 1953, Kinsey was better known in Britain. The *People* quoted the juicier bits but added reassuringly that most of Kinsey's interviewees must be abnormal; well-adjusted women were not promiscuous. A week later the paper had talked to a thousand British women and was able to reassure readers that, far from one in four wives being adulterous, here it was only one in nine. There was just one hesitancy. The paper's survey showed that women's sexual urges were 'greater than is commonly supposed.' Mature women felt the urges most strongly, and were 'not entirely satisfied inside the marriage convention.'

Kinsey remained unacceptable in higher circles. The only relevant entry in *The Times* index for 1953 refers to a sermon preached by a Jesuit at Westminster Cathedral, accusing newspapers of seeking to 'transform what was meant to be a scientific inquiry into cheap pornography.' The inquiry itself was ignored. In Home Office papers, a long minute comments on the 'disgraceful furore' over the book, and suggests what official policy should be when it is published in Britain. Passages about petting (when 'a young girl allows herself to be lasciviously mauled') would give offence and might encourage immorality. Material about masturbation was 'hardly edifying', and as for the sections about homosexuality, they would be 'interpreted as encouraging vice.' What upset the writer most was a statement in the book that modern cures for VD meant that it mattered little if the diseases were spread by sex before marriage. The official wrote:

> Fear of disease is perhaps the most potent factor in restraining many
> young men from promiscuous immorality — at any rate it is the factor
> on which the armed forces principally rely — and to remove that
> deterrent gratuitously (even if, which I doubt, the assumption is valid)
> seems to me to be monstrously irresponsible.

Having got this off his chest, he concluded that action by the government
might do more harm than good. Although it was a work that 'few
parents would care to see in the hands of adolescent children,' prosecution
might fail, and serve only to publicize the book. The Director of Public
Prosecutions felt the same, and, apart from a spasm by the Doncaster
police, who took it upon themselves to seize a copy, nothing was done
about Kinsey, except to hope that he and his kind would soon be forgotten.

Optimism was growing in the early fifties. The privations of the war and
its aftermath were disappearing. Rationing of petrol and tinned food
ended in 1950, and other items were freed year by year. In 1951 the
Festival of Britain provided a middle-class carnival that hinted at better
times to come. A stable home life, built around the honeycombed cells of
happy marriages, would benefit from the new prosperity based on the
Welfare State which the Labour Government had spent six years creating.
Marriages were presumably more likely to be happy in a land of full
employment and free medical care. By now illegitimacy had returned to
its pre-war level, around one birth in twenty-five, and the divorce rate
continued to fall. Family planning, the euphemism that was replacing
birth control, had been available at a few charity clinics since 1930. There
were now a hundred or more of them — run on ladylike lines and
desperate to appease their many critics — that were willing to prescribe
the cap for married women; being married was essential. Clients had to
sit in a row with their stockings round their ankles, waiting to see a
doctor. As usual with sex, those who indulged in it were expected to
suffer a little.

  Marriage was the thing, then as always. Engaged couples might have
sex before it, but 'living together' was rare. It meant loose morals, an
affront to decency. The unmarried didn't think in terms of a place of
one's own. In any case, few engaged couples could have afforded a flat or
a furnished room, even if they were lucky enough to find one in those
days of housing shortages.

When they married, many of them would live for months or years with parents — usually hers — before moving on. But at least they then had a bed. That was the dividing line. What the unmarried had were walls in back lanes for knee-tremblers, grass in parks, and sofas for five minutes when a parent had gone to the shops. They were continually reminded that comfortable, naked sex would have to wait until after the wedding. Petting was more practical, and risk-free. Writing in 1990, a Mass-Observer recalled her early sex life. She was a virgin when she got married, aged twenty-one, in 1950, but admitted to 'a few near misses with previous boy-friends before "falling in love" with my husband. Heavy petting was the general rule . . . and a friend of ours came up with a saying that suited the day, "Feelies for feelies but no putties in", which still amuses us.'

Harry the diarist kept a record of five months' sexual activity in 1950, a year or two after he finished his National Service. At the time he was working for a printer and living at home with his mother, who was in the process of getting a divorce. For the first time he had a regular girl-friend who was willing to sleep with him. They had petted for a year before they took the plunge with a covert trip to London. He stocked up with Durex, bought her a wedding ring in Woolworth's, and got her to memorize a false surname and a non-existent address. They stayed in a small commercial hotel near Waterloo Station, where the manageress asked them how long they had been married ('I recall her narrowing her eyes,' wrote Harry, 'but I confess I was pretty paranoid'). The ring was too big and fell into the cornflakes at breakfast; no one saw. The first night he was nervous and found himself in difficulties as soon as he donned a condom. 'I had read about impotent men, and I thought *this is it, my life is going to be a flop.*' Fortunately his partner murmured, 'Let me take it off,' and her fumbling restored the power.

Harry's record of five months' sexual intercourse reads: three nights at the hotel, sixteen times; after that it was nearly all in singles — sundry commons and sand dunes, ten; at a party, two occasions, on the floor; baby-sitting for a journalist and his wife, five occasions on the floor, twice in bed; at home, nine times, on sofas and the floor, never in bed; against a wall, once. He says it never occurred to him — or the girl, who left him before the end of the year to have an affair with a theological student — to complain about the discomfort.

As long as the unmarried realized that what they were doing went against the grain of social order, no one worried too much; discomfort and guilt did the remonstrating. But Kinsey suggested deeper sexual instabilities, threatening the family of the future. Did that thought simmer in the unconscious of both the ruling class and the ruled? There were to be odd authoritarian outbursts in the fifties, which must have been caused by fear of something. Publishers were harassed; prostitution on the streets was denounced; homosexual men had a bad time of it, because theirs was the perversion that dangerous voices (like Kinsey's) were beginning to say was not a perversion at all.

What to do about homosexuals became a test case for post-war moral values, soon to be followed by other test cases, about books and then abortion. At first hardly anyone supposed that the habits of 'queers' (the universal word for them at the time) deserved any response beyond sending them to prison when they were caught doing it. 'It' could be a variety of acts. Manual and oral sex, whether in public or in private, were punished under a law that defined such acts as 'gross indecency', and most convictions came into this category; the maximum prison sentence was two years. For penetrative sex, 'sodomy' or 'buggery', the sentence could be life. Convictions rose sharply in the early fifties. Most comment-ators agree that this was because the police were increasingly zealous. Once they began to uncover homosexuality, they created a case for uncovering more. One (heterosexual) author, Richard Davenport-Hines, describes a 'pogrom' at Taunton in 1954 and 1955, where younger men were frightened into giving evidence against older men. Sometimes the courts were more compassionate. Alan Turing, the mathematician who did more than anyone to break the Germans' 'Enigma' machine-codes in the Second World War, was a homosexual. Arraigned for an 'act of gross indecency' in 1951, he escaped with probation and medical treatment; and committed suicide three years later.

The Director of Public Prosecutions since 1944 had been Sir Theobald Matthew, who was a Roman Catholic. Matthew is said by his colleagues to have believed that the law had no business to interfere with people's private behaviour. If so, he interpreted that belief oddly where homosexu-als were concerned; prosecutions went ahead merrily under his regime. The Home Secretary in the Conservative Government was not keen on homosexuals. This was Sir David Maxwell-Fyfe (later Lord Kilmuir), a Scots lawyer who was appointed to the Home Office in 1951. Fyfe had moralistic leanings, and was a friend of the Public Morality Council. 'Homosexuals in general,' he said, 'are exhibitionists and proselytizers and a danger to others, especially the young.' Occasional voices were heard seeking a review of the law. Fyfe was unmoved.

It was never clear what caused him, early in 1954, to change his mind and propose an inquiry into the law on homosexuality. The inquiry was also to be into the law on prostitution. Soliciting by women had been an embarrassment in 1953 when London was full of visitors for the Coronation. Kinsey, in London on a private visit in 1955, thought he had never seen so much blatant sexual behaviour; a British friend showed him around the West End on a Saturday night, and he claimed to have counted a thousand prostitutes at work. Fyfe now lumped queers and tarts together, two aspects of the same sexual decline. But at first the Cabinet was not keen on an inquiry of any kind, and Fyfe had to persuade his colleagues.

While they were still considering the proposal, in the spring, the newspapers were full of the trial for homosexual offences of Lord Montagu of Beaulieu, his second-cousin Michael Pitt-Rivers, and a Fleet Street journalist, Peter Wildeblood. Two RAF servicemen were promised immunity (by Sir Theobald Matthew), and the case consisted entirely of the servicemen's evidence of homosexual acts in which they had been willing partners. The three accused were sent to prison, Montagu for a year, the other two for eighteen months. It was widely supposed that the real reason for the prosecution was to catch someone who had a title, thus making an example and ensuring publicity.

Perhaps a case so unnecessary and vindictive disposed the Cabinet to think again. In April Fyfe was told he could have his inquiry, and a 'departmental committee' of outsiders was set up within the Home Office. The chairman was John Wolfenden, who had been headmaster of Shrewsbury and was now vice-chancellor of Reading University. A heterosexual, he checked with his wife and the university before accepting Fyfe's offer, and later 'thought it prudent to avoid public lavatories in the West End,' where, as he would have known, plain-clothes policemen acted as *agents provocateurs*, and an absent-minded smile could have consequences.

Wolfenden was anxious to show himself as the plain non-expert, once describing his committee as 'we poor innocents'. He insisted in his memoirs that in 1954, 'most ordinary people' had never heard of homosexuality, and were probably unaware that there was such a thing as a homosexual offence. Judges had often said the same. At an obscene publications trial in 1942, the judge mentioned in passing that 'in these courts every session we have a number of filthy and disgusting cases with regard to homosexuality, and I suppose most of the members of the juries who come into these courts for the first time are horrified when they hear the evidence that is given. They do not believe that any such thing ever exists.' The public was better informed than judges supposed. In the same year, 1942, a notorious case was heard involving a 'vice ring' in the market town of Abergavenny, where police had raided a cinema and charged twenty-four men; one public figure was lucky to escape. A coarse joke circulated through South Wales. A man had only to bend over to tie his shoelace for someone to say, 'You wouldn't do that in Abergavenny.' Alternatively, if you dropped sixpence, 'Kick it as far as Brecon before you pick it up.' The jokes lingered for years. Every schoolboy knew them.

The pretence of ignorance, others' and one's own, was part of the business of keeping the dangerous facts at a safe distance. Who could risk being tarred with the brush? It was Lord Snow, during a House of Lords debate years later, who commented that his colleagues all spoke as if they had never met any homosexuals – 'as though these were something strange, like the white rhinoceros.'

Wolfenden never tired of explaining to his critics that his committee's task was to examine the law on the two subjects, not the subjects themselves. Nor was he concerned with sin. Three years later, in 1957, the report concluded in effect that it was the law's business to prevent public affronts to decency, not to interfere with private behaviour. This 'unsentimental logic' was then applied to the matters in hand. To curb the public excesses of the prostitutes, and stop them making a nuisance of themselves on the streets, Wolfenden recommended heavier fines and if necessary imprisonment. For the homosexuals he recommended that what they did in private should be their own concern, as long as they were over twenty-one. Punishment for cases not covered by his reforms would stay the same.

The Wolfenden plan meant liberalizing the law but leaving homo-sexuals as a special case, in a twilight zone. The age-limit was imposed because of fears that the young might be corrupted. The word 'private' was left undefined. When (after ten years) the law was changed as Wolfenden suggested, 'private' was taken to mean a situation where not more than two people were present. The law has nothing comparable to say about heterosexual behaviour.

When the report was published, more than half the press, measured by circulation, was on Wolfenden's side. The opponents were vociferous: the committee had produced a 'Pansies' Charter'. The churches were surprisingly liberal, perhaps aware of numerous homosexual clergy. The Archbishop of Canterbury thought that if legal penalties could restrain adultery and fornication as well, then homosexual behaviour should continue to be outlawed. Since it was sadly impossible to stop hetero-sexuals sinning, Wolfenden's logic, he agreed, was correct.

Of the ten years that passed before anything was done about homosexual reform in 1967, seven were under Conservative government, the last three under Labour. Campaigners for the cause worked to modify public opinion, at one point being called 'a rich and powerful lobby of perverts' for their pains. Important names associated with the cause included Lord Attlee, two bishops, Julian Huxley, Barbara Wootton, J.B. Priestley, Bob Boothby, the doctor Kenneth Walker, the writer C.H. Rolph, Bertrand Russell and Isaiah Berlin. For obvious reasons, most of those in the forefront were heterosexuals.

The aggressive hunting-down of homosexuals had stopped, but the underlying position was unchanged. In those days no one dared admit to being a homosexual. The novelist Angus Wilson (1913–1990), one of a number of literary figures who supported reform, was a homosexual who in private had never made much secret of his inclinations. While he was deputy superintendent of the British Museum's Reading Room, between 1949 and 1955, he was blackmailed for considerable sums; the police weren't told. A man of Wilson's sexual character was not seen as a fit and proper person to appear on television. When an item about him was proposed by a producer for the BBC arts programme *Monitor* in the late fifties, its editor, Huw Wheldon, an aggressive heterosexual who understood the BBC mind, ruled that 'we can't have someone who's overtly queer on the programme.'

Whether the ten-year campaign had any effect on the deep and abiding core of prejudice against homosexuals is doubtful. But the tone of public utterance changed. After a series of failed attempts at reform, the Labour-dominated Parliament that followed the 1966 general election was ripe for the Bill that Leo Abse introduced. Abse, a South Wales solicitor (and heterosexual) with Freudian interests, mobilized enough support to get it past the horrified opponents of reform, and it became law the following year. Thus a process begun in difficult times by an illiberal Home Secretary turned into a showpiece of the decade of reform. Wolfenden himself, insisting that 'our objective was not social reform,' found himself seen as the instigator of precisely that.

*

Women on Call

The prostitution part of the report didn't frighten MPs – prostitutes were held to be normal, homosexuals were not – and was implemented within two years. The Street Offences Act, 1959, made life more difficult for prostitutes and had the desired effect of shifting them out of sight. This was supposed to make everyone happy.

Since the early part of the century, when prostitution was seen as an evil, it had dwindled to a nuisance. London still had its networks, kept in check by the police but not unduly harassed. Few thought that stamping them out would change society, even if that were practicable. Between the wars prostitution was becoming a subject that could be reported on without the old air of horror. A public health official in Salford, Manchester, a retired lieutenant-colonel with the title of 'VD Officer', was briefly famous for discovering the mobile prostitute in 1935. Using statistics from the local VD clinic, he identified 'lorry girls', who obliged at transport cafés for modest sums, from a shilling upwards. There was deep poverty then, and a shilling bought a meal or twenty cigarettes. 'Too often', wrote the VD Officer, 'does the driver succumb.' The Home Office sent out a questionnaire (courtesy of S.W. Harris) about 'road transport and its effect on morality.' It was remarked that cars were more of a menace in the matter of sex on wheels, and there was a report of immoral behaviour in a caravan.

Business perked up in the war. The presence of overseas servicemen, especially American, raised prices. Newspaper reports of prosecutions suggest three or four pounds was often charged; this was too expensive for British troops, who presumably paid less and received less attention. A few decades later, when sexual misdemeanours were popular with the media, a prostitute was sometimes able to achieve a kind of glamour, or at least an acceptable notoriety. There was no modern equivalent of Henry Mayhew, who reported on mid-Victorian prostitutes, along with the rest of the London underworld. It was an individual who would be publicized, and made into a representative heroine. A modern Queenie Gerald would be able to write her life story for a newspaper or appear in a television documentary. Cynthia Payne – the madam of Streatham who went to prison in 1978 for keeping the brothel that took luncheon vouchers – had her biography written by Paul Bailey, which inspired a feature film, *Personal Services*; her early life inspired another feature film, *Wish You Were Here*. She appeared on *Blankety Blank*, wrote for the *Independent* and contested a by-election, her slogans including 'Win with Cyn, otherwise I'll cane with Payne.'

But most prostitutes were the same equivocal figures, struggling to make the best of things on the margins. In 1959 they saw Wolfenden as just another attempt to mess them about. Men were still beasts. Bessie, a tart in Soho, talked to a woman researcher:

> You don't know the things [men] do and the things they want. Be all right walking down the street, talk to you ever so nice, but when they get alone with us women, well, some of them are like rats in holes. A woman doesn't know a man. If a wife knew what her husband was really like she'd never live with him no more. We have to chain them up and beat them and jump on them . . . Of course I had to learn it all. Didn't know what the men meant sometimes. Sometimes a man sits beside me and I shudder away from him, if only people knew what you were like, you awful slimy toad, I think.

Margaret described her customers as 'silly old fools'. Gwyneth took men into Hyde Park, charged them ten shillings and then said the grass was too wet to lie down, so 'you don't have the full intercourse . . . You keep your legs together and the men don't know any different.' Strange men. Janet boasted of earning twelve pounds the previous Saturday from an all-night session with a client – 'set my alarm three hours fast and kicked him out early.' Women were beasts, too.

Pimps were still in business. The 'flogging' provision of the White Slave legislation in 1912, which was supposed to have done away with them, had been repealed along with all corporal punishment by the Labour Government in 1948. They still maltreated prostitutes and were endlessly forgiven by them. There were always stories of innocent girls ruined by men who tempted them in Piccadilly. 'They write a lot of nonsense about us in the papers,' said Eileen, another Soho woman, 'but it's an arrangement of our own choice.'

Preparing a newspaper article in 1958, I listened to a heartless young villain, not long out of Dartmoor, talk about the 'mysteries', the fresh new girls who arrive at main-line stations for men like him and his friends to pick up. He told me he did it for fun, not profit; I was innocent enough to believe him at the time. He said he could always find mysteries in cafés near Euston or King's Cross 'about half-past twelve of a night, thirteen or fourteen girls there. Just go up to them and say, "What's the matter?" or "Where you come from?"'

Usually they said Manchester or Birmingham. They had caught the last train down, and in the morning they would look for lodgings. So he and a pal would take four or five of them to a dodgy club, 'have a bit of sport with them', take them home because they had nowhere else to go:

> They get shuffled. We used to shunt the mysteries up to Highbury, leave 'em there, pick 'em up a couple of days later, shunt 'em back to Euston, so they'd go backwards and forwards for three or four weeks, and they used to finish up down the Commercial Road.

By which he meant, as third-rate prostitutes in the East End. They were certainly exploited and arguably ruined; but hardly innocent.

When prostitutes found the streets too uncomfortable after the Act of 1959, they had to find alternatives. The age of the 'call girl' dawned, ultimate in naughtiness in the sixties, though the specialty was not new. Queenie Gerald, in business in Maddox Street after the First World War, had four Mayfair telephone numbers; at another of her addresses she acquired the useful 'GROsvenor 1999'. A madam's 'luxury flat' in Duke Street, raided in 1938, was described by police as 'a house of assignations, where appointments were made by telephone.' Officers keeping watch would see the madam answer the phone in the sitting room, then make a call. A man would appear, and shortly afterwards, the woman who had been telephoned. Four smart young women were observed, together with the eighteen men they serviced, who were 'very much older, and seemed to be of some position.' The madam's address book listed a hundred and fifty-four clients and fifty-two prostitutes.

Tom Harrisson, who founded Mass-Observation, wrote in the forties that 'the "best" (on their own rating) London girls never appear on the streets on business and seldom go out of doors at all ... A regular telephonic clientele is their ideal.' After the Street Offences Act this elite was diluted by girls who used cards in shop windows to attract passing trade. Usually the wording was banal, 'French Lessons' or 'Miss Cane' or 'Advertiser, 20, has Big Chest for Sale', followed by a telephone number. Original-sounding ads were widely copied. One said, 'Lost: ring inscribed "I love Dick".' Efficient call girls' numbers were known to hall porters, night-club managers, firms offering 'hospitality', dubious travel agencies, existing clients and friends of friends. As prosperity spread and standards of living went up, the call girls flourished.

Another course open to the harassed prostitute was an advertisement in a magazine. The *Ladies' Directory* was obligingly brought out to meet this need at the end of 1959, price five shillings from kiosks in the West End, or circulated to night clubs and restaurants for customers wanting to prolong the evening.* Prostitutes paid to advertise in it, from two guineas for a quarter-page advertisement to ten guineas for a full-page with a photograph, nude or clad in underwear. Several issues were produced before the police took action. Like the writer of humorous tales who was punished for publishing *The Link* in 1921, the man behind the *Ladies' Directory*, Frederick Shaw, was prosecuted and sent to prison. Creative lawyers, re-instituting a crime that had not been alleged in living memory, had had him charged with 'conspiracy to corrupt public morals', which he was supposed to have done by inducing readers to visit the ladies of the Directory

> for the purposes of fornication and of taking part in or witnessing other disgusting and immoral acts and exhibitions, with intent thereby to debauch and corrupt the morals as well of youth as of divers other liege subjects of Our Lady the Queen and to raise and create in their minds inordinate and lustful desires.

The medieval language was appropriate to the prosecution. The defence tried to argue that no such offence existed in common law, but Lord Simonds, rejecting the appeal in the House of Lords, insisted that judges had 'a residual power' to 'conserve not only the safety and order but also the moral welfare of the State.' Whatever laws Parliament passed, he said, there would always be gaps, 'since no one can foresee every way in which the wickedness of man may disrupt the order of society.'

Tarts' telephone numbers were now added to these wicked disruptions. In case of any uncertainty about the public-morals charge, the police had also accused Shaw of living off the earnings of prostitution, the pimp's offence. The argument, accepted by the courts, was summed up by Lord Simonds: a man could fairly be said to offend 'if he is paid by prostitutes for goods or services supplied by him to them for the purpose of their prostitution which he would not supply but for the fact that they were prostitutes.' They paid to advertise in his magazine; thus he was living

---

* As the barrister Geoffrey Robertson QC observed, prostitutes' listings were not new. The *Man of Pleasure's Kalender* (1788) gave brief descriptions ('Descend a little lower and behold the semi-snow-balls,' a Miss Wilkinson) as well as other useful tips ('Such an habit of intimacy with the gin bottle, that unless a person is particularly partial to it, it is almost intolerable to approach her,' a Mrs Howard).

off their earnings. The idea of pimping still excited the same aversion it had done in the days of the floggers, even when the facts had to be manipulated to make them work.

Logically the *Ladies' Directory* argument might have been applied in other directions, such as shops where prostitutes went to make their intimate purchases by the gross. Condoms were specially packaged for bulk sales. Prostitutes bought them for their trade. Was a shop that sold them condoms, sufficient to last a respectable citizen for years, not profiting from the business of prostitution? Nothing is too much for a determined lawyer.

Soon no one was bothering about contact magazines, there were so many of them. They were part of the seedy underside of 'swinging London', and the authorities had bigger things to worry about.

'Jiggle and Titter'

Literature in the Dock

PORNOGRAPHY BY THE middle of the century was cheaper than it had ever been. Paperbacks and comics, often American, nudist magazines and saucy booklets with black-and-white photographs of girls in their underwear, were widely sold by small newsagents and kiosks. This was not serious pornography, some of which was still old Victorian material recycled, but it provided the same quick fix of sexual excitement; with the difference that now it was available to a wider, less affluent readership. The porn market was being democratized.

Obscene books and pictures, though intended as an adjunct to private lives, were frowned on by English common law. Once you had them in the library or under the pillow, you could do as you pleased. But author, printer, publisher and bookseller might be prosecuted and sent to prison for the common-law offence of publishing an 'obscene libel' (the phrase simply meant 'obscenity'). Since 1857 a useful statute had been added to the common-law provision in the shape of Lord Campbell's Obscene Publications Act. This gave magistrates the power to order the destruction of material they thought obscene when it was presented to them by the police. It was not, strictly speaking, a criminal prosecution. No penalty could be imposed, beyond the loss of the books or prints. But nor could any meaningful defence be made. The magistrate already knew what the material was likely to consist of because the police told him when they applied for a warrant to search the premises. He had merely to read an impure page, sniff a subversive trend or spot a wisp of pubic hair, and (if he chose) the destruction order was granted.

In this way *The Well of Loneliness* and *Sleeveless Errand* (but not *Boy* and *Bessie Cotter*, which were prosecuted under common law for 'obscene libel') were dealt with. Thousands of titles, both books and magazines, some of them literature but most of them porn, were sent to the incinerator by Lord Campbell's Act over the years; though interesting items found their way into policemen's pockets. In recent years a magistrate at Wells Street court in the West End would tease the police – 'watching a po-faced sergeant I used to say, "Shall I attend the burning, officer?" They knew and we knew.'

The destruction-order procedure was swift and efficient, and when introduced drove the posh end of the trade abroad to Paris and Brussels, where a postal business flourished. There is an old tradition of misprints in English pornography, due to typesetting by foreign operators. As late as the nineteen-forties one could read of a young woman on a couch in a 'loluptuous attitude', or thrill to an account of how her lover's ardour 'caused her to ondulate her back and raise her uttocks.'

Once the Campbell Act was in force, it came to be the method of choice for most obscene material. The statute didn't define 'obscenity', any more than the common law had been able to. That was done eleven years later in a case involving a man called Hicklin. The Lord Chief Justice said in passing that 'the test of obscenity is this, whether the tendency of the matter . . . is to deprave and corrupt those whose minds are open to such immoral influences, and into whose hands a publication of this sort may fall.' The definition has been a boon to obscenity prosecutions ever since, though all it does is to shift the uncertainty on to the words 'deprave and corrupt'.

When the 1857 Act was passed, Campbell was anxious to point out that it would not apply to works of art or literature; the poems of Rochester, the plays of Congreve, were safe. The Act was aimed only at those who set out to corrupt 'the morals of youth'. Well before the end of the century, police and courts were ignoring this, and applying the Act whenever they chose. If it seemed to somebody somewhere that Zola was obscene, that was the end of the matter. The law's willingness to harry 'serious' writers was to make it easier for pornographers later in this century. The authorities had weakened their position by bringing cases against books (like those of Hanley and Radclyffe Hall) whose only crime was to be frank about sex. When a more liberal climate changed the law at the end of the nineteen-fifties, the distinction between such 'serious' writing and the crudities of porn had been blurred by decades of petty persecution. If the former were now to be protected, it became harder to stop the latter nipping in under the same umbrella.

At the start of the nineteen-fifties, there was little talk of protecting anything. Smutty books were on the increase. An underworld of men in dirty macs was presumed to buy them. The connection between this mythical brigade and the wealthy who had collected pornography in the past, and indeed still went in for it, was rarely made. The most famous work of English pornography is *My Secret Life*, published anonymously in the late nineteenth century, an autobiographical work of fastidious detail by a man who wrote that 'Women were the pleasure of my life . . . I liked the women I fucked and not simply the cunt I fucked, and therein is a great difference.' There is a case for identifying the author as Henry Spencer Ashbee, a wealthy bibliophile whose private library of erotica was left to the British Museum, where (in the restricted shelves of the British Library) it remains. His descendants are said to accept that he was the author, while insisting the book is fiction. Either way he was a man engrossed in the literature of sex. He pursued his interests in ways more elegant than those of the men in shabby macs. But it came to the same thing in the end.

Through the fifties, American magazines with titles like *Razzle*, *Eyeful*, *Flirt* and *Silk Stocking Stories* were being shipped to Britain in increasing numbers; from time to time police seized them. An American catalogue issued by 'The Pin-Up King' lists goods of a variety presumably unheard of in post-austerity Britain, though available to anyone with dollars, then very scarce. 'New cheesecake photos!' were fifteen cents each. Twelve dollars bought 16-mm films like *Peggy Disrobes* and *Chris Strips for Bed* ('There is a close-up of the high heels, and Chris is attired in rolled dark stockings').

Darker strains of material were on sale in London for those who knew where to look. The rape and flagellation that went down well with the Victorians was available in hard covers, or in the 'Soho typescripts' that flourished as demand increased but proper printing remained too dangerous and expensive. A title page on grubby pink paper announces *Discipline in the home. Text book*; seventy-two poorly duplicated pages work their way through chastisement that would hospitalize an elephant.

A more general sort of violence could be found in the stories of Hank Janson, a person to begin with and then perhaps a syndicate. Janson was much reviled by newspapers, preachers and the law, and dozens of destruction orders were made. The books had titles like *Broads Don't Scare Easy* and *Sister, Don't Hate Me*. The original author's real name was Crawley, but when a prosecution was attempted in 1955 over seven of the Janson books, it emerged that he had sold the pen-name years earlier. With their gaudy covers, cheap paper and B-picture dialogue they sold millions. *Vengeance* showed a blonde in a low-cut dress, lying back in a chair with her hands behind her head. It was supposed to be the biography of a hardboiled Chicago reporter. Trying to persuade a blonde floozie called Gloria to sleep with his friend Frank, not him, he announces, 'I'm having trouble with my bowels.' He and Frank dance with Gloria and Za-Za, who are both in their underclothes:

> Their stockings were drawn up tautly by long, black suspender tabs; black suspender tabs that contrasted sharply with the creaminess of soft skin. As they continued dancing and kicking I felt sickened and nauseated. Because those suspender tabs changed everything, transformed what was natural into something shameful.

This seemly attitude did Janson no good. His books featured on the Home Office list of titles that were fair game, compiled for the guidance of chief constables. It was a long list. A minute with the 1952 edition says that its predecessor of 1950 'helped the police considerably in their efforts to stamp out the spate of pornographic novels and magazines which were being sold by the less reputable type of bookseller.' Everything listed had been the subject of at least one destruction order during 1951. More than a thousand books were named, *My Way With Pretty Girls*, *Lips of Death* and *Two Smart Dames* rubbing shoulders, or bosoms, with a Maupassant, *The Artist's Model* (case brought at Glasgow), a Daniel Defoe, *Moll Flanders* (Liverpool), and, still haunted by its asterisks, the James Hanley *Boy* (Hull). About four hundred magazines were named, including *Jiggle*, *Titter*, *Oomph*, *The Romance of Naturism*, *Fads and Fancies* and *A Basinful of Fun*.

Most of the magazines were unpretentious, illustrated with drawings of half-dressed women or shadowy air-brushed nudes. *A Basinful of Fun*, which Harry remembered from his youth, described itself optimistically as 'The Family Magazine. Sixpence', and was published in Leeds. The nudes were blurred and lacked nipples. Wholesome young women, fully dressed, were pictured as winners of *BoF* competitions for the Factory Girl or the Natty Swim Suit or even the Pleasant Face. Cartoons were on seaside-postcard lines. A girl addresses her boy-friend as they enter the Tunnel of Love at a fairground: 'Cheer up, Arnold – you'll be feeling much better in the dark!' Advertisements promised that *'fascinating curves'* adding as much as six inches to the bust could be produced by rubbing in 'BEAUTIPON, the amazing Vegetable Flesh Former'; if the problem was the contrary, *'Slimcream*, the remarkable Vegetable Reducing Cream', would remove up to five inches. Both treatments were available from the same box number at ten shillings a course. Apart from taking fraudulent advertisers to court, which didn't happen, it is hard to see why the law needed to bother with *BoF*.

The same was true of *Fads and Fancies*, a few copies of which, dating from 1950, survive on the British Library's restricted shelves. The magazine described itself as 'The smart sports and fashions monthly', and seems to have been for clothes fetishists, with excursions into mild sado-masochism. Hobble skirts, wasp waists and black patent shoes were featured. Key words included 'gusset', 'elastic', 'stocking tops' and 'tight skirts'.

A thin line or no line at all separated the fetishist, whose lugubrious magazine might be taken away and pronounced filth by the Beak, from the newspaper reader looking at a photograph of a woman tennis player whose skirt was short enough to reveal frilly underwear. In 1950 this made 'Gorgeous Gussie' Moran, an American player, briefly famous when she appeared at Wimbledon. The papers were full of her, specifically her underclothes. The *Fads and Fancies* readership was riveted. One wrote, 'I think we Fadists, especially those of us who are Lingerie Lovers, ought to adopt [her] as our Pin Up Girl in chief. I admire this girl immensely, for she always seems to wear very pretty knicks . . .'

Few readers were not lingerie lovers. 'Embarrassing moments' were recalled (a skirt blows up in the wind), punishments were dwelt on (a teenage girl has to wear 'a very short gym tunic' and stand in the corner, another has to wear nappies). The readers' letters may be fantasy, either theirs or the editor's, but the air of solemn absorption in trivia, like stamp collectors comparing watermarks, makes the voices sound authentic. They are the lonely and excluded, clinging to strange dreams. 'For heaven's sake give us a picture of a really fat lady,' wrote someone. Such a magazine must be dangerous. The chief constables had it on a list.

The cinema was edging towards indecent films, but still had a long way to go. Queues formed outside a news cinema in the Charing Cross Road on winter afternoons in 1949 to see an American production, *Body Beautiful*, where clean young women paraded in bathing costumes and did physical jerks. A girl being massaged showed half a breast but that was about all. Most of the audience consisted of men and boys. A Mass-Observer observed a man in his thirties with 'his mouth half-open, licking his lips.'

Nude women were the next step, still permitted only in the distance until another American movie came along, *The Garden of Eden*, which attempted to earn an honest dollar in 1953 with its heart-warming story: a cantankerous old man becomes lovable as a result of visiting a nudist camp. Flesh but no pubic hair was visible. The British Board of Film Censors refused to give it a certificate, but when the exhibitor sent it direct to local authorities, most of them passed it. S.W. Harris, late of the Home Office, who was now Sir Sidney and president of the BBFC, conceded the point, and the absolute ban on nudity was relaxed. The *Daily Mirror* denounced this as 'an outrage to public decency', accompanying its denunciation with four stills from nudist films.

Pubic hair was still forbidden, the bodies on display had to appear to be those of nudists at a nudist camp, and the film had to be a documentary, not a story, if necessary with shots of a notice-board saying 'Nudist Camp' to leave no doubt. Sir Sidney still had influence at the board when serious sex films came in with the sixties – by which time he had been influencing public policy on indecency for forty years – and is said to have remarked, of a French film, 'I suppose we shall have to pass it. But men and women don't go to bed together with no clothes on.'

Nudity had a good innings before stronger films took over. British contributions to the genre included the work of Harrison Marks, who had already made his name as a photographer, as well as a lot of money, with calendars and albums of tasteful nudes in black and white, gleaming figures, devoid of body-hair, posed on beaches and up trees. His film *Naked as Nature Intended*, comedy sketches with some nudity, was another work that the board refused to pass, until local authorities took a more robust view. When it came to creative nudity, however, there was no touching the Americans. In the years between the end of total prohibition and the beginning of total licence, Doris Wishman made a series of nudist films, among them *Nude on the Moon*. Two scientists journey from Earth, and the first thing they find when they arrive is a nudist colony. As a friend of hers told Jonathan Ross on television, 'There were fifteen million horny people in New York ready, able and willing to pay a coupla bucks to see some broads with no clothes on.' There were some in London, if not quite fifteen million.

Films, which came under public scrutiny, were not a serious problem. Books were, however. In 1954 there were moves to prosecute 'literary' novels, charging them with obscenity and not simply seeking destruction orders. Examples were to be made; the rot was to be stopped. Various theories were put forward to explain the harassment. It was the work of

David Maxwell-Fyfe, or it was because Interpol had held a conference on obscene literature the year before. Sir Theobald Matthew, the DPP, said it was because the lawyer representing Hank Janson's publishers in an obscenity case put forward a defence that his client's books were no worse than some of those on the lists of famous London publishers, which he produced in court. Not only did the defence fail, but Lord Goddard, the unkindly Lord Chief Justice, suggested that someone should look at the famous publishers' books, and the DPP took the hint.

Accusing reputable firms of obscenity went logically with accusing reputable men of homosexuality. Success in court would frighten the faint-hearted and lead to a cleaner Britain. As things turned out, neither judges nor juries in 1954 were quite as disgusted by forthright books as in the past. Had it been left to local police and magistrates to act under the destruction-order provisions, there would have been no problem about having books condemned. Works by Rabelais and Flaubert (as well as Maupassant and Defoe) had been destroyed in recent years, usually in provincial towns with little publicity; so had the works of other respectable authors, including Angela Thirkell, Edgar Lustgarten and Erskine Caldwell. Magistrates, as figures in the community, couldn't risk being seen to condone material that the police thought immoral. Customs and Excise, too, could be relied on to look for filth. They operated under their own legislation, and could define 'indecent and obscene articles', which the law empowered them to detain, more or less as they pleased. Their black-list included many novels published by the Olympia Press in Paris (run by Maurice Girodias, the son of Jack Kahane), though thousands of travellers succeeded in bringing them back to Britain.

But to ensure that an example was made of publishers, full prosecutions for obscenity, with judge and jury, were required. A novel from America, *The Philanderer*, published in 1953 by Secker & Warburg, led what the authorities hoped would be a parade of shame. The book, by Stanley Kauffmann, is a well-written tale about a middle-class New Yorker who can't leave women alone. One or two phrases like 'lovely lemon-shaped breasts' are as far as Kauffmann goes in physical description. What he is interested in, and what the book is about, is the hero's sense of loss and self-loathing as lust puts his job and his marriage at risk. Is he doomed, with every woman he meets, to 'sift her down only to organs and heat, like a brute on whom everything else is wasted?' The answer unfortunately is yes: men are beasts, but in his case they regret it.

At the end we see him sidling towards doom, a decent man

incapacitated by his lust. A more moral tale would be hard to imagine. Perhaps Sir Theobald Matthew's objection was precisely that it suggested the urge to philander can seize ordinary men who love their wives. Sir Kingsley Amis was once quoted as saying, 'The end of the urge to have sex is an enormous relief. Someone, I think it was Sophocles, said it was like being chained to a lunatic.' But moralists like Matthew didn't want to hear that sexual behaviour was complicated, only that deviations from Christian doctrine were wrong.

The judge, Mr Justice Stable, made it plain to the jury that he favoured an acquittal. Should contemporary writing, he asked, be measured by what was suitable for a schoolgirl?

> I don't suppose there is a decent man or woman in this court who does not believe wholeheartedly that the pornographic, filthy book ought to be stamped out. But in our desire for a healthy society, if we drive criminal law too far, further than it ought to go, is there not a risk that there will be a revolt and a demand for a change in the law?

The answer to this turned out to be 'Yes'. In the short term the jury acquitted the publishers, who promptly brought out a new reprint that carried useful extracts from the judgment on the back jacket ('Members of the jury, is the act of sexual passion sheer filth?'), and printed the entire summing-up as a pamphlet, price one shilling. Secker & Warburg did very nicely out of the case.

Other publishers and other books followed. Hutchinson were fined a thousand pounds for a novel about a rich man's escapades, Vivian Connell's *September in Quinze*, and heard the judge commend the jury for protecting our youth by ensuring that 'the fountain of our national blood should not be polluted at its source.' That was the authorities' only victory. Charles McGraw's *The Man in Control* (Arthur Barker) concerned a teenage girl corrupted by a Lesbian; verdict, not guilty. *The Image and the Search* by Walter Baxter (Heinemann) was about a nymphomaniac; two juries couldn't reach a verdict, and a formal not-guilty verdict was returned.

While this feeble purge was in progress, the justices at Swindon provided entertainment by deciding that a copy of the two-volume Navarre Society edition of *The Decameron*, seized from a shop opposite Swindon market, should be destroyed. Two hundred and sixty other books and magazines were scrutinized by the same justices, who included a grocer, the secretary of a hospital management committee and a former chief mechanical engineer of the Great Western Railway. The Navarre edition's coloured plates from drawings by Louis Chalon include a couple of bare breasts and a bottom, and these may have influenced their worships. The Home Office was irritated by the scope that the case provided for jokes. The file includes a cutting from the *Observer* of an impassive article by John Gale which listed some of the titles condemned with *The Decameron*. These included *Ahaaaaaa!!!*, *Desirée*, *Flip*, *Nifty*, *Monsieur*, *Tricky*, *Wink*, *Pidgy*, *Radiant* and *Oooooo!!!*. Also listed were titles that the justices reprieved, among them *Pam Slipped Up*, *Wedding Night*, *They Say I'm Bad* and *Don't Mourn Me, Toots*, the latter one of Hank Janson's; alongside the title someone in the Home Office has scrawled, '42 destruction orders elsewhere!'

An internal minute complained that public ridicule was being directed at the Home Office, 'most unfairly', since it was the DPP who had approved the Swindon prosecution. The senior official at the Home Office, Sir Frank Newsam, duly wrote to Theobald Matthew to suggest that a policy for dealing with erotic classics by dead authors be established. Newsam, like the *Philanderer* judge, feared precipitating a change in the law — 'I am anxious to avoid giving rise to a clamour for legislation,' he wrote. The Director was unmoved. Eventually the conviction was quashed.

It was already too late to avert the clamour. Authors began writing to *The Times* — Graham Greene, J.B. Priestley, Somerset Maugham, Compton Mackenzie — talking of police censorship. But it took hundreds of newspaper articles, a Select Committee and years of arguing, lobbying and drafting before a new Obscene Publications Bill — sponsored by Roy Jenkins, then an Opposition MP — became law in 1959. The Conservative Government's law officers had been obstructive throughout, and the Bill was a compromise. It gave the police increased powers to search for and seize pornography, in return for a defence of publication for 'the public good', meaning the good of science, literature, art or learning. The loophole was soon exploited, in retaliation for all the years when the moralists were in charge. The reformers were just as devious as the moralists. Both dressed up their private preferences as matters of principle.

While law reform was under discussion, new novels continued to drift in the direction of licence. J.P. Donleavy's *The Ginger Man* (1955) has a ruttish hero whose adventures were shocking to some at the time. In 1957 John Braine's *Room at the Top* had a hero who used his lecherousness to help him get on in the world, and William Camp's *Prospects of Love* a hero who was lecherous but defeatist. Camp, an administrator and publicist by profession, published a more explicit novel two years later, *The Ruling Passion*, in which a rising young civil servant has an affair with his Minister's wife that causes pain all round. The publishers, McGibbon & Kee, were owned by the left-wing businessman Howard Samuel, who was nervous of being prosecuted for obscenity. In theory rapture on the sofa and casual lines like 'I used to have the most tremendous erections just thinking about her' might still have brought a policeman with a warrant. But nothing happened; and within a year or so the *Lady Chatterley's Lover* case had been brought, and everything was different.

After its first appearance in Florence in 1928, Lawrence's novel had led a clandestine life in Britain, of little interest outside literary circles, though it was vaguely acknowledged by the newspapers as a daring work with indecent passages. The book is a long sexual statement dressed up as a story. The 'lover' is Mellors, a rich landowner's gamekeeper, a working man with noble qualities who sexually awakens Constance Chatterley, the landowner's wife. Sir Clifford Chatterley, poor chap, is impotent and paraplegic as a result of battle wounds in Flanders. He gets little sympathy, being merely a stage-prop to help represent the dismal sexual condition of the British.

The positive side of the novel is where Mellors discusses and carries out the 'fucking with a warm heart' that will cure us all. Lawrence wants us to see a passionate woman as well as a passionate man in action. In inhibited times there is a lot to be said for demonstrations of enjoyable sex. But Lawrence, with sexual problems of his own, had odd theories that got in the way. There was a bitter resentment of women who employ 'self will' to frustrate men, by using them to obtain a clitoral orgasm instead of letting the he-man do it his way. The clitoris enrages Mellors, who can't stop telling Connie how his wife used to 'tear, tear, tear, as if she had no sensation in her except in the top of her beak, the very outside top tip, that rubbed and tore.' Part of Connie's appeal to Mellors is that she has 'some of the vulnerability of the wild hyacinths, she wasn't all tough rubber-goods and platinum, like the modern girl.' A womanly woman, it seems, has to surrender herself to a manly man, who will give her a good seeing-to and make her better: an element of that simple philosophy runs through the book.

A paperback edition of *Lady Chatterley's Lover* was perhaps not what reformers had in mind as a test case for the 'public good' provisions of the 1959 Obscene Publications Act. But Penguin Books, which had already brought out most of D.H. Lawrence's novels, included *Lady Chatterley* in the titles to mark the thirtieth anniversary of his death in 1960. The decision was taken by Sir Allen Lane, who had invented Penguins in 1935 and still ran the firm. *Lady Chatterley* had been published not long before in the United States, where Grove Press was prosecuted for obscenity but acquitted. It was Lane, when he was at the Bodley Head in the mid-thirties, who was behind the first British edition of *Ulysses*, also in the wake of American publication. He is said to have thought a prosecution unlikely. But he knew the potential of literature with a bit of dirt in it, and ordered an enormous print of two hundred thousand copies.

In the first year of the 1959 Act, thirty-four cases were brought, most of them against magazines, films, photographs and typescript 'books'. The only real books involved were Olympia Press imports from Paris, and everyone knew they were either pornography or dressed up as such. The first the authorities heard of *Lady Chatterley* was in letters to the Director of Public Prosecutions from the chief constable of Peterborough in March 1960. He sent an unexpurgated copy and said it was going to be on sale in high-street bookshops. This was before publication had been announced, and it is not clear what copy the police had seen — perhaps of the American edition. But their information was correct.

The DPP's office was cautious.* Maurice Crump, the deputy director, replied that he wasn't prepared to say that a book by 'so distinguished an author' was necessarily obscene, though it might be. He drew the customary distinction between cheap books and expensive books: if it was 'hawked around schoolchildren, that is one thing. If it is offered by responsible people for sale only to responsible people, that is quite another.' There is also an undated minute by Crump where he criticizes passages of 'novelettish trash' in *Lady Chatterley*, but contrasts them with 'the finely written sex bits'. Perhaps, after all, nothing was going to happen.

By June press reports made it clear that the book was going to cost a mere three shillings and sixpence; readers at that price were not all going to be responsible people. The DPP himself, still Sir Theobald Matthew, was now involved, discussing with Home Office and Customs how the

---

* The account that follows is based on the DPP's file, which had not been made available before I read it in 1991.

departments should present a united front. Treasury counsel had to be consulted, one of the barristers who act for the Crown, and whose advice is sought on any proposed prosecution. Mervyn Griffith-Jones QC was the choice, a senior lawyer with wide experience of obscenity cases, including *The Philanderer*; a family man of fifty-one, educated at Eton and Cambridge, gallant soldier in the war, member of Pratt's and White's; someone used to inner circles. Crump wrote to him on 13 July to say that although the usual practice was to refuse to tell a publisher, in advance of publication, whether or not a book would be prosecuted, in the case of 'an old timer like *Lady Chatterley's Lover*' it seemed only fair to reach a decision promptly. This would not be announced, for fear of creating a precedent, but could be 'percolated' to the publishers via the Home Office.

Griffith-Jones replied two weeks later. He wrote briefly from Temple to say that in his opinion the proof copy he had read was obscene, 'and a prosecution for obscene libel would be justified. Indeed if no action is taken . . . it will make proceedings against any other novel very difficult.' So the battle began. The Attorney-General, Sir Reginald Manningham-Buller, added his approval in August. He started reading *Lady Chatterley* on a train, bound for Southampton to board a cruise ship, and wrote to Matthew to say he had 'read up to Chapter IV'. If the rest of the book was going to be on the same lines, 'I have no doubt that you are right to start proceedings, and I do hope you get a conviction.' It has been argued since that the prosecution was wrong-headed from the start, because it sought to deny a book of obvious literary merit the 'public-good' protection afforded by the Act. But such a vague concept as literary merit had to be tested in action. By the standards of the time, and the narrow cultural sympathies of his class, it would have been hard for Griffith-Jones to make any other recommendation.

By this time the book had been technically published, to police officers who collected a dozen copies by arrangement at the Penguin offices on 16 August. Copies were already being distributed to the trade, but publication was halted until the case came to court in October. Penguin's solicitors, Rubinstein, Nash & Co., busied themselves writing to more than three hundred possible witnesses who might give evidence. They had no difficulty in finding thirty-six, with a further thirty-six in reserve. The literati were getting their own back for decades of censorship. When the DPP tried to do the same thing, on a smaller scale, he was unlucky. He approached Noel Annan, provost of King's College, Cambridge, and

Helen Gardner, the Oxford critic, telling them both that it had been 'suggested' they might be willing to assist on the question of literary merit. Both declined, and gave evidence for the defence.

Adverse texts were raked through, to find ways of disparaging the book. T.S. Eliot had written in the *Criterion* in 1931 that Lawrence was not a 'pure artist'. In 1932 Lord David Cecil had used the words 'uncontrolled egotist' and 'guttersnipe', though the words seem to have been taken out of context. Might Eliot and Cecil be recruited by the Crown? Clippings went round to Griffith-Jones, together with a sad little note to say that 'attempts are being made to obtain an introduction with a view to sounding them as to the possibility of their giving evidence for the prosecution. So far no progress has been made.'

Fine legal minds at the DPP's office wrestled with textual problems. Lawrence wrote three drafts of the book. The first was published in America in the nineteen-forties as *The First Lady Chatterley*. This was a thinner, genteel version. Could it be that Lawrence had beefed it up between Version 1 and Version 3, the one published in Florence in 1928, for improper reasons? There are broad hints in the DPP's papers. Passages from both versions were sent round for Griffith-Jones to look at. In Version 1 Lawrence wrote, 'He was in the torment of passion, almost brutal now. She went home alone in the dark, feeling a little bruised.' In Penguin's Version 3 there is a page and more, full of dangerous phrases, 'she lay down on the blanket', 'his hand groping softly', 'he drew down the thin silk sheath', 'the intense movement of his body', 'the springing of his seed in her'. To Sir Theobald Matthew there was something fishy. 'Counsel will bear in mind', said the note sent round with twin versions of half a dozen passages, 'that the three drafts culminating in *Lady Chatterley's Lover* were written over as short a period as three years (1925–1928) ... and he may consider it strange that Lawrence's opinion as to the exposure of intimate details of sexual intercourse as expressed in this passage, as compared with that expressed [previously], could have *genuinely* changed in such a short space of time.'

There were plenty of people who would continue to oppose the publishing of *Lady Chatterley*, whatever the court decided. A man who said he had been an assistant at the gallery where Lawrence's paintings were seized in 1929 wrote to the DPP to say he remembered seeing a letter from Lawrence to the woman who owned the gallery, saying, 'For God's sake, do buy as many copies of my new smutty novel Lady Chatterley as you possibly can afford. I am desperately hard up.' The book had literary merit, but as a young man 'it did me much moral harm.' The critic Dr Leavis was quoted in the press as saying that the publishers had written to him, but that *Lady Chatterley* was 'not at all a book for publication by Penguins. I have worked for thirty years to dissociate Lawrence from talk about sex. The less squalor the better. Nothing decent can come out of it.'

But a mood was waiting to be changed. What the trial achieved, in the muddled and sometimes farcical way of large-scale legal proceedings, was a lurch towards sexual freedom. Almost any book would have done, as long as it was the robustly sexual work of a 'serious' writer who could be attacked and defended as a threat to or an asset of a civilized society. In his opening speech Griffith-Jones calculated that thirteen acts of sexual intercourse were described: 'One follows them not only into the bedroom but into bed.' Nor did he fail to touch on the dirty words in the book, adding them up for the court, thirty 'fucks' and 'fuckings', fourteen 'cunts', thirteen 'balls', six 'shits', six 'arses', four 'cocks' and three 'pisses'. No doubt he hoped to shock the jury (which included three women) into an early distaste for the book; forbidden words offend people as much as forbidden acts. In the same speech he made the remark that attached itself to him for the rest of his life, 'Is it a book that you would have lying around in your own house? Is it a book that you would even wish your wife or your servants to read?'

The prosecution had an air of outrage. An unsigned typescript memorandum from within the DPP's office, headed 'Notes on Mr Gardiner's opening address,' suggests how badly the authorities wanted to hold the line on obscenity. In his speech for the defence, Gerald Gardiner QC had suggested that Lawrence was a moralist, in favour of marriage and against promiscuity; that he preached the doctrine of a sick society which could be healed only by personal relationships; and that there was 'nothing in words themselves which can deprave or corrupt.'

On the four-letter words that Gardiner was defending, the DPP's 'Notes' commented,

> Why is it that even the most cultured and would-be 'progressive' people would probably not like their children to ask them at breakfast, 'Well, did you have a good fuck last night?' Is it not that basically – so far from condemning sex – ordinary people do indeed regard it as a revered mystery which they do not wish to be cheapened? Cheapening is, of course, a kind of corruption.

A conclusion that young people would draw from the novel, suggested the Notes, was that a young man mustn't risk marrying a virgin, 'for how then could he tell whether "'er's deep ter fuck, and cunt's good" (text, page 221)?' Obviously the bride must try out her proposed husband beforehand. *Lady Chatterley* implied that trial marriages were essential – 'part of the dated nonsense of the thirties, which even most of the sexual psychologists have thrown over.' Beside themselves with righteousness, the Notes challenged Gardiner's sardonic remark to the jury that no one ever suggested that DPP or judge or counsel or jury were corrupted, that it was 'always somebody else. It is never ourselves.' Certainly, said the Notes, the book could corrupt 'you or me . . . Inevitably we are coarsened by it.' Defence witnesses no doubt held views on sex which differed from the conventional moral standards by which they were brought up. In that case, 'Is it not likely if – as they will say – this book had such an effect on them, that it helped to twist their views?'

These arguments were never presented in court; they simmered behind the scenes. Perhaps it was just as well that Griffith-Jones didn't listen too closely to the DPP, whose moralizing might not have helped his case. The Notes suggested it was 'not strictly irrelevant to inquire how many of [the defence witnesses] have been divorced, and how many times,' and thought it worth telling counsel that the same woman had been married at different times to the writer Cyril Connolly and the publisher George Weidenfeld.* (Connolly and Weidenfeld would have been in the second wave of witnesses, but were not needed.)

As the procession of critics, clergymen, teachers and authors passed through the witness box – praising Lawrence for saving four-letter words from vulgar associations, finding the book suitable for teenagers, declaring Lady Chatterley's urge for copulation to be perfectly natural – what Griffith-Jones did was to appeal to the standards of propriety that the average person was supposed to possess. The jury were meant to be as shocked by the book as he and the DPP and the Attorney-General had been.

No one knows how much the jury were swayed by the views of distinguished literary figures, or by attempts to give Lawrence a religious dimension. Dilys Powell, the *Sunday Times* film critic, said that in *Lady Chatterley* sex was taken 'as a basis for a holy life.' ('Did I hear you aright?' asked Griffith-Jones.) An Anglican clergyman who was director

---

* The wife was Barbara Skelton. Having been divorced by Connolly she married Weidenfeld, who later divorced her, citing Connolly as co-respondent.

of religious education in the Birmingham diocese, when asked about the word 'phallic', said that 'like many words taken over from a pagan world, it has been baptised by Christians and made into a sacred word.'

The Bishop of Woolwich, Dr John Robinson, a liberal theologian, was remembered ever after for having said that 'I think Lawrence tried to portray [the sexual] relation as in a real sense something sacred, as in a real sense an act of holy communion.' Agreeing with the judge that *Lady Chatterley* showed a woman in an immoral relationship, he added, 'in so far as adultery is an immoral relationship.' Asked by Gerald Gardiner if it was a book that Christians ought to read, he said 'Yes.' For many people the permissive churchman, complete with catch-phrases, first appeared at the *Chatterley* trial.

The jury, according to the writer C.H. Rolph, who was in court, consisted of five members who stumbled when reading the oath, and seven who were 'manifestly literate and educated persons.' When they found Penguin Books not guilty, was it the literary criticism that impressed them? Did they believe the humbug about 'something sacred'? Or was it just a feeling that sexually the world had moved on from the one that Griffith-Jones stood for? Reports that nine of the twelve had been in favour of acquittal from the beginning suggested it was the last. It is not known whether the jury meant by their verdict that the book was not obscene, or that it was obscene but justified by the 'public good' defence.

One issue that might have affected the outcome, Lawrence's fondness for a forbidden sexual practice, was barely touched on at the trial. John Sparrow, the warden of All Souls College, Oxford, who was no lover of *Lady Chatterley*, wrote about it eighteen months later in the literary magazine *Encounter*, demonstrating that in the book's last sexual episode, Mellors commits an act of buggery on the 'startled and almost unwilling' Connie. This has the effect of bringing her 'to the very heart of the jungle of herself,' and is seen by Lawrence as a purifying act, burning out shame and inhibition.

Anal sex with a woman remains a criminal offence, whether or not the participants are married (men can commit buggery with men in private; men who do it with women, however secretly, can be sent to prison if detected, and have been). It has been widely practised, often as an alternative to normal intercourse that carries no risk of conception; this may be one reason women have consented to it — that they found it the lesser of two evils. Another reason, not popular with feminists, is that some women enjoy it. It is still a difficult subject.

Penguin's lawyers knew what Lawrence was getting at in the scene, and hoped that the prosecution had missed it. Griffith-Jones didn't mention it until his closing speech, and then only indirectly. According to one of the two junior defence counsel, Jeremy (now Lord) Hutchinson QC,

> Some of our expert witnesses could not see that it implied intercourse *per anum*. Du Cann [the other junior] and I being good Old Bailey advocates thought otherwise. So we avoided the passage but were prepared to put it to our experts if the prosecution raised it. I don't think Griffith-Jones saw the implication until it was too late to put it to our witnesses. It was therefore not open to him to make any positive suggestion as to its meaning to the jury in his final speech. So he hinted at it, which was all he could then do.

Witnesses might have been disconcerted by anal sex; so might the jury. But its omission by Griffith-Jones was apparently deliberate. The prosecution may have chosen to make only half-hearted use of the episode, but they seem to have known about it from the start. In the copy of the Penguin *Lady Chatterley* used by the DPP, pages 258 and 259, where the scene occurs, have almost every line underscored in red ink. Alongside the words 'Burning out the shames, the deepest, oldest shames, in the most secret places,' someone has written in the margin in large capitals, 'BUGGERY.'

The jury's verdict, coming neatly at the start of a decade, has come to stand for changes beyond the mere publishing of books. Its importance was recognized at once. Some cheered; some were appalled. The sole survivor of the Home Office's *Chatterley* files contains letters from members of the public complaining about the decision. 'England needs your help,' someone wrote to the Prime Minister, Harold Macmillan, adding, 'You also are a publisher.' A 'family man and a grammar schoolmaster' from Essex deplored the verdict and said that his pupils told him it was 'almost impossible to buy "proper comics" in local shops, their place being taken by sex-filled trash.' A woman in Surrey cunningly addressed her letter to Mrs Butler, the Home Secretary's wife, saying she had a daughter aged thirteen at a boarding school, and 'day girls there may introduce this filthy book at only three and sixpence ... If a mistress protests, girls can reply that a clergyman has said, "Every Christian should read it".'

In Nottingham, a bookseller who thought *Lady Chatterley* was 'muck and filth' carried an expurgated edition –

I have a notice in my window which states 'Lady Chatterley clean edition now on sale. Dirty edition must be ordered.' We have orders for over 700 Dirty edition and only 31 copies of clean edition have been sold.

But that was only to be expected.

10

'Darling'

The New Eroticism

THE NEW AGE OF Eros took a few years to dawn. Lurching towards sexual freedom, the British constructed two myths of what was happening to them. In one the nation was maturing, searching its heart, changing its ways. In the other, self-indulgence and anarchy were going to triumph unless there was drastic action. The matter has never been resolved.

People wanted more than was supposed. Some requirements could be met by Act of Parliament, among them simpler divorce, easier abortion and better facilities for contraception. Others were beastlier. A substantial minority wanted to read smutty magazines and watch smutty films. Millions of the young wanted to fornicate. These appetites were generally deplored. It made no difference. Once the national mood had changed, which it did within a few years of the *Chatterley* trial, discussing sex in public became a non-stop activity to which everyone could contribute, if only through radio phone-ins and letters pages. We were all our own sexual masters; or hoped to be.

Harry, in his diary, said he dated his awareness that things were happening to a visit he paid to the Raymond Revue Bar in Soho about 1958, where, in a glitzy atmosphere, with a couple of fellow-lecturers from his institute of technology, he first had a clear view of the female pudenda on a stage, part of a parade of nattily dressed showgirls. Paul Raymond didn't believe in G-strings and sticking plaster. Once a variety performer himself – he had a mind-reading act – he became a producer and found he could pack a provincial theatre by letting girls show their bosoms. As the climate changed, he changed with it. The sixties made his fortune. His premises, close to porn bookshops and a street market, were operated as a club. He was prosecuted and fined in his real name of Geoffrey Anthony Quinn for shows that went too far, but he survived. It was the old naughtiness adapted for the new age.

The Bishop of Woolwich was given the role of dissident priest, not only for his defence of a forbidden book but for the way he opened up instant rifts in the Church of England. The Archbishop of Canterbury, Dr Fisher, said that Dr Robinson had become 'a stumbling block and a cause of offence to many,' and Church newspapers called for his head. The Bishop, born 1919, sailed on happily, serialized in newspapers, looking youthful on television.

A Scottish psychiatrist, Professor G.M. Carstairs, born 1916, was another stirrer-up, using his Reith Lectures on BBC radio as a platform in 1962. 'Is chastity the supreme moral virtue?' he asked, and answered himself by suggesting that for Christ the cardinal virtue was charity.

> It was His intemperate disciple, Paul [said Carstairs], an authoritarian character, who introduced the concept of celibacy as an essential part of Christian teaching, and centuries later it was the reformed libertine St Augustine who placed such exaggerated emphasis upon the sinfulness of sex. It has always been those whose own sexual impulses have been precariously repressed who have raised the loudest cries of alarm over other people's immorality.

References to fallible saints and their jaundiced views sounded less novel as time went on, but in 1962 Christians found it unsettling to hear them on the BBC. Carstairs spoke matter-of-factly about adolescent sexuality, a forbidden subject. Young people, he said approvingly, were turning our society into one where 'sexual experience, with precautions against conception, is becoming accepted as a sensible preliminary to marriage.' Had he proposed cannibalism, the outrage could not have been greater.

In 1965 Michael Schofield published his survey of *The Sexual Behaviour of Young People*, an academic's inquiry that would have been too daring a few years earlier. One interviewer (wearing a mackintosh) was arrested briefly. Schofield's sample of nearly two thousand suggested that one in three boys and one in six girls had lost their virginity by the age of eighteen. Heavy petting, broken down into interesting categories for the first time, was enjoyed by half the boys and almost as many of the girls. No consensus on what the young were up to had emerged. The *Newnes Manual of Sex and Marriage* (1964), kept to the old proprieties. Intercourse before marriage was wrong, and that was that. Furthermore, 'It can be said with confidence that any manipulation of the genital organs is overstepping the mark and these might well be thought to include the breasts.' If *Stimulating breasts under clothes* (a Schofield category) was overstepping the mark, then nearly two-thirds of adolescent girls were guilty. According to Harry, plenty of teenage middle-class girls were guilty twenty years earlier, too.

Schofield found casual attitudes to contraception, and his account is a long way from Carstairs' idealized picture of teenagers making responsible experiments in order to guarantee happy marriages. Anyone sympathetic to change hopes to make the changes sound high-principled. A Reith lecturer could hardly say bluntly that teenagers were doing it because they liked it.

Newspapers were quick to write about promiscuity among the young. It proved nothing, but proof was hardly needed. Some of those who talked about sexual exploits learned to distance themselves from their behaviour, to season the story with enough self-disgust to make older readers feel safe. In Birmingham in 1966 I heard the Butlins Summer Worker's Tale. He was in his early twenties, a virgin (he swore) when he went to Butlins.

> I became sickened, it was so totally available. The first time it happened the girl said, 'Let's go back to your chalet.' I had the top bunk and we climbed over the chap below. She took her clothes off and we had sex seven times. Quite honestly, when I went there I thought sex was a sort of love, but afterwards I thought differently.

Precautions, if taken, meant condoms. (The Pill, still a novelty, was difficult to obtain for single women.) Did the girls worry? 'No, they were on holiday.' Sex meant nothing to him now. 'It's like a cup of tea in the morning. You see a girl in a bathing costume and say, "Ah, Christ, she's nice, let's have her." One girl was fucked by thirty-eight blokes in her fortnight. Quite honestly I'd rather sleep in the same bed as a girl and not have sex with her.' His tale didn't appear in print, but many like it did.

The Profumo scandal of 1963 fitted the expectations of the time. Was it reflecting a mood or helping to create it? The War Minister, John Profumo, had sex a few times with a showgirl and part-time prostitute, Christine Keeler, in the summer of 1961. He was quickly warned off her louche social circle, indirectly by the security services, because it included a Soviet naval attaché who was also a spy. His relationship with Keeler herself was unknown to them, and the affair, some of it conducted inside small motor cars, was over before the end of the year. This could have been the last of the matter. But a year later a stray event that had nothing to do with Profumo – a shooting incident outside a flat that

Keeler was visiting – drew attention to her and her circle. She talked to people about her liaison with the War Minister. Rumours began, resulting in his resignation and disgrace in July 1963, and damage to the Conservative Government of Harold Macmillan from which it didn't recover.

The story had enthralling ramifications, since gone into in several books and a film, and it was unfolding at a time when newspapers felt freer than ever to dwell on sex. It involved 'call girls', in vogue since the Street Offences Act curbed open soliciting. It was about sex in reasonably high places; the social discretion that might have confined gossip about this to a smaller circle no longer existed. There were true stories of 'kinky sex', though not involving Profumo and Keeler. Two-way mirrors, improper photographs, orgies and sado-masochistic activities were just what readers expected (or feared) of the permissive age. Matters that might have been suppressed by newspapers themselves in the past as obscene or tasteless, or at least interpreted in more respectful terms, were now sought after by editors.

At the same time prostitutes came into their own for the media: they were immoral, but when referred to as 'models' and 'call girls' were quite glamorous, too, and as good a source of information as anyone else. The modern style of kiss-and-tell journalism ('Model tells of naked romps with football star') began when Christine Keeler signed a contract with the *Sunday Pictorial* in exchange for her story and a copy of a letter that Profumo wrote to her on War Office paper beginning 'Darling'.

'Darling' itself was a word for the times, part loving and part meretricious. Harold Macmillan, puzzled by the world of non-gentlemen, wrote in his diary about a society 'where no one really knows anyone and everyone is "darling".' It was the title of a screenplay that Frederic Raphael wrote for John Schlesinger to film in 1965, then turned into a novel. The darling of *Darling* is a genuine model, not a prostitute. She and a journalist fall in love, leave their spouses and live together, but her natural promiscuity triumphs in voluptuous London. The sexual relationships are described without apology. The difference between the journalist and the girl is that he retains his integrity and she doesn't.

For Raphael and many writers the new erotic London was an ambiguous place. When Ann Veronica/Amber Reeves coupled with Capes/H.G. Wells in 1908, sexual freedom was an exciting but distant prospect. By 1965 it had arrived, a rose with thorns. To the puritans there was no ambiguity. They queried the new order from the start. How free was free? Where would it all end? Sometimes the hum of questions was louder than the cries of pleasure.

Mrs Mary Whitehouse (b. 1910) emerged from rural Shropshire in 1964 to wallop progressive attitudes and in particular the BBC's. She began as a schoolteacher; had an unhappy (but non-sexual) experience with a married man in her late twenties; was helped through it by MRA, the Moral Rearmament movement, where she met her husband. She said she was never active as a Moral Rearmer, but her manner caught the movement's naïve insistence that positive acts at strategic points would prune the evils of society. To her it was not just a question of people turning to immorality. She saw them being manipulated. Forces ('the enemies of the West') were out to destroy us by undermining the nation's character. Some were moved by greed, like the pornographers; others were supposed to have sinister ideological motives, like Sir Hugh Greene, director-general of the BBC.

Greene, who liked women and could never see what the moralists were making such a fuss about, wouldn't concede that Whitehouse's Britain mattered. It was middle-aged or older, often Christian and preponderantly female. The 'Clean Up TV Campaign' that Whitehouse began with a clergyman's wife, then turned into the National Viewers' and Listeners' Association, linked him with the new satire shows and social-realism plays. These came from young writers and producers. Greene's contribution was a benign silence that created a climate for them to flourish in. In November 1965 he ruled that Whitehouse should not be invited to appear on television.

By nature Greene was nonchalant, fond of cricket and beer (his family were East Anglian brewers), often preoccupied with his private life. He was in the line of cheerful English pagans who irritate and are irritated by moralists. But they rarely occupy such a commanding cultural height as he did between 1960 and 1969. The same freedoms were in the air at independent television, but it was Greene's BBC that made the most of them. To combat this enemy, the National Viewers and Listeners did like William Coote and the National Vigilance Association, and painted pictures of depravity. Its first conference in 1966 praised the BBC for many of its programmes, only to denounce the 'torrid love scenes' and 'foul language', the tide of decadence, the armies of 'long-haired youths and untidy girls', and the underlying assumption (so they claimed) that promiscuity and infidelity were the norm.

Descriptions of change in the nation ran ahead of change itself. Side by side with stories about avant-garde mothers (usually described as living in 'fashionable Chelsea'), who put their sub-teen daughters on the contraceptive pill, were better-documented stories about the Family Planning Association, whose clinics refused to see unmarried women. It was 1965 before Boots the Chemist could bring themselves to sell condoms, because of the association with 'promiscuity, vice and prostitution.'

Harry, who married Sheila in 1954 and had two daughters, wrote in his diary, Saturday 18 February 1967,

> I have had S. *up to here* and the last straw is to be accused by her of deserting her and the girls in order to *live out a pathetic fantasy* about younger women. Grace is not particularly younger. She is thirty for God's sake. This was last night: S: 'I don't care who you go off with, but I wish you would not make a fool of yourself.' Me: 'That's my problem.' S: 'Your hair's too long, are you trying to be trendy? That's what Grace is, isn't it, trendy?' Me: 'If you say so.'
>
> God knows it is considerably more than sex but it is that too. At one time Sheila used to beg me to secure her to the bed with dressing-gown cords, belts, ties – anything that was to hand, when she was in the asking mood. I did it once when she was fully clothed after she returned from an NUT conference and I pretended I knew that she had been shafted nightly. I trussed her up and used a scissors to cut away crucial underwear. I didn't actually need to touch her. On the last occasion I attempted Bondage Games, I believe in 1963, she claimed that she had grown out of them, and when we did it it was only ever to please me. I play super games with Grace, her body smells sweeter than Sheila's, but things like that can never be mentioned. I feel ashamed sometimes.

The entry has a postscript, added nearly seventeen years later.

> In retrospect I admit to there being some truth in S.'s fantasy theory. Ipswich was dead as far as I was concerned. Every time I saw young girls doing the Twist I had an erection, or it would be truer to say that I desired to have an erection, and in some cases I succeeded. I was aged thirty-nine. The dentist took out a front tooth and I had my first attack of piles both on the same day. Grace saved my life. Why I said I was ashamed I cannot imagine. S. has had a far happier life without me. I am writing this with difficulty because Tracey is tying up my other arm (Joke).

*

The Abortion Wars

A fierce campaign to reform the law on abortion, and an equally fierce campaign to stop the reformers, was in the news for years. Women had always sought abortions. In Britain a small group of activists, their case logical and humanitarian, had kept itself alive on hope since the nineteen-thirties. Before that time it would have been difficult for such a group to exist and claim to be reputable. As it was, they continued for years to be seen as middle-aged, middle-class cranks.

A multitude of women had their pregnancies terminated. Some did it themselves, others went to women (occasionally men) who did it illegally for a few pounds on a couch or in the kitchen, using simple implements. Some general practitioners would do it. The abortionist was an odd combination, the sinister figure with the Higginson's syringe and the mackintosh sheet, but also the friend and confidante who was herself vulnerable to blackmail or medical mishap. Infection and illness were not uncommon, and thirty or forty women were known to die each year from the after-effects of criminal abortion; other deaths were concealed.

The annual total of illegal abortions could only be guessed at, and the reformers, seeking a nice round figure to strengthen their case, guessed at a hundred thousand. I was on their side; I guessed the same. In debate, reformers concentrated on the Old Woman who Lived in a Shoe principle, the poor, harassed mother driven to find help in the backstreets. As with birth control, it would have been unwise to talk about the unmarried, who had no business being pregnant in the first place.

No one took much notice of the reformers, whatever they said. Under a law of 1861, an attempt to induce miscarriage unlawfully was a felony punishable by life imprisonment. Abortion was seen as a dirty business. An occasional liberal voice was heard. A judge (McCardie) who heard a series of abortion cases in the early thirties declared that the law was out of touch with reality, adding later, 'I cannot think it right that a woman should be forced to bear a child against her will.' But the zealots who still tried to rule Britain as if it was a glorified public school where the greater kept the lesser in order were unrelenting. Abortion meant sex, pregnancy, crime and even death. Politicians edged away from such a grisly topic, charged with such moral implications, so there was little chance of a change in the law. Despite kindly coppers-on-the-beat who sometimes looked the other way, dozens of illegal abortionists were prosecuted each year.

Yet a parallel world existed in which abortion was not illegal at all. Those who were tacitly allowed to terminate pregnancies for fee-paying patients had to be consultants, or − medicine being a class-conscious profession − they had to act as if they were, with premises in the West End. The escape-hatch in the law of 1861 was the word 'unlawfully', which implied that there were circumstances in which an attempt to induce miscarriage could be lawful. A case of 1938 involving a girl made pregnant by rape, where the surgeon who performed the abortion was tried and acquitted, widened the loophole. The judge (Macnaghten) said that a pregnancy could be ended if it meant preserving the mother's life, in which connection it was sufficient to believe that had the pregnancy continued she would have become a physical or mental wreck.

From then on, mental wrecks were Harley Street's friend. A distraught woman could be sent to a reliable psychiatrist, who would give it as his opinion that unless her pregnancy was terminated, she might commit suicide. The fee for the operation would be large, usually around fifty guineas, sometimes more. Fifty guineas is well over a thousand pounds today, but it could be demanded without seeming like extortion. It was inadvisable to ask for cash, and fatal to tamper with the records. The essence of the West End abortion was that if questions were asked, the case should have an air of legality.

Dr Francis de Caux, a New Zealand anaesthetist who had set himself up in Mayfair to practise gynaecology, came to grief in 1942 because he had been devious. He used a dubious consent form for a Miss K, kept no notes that indicated why she was in his consulting room, and was charging her seventy-five pounds in cash, which she had with her in a suitcase when the police arrived. 'Was there something to conceal?' asked the judge, and sent him down for five years.

Most of the gentlemen abortionists were more prudent or luckier (de Caux was shopped by a theological student, who told the police what was going on in Green Street). Thousands of women with the money and the right connections came to their shadow-world and were 'helped', as the phrase went. Every doctor knew what a woman meant when she said, 'Can you help me?' Meanwhile the reformers chipped away at official indifference. A Bill of 1953 sponsored by Labour MPs aroused the displeasure of the Roman Catholic hierarchy and was talked out. The same thing happened in 1961, with Catholic MPs wrecking the measure in its early stages, and again in 1965 and 1966. But the scene outside Parliament had changed. Middle-class women were becoming aware of the law's anomalies. No feminist movement as such existed; but unwanted pregnancies, at a time when sex was daily seen to be shedding the old shame and secrecy, could now arouse anger as well as terror.

Mrs Diane Munday, married to a professional man, lived in the Hertfordshire village of Wheathampstead. She had three children under the age of three and a half when, in 1961, she found herself pregnant again. Some years previously L, an acquaintance, had died after a criminal abortion. Mrs Munday sought out Professor Nixon of University College Hospital, one of the rare gynaecologists who sometimes terminated pregnancies within the Health Service; 'I am the abortionist of Gower Street,' he would tell bemused colleagues. Nixon turned her down. She got the address of a West End doctor, the famous Teddy Sugden, whose practice was in Half Moon Street. He was said to keep alligators there; an amiable, rumpled man, like a professor of some obscure humanity, who liked parties and women. All she saw in the waiting room were tanks of tropical fish and an aviary. Sugden had told her to go there late in the evening.

She was on edge. When she was shown in to him, he said, 'You look whacked, my dear,' and gave her a glass of gin. Stories of gin and hot baths as a means of abortion came to mind; had he started on her already? They went through the charade of discussing her mental state, and he said that if a psychiatrist concurred, he would terminate her pregnancy at a nursing home in north London for a hundred and fifty pounds. Later he agreed to take ninety. When Mrs Munday came round from the anaesthetic, her first thought was, 'L is dead and I'm alive.'

She had already joined ALRA, the Abortion Law Reform Association. Now she emerged as one of its leaders when it rejuvenated itself and became an effective political pressure group. She may have been the first woman to say on television that she had had an abortion. This helped to give her a local reputation. In Wheathampstead people would cross the road to avoid her when they saw her coming. She stopped using the village shops and went to St Albans instead. In 1969, when the reform had been won, the liberal network, in the shape of the Labour Government's Lord Chancellor, Lord Gardiner, appointed her a justice of the peace. This was the Gerald Gardiner QC who defended *Lady Chatterley*. Diane Munday was rehabilitated in the village high street.

The reform movement succeeded because it ceased to be untouchable. The subject was no longer reserved for the medical profession (which by and large wanted no change in the law) and the lawyers. Once television and newspapers began to deal with it, the ramshackle system came under the public eye. Women felt encouraged to seek help; one result was that convictions for criminal abortion, thirty-three in the first year of the decade, doubled. The abortion networks were busy.

A woman went from a suburb on the west of London to a GP on the east. He told her to return home and forget she had seen him. A day later the phone rang, and a man who didn't give his name made an appointment. When he came, thirtyish and casually dressed, he left his car parked round the corner and brought a picnic basket with his lunch. Among the sandwiches, a vacuum flask; inside the flask, the instruments. Ten minutes in the kitchen and it was all over. A friend, waiting in the sitting room, heard nothing. The visitor was vague about the fee; she could pay what seemed appropriate. It was a nice house near the river, and forty pounds would be fine.

GPs who dabbled in abortion risked their careers, yet few towns lacked a doctor who might be persuaded by money or pity or even lust — stories were told of doctors taking advantage. But they were always cautious, having more to lose than the retired nurse or midwife.

A reporter has come to interview a doctor in a poor district, near the Elephant and Castle in south London, late on a July evening in 1965. The doctor is elderly and speaks with a slight accent, perhaps German. He mentions Berlin. Perhaps he practised in the Weimar Republic, in the years that Koestler wrote about.

The reporter asks, 'How far can I go?' 'Ask and see,' says the doctor.

'Under what conditions are you prepared to do terminations?'

'Already you have gone too far.'

He speaks of an imaginary doctor who is selective about his patients. The reporter knows this already: a friend of a friend was refused. Most of the women, says the doctor, are middle class; the working class go to their own kind.

'I think I have met some of them, these backstreet women. They are not afraid to face me, posing as friends. Yet I don't know a single address.'

'What are the medical dangers?'

'A paste of aromatic oils may be introduced into the womb by cannula. If the operator squeezes the paste and it enters a vein, the woman may drop dead because the substance contains fat. Again, if he is not using an anaesthetic, he risks her crying out — not with pain, with anxiety.'

'What are patients like when they arrive?'

'Some may be afraid to open their mouths from fear. Some may say, "Doctor, I want an abortion!" Only a fool does neurotic patients. Or those light-hearted girls to whom the whole thing is a joke. These people will give his address too readily, possibly over the counter in a public house. A level of seriousness and felt distress is important.'

'The police?'

'Sometimes they use decoys. They want to know the man they're dealing with, to test his capacity and courage. Other times they turn away, do nothing. They can be far more understanding than one section of the public. Whether that is on instructions from above, or just the human kindness of the lower ranks, I've not been able to discover.'

'How does a doctor say "No" to a woman?'

'He tells her quite coldly, "You must be mistaken".'

He sits with his back to a darkening window, explaining why it is that a doctor will complicate his life with these difficult matters. He will have a feeling for the women. There will undoubtedly be financial considerations as well.

The telephone rings and he listens to the caller for a moment. He says 'we shall have to see' and then 'perhaps a little later.'

He shows the reporter out through the empty waiting room to the street. 'Remember,' he says, 'I have told you nothing about myself.' He remains on the doorstep, staring towards the lights of the Elephant, looking out for whoever is coming.

A few doctors did legal abortions inside the Health Service. Sir Dugald Baird, a Scottish professor of gynaecology who retired in 1965, had run a free fertility service for the women of Aberdeen for nearly twenty years, offering contraception, sterilization and (where necessary) abortion. Whitehall, far away, turned a blind eye. Using his freedom as a university professor, Baird was ahead of his time. From the middle sixties the political debate in London about abortion expended much energy on the question of whether a woman's 'social' as well as 'medical' circumstances might properly be used as grounds for allowing legal abortion. Baird had no time for such nonsense. People were people, making the best of their circumstances. 'When a trawlerman comes home after a fortnight,' he said, 'it's a lucky woman who avoids getting pregnant.' Peter Diggory, a consultant gynaecologist, was the first English doctor to say in public that he had done abortions, a hundred and ten within the NHS and privately.

Eustace Chesser was another pioneer, a psychiatrist and sexologist with liberal views who was also a leading Harley Street abortionist, nervous of prosecution, yet driven to do it for principle and profit. He was a busy author, writing books about sex and marriage, philosophic and sometimes explicit, beginning with *Love without Fear* in 1941, for which he was prosecuted. A paperback edition of 1970 claimed that more than three million copies had been sold. Chesser was doing no more than Van de Velde, though in a simpler style and fewer pages. This was probably his offence. Promiscuity was not hinted at; even the 1970 edition is carefully described as 'A plain guide to sex technique for every married adult.' But in 1942, after the book had been out for a year and a half, the DPP decided to mount a common-law prosecution for obscenity, the kind that might result in prison.

The war was going badly, but the nation still had to be protected from filth ('Do you think it was really necessary to go into minute descriptions of the organs of sexual congress?'). Particular attention was drawn to descriptions of 'kissing all parts of a woman's body' and 'manual stimulation of men by women', and to accounts of lesbianism and flagellation. The jury were unimpressed; perhaps the war was too much in their minds. They took less than an hour to find Chesser not guilty.

His career as an abortionist was more covert, but, like all of them, he helped to wear away the opposition. 'They could have caught me in the early days,' he said (in an interview of 1965, never published because the events were too close).

> When I was younger I was more fanatical, and the money played a bigger part. I can assure you it's been a very thorny path. I've been lucky, maybe I've been clever. It's not that I don't believe in the cause. In my not so humble opinion there is no greater sin than to force an unwanted pregnancy to continue into the birth of an unwanted child. But I liked the money and the power.

It was a year since he had given up abortions, to concentrate on books and campaigning. His son, also a doctor, had just taken his Diploma of Psychological Medicine; it was time to change trains.

Chesser was born in Edinburgh, into a disciplined Jewish home; both his parents' families had fled from Russian pogroms. His childhood and a public school left him isolated, an outsider, contemptuous of systems but intimidated by them as well; a natural enemy of authority. He must have started out as an abortionist a year or two after the *Love without Fear* trial, perhaps encouraged by knowing he could make a living as a writer if he was ever struck off the medical register. One minute he would be a psychiatrist in Wimpole Street, the next a surgeon at a nursing home in the Cromwell Road.

Every safeguard was double-bolted, but he was rarely free from anxiety that 'they' would catch him out, put on to him by a meddling Roman Catholic. An exception was when a woman came via a titled doctor, or when the woman herself belonged to a titled family. 'Then', said Chesser, 'it was in the bag, given the nature of back-scratching relationships. And I suppose it is perfectly true that the trauma of Lady Piddle's daughter bringing an illegitimate child into the world may be greater than that of a girl in Soho.' His maximum fee (so he said) was seventy-five pounds, 'or a hundred for a millionaire.' On two occasions he had refused a thousand guineas to abort a girl, both times from a magistrate; he smiled as he said it.

Near the end of his life, in 1972, Chesser was called as an expert witness in an obscenity trial, and was probably the first person to stand up in court and say that pornography was good for you. This ingenious defence, which meant that the dirtier the book the more successful it was at promoting therapeutic masturbation, had a brief, colourful life. The judge in 1972 reminded jurors of the fate of the Roman Empire, but the publishers were acquitted; Chesser must have smiled again.

If one or two old-stagers like Chesser were stepping aside in the middle sixties, many more recruits were making the most of the new freedoms. There was a dentist who ran a clinic, several GPs who put up their plates in fashionable streets, anaesthetists who fancied richer pickings. Few of them wanted the law changed to make abortion easier, let alone — God forbid! — widely available under the Health Service. That would ruin the market. The delicate balance suited them. In the expensive consulting rooms, the business was pressing ahead. Dozens of gynaecologists in Harley Street and its environs sent patients into other liver-coloured houses to be examined by psychiatrists, to return with their certificates and have an appointment made for them to enter a nursing home in Stanmore or West Hampstead or Ealing. Some of the operators were eminent then; some have become eminent since. The hard core with the big turnover were out to make money, but that was nothing new in Harley Street. A few were undeniably rogues. Others were entertainers. Mr X, Member of the Royal College of Obstetricians and Gynaecologists, who dressed soberly and drove a fast car, was so anxious to be thought above-board that he showed me his accounts, or some of them. He is still alive.

The surgical side of X's work took him three and a half days a week, averaging about ten abortions a day, most of them in his private operating theatre on the premises. His gross turnover in 1966 was a quarter of a million pounds a year, all of it in cash. The old caution had gone. Cheques paid the day before an abortion were likely to be stopped the day after. He had no secrets; why should he worry about insisting on pound notes? A need had arisen and he was meeting it legally.

Most of the women he saw were unmarried. In the first week of January 1967 he operated on twenty-five, the youngest a girl of fifteen with a lover twice her age, for a fee of a hundred and seventy guineas. The most expensive abortion was procured on a married woman, separated from her husband; her age (forty-one) and the length of the pregnancy (eighteen weeks) meant a fee of three hundred guineas. 'If a woman can afford to pay,' he said, 'I have no hesitation in jacking up my fee.' The cheapest was for an Indian woman, and was only thirty-nine pounds. That week the single women included six secretaries, two clerks, a typist, a receptionist, a nurse, a teacher, a dressmaker, a singer and a stripper.

Later I was in touch with the three hundred-guinea patient, who said that X was 'very hard-hearted . . . He also spins a yarn on how hard it is to do etc. etc. Also the "nursing home" is a basement in New Cross [she was unlucky; there were better places] and I had a bed on the floor for my three hundred guineas. Even though you don't feel well you are chucked out one hour later.' Others rather took to Mr X. But it was not a business for the squeamish.

More babies were being born 'out of wedlock' – about twice as many in the mid-sixties as a decade earlier. At the same time, more were being aborted, both illegally and in Harley Street. The obvious conclusion was that X and the rest were making a fortune because some groups of the young were fornicating more, or more recklessly, than they used to. Moralists said, 'Of course.' Progressives made excuses.

At that time, anyone who broadcast or wrote on the subject, in a way that suggested knowledge of Harley Street's facilities, was bombarded with letters. 'I am an unmarried teacher of twenty-three yrs and my career will be shattered if . . .' 'The fact is that I have made a young woman pregnant . . .' 'I am forty years of age, with a sick husband. I am now two months' pregnant, and we have no one to turn to for advice

...' 'I cannot go to my own family doctor, who would be completely unsympathetic ...' 'How does one get to know of these Nursing Homes? ...' 'I left my husband ('cos he was very violent) before Christmas and now I find I am three months' pregnant ...' 'I am just about on the verge of panic ...' 'I am in a terrible state ...' 'I am eighteen and need now to save, not me particularly but my family, the shame and ignominy of it all. In early November I have three days' holiday from the bank and must in this time find some opportunity to get an abortion ...'

No doubt they were much the same as the letters Marie Stopes was receiving, in greater numbers, forty years earlier. These were bad times, but for women in trouble, when had they been anything else? The difference in 1966 was that something could be done. A name, an address, a phone number, would give admission to the network. Most women relied on word of mouth. Those who had to write to a stranger were the desperate ones, often in small towns or distant suburbs, who had no friend who knew the ropes. I told them what they wanted to know. Others were doing the same.

Abortionists were raking in money. Some of the greedier ones sent me bribes in plain envelopes, not much, five pounds here, ten pounds there, trying it on. I told them to stop, and forwarded the money to ALRA. But I went on sending them women, since there was no alternative; the greedier the doctor, the more likely he was to say yes. I interviewed a clinic proprietor in the West End. 'One could make a nice income, referring patients to us here,' he said as I was going. It was an unlovely business. One heard the horror stories, the blood-filled buckets, the cruel nurses, the dirty bed-linen, the lascivious doctors who were all fingers and smiles as they talked of 'naughty girls' and what they must expect. They were more acceptable, to the women who endured them, than the alternative, of not obtaining an abortion. If society wanted to do better, no one was stopping it.

Society, in the shape of the reforming Labour Government of 1964 to 1970, was finally moved to action when David Steel, the Liberal MP for a Scottish constituency, was persuaded by ALRA to sponsor a Termination of Pregnancy Bill, and Roy Jenkins, the Home Secretary, promised a benevolent neutrality. The measure was debated in and out of Parliament for more than a year from the summer of 1966. The diligent lobbyists of ALRA spent much of their time denying that the Bill they sought would mean that anyone who wished could have an abortion. This was disingenuous. The heart of the Bill, which was to survive undamaged, was a clause that permitted abortion if two doctors agreed that a woman's life or health, including mental health, was at risk; it confirmed the case law set out in Macnaghten's judgment of 1938, and (the medical profession being in clinical matters a law unto itself) it was left to the abortionist and his pal to evaluate 'risk' and 'health'. For obvious political reasons ALRA had to deny that abortion on demand lay at the end of this road. But effectively it did.

Few public controversies have said so much about the secret lives of women; none, till then, had been accompanied by the lurid detail that was now permitted reading. But the debate consisted largely of men — bishops, politicians, gynaecologists, journalists — arguing about what was best for women. Should 'social' conditions be taken into account? Would it be wiser to insist that one of the doctors involved in each abortion be a Health Service consultant?

Religious moralists, principally but not exclusively Roman Catholic, told women that to destroy the foetus was sin. For good measure women were warned that a foetus felt pain. They were confidently informed by psychiatrists opposed to abortion that the desire to end a pregnancy was a passing phase. A Society for the Protection of the Unborn Child was formed. Anti-abortionists spoke of souls and butchers, and used foetuses in plastic bags to frighten politicians and pregnant women. Even the progressives found it hard to say a good word for the Xs and Sugdens; and everyone joined hands to denounce the backstreet abortionists. Yet the women, who knew their own wishes, continued stubbornly to buy abortions of their own free will, as they had always done.

Even Leo Abse, the reforming Labour MP from Cardiff, decided he knew better than women. Abse is aptly described, in the blurb to his autobiography, as 'a colourful backbencher revelling in his minority role as a Welsh Jew.' His record as a sexual progressive is distinguished. When the abortion debates were going on, in 1966 and 1967, Abse was manoeuvring to get his Bill legalizing homosexuality through Parliament, ten years after Wolfenden had proposed the reform. He had a hard time. Quick to look for psychological truths behind public rhetoric, he wrote in his autobiography about the number of MPs who react violently to the idea of tolerating it because they are 'ever fearful that they may yield to its attractions.'

This is very likely true. But while Abse's conscience led him towards reform in one case, it made him oppose the abortion Bill with equal vehemence. The early pioneers of ALRA were, he wrote, 'intelligent shrill viragos.' Abse married late and had two children, one of whom suffered serious early illnesses; he likes to quote the Jewish precept that 'the world survives in the breath of little children.' To Abse, abortion on demand seemed like a triumph, not for women but for 'the thwarted men who, evoking their initial feelings of rejection as babes, release their hate upon all womankind.' In practical terms he did everything he could to oppose Steel's Bill, and ceased to fight it only because he was politically blackmailed: some of the supporters he needed in the House of Commons for the homosexual Bill to succeed resented his attacks on the abortion Bill, so he stopped the second in order to achieve the first.

Sexual reform of any kind aroused fierce questions of conscience. Freudians like Abse were entitled to view opponents as the prisoners of their unconscious, but the process works both ways. Abse, however sincere, was blind to the need for abortion that women have always felt. We all have our silent reasons; even for writing books about sex and the British. What matters is that a conflict was resolved. Parliament was persuaded and the law was changed, and quickly taken advantage of.

What was achieved was the de facto right to an abortion somewhere, not necessarily to an abortion within the NHS, which has always been unable or unwilling to cope with the demand. Few gynaecologists like the operation, and they may have religious objections. So charitable services were set up, charging modest fees, and came to carry out half the abortions. The system was imperfect, but for most women it felt like progress.

Buy Me and Stop One

Contraceptives still aroused sniggers in post-Chatterley Britain. The subject verged on indecency, as it had done since before the time of Marie Stopes, who died in 1958 a few days before her seventy-eighth birthday, convinced almost till her death that she was destined to reach a hundred and twenty. Her influence had made the subject discussable, but in a way (which was not her fault) that separated it from sex, or at least from anything remotely enjoyable.

It was generally thought to be all right for a married woman to visit a clinic and have a diaphragm fitted. The Family Planning Association, a charity set up in 1930, now ran hundreds of clinics, which provided an efficient but spartan service. There were nurses and part-time doctors (usually women) and the setting was medical. The patients sat half-dressed on hard chairs, waiting to have their problem attended to. It embarrassed them to have attention drawn to their sexual lives.

> We all looked at one another in silence because we knew that we were going to have the same thing done to us. It seemed sort of funny us all sitting there, showing one another publicly that we have sex with our husbands and all that.

The embarrassment was part of the safeguard. The FPA couldn't risk being tainted with dirt, lust and sin. Even its original title, the National Birth Control Council, was thought too explicit, and the blander version replaced it in 1939. Caution was part of its style.

> When I worked in a branch I used to go and sit with some of these poor souls – a woman crying, saying 'The doctor'll not see me. I'm to bring my man and he'll not come.' There used to be something on the form they filled in, *How many times do you have intercourse in a week?* If it was more than three times, the doctor used to get the woman to bring her husband, and tell him to behave himself. I'm being unkind. On the whole the FPA did a very good job. But it's absolutely true. It was burnt into my brain.

The FPA provided a network of clinics. Governments did nothing. When the Labour Government of 1945 was creating the National Health Service, the provision of birth control by the State was not considered. Presumably a government of national reconstruction thought it had better things to do. The chance was lost. It was 1966 before the Ministry of Health (under another Labour Government) told local authorities to improve their family-planning service, and implied that no distinction should be made between married and single. The previous pronouncement by the Ministry had been its memorandum of 1931. Also in 1966 the Royal College of Obstetricians and Gynaecologists said it approved of contraception; it was the first statement on the subject in its history.

The most popular contraceptive was the condom, tainted because it was available in packets to anyone who could afford two or three shillings. Prostitutes and men bought them, the latter mostly in men's hairdressers, where the only women to be seen were mothers accompanying infants. The barber's murmured 'Will there be anything else, sir?' as he brushed a customer's lapels was equalled in tactfulness only by the way he would palm a packet of three into the hand, if a Roman priest or a small boy were in the next chair. A small electric clock with the word 'Durex' on it was as far as point-of-sale advertising went. The London Rubber Company had to bribe shops to compensate them for the embarrassment factor. In 1960 condoms which cost a retailer fourpence-halfpenny each, when bought by the gross, cost the customer a shilling, giving the shop 166 per cent profit.

'Surgical stores' or 'rubber shops', offering their medley of sprays, douches, incontinence pads, pills (female and virility), creams, herbs, tonics and dubious literature, did a profitable trade in condoms with those who didn't mind being seen to enter such premises. Ordinary pharmacists were less keen. The only notice the Pharmaceutical Society would allow its members to display was a small sign in the window saying 'Family Planning Requisites'. Some wouldn't stock the beastly things at all; others stocked them but displayed no notice, so that the buyer in a strange town was never sure if he would be rebuffed.

The London Rubber Company's directors found this distressing. They spoke of 'protectives' and felt misunderstood, insisting that most people who used them did so chastely, in the marital bed. The company's literature was discreet. A booklet of 1958, 'Planned Families are Happy Families', gave warning on an outer envelope that it was only for the married, or those who soon would be. The booklet itself gave further warning of 'a sealed section at the end,' where, finally, after pages about the population problem, the responsible citizen came face to face with 'Durex Protectives: the Modern Method,' and all was revealed.

Advertising was so discreet that posters on the London Underground spoke only of 'Durex Housewear and Surgeons' Gloves.' Even this oblique approach was too much for the British Transport Commission, which banned the posters in 1960. Another of the company's tactful initiatives was an offer to give the infamous rubber shops of the Charing Cross Road smart new façades if only they would stop displaying sordid wares alongside the honest protective. The rubber shops were not interested.

Serious publicity came the way of the contraceptive industry in 1963, when the Consumers' Association decided it would test everything there was — condoms, caps, suppositories, creams, jellies, pastes. The results were published in a supplement to the magazine *Which?*, creating an acceptable news story that contained the kind of detail that popular newspapers would have shrunk from printing of their own accord. The *Daily Mirror's* Marjorie Proops called the report 'brave, splendid and incredibly frank,' and the paper devoted its centre-spread to a summary, with a warning on page one that readers who wanted it kept from their children should remove the pages.

Which? criticized the price and reliability of rubber goods, their testers having filled condoms with pints of water to see if they could make them burst, which London Rubber said was ridiculous. But the breaking of taboos was what mattered. The *Daily Herald's* headline was 'PLAIN WRAPPER COMES OFF BIRTH-CONTROL.' Caution, however, was still called for. Proops, the *Mirror's* family conscience, wrote primly that the allegedly faulty condoms had their merits. 'One thing about the report which pleases me: it may make those "unofficial" users of contraceptives – the unmarrieds – who slink into rubber goods shops think twice before taking a chance.' Contraceptives were not for the likes of them.

The condom could have remained a pariah for years if it had not been overtaken by 'the pill', which made all other forms of contraception look obsolete and so less threatening. Later events showed there was plenty of life in the condom, but in the beginning oral contraception seemed to be the solution that progressives had hoped for and moralists feared. It became part of the mythology of the 'permissive society', and it could be discussed with less embarrassment than other methods, especially condoms. The pill sounded like medicine, the condom was a reminder of the penis in action.

If the subject had not been so controversial, oral contraception might have been developed sooner. Farmers and veterinarians knew long before that a substance secreted by the ovaries made cattle barren, and that when its source was removed the beast became fertile. Doctors in Vienna were using the substance – eventually identified as a hormone and named progesterone – in animal experiments at the start of the twentieth century. Later an Austrian, Haberlandt, found a pharmaceutical company that would make an extract to be taken orally by women. He called it 'Infecundin', and it was briefly on sale, a nice idea but technically deficient, before he died in 1932.

By 1945, many experiments later, the idea that hormones might be used to inhibit ovulation, and thus pregnancy, was widely known, and could be read about in a leading American textbook. But it was a delicate subject. Research scientists or their institutions didn't care to pursue it, and the cause was left appropriately to the energies of two women, one radical and one rich. Both were elderly. Margaret Sanger was the radical. Earlier in the century, when the United States had a horror of contraception, she went to prison for advocating it. A former nurse, she invented or at least popularized the phrase 'birth control', and, unlike Marie Stopes the dreamer, fought the system with everyday polemics and anger. At times she had a touch of the Christabel Pankhursts ('Three out of every five married women in New York have gonorrhoea'). H.G. Wells had an affair with her when she visited Britain in 1920.

Sanger's friend was the wealthy Katherine McCormick, a biologist by training who had married money and seen her husband become insane. In the twenties she contributed to the birth-control cause, and both women kept an eye on technical developments. Sanger visited the Soviet Union in the thirties and discussed experimental work being done with chemical contraceptives, later abandoned when the regime decided (like the Nazis) that more births were required, not fewer.

The project that finally produced the contraceptive pill got under way in 1951. Sanger and McCormick conceived it with a biologist, Geoffrey Pincus, who was doing research into reproduction at Worcester, Massachussetts. McCormick had known him since he worked on schizophrenia, her husband's disease. No one else seemed interested in an anti-pregnancy pill. Given the unwavering opposition to birth control of the Roman Catholic Church, and some of the powerful Protestant fundamentalist sects, neither laboratories nor research foundations cared to risk making enemies. Kinsey was already incurring the moralists' wrath for asking inconvenient questions, and was soon to lose the support of the Rockefeller Foundation. McCormick, however, was a free agent. She agreed to finance Pincus; eventually the work cost her two million dollars.

G.D. Searle, one of the pharmaceutical firms that was producing the compounds to be tested, was at first uncertain whether it wanted to be seen as a maker of contraceptives. Its public relations department warned that the company's hitherto 'impeccable reputation' might be damaged. The first human trials were done in Puerto Rico and Haiti by Pincus and his colleagues, so soon after the initial research that the consequences to women were far from certain. The researchers argued that the extreme poverty sanctioned the tests. 'The gratitude of those selected', it was said, 'was pitiful.' There were no disasters; the pill worked. By 1961 oral contraceptives were being prescribed by doctors.

In Britain the pill took longer to be accepted than in America, and it was five or six years before it came into general use. At one manufacturer's symposium in London a doctor assured his audience, 'It is not enough to think of this contraceptive as just an anti-baby pill. It is more a wafer of love.' Nirvanah lay ahead. Young middle-class women were the first and most enthusiastic users, and it was more popular in the south of England than the north. Like the diaphragm, it allowed women to decide whether or not they became pregnant, but less messily and more efficiently. The idea of decrying the pill because it enabled men to pleasure themselves at women's expense – aired by feminists a generation later – would have seemed ludicrous to those in the sixties and seventies who saw it as the essence of liberation.

Germaine Greer wrote in 1984:

> I and my fellow fighters for sexual freedom strove to like our diaphragms, to the extent of wearing the springs from worn-out ones as ceremonial jewellery and marks of caste. Long before its use as a contraceptive was officially authorized, we were wheedling the oestrogen pill out of our doctors. No one who has ever forced herself to carry her dilly-bag with spermicide and diaphragm at all times and gamely tried to squirt and insert in the woods and on the beach . . . has not longed to do away with the whole kit and caboodle.

The merits of the pill were balanced against fears about what it might do to morals. Millions of people still took it for granted that contraceptives were dangerous if they 'got into the wrong hands.' Promiscuity worried the ladies who ran the FPA's clinics, and who had been brought up in beliefs unchanged since the nineteen-twenties; one headquarters official dropped her voice when she said 'french letters'. A generation of teenagers was beginning to toy with serious sex, but it went against the grain to help them. 'We are here to plan families,' was the line, which had to be maintained lest a more lenient view gave hostages to the enemies of contraception. In private some of the FPA's professionals knew it was a pretence, but for a long time they had to maintain it.

One of its members, Helen Brook (b. 1907), had the energy, and access to funds from a family friend, to go off in 1964 and found clinics of her own, the Brook Advisory Centres. The FPA's deputy director, Freda Parker, abetted her. Brook clinics saw women under the age of twenty-five without caring if they were married; girls of sixteen could go there. Mrs Brook was a heroine to those who agreed with her, evil to those who didn't. Her detractors spoke of 'the fornication lobby' and 'pedlars of promiscuity.'

None of this worried her. Educated at the Sorbonne, she married a banker before the Second World War. Her background would have annoyed any moralists who knew about it. Bored and well-off, she let herself be drawn into family planning in 1952. Ministering to the sexual needs of the poor in Islington seemed to her a peculiar business. When a woman first visited an FPA clinic she was shown how a diaphragm worked and given one to take home and practise. But it had holes in it; only later would she get the real thing. Women were advised to insert the device with one foot on the bath, but they had no baths. It was a bit like Marie Stopes forty years earlier, telling them to prepare for sex before they dressed for dinner. Women loaned their diaphragm to a neighbour and then became pregnant. Men refused to let their wives use an appliance because they said it got in the way. One man dragged it out of his wife and threw it in the fire. As they listened to all these tales, the interviewers wore hats.

Under the FPA's rules, only the married could be seen. This produced difficulties in the nineteen-fifties when young Caribbean women, immigrants to London from a society that cared less about virginity at marriage, began to visit clinics. The FPA, prodded by Helen Brook and others, got round the problem by making an exception as long as the women were in a stable relationship. The British remained bound by the rules. Every move towards freer policies had to be finessed. As time went on, FPA workers often bent the rules. But the official line was unyielding.

Marie Stopes was made to do a good work, after her death, of which she would not have approved in her life. Part of her estate, including the house in Bloomsbury where her clinic had been for many years, went to the Eugenics Society; she hated the FPA. The eugenicists (now a shadow of their old selves) and the family planners had friendly connections. A Marie Stopes Memorial Clinic was set up in the house, chiefly for unmarried women. Helen Brook became the director. In the basement, used for fitting contraceptives, Stopes had made her pastes and suppositories. Upstairs, shelves still held dusty volumes about controversies that no one remembered, *Nature Hits Back* and *Birthrate and Empire*. The grandchildren of Stopes' revolution, whose sexual lives she would have deplored, arrived in the shape of students from London University, a few streets away.

The Stopes clinic was the forerunner of the Brook centres, funded with a gift of fifteen thousand pounds. Sex, Mrs Brook used to say, rarely entered into old-fashioned family planning, which was about preventive measures, not enjoying oneself. The Brook philosopy stressed, as it was entitled to, the anomaly of a society that promoted large-scale sexual titillation but preached pre-marital chastity. The Brook board included Lord Brain, a leading physician; he was also president of the FPA. FPA rank and file were unmoved by his example. Two annual meetings refused to change the married-only rule.

Moralists saw the Brook concept as shameless. Lustful boys slinking into rubber shops were bad enough. Now lustful girls would be able to slink into Brook clinics. When one was opened in Birmingham, the fourth in the country, in 1966, the local branch of the British Medical Association said it was 'undercutting the whole basis of family medicine,' and felt sure that parents wouldn't want to see their children 'sneaking off' to what it described as a 'teenage sex clinic'. The Brook management was infuriated, not least because of the profession's own dismal record in family planning.

Clinic doctors (though few of them at first) were sometimes willing to prescribe the pill for a girl under sixteen, the minimum age of legal consent. Could they then be accused of aiding and abetting the serious offence committed by her lover? The answer seemed to be no, but there were uncertainties. Brook's advocates pointed to the rising number of under-age abortions and births. Its detractors, using the argument that was heard in other sexual contexts, said it was the wickedly permissive attitudes of people like Mrs Brook (and presumably Lord Brain, DM, FRCP, FRS) that produced the illicit sex in the first place. To blame the liberals of the sixties meant ignoring the long curve of sexual awakening among ordinary people that could be traced back through the century. But the accusation rolled easily off the tongue.

The cause of contraception was advanced by Parliament, up to a point. A Labour MP, Edwin Brooks, drew a place in a Private Members' ballot, and consulted Leo Abse about a family-planning Bill. Abse, busy pursuing homosexual legislation while his friends were blackmailing him over abortion, gave his support. It was a simple measure allowing local authorities to set up or support birth-control clinics for women, married or single. Harold Wilson's Government made room for it. Opponents talked of 'sex on the rates', but there were not many of them.

There was something artificial about the protests; it was characteristic of the long struggle over birth control that while churchmen, politicians and leader-writers debated the subject till they were blue in the face, people just went on using contraceptives; especially after 1945. In the end the State had to buck up and follow their lead.

While Abse was drumming up Parliamentary support, he was disappointed to find no opposition. He thought his colleagues' enthusiasm for the cause was morbid, deciding that what he had to thank was not their charitable nature but their unacknowledged castration fears, as a result of which they were 'demanding the symbolic castration of all others through state population control policies.' Perhaps they just thought it was easier to say yes.

The Bill was passed in 1967. Local authorities showed varying amounts of enthusiasm, sometimes none. By the end of the decade the FPA, which most authorities hired to provide the service, had a thousand clinics. Until the FPA changed its rule about the unmarried, which it didn't do until 1970, these clinics were officially unable to see the unmarried women that the law now permitted public money to be spent on.

Within itself the FPA reproduced wider conflicts in British life. An FPA pamphlet of 1971, *Straight Facts about Sex and Birth Control*, caused trouble out of all proportion to its modest intentions. It was published in the aftermath of a case in Birmingham where a doctor told the parents of a girl of sixteen that the local Brook Clinic had put her on the pill. He was a religious man, and believed it was 'not God's will for them to have intercourse before marriage.'

Birmingham was always a difficult city for reformers, with an innate conservatism among civic and professional figures, who resented being told by outsiders (as they saw it) how to run their affairs. Family-planning liberals in general were worried about the religious doctor, the Brook managers in particular; three-quarters of the clients attended without their parents' knowledge. Unwisely they reported him to the General Medical Council, a conservative body that was apt to be merciless towards a carnal act with a patient, and by the same token responsive to old sexual values. When the GMC cleared the doctor of misconduct in disclosing information, the verdict threatened to wreck the confidentiality on which clinics prescribing for teenagers relied.

Unless they married, few children in those days left home before they were twenty. It was only in 1969 that the Family Law Reform Act fixed the minimum age for marrying without parental consent at eighteen; previously it was twenty-one. The long march of the young towards early freedom was only beginning. The sense of independence for a boy might be related to his first job, but a girl's 'real life' traditionally began with marriage. Those who experimented with sexual relationships did so under the eyes of their families. Yet they were the ones, according to the new wave of family planners, whose need was greatest. Under the Abortion Act, more than twenty thousand teenagers a year were now having their pregnancies legally terminated.

The FPA's *Straight Facts* pamphlet was rushed out, not long after the GMC's verdict, with a slip-in leaflet headed 'You Can Trust the FPA', the idea being to hearten both the family planners and the young clients they wanted to attract. On the cover was a picture of a teenage boy and girl, her head on his shoulder. The contents were practical and explicit. Some of the rank and file were shocked; branches refused to handle it. What upset them was not so much the explicitness as the absence of references to 'immorality'. Teenagers were warned of 'several very unpleasant things' that could happen if a girl became pregnant by mistake, such as an abortion or a forced marriage, but that was the nearest it came to suggesting that unchastity was a punishable offence. I heard an old hand who was disgusted by *Straight Facts* say, 'I had to wait till I was twenty-five before *I* had sexual intercourse. Why shouldn't they?'

The pamphlet came out under the aegis of Caspar Brook (not related to the other Brooks), who had been Director of the FPA since 1968. Brook (b. 1920), a dashing fellow with experience in publishing and consumerism, had no time for fools. He saw himself as the chief executive of a business, which is what the progressives in the movement wanted. When he read the pamphlet in typescript, a sentence in a section on VD caught his eye. It said that the chances of infection were reduced if both partners 'pass water' as soon as possible after having sex. Brook saw no reason for this old-fashioned euphemism. He crossed it out and substituted 'pee'. This, too, caused offence. FPA clients didn't pee.

Because of strong feelings in branches, a revised edition of the pamphlet was published. It now included a section about the chaste approach to sex, summed up by the sentence, 'There is no reason at all to feel that you must have sex because you think everybody else is doing it all the time.' Standard disclaimers of this kind are now common, but progressives were more doctrinaire then, and they resented having to use platitudes that they suspected would have no effect on morality but might alienate teenagers who were preached at often enough as it was. 'Pee' reverted to 'pass water'.

The revised *Straight Facts*, in July 1971, coincided with another embarrassment for the FPA as alternative views collided. The Association was to hold a three-day conference at the Festival Hall, 'New Frontiers of Birth Control', with speakers from government, medicine and education. It was to mark fifty years of progress since Marie Stopes opened her first clinic. Someone, probably Caspar Brook, decided to mount fringe events that might attract the young. Music, films and information booths were promised. The FPA advertised it in *Time Out*, then an underground magazine: 'Birth Beat − giant talk-in on sex and sensibility.' Alongside the ad was another for Swedish condoms, 'with free pin-up calendar.' London Rubber had donated ten thousand balloons to be filled with gas and floated over the capital, a wheeze on the lines of the rubber gloves in the Underground advertisements.

None of this educational jollity came to anything. When the *Daily Express*, still finding mileage in prudery, got wind of Birth Beat and mounted an attack ('Pop and the Pill: This is no way to teach the young'), the FPA abandoned the fringe within hours, rather than risk compromising the rest.

These were rearguard actions. In the main contraception flourished, yet never as neatly and conclusively as its advocates had hoped. Family planning became part of the Health Service in 1973 and the FPA's thousand clinics were taken over by the State. What women failed to do was become logical birth controllers, organizing their fertility with the aid of science. Something in them rebelled or was indifferent. Soon more than a hundred and fifty thousand of them a year would be having abortions, ending pregnancies that they might, in theory, have avoided. There is evidence from many countries that a high incidence of birth control means a high rate of abortion; use one, why not use the other? It was more complicated than the world of Marie Stopes.

Never So Much Together

Marriage was the substance around which the nation was built, and in the first half of the twentieth century only a few dissidents questioned the need to make marriages last. Church and State agreed that it was the institution whose rituals and regulations protected people against themselves, within which they were safe to confide, dream, make love and bring up children to do the same again. But it proved as vulnerable as everything else to the desire for change. An appetite for divorce overwhelmed the system that was supposed to control it. In 1969 the law was reformed, making divorce easy and leading to what has been called 'the most profound and far-reaching social change to have occurred in the last five hundred years.' Marriage still thrived but now it was negotiable.

The essence of getting into marriage had been for centuries that it was impossible to get out again except through death, which often happened sooner rather than later. Until the latter part of the nineteenth century, one marriage in three was ended by bereavement within twenty years. My forebear James Ferris, a woollen worker of Trowbridge, in Wiltshire, married Mary Ann Barnes in 1825. He was twenty-five, she was twenty-three, already a widow. Mary Ann bore him at least four children before he died of tuberculosis when he was forty-four, leaving her widowed for the second time. When last heard of she was sixty, living with a grown-up son and daughter, working as a washerwoman.

Divorce was beyond the comprehension of the poor. Divorce courts were created by the Matrimonial Causes Act of 1857, and thereafter a hundred or two decrees were granted each year in England and Wales (the Scots had their own more civilized arrangements), the numbers climbing slowly, reaching five hundred early in the century, a thousand at the end of the First World War. By the early thirties it was about four thousand a year, still a negligible figure, despite much wringing of hands. But it was enough to keep marriage in the frame, an institution that had to be defended.

It was assumed that women were not the problem. Women romanticized marriage. Reformers who had been talking about it since the nineteenth century as 'legalized prostitution' didn't get much of a hearing from those they were trying to help. Women could be trusted to dwell on marriage; it was their career. (It had to be, when jobs for married woman were difficult to get, and in any case were disapproved of. Marriage was a way to earn a living.) When a wedding involved an important family, local newspapers reported the minutiae for women readers, down to the presents. An evening newspaper told its readers (January 1925) that a Miss Bostock was receiving

> from the groom, pearl necklace. From her mother, fur coat and Minton tea set. Pair of brass water jugs, case of two carvers, riding crop, silver cigarette box, old Chippendale bookcase, four glass bon-bon dishes, crocodile handbag, ostrich-feather fan, leather blotter . . .

The groom, Mr Glasbrook, was not forgotten:

Shooting stick, water colour, pair of old Sheffield candelabra, old china dessert dishes, silver inkstand, hunting crop, brass chestnut roaster, snow-leopard rug, glass coffee machine, fountain pen, silver cigarette box . . .

Women were the preservers of marriage ritual that took them from one state of life into another. The charms were to ward off evil spirits, the veil was part of the bride's protective wrapping; she was not supposed to look back at the house when she left it to get married. Weddings generated an energy. Philip Larkin (who never married) wrote in his poem 'The Whitsun Weddings' of seeing newly-wed couples on a Saturday join his London-bound train – 'and what it held/Stood ready to be loosed with all the power/That being changed can give.' Harry wrote of his first wedding, 'I felt not myself. I came-to some three days later. Sheila was not the same, I couldn't say in what way, precisely. She said (*of course, she would*) that SHE was exactly the same, I was the one who had changed. How typical.'

Women were said to look different after marriage, to fill out and enjoy better health. A verse by Catullus says of the wedding night that 'the nurse, revisiting her charge at daybreak, shall not be able to encircle her neck with yesterday's thread.' The custom of measuring a bride's neck before and after the wedding night was still in use in rural France a century ago, according to Havelock Ellis; if the thread still fitted in the morning, it meant the marriage had not been consummated. Professor Arthur Thomson, an Oxford anatomist earlier in the century, thought the thyroid gland might be stimulated by male secretions – the magical semen and accompanying substances that Marie Stopes thought so highly of. Thomson wrote that 'among musicians it is recognized that the female voice never attains to its full pitch of excellence until marital relations have been established.' More likely the crucial event, if any, is (or was) the ending of sexual frustration, not the magical male secretions.

Marriage, anyway, was a women's event. Romantic fiction that ended in happy marriage had been devoured by women readers since the nineteenth century. Even the adventure stories in Harmsworth's magazines were likely to be rounded off in church. 'This was the beginning of a happiness for bride and bridegroom which no cloud of sorrow ever came to mar' (*The Marvel*, 1890s). While the Suffragettes were denouncing men before the First World War, soft-centred romances in limp covers featuring clear-eyed heroes and swooning women were already being devoured by non-feminist readers. The genre has survived, though not unscathed. Mills & Boon, publishers of romantic fiction, asserted in their style-sheet for authors (1988) that 'It is all right for the hero and heroine to go to bed together, although a wedding should follow almost immediately.' References to the heroine's 'hidden places' and the hero's 'hard male strength' are also apparently in order. The cinema was not explicit for fifty years or more. Films conformed to strict moral regulations, as in Hollywood's Production Code dating from 1934, which ruled that 'the sanctity of the institution of marriage and the home shall be upheld.' Women who went to the pictures expected nothing less.

Early in the century, writers like Wells and Shaw were dismissing the false promise of the perfect marriage, without their words having any effect on the people, mainly women, who wanted their romance. In his *Marriage and Freedom* (1946) Eustace Chesser attacked 'romantic rubbish' with its myth of 'marriages made in heaven' that was often commended for its suitably moral tone. Men, too, he suggested, could be enslaved by the quest for non-existent fairy princesses, an attitude 'drilled into them by a score of agencies, ranging from home influence to the BBC.' But Chesser on romance wasn't as credible as Chesser on sexual intercourse. The idea of a marriage as something ordained by fate has persisted. 'Marriage is destiny,' said a sixteenth century proverb.

Men were supposed to get the best of marriage in material things, but paradoxically marriage made men feel hard done by. Any comedian could raise a laugh by walking on to a stage and saying, 'I am a married man.' The Clerkenwell magistrate, dealing with a marital dispute (February 1921), said that he had

> invariably found that where a man knocked his wife about, it was the wife's fault . . . Under the good old law a man could thrash his wife so long as the stick was no thicker than his thumb. But now the law is wobbly, weak-kneed, and we have instead these miserable maintenance orders. There is no domestic happiness.

Sexually it was men who had the freedom in marriage. Suffragettes and other early feminists complained about prostitutes because men, certainly those higher up the social scale, enjoyed commercial sex as a matter of course. Sleeping with a prostitute was not 'real' infidelity. In Roman law a harlot could not commit adultery; thousands of Edwardian Englishmen felt the same.

Until 1923 a man's adultery with anyone, harlot or mistress, was not enough for his wife to divorce him; there had to be additional aggravation in the shape of cruelty, desertion, incest, bestiality, sodomy or rape. A single proven act of adultery by her, however, and the husband got his divorce. When the reform of 1923 was being discussed in Parliament, only a few MPs were brave enough to say outright that a man's casual infidelity, perhaps while away from home, was not to be compared with a wife's fall from grace. No doubt many thought it, while voting for the same standard, divorce for adultery, to apply to both.

The sexual side of marriage was more easily discussed as time went on. Within living memory marital sex had been a kind of imperfection, or had been made to sound it. It was base and animal, whereas marriage was spritual and hygienic. Before the First World War the marriage manuals enjoined caution. A. Dennison Light wrote in *Marriage: Before and After*,

> To act in the marriage bed like the beasts that perish is to rob married life of its joy and peace. Nothing can so easily break up happy married life as an insistence in either party on too frequent indulgence in sexual intercourse.

There wasn't much of that in print by the nineteen-thirties. Sexual pleasure for married women (not for spinsters, of course) was having to be conceded. Marie Stopes had no time for 'Lord X', who told her – she wrote in 1928 – that with *Married Love* she had 'broken up the home; you have let women know about things which only prostitutes ought to know; once you give women a taste for these things, they become vampires, and you have let loose vampires into decent men's homes.' But the fact that a more realistic approach to marriage was emerging didn't stop the romantic view continuing to flourish, and perhaps made the romance seem all the more necessary.

The modern industry of worrying about marriage got under way. The unfailingly sober reports of the Marriage Guidance Council (founded 1938) were typical, with their almost religious air; social workers were taking on the authority that used to belong to clergymen, who were themselves well represented in its ranks. The 1952 report had a photograph of the young Queen and Prince Philip, holding the infant Charles and Anne. Otherwise the pictures were of bald middle-aged men. The report noted with relief that divorces were falling from their post-war peak of sixty thousand in 1948; they were now about half that figure.

Ten 'General Principles' were listed, describing how best to safeguard 'the family unit' which was 'of vital importance to the future welfare of the nation.' Only 'permanent monogamous marriage' would do. The right basis for personal and social life was to avoid sexual intercourse outside marriage. 'Scientific contraception' could help married couples space their children, but was dangerous when 'misused . . . to escape the duties and disciplines of marriage and parenthood.' A phrase about parenthood fulfilling the 'racial end' of marriage echoed the old eugenic litany.

The quiescent style of the fifties enabled this idealized version of a moral marriage to sustain itself a little longer. Fears, conscious or unconscious, about threats to family life may have been a factor in the authorities' harassment of homosexuals. The annual divorce figures were down to 24,000 by the end of the decade, in spite of the fact that legal aid for matrimonial work had been available to the poor since 1948. Perhaps the nation had taken a grip of itself. But by 1962 the figures were climbing again. The sadness of the empty marriage, the artificial holding-together of relationships that were over, seemed more culpable now than in the past. In the words of Louis MacNeice's poem *Les Sylphides*, written twenty years earlier,

> So they were married – to be the more together –
> And found they were never again so much together,
>   Divided by the morning tea,
>   By the evening paper,
>   By children and tradesmen's bills . . .

Marriage had been realistically assessed by tens of thousands of spouses who wished to get unmarried after the upheavals of the Second World War. In the early fifties a Labour MP, Mrs Eirene White, promoted a Bill to allow divorce after a separation of seven years, against the wishes of one party if necessary, and so introduced the idea of 'matrimonial breakdown' instead of 'matrimonial offence'. It failed because the Government wouldn't support it, but a preliminary vote showed strong support. Officially, if one listened to the voices of authority, monogamy remained the only decent way of life. But people were changing their minds.

After an inconclusive Royal Commission, another private Bill with a seven-year-separation clause, this time Leo Abse's, failed in 1963. Soon after, the advice of the Church of England was sought on a crucial matter of social policy, perhaps for the last time in its history. The Archbishop of Canterbury, Michael Ramsey, formed a committee to 'review the law of England concerning divorce.' Of its thirteen members, ten were lay and three clerical. To most people's amazement (including Abse's), its resulting report, *Putting Asunder* (1966), proposed that 'irremediable marriage breakdown' should replace the concept of matrimonial offence as the basis for divorce. In future, it would be nobody's fault.

Three years earlier the Church of England had dismissed Abse's 'seven-year' proposal because it undermined Christian marriage. Now, without the established Church on its side, the moral opposition to divorce reform became politically irrelevant. A report by the Law Commission, which was composed of judges and lawyers (who had seen the inadequacies of the divorce law at first hand), made their own proposals, which went too far for many Anglicans. But the Church, having performed its function of sanctioning a secular innovation, was now dismissed from the debate. The Labour Government that would deal with abortion and homosexual relations was in power; divorce joined the queue. It was a momentous shift in informed opinion, hard to pin down, but the process must have been going on for years, under the moralists' noses. As with abortion and contraception, the true level of demand was concealed by the opponents of change.

Women fought a rearguard action of sorts. Wives (or some of them) came out with the same accusation whenever divorce reform was in the air: men were beasts, men were promiscuous, men would swap a middle-aged wife for a young one. The charge was made before the Act of 1857 (and endorsed by Gladstone), and again at the time of A.P. Herbert's reforms of 1938, when desertion and cruelty were being added to the grounds for divorce, and the Mothers' Union was opposing him. In 1969, when the Divorce Bill was being argued through Parliament, the attack was headed by a Labour life peer in her late sixties, the former Edith Summerskill, 'once beautiful', as Abse put it unkindly, and 'singularly equipped to tune in to the latent apprehensions of fading middle-class, middle-aged women.' The fading Lady Summerskill gave him a run for his money, coining the slogan 'Casanovas' Charter' and delaying the Bill; but only for a while.

Under the new law there were no guilty parties. From 1 January 1971, the old matrimonial offences − adultery, cruelty − survived only as evidence that the marriage had broken down. Desertion for two years would do equally well. Living apart for two years guaranteed a divorce, as long as both parties agreed. After five years of separation no agreement was necessary: either party was entitled to a divorce.

In theory, as with the Abortion Act, the citizen had no absolute right of demand. Legal requirements had to be satisfied; divorce was not automatic. In practice those who sought it found they could obtain it. 'Cruelty', too, was no longer cruelty, having recently been redefined by the law lords as the vaguer 'intolerable behaviour', which could include almost anything. Within a year of the Act divorces went beyond a hundred thousand a year, and are now around a hundred and sixty thousand. Three-quarters of the petitioners are women; the Act was not a Casanovas' charter after all. Other predictions, too, were proved wrong. The Divorce Act was supposed to help people escape a life of sin and get re-married, thus reducing births outside wedlock. Instead, cohabitation and the one-parent family were to become part of normal society.

Abortion and divorce, and to a lesser extent contraception, had always been regarded as issues that were too important to let the individual settle on the basis of his personal preferences. They involved the duties and obligations of a society that knew its destiny, or used to think that it did. When the debates of the sixties were in progress, the responsible side of human nature was constantly emphasized by progressives. Legal abortion would sweep the backstreets clean, universal contraception would eliminate abortion, easier divorce would make marriage a healthier institution. No one would act *lightly*. Most of this was expedient window-dressing. Sexual autonomy, once achieved, can be used for whatever people want it to be used. The reality is that many women have found abortion a useful palliative, that marriage can be important or expendable as individuals choose, that contraceptives help millions to fornicate in safety. One doesn't have to pretend that human nature is any better than it was.

Quintin Hogg, later Lord Hailsham, remarked in a debate on the Divorce Bill that the number of divorces had risen tenfold in the past thirty-five years. 'Are we sure how much human happiness has increased during those thirty-five years?' he asked. 'Would anyone care to dogmatize?' But happiness is something else.

Harry's diary, Tuesday 28 March 1972:

> Grace has been quarrelling with me concerning (a) Sheila, who sent me a birthday card last week showing yachts in the Solent, which according to Grace is code for telling me, *Do you remember how happy we were?* etc. etc. etc., (b) the visit of her friend Kath, who teaches R.I. at a C of

E school, and has been engaged twice but is still not married. The sins of Harry are as follows: Knowing that the said Kath was having an early night because she was driving to Gloucester in the morning, he made it his business to go out to the car in the drive on a pretext (consult a road map), from which he could see into the downstairs bathroom where the frosted glass is cheap stuff and the outline of Kath could be detected (Grace: 'I saw you from upstairs. Don't deny it'). I didn't, I didn't. I told her she was excited at my seeing Kath naked, even if through a glass darkly. She asked if Sheila had known I was a voyeur. I said, I am worse, I rummaged through the dirty clothes basket when you were both out yesterday and found a pair of Kath's pants. (This was not true. It might have been true.) She said I was a pervert. I said, go ahead, divorce me, I'm sure it counts as mental cruelty, Tom B— says that his wife is alleging he humiliated her conversationally in front of friends and colleagues, and her solicitor says that may be sufficient. Grace came back to my birthday card, and I said that Sheila and I could never live together again. Never, never, never. She kissed me and I put my hand on her breast and could feel her heart going. So that was all right.

11

'Letting it All Hang Out'
Radical Voices

RADICAL IDEAS ABOUT SEX were becoming so common that the 'official' reforms emerging from Parliament lost some of their novelty as they were swept into wider currents and diluted. Women's Lib got under way in America, at first with the unpromising title of Chick Lib, a reference to the chicks who made coffee, typed letters and took their clothes off for the male activists, protesting against racial segregation and the Vietnam War.

As they struggled for an identity, the radicals, like the Suffragettes, knew the importance of going to extremes. But the movement had no single political aim, like votes for women, that lay within the gift of a government; arson and bombs were not appropriate weapons. It was a time of stunts. WITCH, the Women's International Terrorist Conspiracy from Hell, invaded the New York Bridal Fair wearing black veils. They sang 'Here come the slaves, Off to their graves,' and let loose two hundred white mice. In September 1968 women picketed the Miss America pageant in Atlantic City. An unfortunate sheep was crowned, and liberated women were invited to fling items of clothing that symbolized oppression into a dustbin. Stiletto-heeled shoes, suspender belts and bras were collected. Bras were not actually burnt, but the idea of women doing it was a good joke, no doubt coined by a man who had in mind the serious business of burning Vietnam War draft cards.

As with the Suffragettes, men had to see feminists as either comical or a menace, preferably the former. A British newspaper cartoon showed a woman on a soap-box demanding freedom from the 'eternal drudgery of switching on washing machines, spin driers, dishwashers and vacuum cleaners.' Angry feminists invited mockery. In 1970 a gynaecologists' conference in Holland was invaded by a group who pulled up their blouses to show the slogan 'BOSS OF OUR OWN BELLY' crayoned on their stomachs. Women disrupted a Miss World contest in London with football rattles and stink bombs. Like the topless-dress craze of a few years earlier, it was seen as outrageous exhibitionism. One had Prince Charles' word for it. 'Basically,' he said, 'I think it is because they want to be men.'

The movement established itself in an oddly retrospective way, calling up ghosts from the past so that the present aligned itself with an unwritten history of women that had been there all the time. Whatever the temporary absurdities of the feminist revolution, it had always to be measured against a long collective memory. In one obvious example, abortion-law reform, women played a significant part, although in Britain, none of those who helped achieve the Steel Act regarded themselves as 'liberated women', since their efforts predated the phrase. The long and honourable list includes Stella Browne, Dora Russell, Joan Malleson, Janet Chance and Alice Jenkins earlier in the century; Madeleine Simms, Vera Houghton, Dilys Cossey, Diane Munday in the crucial years of the campaign. But in modern accounts the chronology is blurred, and not surprisingly, militant feminism is seen reaching back in time to include those who had done their work before a single mythological bra was burnt. (By their nature militant texts have also had to ignore the men who contributed to abortion reform, Haire, Baird, Diggory, Steel and others; even Chesser and Sugden and Mr X, in their fashion.)

Views about women's sexual nature were revised. Among the accidental contributors to the debate were the American researchers Masters (a male gynaecologist) and Johnson (his woman assistant), who concluded that women's capacity for sexual pleasure was as great as men's. Any number of people, including poets and the writers of pornography, had always assumed this to be so. But studying sex was now a serious academic subject and needed its own evidence, which, presented as scientific truth, did, in fact, change people's perception even when they said in the same breath, 'We all know that.'

Following on Kinsey's feats of persuasion, Masters and Johnson had no difficulty in finding couples who would lie naked on a bed, electrodes attached to them, having sexual intercourse in the presence of a camera crew as well as Mr Masters and Mrs Johnson. *Human Sexual Response* (1966), based on work that began in 1954, led to further studies and an industry devoted to 'sex therapy' for both men and women; a poor sexual response became a disability. The delicate matter of vaginal lubrication and whence it came was solved; science enabled the unspeakable to be put into print for the layman. The clitoris would soon be regarded as dispassionately as a thumb; Masters and Johnson said it was invariably the source of a woman's orgasm, though later researchers (and Harry) queried the 'invariably'.

But the clitoris became political. 'Many men are not able to find this tiny organ,' wrote the popular sexologist Rennie Macandrew (1941). The tiny organ now found itself regarded as a power-centre that worked regardless of men and their penises. The way was opened for the rise of the lesbian, backdated to take care of history; Christabel Pankhurst was made a retrospective lesbian, with hints that her mother Emmeline may have been one as well.

The main stream of sexual reform was not feminist at all, though it always had feminist implications. Pleasure and freedom were the stated aims, and a series of people and episodes helped to dramatize what was happening. Early populist figures in Britain among the permissives included Dr Martin Cole (b. 1931), who became famous for a film of 1970 called *Growing Up*, an awkwardly made exercise in sex education which featured fifteen seconds of intercourse and two bouts of masturbation, one by a boy aged fifteen, the other by a young woman of twenty-three. The film was meant to be shown at schools and universities, as an antidote to what Cole saw as the sexless sex-education films of the time which 'began and ended with pictures of babies and mothers pushing prams.' In later years he conceded that the film's real intention was to 'make a statement', which is what Mary Whitehouse and the irate city fathers of Birmingham (where Cole was a lecturer in genetics) suspected all along.

The statements that Cole made were related to his own life, in which his sub-career as a sexual reformer, adviser and propagandist played a central part. He made contact with abortion-law reformers in 1963 when he thought that a woman with whom he was having an affair was pregnant; his first marriage had ended as a result of the affair. The network passed him on to Mr X, and although the pregnancy turned out to be a false alarm, he became involved with the abortion reformers, and began a branch of their association in Birmingham.

By the end of the sixties he had helped start the local Brook clinic (contraception for the single woman) and the first pregnancy advisory service (cheap private abortions under the Act), set up an Institute for Sex Education and Research, and ended a second marriage. It was the Institute that made *Growing Up* and other films, among them *Sexual Intercourse*, thirty-three minutes of explicit activity, which brought detectives to see him after he had shown it to the Law Society in Liverpool. The DPP studied a print, but it was sufficiently instructional, and no action was taken. Cole saw no point in being coy about sexual arousal, arguing that sex education needed it in order to make sense. He thought that society subjugated the young (which it did); his critics thought him subversive (which he was). There was not much room for manoeuvre.

From 1972 the Institute was involved in 'surrogate therapy', the wondrous method of improving people's (usually men's) sexual performance by providing a temporary partner. The idea came from Masters and Johnson (1970), who had to stop using surrogates because of bad publicity. Denuded of its jargon, the method involves little more than the aphrodisiac effect of a new lover. Not surprisingly, it often works. Over the years the Institute 'treated' several hundred people, most of them men. Cole himself sometimes acted as a surrogate, and on one notable occasion, during the early eighties, he had embarked on therapy with an attractive young woman when a neighbour reported seeing a car parked outside, containing a man and, on the back seat, a camera with a telephoto lens. This turned out to be from the *News of the World*.

Charming Tina, housewife, and her husband Bob, insurance broker, were not what they seemed. They had written from Wolverhampton to say that 'making love has always been awkward, although there is nothing physically wrong.' After completing Eysenck Personality Inventories and telling Cole they had gone off one another, each was given an appointment for a surrogate session. Tina and Cole proceeded to lie, fully dressed, in, or on, a bed. He had her wired up to a machine that measured galvanic skin response and was surprised to observe, when he undid her bra, that the apparatus registered no change. They did not, in the jargon, proceed to intercourse; nor did Bob with his surrogate. A week later, having rumbled their identity, Cole wrote stiffly to say that therapy was off. He has continued to be a sexual propagandist; of late without expecting too much of the propaganda. His third marriage has long since ended, but he is not short of companionship.

Pornography was providing another kind of subversion. Books that would have frightened publishers before *Lady Chatterley* were now worth attempting. In 1963 Mayflower Books tried a paperback of *Fanny Hill*, Cleland's decorously written erotic novel of 1748, hoping it would be regarded as a classic. The authorities didn't risk a prosecution with a jury, which Mayflower requested, but had the book brought before a magistrate, who thought it obscene and made a destruction order.

Technically such orders are effective only in the district covered by the court. Shops went on selling *Fanny Hill* surreptitiously. Harry bought a copy in Leicester and started reading it on the bus going home. He said it was the first book he had encountered for years that gave him an instant erection; evidence perhaps of the book's power to corrupt, except that, as Harry remarked, he had doubtless been corrupted for years. (This was an argument that appealed to Southampton justices in 1971, when they refused to convict a bookseller for stocking such titles as *Dingle Dangle No 3* and *Oral Artist*, on the grounds that his customers were likely to be 'inadequate, pathetic, dirty-minded men seeking cheap thrills,' and presumably wearing long mackintoshes. The House of Lords entertainingly restored the original conviction, declaring (by three to two) that even the corrupted could become more corrupt.)

Books were beginning to creep through the gap that *Lady Chatterley* had opened. The big literary prosecution of the sixties concerned Hubert Selby Jr.'s novel *Last Exit to Brooklyn*, which John Calder issued in 1966. Calder, a Scot, born 1927, at first a dilettante publisher with family money (timber and whisky) in the background, had come to specialize in progressive fiction, usually by non-British writers. Samuel Beckett was one of his authors. Calder dealt in books that were unsettling influences, and it would not have been surprising if someone had him on a list.

In 1963, when Henry Miller's erotic thirties novel *Tropic of Cancer* was openly available in America and France, he published it in Britain, first writing to the DPP and listing the literary witnesses he proposed to call if necessary. There was no prosecution. Calder also published fiction by the American William S. Burroughs in which drug addiction and sadistic homosexuality might have interested the authorities, but didn't.

Last Exit to Brooklyn offered further glimpses of urban squalor, this time in New York slums where bad characters come to sticky ends. The violence and sex (much of it homosexual) was painfully explicit, but the book was seriously written and respectable shops were selling it, so the DPP decided to leave it alone. This was summer 1966. An agitation against the book then began in Parliament, led by religious-minded MPs. A predecessor to Abse's homosexual reform Bill, which was passed the following year, was attracting support, and its opponents may have seen their fear of unnatural vices realized in *Last Exit*. Having failed to convince the authorities, Parliament's arch-Christian, Sir Cyril Black MP, began a private prosecution.

Occasions where the sexual wars of the time went further than words were rare. Black (1902–1991) was just the man for a fight with the forces of darkness, a puritan with money. He was a property-developer, a fact his opponents liked to remember. A Baptist lay-preacher, in his time he had opposed mini-skirts, the advertising of alcohol on television, the opening of most things on Sundays, and the sale of condoms from slot machines. His views on homosexuality were the Bible's — 'Thou shalt not lie with mankind, as with womankind: it is abomination,' Leviticus 18, verse 22. Black's steely uprightness earned him respect from many, though not Calder, who suggests that *Last Exit* was precisely 'a book about the kind of people created by Black,' meaning Black the property developer.

Black sought a destruction order from the Marlborough Street magistrate, Leo Gradwell, who allowed expert witnesses to give evidence before making up his mind. Men of letters (Anthony Burgess, Frank Kermode) defended the book, but the opponents of filth had rallied their forces since *Chatterley*, and the prosecution called witnesses. The author Montgomery Hyde, a former barrister and MP, said *Last Exit* was nauseating. Sir Basil Blackwell, the Oxford bookseller, made the almost unheard of admission that 'to some extent' it had depraved and corrupted him; he was seventy-seven. Captain Robert Maxwell MP, as he then was, thought the book muck and filth, but spoiled the effect by replying, when asked if he thought *The Decameron* should be published, 'The what?'

The magistrate observed that Shakespeare's *Antony and Cleopatra* contained an obscenity, and gave the reference, Act I, Scene II. One of Cleopatra's attendants remarks,

> Well, if you were but an inch of fortune better than I, where would you choose it?

and another attendant replies,

> Not in my husband's nose,

But Gradwell (b. 1899) was not on the side of *Last Exit*. An old naval man, who had served in both world wars, he referred to the brutality he saw when he worked as a deckhand on trawlers, and may have been, as many were, nervous about homosexuality at sea. The three copies seized were ordered to be destroyed.

So Black had his victory. But, since the prohibition applied only in the Marlborough Street area, Calder said the book would continue to be distributed. The Attorney-General was driven to bring a full prosecution, and in December 1967 a jury at the Old Bailey found *Last Exit* guilty, and the judge imposed a nominal fine. Six months later the court of appeal reversed the decision because of misdirection by the judge, and Calder was free to sell a book whose title must by now have been known to a million or two people, thanks to Cyril Black.

Fellow-Christians criticized Black. He admitted that no constituent ever complained to him about the book, and that many clergymen were lukewarm in their support. But he was indifferent. Not long before his death, an ancient figure in a sombre suit in the back room of an office in Wimbledon, where he attended assiduously to his properties and companies, he said that perhaps there was not as much pornography to be seen as at the time of *Last Exit*, though he admitted he might be wrong; he was not in the habit of reading that kind of literature. But no matter, what he did was 'a blow struck for righteousness.'

Immediately after the Old Bailey trial, the *People* began an investigation of pornography in London. Montgomery Hyde, who had told the court how vile *Last Exit* was, toured Soho and reported on the thriving industry, noting that one of his own books, *A History of Pornography* (1964), was on sale, and taking another stab at Calder's book. But publishers were no longer cowed by adverse verdicts, and certainly not Calder, who wrote briskly to the *People*, suggesting that the book's only crime was that it pointed out unpleasant facts of modern life, and that most people in porn shops looked rather like Hyde, 'elderly gentlemen of comfortable means.' Calder teased Hyde (1907–1990) about his interest in sexual subjects, as in his book about pornography ('It is, I suppose, a contribution to knowledge'), bringing a slightly too furious reply from the author —

> Mr Calder's suggestion that I was prompted to write my 'History of Pornography' because of the same kind of interest in dirty books as that of the customers of the dirty bookshops, is thoroughly despicable. Nothing could be further from the truth. The book was commissioned by a leading firm of publishers ... My 'fieldwork' – not a particularly agreeable exercise, I may add – was carried out not in the sleazy Soho bookshops, but in the library of the British Museum, where the literature of pornography is made available to students under the strictest conditions.

If it was hard for people born in a distant England to cope with a book like *Last Exit to Brooklyn*, it was even harder for them to see any reasonable cultural purpose in the underground magazines that were circulating by the early seventies. Several were prosecuted, the most notorious being a 'schoolkids' issue' of *Oz* in 1970, edited by teenagers. In the dock were the three adult editors, the Australian Richard Neville and two colleagues. It was said half-seriously that what offended the authorities most was a comic strip showing Rupert Bear, cartoon friend from many a middle-class childhood, perform a running rape on a grotesque woman called Gipsy Granny. The *Oz* pictures were based on a strip by the American artist Robert Crumb, with Rupert Bear's head substituted for the original character's; the more that middle-class childhoods were derided, the better.

The underlying tone was that of the alternative society, so-called, which had begun in California half a dozen years earlier, offering an easy-going culture of soft drugs, long hair and casual sex. It was the 'Love Generation', telling the young (meretriciously, as it turned out) that men in suits had had their day. Neville defended himself with long brilliant speeches, and the trial, which extended over six weeks, the longest obscenity hearing in a British court, provided an unparalleled platform for the alternative viewpoint. The suits struck back by ensuring that all three defendants had their heads shorn while remanded in custody, a practice that was later forbidden. They were found guilty, and given prison sentences.

The case went to the court of appeal, which picked its way carefully through the pages of *Oz*. The back cover, said Widgery, the Lord Chief Justice (b. 1911), showed five nude women, attractively drawn.

> Closer inspection, however, shows that these women are lesbians or at least are indulging in lesbian activities. One of them has what appears to be a rat's tail protruding from her vagina. In another case a woman is wearing strapped to her thighs an artificial penis or dildo, as apparently it is called, and other pairs are indulging in what are clearly lesbian activities. Attention has not unnaturally been drawn to that as an example of material in this magazine which might deprave or corrupt.

Other material cited by Widgery included a small ad that said

> Voyeurs . . . Homosexuals, Lesbians, Heterosexuals, all Erotic Minorities . . . Join Contact Club International . . . Membership £2 only. 100% Confidential. Free Fucking, Sucking, Hardcore Pornzines of your choice! Excellent for Masturbation and Fuckstimulation!!

In spite of such wickedness the appeal court quashed the more important convictions, together with the prison sentences, once again because of misdirection by the judge, who had led the jury to believe that 'obscene' in the 1959 Act could also mean 'repulsive', 'filthy', 'loathsome' or 'lewd'. It was getting harder to define obscenity as standards relaxed. As for people (like the *Oz* defendants) who wanted to publish lewd material as part of an argument with conventional society, they were a new breed, difficult to assess; while the law grappled with them, the young who were supposed to need protecting were laughing at the jokes or experimenting with forbidden sex. *Oz* didn't invent the tide, it went with it.

Another *Oz* item that bothered the Lord Chief Justice was an advertisement for a magazine (his lordship said, 'What seems to be a magazine') called *Suck*. The ad incorporated

> a salaciously written account of the joys from the female aspect of an act of oral sexual intercourse. It deals with the matter in great detail. It emphasizes the pleasures which the writer says are to be found in this activity, and there is in it no suggestion anywhere which would imply that this was a wrong thing to do or in any way induce people not to do it.

The gulf between the kind of people who produced *Oz* and *Suck*, and a judge who thought oral sex in 1971 — forty-odd years and several million copies after Van de Velde had endorsed it — 'a wrong thing to do' was unbridgeable. The lurid representation of oral and every other kind of sex was part of the armoury of protest used by those who dreamt of an 'alternative society'. They wanted, in the phrase that lingers on, to 'let it all hang out.' The bourgeois family was, they thought, finished; the old liberals as fraudulent as the old reactionaries. *Suck*, published in English in Amsterdam, was one of the short-lived manifestations of the short-lived dream.

What might the court of appeal have made of *Suck*, had it come before them? Perhaps something on these lines: 'The publication, of which we have several issues to consider, describes itself as "the first European sexpaper," and deals with the matter of sexual relations in great detail. Intercourse, fellatio, cunnilingus, masturbation, flagellation, anal sex, orgies, bisexuality, homosexuality, incest and sex with children are portrayed in photographs and drawings without any suggestion that any of them is wrong. It is as though every activity is permitted except moral restraint. The text is blasphemous, scatalogical, depraved and occasionally, one must concede, funny. Little of it is accessible to coherent quotation, resembling rather the disconnected voices of a nightmare. Headlines such as ORGASMS EXPAND CONSCIOUSNESS, WHY THIS FEAR OF BEING SEXUALLY LIBERATED?, WE PUT COGNAC IN OUR VASELINE, MAN PULLS TRUCK WITH COCK, TRUE LOVE IN A NAZI YOUTH CAMP and MY OWN DAUGHTER WAS DEFLOWERED BY MY SON abound. Boy Scouts, the Christian religion and the nuclear family are mocked. Typography, layout and picture-quality are dangerously professional.'

Among the editors of *Suck* was the Australian Germaine Greer (b. 1939), whose book *The Female Eunuch* (1970) was wiser and sharper than most of the early feminist texts; *Suck* also printed a famous nude photograph of her. The magazine called her 'Dr Gee', because of her PhD and her English lectureship at Warwick University. She wrote in the magazine:

> Our cause is sexual liberation. Our tactic the defiance of censorship . . . [but] *Suck* is unliberated sexuality, much of it heavy with hatred and cruelty and desire of death. Most of it is fantasy, and hugely derived from the fantasy machines developed by commercial pornography to reinforce the sexual status quo. *Suck* too must carry its burden of whips and chains and iron-hard cocks ploughing the wombs of women in agony, because we have rejected all censorship, even our own.

Once the radicals had delivered their message, that sexual repression distorts and punishes, there was nothing for them to do but repeat themselves in wilder, messier, more brutalized images. Sexual de-repression offered no programme except itself. In this it was more honest than the old optimism which suggested that an account of sexual intercourse in plain language and a reassurance that masturbation didn't make you blind would set a child on the road to well-adjusted sexuality.

Suck organized erotic film festivals in Amsterdam where the love children gathered to watch, touch, fornicate and live out their fantasies in front of fantasies on the screen. One film that attracted attention was about a Danish woman in her twenties having sex with animals — dogs, horses, pigs. She was much written about and interviewed. Her mother, it was said, beat her as a child because of her interest in sex, so she turned to beasts for affection. 'I sweeten the life of my animals,' she said, 'and especially today, when most of it is artificial insemination, it must be nice for a boar to get into a warm lap.' But her heroic exploits had already been turned into commercial pornography. Ancient copies of the original Danish films can still be seen. She and the animals (especially the pigs) appear to be enjoying it. What has survived is some bizarre pornography, not the *Suck* philosophy that embraced bestiality because everything had to be embraceable.

Those who disliked the new freedom thought that the authorities (or parents, or God) were losing control. Fornication was becoming widespread among the young. In 1970 about half the brides in Britain were still virgins when they married, but they were an endangered species, and in a few years the virgin bride would be a curiosity. Illegitimate births, rising fast, had reached the unprecedented peacetime level of eighty per thousand, although the word to describe the result was going the same way as the offensive 'bastard'; the concept of 'illegitimacy' had been under attack since the war, most recently in the Family Law Reform Act of 1969, which established the principle of equal rights for those born outside marriage. The phrase now was 'extra-marital', or, better still, 'children of one-parent families.'

The moralists saw immorality everywhere, and it was true that ideas, words and pictures that had been indecent for most of history, and kept out of sight, were now being presented to the country at large. It was no use suggesting to the objectors that people might be rebelling against the constraints of the past, that the increase in erotic imagery and the increase in fornication were parallel developments, not cause and effect. The case was that evil influences must be at work, perverting the susceptible.

Those who seriously worried about it, as many did, were appalled to find how little they could do. 'The "liberators" of the sixties have become the tyrants of the seventies,' wrote Mary Whitehouse, not without justification, and continued to speculate about the motives of 'those' who were behind the 'attack' on values. In reality they didn't exist as conspirators, only as the random expressions of an age. But the anger and frustration that each new event provoked were real enough.

Oz stoked up the outrage. So did *The Little Red Schoolbook* (1971), a short work of impractical mutiny, originally Danish, that a Left-wing publisher brought out in London, packed with details of exciting things that the young could do to one another. Previous books from the publisher had included essays by Che Guevera and the speeches of Fidel Castro. Police seized copies of the *Schoolbook* and a court ordered their destruction; Scotland Yard's Black Museum keeps a copy in a cardboard box, another left-over from the radical dream.

No single event was more effective in offending the moralists than Kenneth Tynan's staging of the erotic revue *Oh! Calcutta!* in 1970. Tynan (1927–1980), the best theatre critic of his generation, had been recognized as dangerous in 1965 when, during a BBC satire show late on a Saturday evening, he used the word 'fuck'. The context suggests he had planned to do it. Asked, in a live conversation about censorship, if he would allow sexual intercourse on the stage at the National Theatre (of which he was literary manager), Tynan said, 'Oh, I think so, certainly,' then changed direction, continuing with, 'I mean, there are few rational people in this world to whom the word "fuck" is particularly diabolical or revolting or totally forbidden.' He was wrong; as broadcasting authorities have discovered. Behind the scenes the BBC agonized about the episode. 'A taboo word except between adult males of similar age,' a senior manager said thinly at one of many discussions. Mrs Whitehouse announced she was writing to the Queen and said that Tynan should have his bottom smacked, which caused Ned Sherrin to say, 'He'd probably rather have enjoyed that.'

On the bottom-smacking scale, Tynan would have been hanged for *Oh! Calcutta!*. Having fought against the Lord Chamberlain's veto, which was replaced with the less oppressive Theatres Act of 1968, Tynan conceived a revue, first seen in New York in 1969, that presented 'sex as play, nocturnal diversion, civilized pastime,' and included sketches about wife swapping, masturbation fantasies, an orgy (of elderly baby-sitters), sado-masochism and women's underwear; together with nudity. The London version opened in June 1970. The liberal barrister John Mortimer advised that there was a fifty-fifty chance of prosecution, given the repeated references to oral sex and sado-masochistic activities. But the authorities decided to leave it alone.

Oh! Calcutta! went on to make a fortune (though not for Tynan, who was not in financial or artistic control), and upset many who saw themselves as liberals. Among them was A.P. Herbert, who had championed divorce reform in the thirties, and was a prime mover in the campaign to promote the 1959 Obscene Publications Act. How sad, he suggested (aged seventy-nine) in *The Times*, that the struggle to give 'reasonable liberty' to 'honest writers' should have led to the right to represent copulation on the stage. Yet Tynan's concept could not have been more honest. As his wife's rigorous biography showed after his death, Tynan the wit and innovator had certain private interests: the caning of schoolgirls, masturbation, the fetishism of underwear. He had the audacity to put his own (and others') fantasies on the stage, dressed up with jokes, and call the result entertainment: which it plainly was, having grossed, according to the biography in 1987, three hundred and sixty million dollars.

In 1971 the moralists began to line up. A group called the Responsible Society announced itself in a letter to *The Times*; the sponsors included Lady Snow, who as Pamela Hansford Johnson was Dylan Thomas' girl-friend in 1934, and wisely refused to sleep with him. A 'Festival of Light' movement began with a well-attended rally in Trafalgar Square, at which Malcolm Muggeridge, a libertine who came late to purity, spoke of 'the squalid abyss of a reversion to animality, megalomania and erotomania,' which had been the theme of Edwardian bishops. Other supporters included Cliff Richard, the Right Revd Trevor Huddleston and Mary Whitehouse, who brought a message from the Pope. Pornography was their prime target, as it was of a committee set up by the Earl of Longford, a Roman Catholic, which produced the Longford Report, published as a paperback in 1972.

A combative man, a former Labour politician who was now a publisher, Longford (b. 1905) set the tone of the report by quoting from a conversation with the politically correct figure of a West Indian bus conductor, who told him that 'if a man sets himself to improve the morals of a nation then he must expect to be called a humbug. But I say let him stick to his line.' Longford took this advice. The five-hundred-page report, with sub-reports from many hands, offered insight as well as prejudice. Curiously, a scholarly essay by a liberal-minded psychologist, Dr Maurice Yaffé, printed as an appendix, concluded that there was little evidence about the effects of pornography. This effectively demolished the entire report, which nevertheless went its own way, proposing that obscenity be legally defined as that which outrages 'contemporary standards of decency or humanity accepted by the public at large,' a definition capable of giving the lawyers a weapon that a William Coote or an Archibald Bodkin would have relished.

No doubt the report was being defiant in the face of overwhelming forces. If there was such a thing as a 'tide of filth', it rose alarmingly in the middle years of the seventies. Not all the Whitehouses and Longfords could stop its progress. Pornography became industrialized. A demand existed and was met, not by sexual progressives but by businessmen; though the progressives had helped clear the way.

Pubic hair, once the litmus-test to indicate actionable obscenity, had first been shown in magazines without bothering the police in the late sixties. Now more intimate glimpses of women, and occasionally men, began to appear, printed in colour to high technical standards. An occasional erect penis could be sighted but this was dangerous for above-the-counter magazines. Under-the-counter material covered every known sexual activity. A 1972 leaflet for 'Pornophone' extended-play records offered 'Screams of Pain', allegedly 'recorded live in a 20th-century TORTURE CHAMBER.' The badly-duplicated 'Soho typescripts', semi-literate stories about women being raped, men being dominated, debauched children, high-living transvestites, coprophiliacs, bonds, chains, whips, enemas and even sexual intercourse were still on sale at five pounds a time.

Until 1972, when the *People* published another exposé, the traditional trade behind the bead curtains in Soho's porn shops was helped by a useful arrangement with corrupt police officers. In one of his 1967 *People* articles, Montgomery Hyde wrote that 'the shops which last longest are those which get tipped off when a police raid is coming.' What he didn't spell out was that the tip-offs came from the police. There was a fixed tariff for services rendered, sixty pounds a week for a sergeant, a hundred for an inspector, a hundred and fifty for a chief inspector. Permission to open a new shop cost a thousand. Seized magazines were sold back to the trade by officers. Eventually numerous detectives were gaoled or forced to resign, and Scotland Yard's Obscene Publications Squad in its old form ceased to exist. It was said that a quarter of a million pounds a year had been paid in bribes; evidence of the buoyant market in pornography and people's willingness to pay high prices for it.

Above-the-counter magazines were beginning to handle forbidden topics with impunity. This was best done by presenting them as educational, a method that was still the publisher's friend. *Forum*, a pocket-sized magazine with few illustrations and an air of professional candour, relied on readers to write in with sexual problems, and had doctors and other therapists on hand with advice. Circulation in 1972 was 200,000. Readers described (or invented) their experiences in the form of detailed stories. A fantasy about voyeurism or transvestites was arguably therapeutic for the person who wrote it, and for those with similar inclinations who read it. This was the new psychiatric dispensation, that pornography was good for you because it aided masturbation. The opinion, cultivated for use by defence lawyers, was held widely enough to be reputable; masturbation was improving its image. Cities had fewer prostitutes now. Perhaps one reason, rather unheroic, was that men masturbated more.

Sexual fantasy was a growing business. In 1953 Gordon Rattray Taylor in his book *Sex in History* wondered what effects the increase in 'vicarious sexual stimulation' would have, noting that illustrated books and magazines, together with cinema and television, were widely available for the first time in history, which meant 'an enlargement in the fantasy life of whole populations.' Twenty years later fantasy lives had a lot more to stimulate them.

Advertising was erotic. So were films. The legitimate cinema showed movies that would have brought the police round a decade earlier. Television pretended to be prudish but loved the flesh. Even in the fifties the BBC was having trouble with close-ups of male dancers. Covert eroticism was everywhere, all the more acceptable now that the deliberate kind was so rampant. The porn industry was busy satisfying demand and helping to create it. Blue movies were condemned by family newspapers, which were read by law-abiding men who wondered how they could get hold of them. The films were often imported from Denmark, where pornography was legally available, in fishing boats and bacon lorries and consignments of chicken offal. Technical standards had improved, with films shot in colour and edited professionally. The Danish 'pig girl' and her animals found a wider audience than the readers of *Suck*. Most of the films were heterosexual, their couplings enclosed in fragile 'stories' or no stories at all. They were shown at cinema clubs in Soho and the East End, or wherever a projector and an audience could be gathered together. Home videos, and a domestic market for blue videotapes, came later.

The authorities grew cautious about prosecuting pornography. Juries were unpredictable. A trial of 1974 involved a cameraman in his thirties, John Lindsay, who had made a series of erotic films. The fact was not in dispute. One of his specialities was schoolgirls. A foreigner had come to him and said he was 'madly interested' in films with English schoolgirls, the only ones who wore uniforms. After the trial Lindsay described what happened;

> I told him, 'That can't be done. I can only use consenting adults.' 'Right,' he said, 'find young-looking models, sixteen to eighteen, have the make-up man scrub any eyeshadow off.' So I did. I dressed them in school uniforms, and I found a real school in Birmingham that the caretaker said I could use in the holidays and at weekends. *Jolly Hockey*

Sticks was the most famous one — girls playing hockey, and the physical training instructor has a go. Some of them had wedding rings on which we forgot to take off. It was all taboo subjects. There was *Convent of Sin*, where there were nuns masturbating with crucifixes, and priests having intercourse with nuns in what looked like a convent. The worst one of the lot was a film called *Anal Rape*, in a classroom, with a very young-looking blonde girl.

Police seized twenty-nine of Lindsay's films in raids up and down the country. He pleaded not guilty at Birmingham to conspiring to publish obscene films (five minor characters pleaded guilty). The prosecution said the films showed 'sex in the nastiest, rawest fashion, bestial and perverted, without any question of love or tenderness.' Lindsay said he didn't distribute them, and believed they were being made for export. Otherwise he stood by his work. He wanted, he said hopefully, to 'make a stand for adult liberty.' Two psychologists (one of them Maurice Yaffé, the 'Longford Report' dissenter) and a woman GP explained the therapeutic benefits of pornography.

The Crown had its own expert witness, a psychiatrist, Myre Sim — famous during the abortion debates for saying there were no psychological grounds for abortion — who thought that *Anal Rape* would encourage sadistic behaviour. As for the sexual guilt that pornography was supposed to assuage, Dr Sim said bleakly that 'if you take guilt out of sex, you take guilt away from society, and I do not think society could function without guilt.'

The prosecution paid special attention to *Anal Rape* and the illegal act it portrayed. Lindsay said it was to have been a simulated ordinary rape, but the girl expressed a preference for a genuine act of sodomy, and his client approved, saying it would 'go down very well on the German market.'

The judge, Mr Justice Wien (b. 1913), was not impressed by the defence. He asked one of the psychologists, who had said that he recommended sex aids under the Health Service, 'Do you recommend lesbianism on the NHS?' ('No,' said the psychologist.) In his summing-up Wien spoke of 'the unnatural and horrible offence of sodomy,' and gave the jury a lecture:

If you have but a passing acquaintance with the Bible, you will know what happened in Sodom when Jehovah called forth fire and brimstone to punish the inhabitants for their unnatural practices. It has always been in this country, and in every civilized country, a serious offence to commit sodomy, which is punishable by life imprisonment. It is as serious as committing manslaughter or grievous bodily harm.

The jury failed to agree, possibly because some of them were in the same camp as the 40 per cent of a sample of three thousand six hundred *Forum* readers — surveyed earlier in the year by Michael Schofield and Maurice Yaffé — who had tried it for themselves, and who were thus technically in line for life imprisonment; a further 14.5 per cent hadn't done it yet but looked forward to the experience. There was a re-trial, and this time the verdict was not guilty. According to Lindsay, the new judge, Mr Justice Ashworth, had declared that to find the films not obscene was to make nonsense of the Obscene Publications Act. When he heard their verdict, he 'threw his papers in the air and stormed out.' The authorities felt much the same in 1976 about the book *Inside Linda Lovelace*. Its publisher was acquitted, to the dismay of the police, who saw the verdict as marking the end of written-word prosecutions.

The defence argument that pornography was therapeutic relied on the 'public good' clause in the Act. It didn't always work, but it gave a jury a respectable excuse for doing what seemed to them sensible. Newspaper reports rarely spelt out that the therapeutic value lay in using pornography to fantasize with while masturbating. Occasionally it became clear:

> Prosecuting counsel: Is it of any value to print articles defining explicit acts of incest?
> Yaffé: Yes, because people have fantasies on this. It does not mean they go out and do it. If material like this gives people relief, it is preferable to someone actually doing it.

John Mortimer QC (b. 1923), as entertaining in court as the Rumpole he invented for television when he gave up the Bar, was a formidable exponent of the 'therapeutic' method. Mary Whitehouse referred to the travelling experts as 'Mortimer's Circus'. Mortimer wrote, 'One such doctor had a joke. This concerned a boy who said to his mother, "If it really makes you blind can I just do it until I become short-sighted?"' (It is a very old joke. A more elegant punch-line is, 'Can I do it till I need glasses?') Mortimer continued, 'Sometimes this joke went down well with juries, sometimes it fell like a lead balloon.'

In many cases juries obstinately refused to see eroticism as obscene. A woman psychologist, Arabella, and a colleague, Colin, who ran a magazine called *Libertine* from a shop in Leicester, were raided on several occasions. They put a notice in the window: 'We are sorry if your favourite magazine is not available but the police like them so much they have taken lots of them away to read.' Eventually, in 1977, they were charged with obscene publication and tried before a jury, where John Mortimer defended them. Among the passages complained of was a girl's dream of anal rape (again), followed by buggery with her father a bit later. The Crown said the magazine was 'tasteless and reached the depth of depravity.' Maurice Yaffé (now described as 'consultant psychologist to Crystal Palace Football Club') and others did their stuff. Mortimer told the jury that his opponent's closing speech had 'all the charm of a wander around an old house built about 1850, when the definition of obscenity was first promulgated.' The verdict was not guilty. As Colin and Arabella were leaving court, a woman juror said to him, 'It's a lot of old rubbish, isn't it, my duck?'

The days of the 'masturbation' defence were numbered, however. The authorities won back some of the ground. The appeal court had already decided in *R v Staniforth* (a Mortimer case) that it couldn't possibly be what Parliament intended; though it added that

> The difficulty, which becomes ever increasingly apparent, is to know what is the current view of society ... society appears to tolerate a degree of sexual candour which has already invaded a large area considered until recently to lie within the forbidden territory of the obscene.

In 1977 the House of Lords confirmed the Staniforth judgment, and, as Mortimer wrote, the joke about going blind was heard no more in the land.

But pornography continued to be sold by backstreet newsagents and through the post. The quasi-medical glimpses of secret flesh, the lewd stories and lewder letters, were part of a popular culture, whether one liked it or not. This was another byproduct of the radical dream.

12

⊷⊃∘⊂⊶

'What Have We Come To?'

Taking Stock in the Seventies

THE 'SEXUAL REVOLUTION', which its friends wrote with inverted commas because they realized the limitations, had slowed down. What was acceptable had changed, but the need for acceptability was as great as ever. The moralists never slept. The innovators kept trying. In between, the public remained enigmatic, torn between options.

The sex shop was an invention whose time was supposed to have come. 'Sex supermarkets' were in business by 1970, promising carpeted decor and soft lighting through which well-adjusted couples would stroll, selecting an eight-inch giant vibrator here, some impractical underwear there; or perhaps the latest in fun-condoms crowned with Micky Mouse's head or Dumbo the Flying Elephant. But however hard they tried to be matter-of-fact, an air of embarrassment clung to the stores, of which there were not many.

Smaller shops offering friendly advice, on the model of an old-fashioned pharmacist with red and green carboys in the window, could be found in the suburbs. Nurse Phyllis and her husband had a shop that suffered because it was opposite a café and a driving school, which meant 'people sitting in the windows with nothing better to do than watch.' The 1977 catalogue ('Please do not leave it where it may be seen by Minors') ran to twenty pages. It referred to dildos as 'hand-held prosthetics.' The 'Female Prosthetic (Artificial Vagina),' hideously illustrated, was on sale with the 'widowed male' in mind. Even worse was the inflatable Female Torso in heavy-duty latex, headless and legless, as though waiting for the Murder Squad.

No doubt such items were needed. Nurse Phyllis said that one of their torsos was at this moment 'servicing twenty-eight men on a North Sea gas rig.' Entire females, in the form of blow-up life-size dolls, were also available, perhaps early versions of the dolls imported into Britain from West Germany in the eighties, and seized by Customs as obscene. In

1977 the rubber women or portions thereof were serious therapy, anyone could open a sex shop, and Nurse Phyllis felt she had a vocation to 'put the sparkle back in marriage.' But the same hint of embarrassment was there; eyes were always staring from the café and the driving school.

The vibrator itself had a few years of glory and tried to escape from the confines of sex magazines. *Over 21* magazine for May 1977 featured a full-page advertisement showing a sulky blonde with arms folded, above the caption 'Some people are never satisfied.' 'Many women' were said to have overcome their problems by using a vibrator – 'It doesn't stay out with the boys. It's never too tired. And it's always available.' *Over 21* was published by the Morgan Grampian group. Some of the directors had wives who didn't like the advertisement. It was not repeated. Nor did the mail-order company that placed it find any other women's magazine that would take their money.

Sex education was another area where optimists expected progress. The scene was confused by the efforts of pornographers to pretend that what they were doing was educative. But the mission to inform was real enough. A new generation argued the old case, that ignorance of sex had led to misery down the ages.

Udi Eichler, a producer at Thames Television, conceived a series of seven programmes, *Sex in Our Time*, that would inform the viewer in plain lanaguage and, more dangerously, plain pictures. There would be sex in history, sex behaviour, sex therapy, homosexual sex, the sex industry, sex and feminists. Eichler was working on the series in 1975, and began to assemble his material the following year. Aged thirty-five, he lived in a community – popular then among progressives – with two daughters and his wife, who at the time was an invalid.

His own sexual problems were mixed up with the film-making. He had been 'outraged' by Dr Alex Comfort's *The Joy of Sex* (1972), the first manual to treat sexual activity purely as pleasure, because he was fearful of the pressure it exerted on people to be what they were not. Eichler wanted to view sex as suffering as well as rapture. 'My innermost purpose,' he said, 'was to cleanse myself of my preconceptions, which through my anguish were closing in on me.'

The programmes were to go beyond anything that had been attempted for television. The production team's argument was that half the drama on television was driven by sex, so why not let the honest documentary have a chance? Andrea Newman's *Bouquet of Barbed Wire* plays, laden with sexuality, had been seen by audiences of fourteen million not long before. *Sex in Our Time* was entitled to the same freedom to address adults.

This argument came unstuck over pictures of women's vaginas. Other matters were argued about, but the vaginas were not negotiable. It was said that a senior person from the Independent Broadcasting Authority walked into a viewing room when genitalia filled the screen. The sequence had been filmed with a radical women's group to form part of programme 2, 'Women, Sex and Identity.' This was the period when zealous feminists made a cult of self-examination, both physical and spiritual, to enhance pride in themselves as women. Peering at their private parts with mirrors, and examining themselves to see what was where, meant doing no more (ran the theory) than men were able to do as a matter of course with their self-evident equipment. Masturbation, as a means of focusing women's attention on their own pleasure, was also on the curriculum.

A woman researcher on *Sex in Our Time* thought it 'the most exciting subject I'd ever researched. There were things the women shared that I'd thought were freaky. It was daunting for me to think about my insides. Now, I don't feel nearly so bad.' This was the effect that the sequence was meant to have on women who saw it. As incorporated in programme 2, there were a few seconds of intimate shots within a much longer section, together with an earnest sound-track. 'We were all quite shy,' one woman was heard to say, 'but once our knickers were down it changed, because we started appreciating one another's bodies.' Information on the lines of 'This very neat, well-defined acorn shape here is her clitoris' was given. The radical women were against any tampering with what they saw as beautiful pictures.

When the Independent Broadcasting Authority realized how explicit the series was to be, the Thames management were told what was being done in their name. George Cooper, the managing director, sat down with a subcommittee to see the recordings. That was the end; even before they reached Programme 2, the committee was bemused by erotic graphics from Eastern cultures that seemed to go on and on. Plastic models of sexual organs caused further alarm. The radical women were the last straw. The series was removed from the schedules, and never transmitted.

The production team felt betrayed. But they and the administrators occupied different worlds. Cooper's job as he saw it was to draw the line somewhere. Discussing it afterwards he mused on small-town life and what the middle-aged husbands and wives he saw with weekend groceries and library books would make of *Sex in Our Time*. 'Once a programme has started,' he said, 'it may be even more embarrassing to get up and switch it off. I can see that embarrassment is what they may have been meant to cure; but they could have caused it instead.'

Fifteen years later, when Channel 4 ran a series of banned films, they included 'Women, Sex and Identity': a bit dated, awkwardly sincere, calling a spade a spade. As might have been expected, since the two worlds remained as far apart as ever, the intimate pictures were blacked out once again by order of the television authority.

Education in sex had other radical manifestations that the moralists hated. The Family Planning Association, lacking a role now that the State had taken over its clinics, turned to advice and information (or 'propaganda', according to its opponents). One of its offshoots was called Grapevine, planned as a friendly service for the young who wouldn't go near a counsellor or a doctor if they thought they would be lectured. Its volunteers were all under thirty. They spent long sessions discussing what they should say to those who telephoned, or who walked up two flights of stairs to their dingy quarters above a fried-chicken restaurant in north London, seeking advice. By definition it was no use their condemning anything the clients did, because then no one would listen, or come back for more.

All that the volunteers could do was find formulas for giving reassurance. Masturbating and not masturbating were equally acceptable. Edward did say that half the crowd shouted 'What a wanker!' when an Arsenal player missed a goal, which made it a term of abuse. But there were historical reasons for that.

Was masochism a bad thing? No, because if a sadist could find a masochist, that was a beautiful thing. Oral sex? 'Some think it's illegal,' said a man with a beard, 'some think it's dirty. Some think they'll get a disease by going down. Some complain their girl won't give it to them. Where is reality?'

No one claimed solutions. The virtue lay in being free to talk. There were no more secrets, in theory. In practice every door that opened revealed another. 'I can find myself in front of a class,' said Rhona, 'and I think "Christ, if they knew what I was thinking!" You can be very honest about sex in your own mind. But not with others.'

On a later occasion, another of the Grapevine volunteers, Sal, faces a mixed class, teenagers and above, at a technical college. Middle-class youths might be different, using conversations to play polite games; here they wind her up, talking about whips and rubber suits and suspenders. 'That's not normal,' says a girl, and Sal tries to get them to discuss what 'normal' means. 'Why are you asking us?' calls a boy, then asks her if it's all right to have intercourse with a cow. She gets them back to their own sexual relations. Do they ever think having sex is bad? 'When me mum and dad come home unexpected,' says a wit from Hackney.

Trying hard, Sal tries to get some mileage from the boys' perceptions of how girls feel about sex. A fat boy sweats and obliges. 'If you went up to a girl as the pub was shutting and asked to take her home, she'd tell you to fuck off. If it was halfway through the evening, buy her a few drinks, maybe she'd go.'

'So what does that mean?'

'It means, like, I'll swap you sex for a couple of drinks and a few fags.'

'Rubbish!' cries a girl.

They turn on Sal. *She's* supposed to know about sex. Why does she keep asking them?

'We're here to talk about attitudes,' she says wearily. 'How could I possibly know more about sex than anyone else?'

'Then what are you doing here?' yells the lad from Hackney. He isn't winding her up now; just angry.

Small, bloody skirmishes in the sex-education war came and went in provincial towns, as each side tested the other. The FPA was active in Basingstoke in 1977, chiefly through a young woman, Elaine, who gave talks at schools and colleges. An apprentice was said to have complained about 'this bint in tight trousers' who 'comes in and crosses her legs and talks about sex.' Elaine sounded and probably was the kind of educationist who would have made the pre-1939 radicals think the good times had come, talking dispassionately about Tampax and intercourse, showing films, letting a class of girls giggle for half an hour if that was what they wanted.

By means that weren't clear, an informal group linking local schools and colleges decided that outside speakers were not desirable. Invitations dried up. The authorities would have been happier had she been less attractive, or married, or both. 'My opponents,' she said, 'think I'm saying, "Cor, it's great!" I'm not. I know plenty of girls who are going to wait till they're married. I'd support them either way. But no, I don't say that sex is for procreation alone.'

Teenage pregnancies rose significantly through the sixties, and so did teenage abortion, where the figure was twenty-eight thousand in 1977. In the same year the total of births to unmarried mothers of all ages reached ninety-seven per thousand, overtaking the century's highest figure, ninety-three at the end of the Second World War. Family planners responded to these trends by urging the need to instruct the young. The Basingstoke initiative was a tiny part of this process. But only a minority of British schools had the stomach for explicit sex education.

For the orthodox, middle-aged, parent-beset educationist, the real sexuality of the young was not on the agenda. 'Moral guidelines' was the phrase to make them happy. Michael Schofield, in a new study, *Promiscuity*, published in 1976, had failed to make the blood run cold on the subject, as the moralists would have liked. Instead he told his readers, 'We take it all too seriously.'

Schofield had studied three hundred and seventy-six young adults and found sixty of them promiscuous. He discussed them but didn't wring his hands, which meant he was no better than Elaine and the FPA. He even poked fun at the moralists by telling them that in the fourteenth century when Langland paraded the seven deadly sins in *Piers Plowman*, Anger got fifty-three lines, Avarice a hundred and fifteen and Lust five. A headmistress at Basingstoke who spoke to me of the 'mystique and beauty' of preparing her girls for life, while not putting too much emphasis on sex education, was not a fan of Schofield, or of outside speakers bringing whiffs of worldliness. 'By talking about these things,' she said, 'you may be arousing their desires.'

Distant figures did their bit for the conservative cause in Basingstoke. Judith Colman, wife of Sir Michael Colman, Baronet, of Reckitt and Colman, was not really distant, but the Elaine camp didn't know she was a governor of two local schools. Her home, Malshanger, was ten minutes away by road. I went to have tea and to agree to differ. With her was a friend, Mrs Jennet Kidd, part-author of a booklet, *Sound Sex Education*, that the Order of Christian Unity had published the previous year. Lady Colman and Mrs Kidd, a nurse who lived in a cottage nearby, had distributed copies throughout the district, and it was likely to be adopted as a standard text in the town. It dwelt on chastity.

We talked about chastity, or rather we stated opposing views and smiled at one another. I said the FPA tried to cope with the real world. Mrs Kidd asked why they couldn't look ahead to happy family life. I said she and her friend were hopeless optimists and they said I was a hopeless pessimist. We got back to sex education. I mentioned oral sex and Lady Colman said, 'What have we come to?' She said schoolchildren wanted to be taught the good things in life, not be over-enlightened on certain subjects. Masturbation was another such subject.

I asked what happened when adolescent girls had sexual desires. The answer seemed to be that they did not. Mrs Kidd said that such girls were 'at the height of their idealistic longings': it was the media's fault for going on about sex. Having a teenage daughter of my own at school, I wondered weakly if Mrs Kidd might be right after all about idealistic longings. She spoke of having come down on the train from London that day. It was March. Through the window she glimpsed sheep with their lambs, and thought, 'The lambs aren't thinking about sex.'

Somehow the lambs were not convincing. We smiled some more and parted. At the Health Education Council in London they said briskly that *Sound Sex Education* was not on their resource list. Yet there were teachers who swore by it in Basingstoke, and in other places, too.

Because it dealt mainly with the young, sex education remained a sensitive issue to which solutions were personal and emotional. The Longford Report thought it 'primarily an affair for parents', ignoring the fact, familiar to most parents, that to tell one's own children about sex in an open, casual manner is difficult. It may be that sex instruction of any kind is a hopeless endeavour, and that learning about it behind the bicycle shed and by experiment is the only practical way. But by the nineteen-seventies there was a case for assuming that to give the teenage children of a highly sexual society information about contraception and behaviour would do no harm and might do some good. Longford, fumbling in a dark of his own making, wanted to curb that sort of thing by rewriting the Obscene Publications Act to make it 'illegal to show children under educational auspices any material which may not be shown in a public place.' The 'lambs aren't thinking about sex' syndrome underlay whole areas of policy that aspired to greater sophistication.

A fear that liberal educators wanted to make sex too ordinary was behind many of the criticisms. Valerie Riches, a former social worker who ran the Responsible Society, said that 'we are virtually teaching our children to be unshockable.' She conceded the achievements of the FPA, but its 'propaganda' distressed her. Like Whitehouse, she had an eye for networks. She had a chart that linked the Inner London Education Authority, FPA, Pregnancy Advisory Service (low-cost abortion), London Rubber (Durex), the Abortion Law Reform Association (then run by feminists, shrilly defensive of the Act), International Publishing Corporation magazines and for good measure the British Council of Churches.

The critics of liberal sexual attitudes always stressed that it was not progress they were against, only particular examples of it. Riches said that in general it was 'good that one can talk freely, that one can say to a chap, "I'm going to the loo".' But we had gone beserk. 'To feel shocked about some things is *right*,' she said. This was much the same point that Myre Sim, the psychiatrist, made at the Lindsay obscenity trial: without guilt, society could not function. In the sense that society needs restraint if it is not to become anarchic, it must be true. The question was whether sexual freedom led to sexual anarchy and the end of social restraints. Many people found this proposition absurd. But to those who believed it, the prospect was alarming, and sex education a crucial issue.

Liberal educationists had modest resources and were always vulnerable. Dorothy Dallas contributed a section about 'The Biology of Man' to a Nuffield Secondary Science book, intended for thirteen-year-olds and upwards. This was the usual age when menstruation began. Boys' bodies changed earlier, too; at the turn of the century their growth wasn't complete until they were twenty-three, but now it was seventeen. Dallas' text was amended. References to masturbation were taken out. In the published version, circumlocutory sentences hinted at the blue pencil: 'When boys first begin to produce sperms, they do not realize it until the sperms leave the overcrowded testes and come out through the penis.' This was reminiscent of, 'There is a tube leading from the spermaries down which the sperms pass. It is the same tube down which the water which the body has no further use for, passes.' (*Towards Racial Health*, 1916.) 'The team,' said a Nuffield official, 'was collectively unable to deal with Mrs Dallas' text in a way they felt was collectively acceptable.'

Dallas took a sanguine view of what had happened. It had happened to others. 'You find me a school textbook that illustrates the clitoris,' she said. 'You can't, because naughty boys might find it, and discover what girls like.' Her idea of immorality was mothers trying to keep children innocent, succeeding only in sending them 'unprepared into a sexy world.' It pleased her to have got a Leonardo da Vinci drawing of sexual intercourse, small but recognizable, into print. She thought it probably survived the censors because of its provenance. The copyright acknowledgement said, 'Reproduced by gracious permission of Her Majesty the Queen.'

Sex education was a drawn game between progressives and moralists; neither got what they wanted. The most extreme attempt to advance a sexual frontier was made by the paedophiles, who surfaced briefly as a lobby to make sex with children legal. An organization called PIE, the Paedophile Information Exchange, was busy with press releases and a magazine in 1977, anxious to dispel what it called myths about child molesters, and show that paedophiles wanted no more than 'gentle, loving and mutually pleasurable relationships' to which children consented.

One of PIE's spokesmen was a teacher in his early thirties who had left the profession after telling a boy aged eleven that he loved him. He would tell any journalist who listened that no lower age-limit existed for the paedophile, that 'people do have sexual relations with children of one or two, but interest really begins at five or six.' Asked how a child of that age could 'consent' to sex with an adult, he fell back on the analogy of food: if a child could say 'I'm hungry', why couldn't it say 'I like to be played with sexually'?

For a while a willingness to discuss the paedophile case was the sign of a serious liberal. Some of the Grapevine volunteers toyed with the idea of paedophilia as a good cause. Hadn't *Suck* included incest and child-sex in its revolutionary acts, or at any rate revolutionary fantasies? As a magazine editor wrote to the press, attacking another journalist who had dared to call PIE 'nasty', 'There is absolutely no reason why paedophiles shouldn't organize themselves into a self-interest group just like homosexuals, journalists or railway train enthusiasts.'

Prudent progressives changed the subject. It was not unknown for Family Planning Association workers to be asked by moralists about their policy towards paedophilia. The answer was to say they didn't even think about it. 'We don't have a policy on bestiality or necrophilia, either,' a member of the executive was heard to snap. All this was long before sexual child abuse became a national issue. The artless paedophiles belong to another age.

One issue that might have been settled after a century and a half of strife was pornography. Following eighteen unsatisfactory years of the Obscene Publications Act, a Home Office committee under the philosopher Bernard Williams was appointed by Jim Callaghan's Labour Government in July 1977, charged with reviewing the laws of England and Wales on 'obscenity, indecency and violence in publications, displays and entertainments.' Broadcasting was excluded. The members included a judge, a former chief constable, a bishop, a psychiatrist and a journalist.

For two years the Williams Committee heard and read evidence from those who made and advocated pornography as well as those who deplored and prosecuted it. One submission wanted obscenity defined by items on a list, among them 'photographic portrayal of the adult female breast.' The committee studied the product in print and on film. Their report gave the first reliable picture of the trade, estimating that about four million people read one or more magazines every month. Four million was also Schofield's estimate of the number of 'promiscuous' people in the population, having sex with more than one partner in a year. No doubt it was a different four million. Most were men, younger rather than older, the readership strongest in the skilled working class, weakest at the top and bottom of the social scale. The poor couldn't afford it, the wealthy didn't need it.

Pornography was seen as an effect of the 'new openness', not a cause. Since the *Linda Lovelace* acquittal the London police had assumed the law was unlikely to be used again against the written word. There were doubts whether magazines could be controlled (although a zealous police chief could still get destruction orders, as in Manchester, where a new chief constable, James Anderton, sent his vice squad off on several hundred raids in 1977). The law was in chaos, given the difficulties of defining obscenity, and the variety of prosecutions that could be brought. It was not – the committee was careful to point out – that an intellectual defence of porn itself, with its 'tastelessness and depressing awfulness', was appropriate. But there was a general presumption in favour of free expression, and censorship was by its nature 'a blunt and treacherous instrument.' Better to permit it than try to ban the unbannable.

If there was evidence that pornography caused harm, that would be different. The Williams Committee failed to find any, thus making it the enemy of moralists, who were now saying it was not only sinful but caused crime and unhappiness as well. Feminists, too, had begun to argue against pornography, declaring that it was anti-women and led to rape.

The arguments remain unresolved. But having resolved them to its own satisfaction, Williams made practical proposals. The 'deprave and corrupt' formula was dismissed as 'useless'. Written pornography should be unrestricted. The rest, apart from old-fashioned pin-up pictures, would have to be sold in sex shops, dedicated to the trade but not requiring a licence, to customers aged eighteen or over. If people wanted to look at pictures of group sex, buggery and bestiality, then let them.

The report was lucid and reasonable. It even found room to smile at itself (and Parliament), when discussing how a clever pornographer might evade restrictions by thinking up 'forms of activity which had never occurred to the wholesome minds of committee members and legislators.'

By the time the report was ready it was October 1979, and the government that commissioned it was out of office. Whether Labour would have implemented such hard-headed and unsentimental recommendations is far from certain. Doing something about its dispassionate proposals would have meant admitting that pornography was a legitimate product. That would never have done. Hypocritical huffing and puffing had served the nation well for a century. Why change now? In any case, Margaret Thatcher's first Conservative Government was in charge, and the decent liberalism that the report expressed had gone into decline. Williams gathered dust. The days of sexual reform by legislation were over.

13

'Insidious and Dehumanizing'

The New Pornography

IF THE MORAL STAIN on society at the start of the century was thought to be prostitution, by its closing years the obloquy had passed to porn. Commercialized sex had less to do with meeting the demand for fornication, now that so many women were emancipated and sexually active, and more to do with feeding the imagination. Erotica was cheaper, more accessible to the sexually timid (probably most of the population) and, an accidental bonus, didn't carry the HIV virus, whose existence was becoming known by 1985. Contemporary moralists fired their adrenalin with pornography.

For all that, prostitution was still a busy profession. One reason for its lower profile was that moralists had stopped denouncing it. Now that 'immorality' had become normal behaviour, the professional misbehaviour of a few women who charged for the favours that most supplied to their lovers free of charge hardly mattered. Nor was prostitution blatant in the way that used to cause offence in Edwardian Britain. It had largely vanished from the streets, except in districts where women waited to be approached by kerb-crawling motorists; usually poor inner-city areas or suburban avenues.

Vulgar creatures with brassy manners didn't cause embarrassment on fashionable pavements (although some street soliciting was evident in the late eighties, as the recession brought in needy housewives who had no telephone network.) Women or their touts left pink and white cards in telephone kiosks and waited for men to ring them up. There was no high-profile profession to denounce.

The cheapest women, charging say ten or twenty pounds for 'love' (the old word, still to be heard), were the only ones likely to look like prostitutes, with micro-skirts and fishnet tights. In London, well over half the whores probably worked for a madam (recommending 'nice clean girls'), an escort agency or a hostess club, and lived in hopes of clients who would buy them for a night and pay a few hundred pounds.

Clubs overlaid with a thin scale of glamour – frilly underwear, canned music, champagne – ran on the same sleazy, profitable lines as they had done since the Second World War, if not longer. But it was now possible to have an 'international clientele', dupes who didn't even speak colloquial English instead of dupes from up north. The 'case girls' on offer to visitors who had paid their five or ten pounds entrance fee had to be stoked up with bubbly or pretend-bubbly at perhaps fifty pounds a time, using large balloon glasses, three of which drained a bottle. If the party consisted of two clients and two girls, a second bottle was needed to complete the round. At some point girls might be willing to 'go out', usually making firm conditions, like a compulsory Durex and cash in advance. Japanese businessmen were said to be popular because they were scrupulously clean, all with families in Japan to think about, and had undemanding genital dimensions.

Some clubs organized the prostitution, negotiating rates with company personnel in advance, taking credit-card payments from clients, two hundred pounds per man-girl session (which she collected at the end of the week, less a large handling fee), and even providing cars to shuttle between the club and a pre-arranged hotel in some backwater. There were prosecutions.

Better-class prostitutes using their own flats in the West End, the 'Mayfair girls', were left alone, and even brothels were not harassed unless they became a public nuisance that brought complaints. An officer said that some of the flats had been in use by the trade since he was a police constable there in the sixties. He thought that only a minority of the Mayfair brigade now did 'straight intercourse'. It was more bondage-and-domination, with 'games rooms', 'dungeons' and 'clinics', the latter no doubt still staffed by women in nurse's uniform. An 'average girl' could make a couple of thousand a week if conditions were right. He knew a girl 'on the other side of Oxford Street' who did 'kinky stuff – transvestite, flagellation' and who boasted she could turn over twelve hundred pounds in a day.

'Away-Day' girls were well publicized, taking the train to London for a day's work, unknown to husband or boy-friend. The magazine *Marie Claire* (1989) interviewed a married woman in her twenties who went up to London regularly, paying £35 on a rail fare but hoping to show a profit of six times as much in a day. She had regulars in London who paid sixty pounds a time. With her 'short red hair, a close-fitting black skirt and a tight emerald-green sweater,' she liked to make a start in the lavatory before they were long out of Birmingham New Street. She had 'had men desperate for it right outside the dining-car on a wet Monday on their way to work.' Short-times on trains were nothing new. Harry's diary, Wednesday 2 July 1958:

> I was alone on the train going to Manchester for the interview when a tough-looking female aged about thirty with sticky red lips and hair to her shoulders looked in from the corridor and asked if I could tell her whereabouts the toilet was. Thinking this very peculiar, I indicated its direction and resumed my seat. Later, when visiting the toilet, I discovered a cheap-looking bracelet in the soap dish. I now realise she must have been a pro, putting out feelers. Pathetic of me not to have seen this at the time.

National contact magazines, now ignored by the police, were sold at extortionate prices, claiming to offer the phone numbers of 'horny young girls, housewives and models', and illustrated with photographs of women in lounges ('Call Mandy, in comfy home,' Humberside), wearing nurse's uniform ('Mistress Paula, experienced and fully equipped,' Birmingham), gown and mortar-board ('Kinky or straight, I am great,' Carla, London), or just looking cheerful in a bedroom ('When in Norwich and feeling randy, ring my number, I'm always handy,' Elaine). A contact magazine could cost up to fifteen pounds. Women were told they could advertise free, no doubt with the Ladies' Directory case in mind.

The only serious attempt to interfere with the trade in recent times was the Sexual Offences Act of 1985, which created the crime of kerb-crawling, and for the first time laid men open to charges over a prostitution-related offence. The Act was meant to stop the 'nuisance' caused by drivers looking for sex, usually in respectable streets where prostitutes went to attract drivers, and where men cruising with intent were inclined to assume that anything wearing a skirt was on the game. Police raids in Soho, designed to improve the area's seedy image, alongside Westminster Council's refurbishing of the district, had driven out nests of prostitutes, who had to go somewhere. One of the places was Bayswater. The gentry and their wives who lived there in leafy terraces a mile away from vice-land soon made their views felt.

Popular with women's organizations as well as residents, the kerb-crawling law was sometimes enforced in districts where the nuisance to residents was less obvious. When Sir Allan Green was cautioned by police for leaving his car and approaching a prostitute behind King's

Cross station in October 1991, and next day resigned his post as Director of Public Prosecutions, he was given a large measure of public sympathy for having been unlucky, trapped by the authorities' fondness for making sex into a crime if it can be arranged. There was the usual speculation about how 'a man in his position' could 'throw it all away'; even suggestions that he might have done better to visit a flat in Mayfair than a tawdry wasteland where (how could he not have realized?) the police were known to be active: as if logic were any guide to sexual behaviour.

Apart from the 1985 Act, prostitution didn't feature in the sexual legislation of the decade, of which there was a steady flow. Just as the Labour Government that returned to power in 1964 had the stomach for sexual reform (or perhaps lacked the will to stop its backbenchers), so Margaret Thatcher's Conservatives arrived in 1979 with a moralistic agenda tucked away behind the main business of economic reform.

Pornography was the blot on society that had been identified by Whitehouse, Longford and the other public moralists. Militant feminists, too, were making pornography an issue, viewing it as symbolic of men's contempt for women. But it could be seen as symbolic in a wider sense, a visible sign of all that had changed in thirty years. Phrases like 'family life' and 'traditional values' were used glibly, but sincerely as well, by those who saw a world decaying around them. The year before the Conservatives returned to office, William Whitelaw, the party's deputy leader, spoke at the annual conference of Whitehouse's National Viewers' and Listeners' Association.

> There will always be those [he said] who regard any action by the State to protect its citizens and maintain standards of society as unjustified censorship and interference. Such people regard as antiquated and prudish prigs those, among whom I include myself, who believe that we have a duty to conserve the moral standards on which our society has been based, and so preserve them for future generations.

This message was to echo through the Conservative Party when they returned to power.

Actual behaviour went its own way; the young were changing the nature of sexual relationships to suit themselves. But pornography was an issue that could be legislated against, and made an example of.

The Williams Committee's idea of unlicensed sex shops that could sell every degree of pornography, leaving citizens free to look in or pass by as they chose, was forgotten. The thought of sex shops selling anything was distasteful. They had never achieved the status that optimists spoke of in the early seventies, unashamed emporia for some new age of openness. By 1981 they were being denounced by feminists, and a group calling themselves 'Angry Women' attacked shops in the north. The following year a section of the Local Government (Miscellaneous Provisions) Act gave local authorities the power to restrict sex shops and sex cinemas in their area. Religious groups and shopkeepers who didn't want unusual neighbours were thus in a position to lobby their town councillors. By the end of the decade, hundreds of sex-shop licences and renewals had been refused. Dirty magazines and sex toys were hardly an amenity that people were going to argue for in public. The number of sex shops fell below a hundred; their image became a steel door in a derelict street.

There were measures restricting the display of indecent material (1981) and the showing of pornographic films by cinema clubs (1982). In 1984 the Video Recordings Act addressed the technology of home video machines. Erotic videotapes, both newly made and copied from celluloid film, were a flourishing business. Rather than leave them to be dealt with by the Obscene Publications Act, to which they were already subject, opponents argued for a special licensing system. This was duly imposed by the Act, with video licensing added to the remit of the old film-censoring body, now the British Board of Film Classification, with the same initials as before, BBFC. As a result Britain had the strictest regime in Europe for controlling sex videos.

The most daring category that could be sold or rented freely, '18', included imported videos, edited from the master tape to produce baffling scenes as characters met for no obvious reason, then parted a moment later, the intervening sexual encounter having been cut. David Sullivan, the ingenious multi-millionaire who began the *Sport* newspapers but had made his fortune earlier with soft-porn magazines and sex shops, once imported a famous American movie, *Desires in Young Girls*. It ran for ninety-six minutes. He had a fifty-eight-minute version passed and certificated by the BBFC.

A modest domestic industry arose to produce video films tailored to the '18' specification. Peter Kay, a former photographer whose Strand International did the best it could for the British market, thought it a return to 'the old days of Hollywood where they had to have one foot on the floor.' By limiting videos to smutty titillation, and ruling out the frank portrayal of sexual activity — which some of those at the BBFC would have allowed if they could — the system was in the best or worst tradition of British prudery. The horseplay and innuendo in Strand's *Riding School Ravers* ('Caused a storm when some of the raunchier details were leaked') were on the edge of the permitted. In the distance a woman lies back on the grass and has her riding breeches pulled down; the man takes off his shirt and they roll about uncomfortably, as if there are ants.

A more adventurous category of 'restricted' videos, labelled 'R18', was also licensed by the BBFC. This allowed simulated sex, or even genuine sex if there was no visible proof that it was genuine. Women could display themselves intimately in strip-tease or aerobic sequences, and be seen to masturbate; here, again, the need to manoeuvre past the examiners made the videos seem grubby rather than sensual. In any case, R18s could be sold only at sex shops, which were ceasing to exist. Having recognized a demand for sex videos, the authorities had now contrived a situation where it was difficult to obtain them. Not surprisingly, a thriving underground trade grew up in explicit videos.

A further category of films was created by the 'sex education' videos that were on sale in large quantities by 1992, a motley collection that was suspected by moralists of being soft pornography in disguise. Some of them may have had an eye on titillation, like the 'sexual encyclopaedias' of the past. But was the matter-of-fact portrayal of sexual intercourse a proper concern of policemen and lawyers any more?

The implied intention of those who sought the Video Recordings Act had been different. They concentrated on castration, disembowelling, cannibalism, buggery, rape and murder. Horror videos had appeared on the scene, 'video nasties' that were said to be attracting the young and warping their minds. Children had to be protected: a premiss that no one could dispute. The young were often produced to clinch an argument. Pornography *about* children, a real but marginal element — since most of it was produced privately by paedophiles and circulated among friends — was sometimes presented as a tide that was about to overwhelm the hard-pressed police.

In general the technique of those who opposed pornography was to make the material seem indefensible. The argument came to concern social and humanitarian consequences, replacing the bald indictment of the past, when pornography was wicked because it was pornography. It now stood accused of tainting the young, inciting men to rape and dehumanizing everyone.

Most pornography was fairly mild — lewd rather than cruel — but enough of it was vicious to put the rest in its shadow. Whether this was an argument for seeking to ban all pornography (an impractical aim, in any case) was another matter. But Scotland Yard indisputably had videos to turn the stomach. 'The material that we have to view on a daily basis is so unspeakable that people don't really comprehend the true nature of pornography' (Supt. M. Hames, head of the Obscene Publications Squad, 1990).

James Ferman, director of the BBFC, had cautionary show-tapes of violent and sadistic extracts from films, faked for the screen but bloodily realistic — women raped, men mutilated, men having their wounds urinated on, women hacked with knives, meat hooks ad lib, crucifixion. The most oppressive, a full-length American feature, followed the sexual gyrations of a woman, supposed to be investigating pornography, who finds herself excited by videos of torture: 'It was all so awful. But what a turn-on!' The lover who has been showing the videos tells her, 'You could make that dream come true. Because things like that really happen.' He takes her to see them really happen, fondling her as they watch through peepholes. People appear to be dying. Film-makers say it could all be faked. At the end we are told that the woman was taking LSD and imagined the scene. The film is truly disturbing. So is the fact that it exists. Someone wanted it; the market supplied it. There were persistent stories from America about Mafia involvement in the trade

Two voices in particular were heard against pornography, the Christian and the feminist. As well as condemning its sinfulness, the churches used the new language of social concern. In the forefront was the evangelical CARE, Christian Action Research and Education, a formidable group. Its sixty thousand subscribing members were organized around local churches, with a headquarters in Westminster staffed by agile clergymen who knew about political lobbying. 'Pray against the influence of pornography in our society,' said the CARE magazine, and 'action packs' went out to churches.

> What in our culture is hailed as liberalism [said a CARE background paper, 1988] is in fact a cover-name for hedonistic selfishness. Our provision for the so-called personal and private sexual tastes of some of our citizens has vast social and public repercussions. At home we

see the injustice of the pornographic portrayal of women resulting in rape and violence. We see increasing adultery and divorce as a result of dissatisfaction and the [sex] industry-fed belief that the myths of sexual libertarianism will bring missing fulfilment.

It was often asserted that pornography helped to cause this 'increasing adultery and divorce', as well as rape. CARE and the evangelicals had assumed the moral leadership in the Church of England, whose upper echelons were bedevilled by doubts about its own attitudes, not least to homosexuals in general and its own homosexuals in particular. It was noticeable that while CARE insisted on rigid standards – chastity outside marriage, no abortion, no homosexual behaviour – it was anxious not to denigrate sexual pleasure as such. The shift was common among Church leaders; what else could they do? When they were more influential they could argue for spirituality. Sex was base, needed for procreation but otherwise best ignored as the worst part of humankind. Now it was reassessed and allowed to be pleasurable and God-given in its own right after all; with hints that this had been a basic truth all along, unfortunately mislaid by western churches for a century or two.

Rob Parsons, a young law lecturer who ran CARE seminars on marriage, cited the case of a woman who said, 'My husband complains I'm not so good at sex since I've started going to church.' The Christian community (he said) had somehow given her a view of sex that was not Christian. Sex was God's idea. There was nothing wrong with making love on the stairs, running about the house naked, having a bath together. 'Only, you have to talk about other things, such as the dignity of human beings, of mutual respect.' Pornography, of course, was beyond the pale, its fantasies forbidden territory.

Dedicated Christians probably influenced more Conservative MPs than did dedicated feminists, but it was the feminists who attracted attention in their war against pornography. Men found their extremism more threatening. Disapproving Christians had always been with us, and many of the active ones were themselves men. The feminists condemned all titillating images, even the girls with naked bosoms in the *Sun*. Protesters came and went in the media, embarrassing W.H. Smith (which sold only the more harmless men's magazines) with raids on top shelves, appearing on television to warn of the male psyche, writing articles that linked rape with pornography.

No one emerged with much credit from these wrangles. Men

diminished the threat they felt by inventing feminist figures of fun (lesbians with boots and cropped hair, or at best women with unhappy marriages and shrill voices, telling men how to conduct their private lives). Feminists inflated male characteristics to create cartoon figures of aggression (despoilers of women, inflamed by vicious fantasies filled with hate), as though unaware of the sexual uncertainties that nibble at men's hearts.

The feminist ideology for the anti-porn campaigns of the eighties in Britain came from America. Prolonged attempts were made there to have pornography defined as a form of sex discrimination, thus allowing individuals to sue pornographers in court and collect damages for the harm they had done. In 1984 the city of Minneapolis approved a local law on those lines (drafted in part by the feminist Andrea Dworkin), only to have it declared unconstitutional by the Supreme Court two years later. American feminists remained divided by the issue. Those who opposed the obsessive concern with pornography − some of them lesbian, some heterosexual − argued that its dangers had been exaggerated, and that feminists had better causes to fight. Besides, pornography could appeal to women as well as to men. The point was stylishly made in a collection of essays, *Caught Looking. Feminism, Pornography & Censorship* (Seattle, 1988), illustrated with hundreds of black-and-white photographs celebrating, also perhaps laughing at, western erotica of the last hundred years.

> Pornography sometimes includes elements of play [wrote one of the essayists, Ann Snitow], as if the fear women feel toward men had evaporated and women were relaxed and willing at last. Such a fantasy − sexual revolution as fait accompli − is manipulative and insensitive in most of the guises we know, but it can also be wishful, eager and utopian. Porn can depict thrilling (as opposed to threatening) danger. Though some of its manic quality comes from women-hating, some seems propelled by fear and joy about breaching the always uncertain boundaries of flesh and personality. Hostility haunts the genre, but as part of a psychodrama in which men often imagine themselves women's victims . . .

The anti-porn women had no time for cosy psychodrama. Their British counterparts, who also met opposition from within their own camp, concentrated on the possibility, which they saw as a certainty, that pornography drove some men to violent behaviour and to rape. Academic studies and anecdotal evidence (much of it from women, the victims) gave them the necessary ammunition, but the facts were conflicting, the case unproven; though not for the feminists, or for many others.

A Conservative MP speaking in the House of Commons drew the 'commonsense' conclusion from the fact that during the past thirty years in England and Wales recorded rape cases have increased by 560 per cent, from 480 in 1957 to 2,288 last year (Gerald Howarth, 1987). 'If women are increasingly displayed as mere sex objects,' he said,' 'it should surprise no one if the readers of such magazines are encouraged to treat them in that way.' Violence of all kinds had shown the same trend. But those who wanted to make pornography a scapegoat were not easily deterred.

Howarth's remarks came during the Second Reading debate on a new Obscene Publications Bill that he had introduced, which would have made it difficult to publish even the mildest pornography, and might have succeeded. In addition to the old test of obscenity, material that could 'deprave and corrupt', Howarth's Bill proposed a further category, material that was 'grossly offensive' to a 'reasonable person'. As Geoffrey Robertson remarked in a legal opinion for the British Film Institute, 'What is meant by "a reasonable person"? *One* reasonable person? *All* reasonable people? A person as reasonable as, say, Mrs Mary Whitehouse?' Howarth wanted the new test to apply also to 'sex aids, bondage items and so on,' though he kindly excluded contraceptives from his list.

This extraordinary measure, if passed in its original form, could have led to a large proportion of modern novels and feature films being declared illegal. The Bill had Government support, and might have succeeded but for lack of time. Few liberal voices were raised in complaint, no doubt because the arguments for 'protecting literature', which came in so useful in the pre-*Chatterley* days, no longer had the same respectability, and couldn't be deployed without suggesting a desire to protect pornography as well, something that few are prepared to be seen doing. Certainly the Labour Party leadership in the late eighties and early nineties had no intention of offending feminists (in particular) by standing up for any notional freedom to buy indecent books and magazines. The honest appraisals of the Williams Committee became less relevant every year.

In 1989 the Home Office commissioned a survey of the available literature, egged on by Conservative back-benchers who had called for an 'urgent study of the impact of pornography,' their motion making it clear that the only argument was about the degree of harm being caused. Two university psychologists experienced in looking at social causes and effects, Guy Cumberbatch and Dennis Howitt, spent six months reviewing the available data, most of it American. The Home Office spent another six months digesting the report before releasing it.

The general conclusion, painstakingly reached, was that 'little evidence exists to show pornography is harmful.' This was not what Government, Christians or feminists had wanted. The Home Secretary gave it as his opinion that pornography had 'an insidious and dehumanizing effect on attitudes to women and family relationships.' Hames of the Yard, speaking from 'bitter experience', declared that 'the sick deluge of pornography' was on the increase, along with violent sexual crime. As usual, no one was any the wiser. The report was shelved, having failed to confirm its sponsors' prejudices.

The Broadcasting Act (1990), long sought-after by the moralists, made television and radio subject to the Obscene Publications Act, without having any obvious effect on the output: which had always been in the hands of large, well-disciplined organizations, where there was no scope for a seedy fringe, as with magazines and books. Satellite TV brought the possibility that programmes unsuitable for British eyes, transmitted by foreigners, could bypass the controls and arrive in the nation's homes without permission. There was shaking of heads, accompanied by assurances that steps would be taken where possible. Those who were interested quietly equipped themselves with decoders, for use when signals not intended for Britain were encrypted for copyright reasons, and viewed films and game-shows — some smutty, a few genuinely erotic — that were beamed up to satellites from sinful transmitters on the Continent.

Among them were short pornographic films made by Candida Royalle, an American woman who used to act in them before she set up Femme Distribution to produce movies intended for women as much as for men. She talked of 'humanizing the sexuality without turning off the heat,' and produced amusing, even gentle fables around the scenes of fornication, which were themselves good-natured rather than vicious; but were of course deeply obscene under British law.

Customs & Excise did their best to exclude what was regarded as filth. The rise of the European Community produced further fears of infiltration, and at the end of the eighties Customs officers were taking a harsher view of imported material than they had at the beginning. Their powers rested on the Customs Act of 1876, which made it illegal to import material that was 'obscene' or 'indecent'. Unlike the police, who had to be able to convince a court that an item tended to 'deprave and corrupt', all that Customs officers had to demonstrate was its indecency; not a difficult matter. The question of 'pornography' as such didn't arise, and officers were told they were not to use the word when describing goods. It was no use asking them how they defined indecency, since they used the bullying principle of letting travellers work it out for themselves, and (they hoped) err on the side of caution.

A Customs instruction that came into unfriendly hands showed that in 1978, officers were being told that in no circumstances were persons to be asked if they had indecent or obscene items, and that single items should normally be allowed in. Ten years later they were stricter, not least because the commonest item coming into the country was the video cassette; one of which could be used to generate copies and make money in the underground porn market.

Publishers producing soft-porn magazines were allowed to import sets of colour transparencies showing women, naked and half-clad, from America and the Continent, on condition they let Customs decide which of the foreign filth was not too filthy for the British. It had to do with the degree to which the crotch was exposed, even the tint of flesh that was visible. This arcane knowledge was never committed to paper; rather it was handed down from one generation of officials to the next, like recipes from grandmothers.

Given the arbitrary powers of Customs officers, it was not surprising that people cooperated with them; and that, if detected in some misdemeanour with a video or a few magazines that were 'detained', rarely took legal action to retrieve the property, lest their bad habits be published to their friends. The one clear defeat that Customs has suffered over a sexual item in recent times concerned some inflatable life-size dolls imported by the publisher David Sullivan, who successfully challenged the Customs' right to seize them. The dolls were made in West Germany, complete with working parts, and when they arrived in Britain were at once perceived to be obscene or indecent articles. Normally that would have been the end of the matter. But Sullivan, a rich man with no love for authority, fought as a matter of principle to get the rubber women back for his sex shops.

Lawyers acting for Conegate, the company involved, argued that –

since sex dolls were not prohibited in Britain — to stop their import amounted to a trading discrimination against a member-State of the European Community. The case had to go to the European Court before it was decided in Conegate's favour in 1986. The Customs authorities were furious. No doubt they found it agreeable to impose their own standards of morality, and knew that Community developments might erode their power. An official spoke of his regret at seeing 'the nice straightforward Customs Act contaminated,' but made himself feel better by adding that when the Conegate dolls finally had to be returned, 'they were perforated, ha ha.'

The fear of being infected by sexual manners from abroad was still ingrained. Whether it was novels by Zola and Balzac, or postcards from Berlin, or Belgian picture-sets, or stories printed in Paris where girls displayed their silken logs, or the actual women who walked the streets and accosted men in voices with funny accents — foreign filth and the efforts to exclude it had a long history. Replying to a critic of puritanical government attitudes in 1989, a Home Office official writing on behalf of his Minister spoke sternly about 'the need to protect public sensibilities from the worst [pornographic] material which is available.' S.W. Harris couldn't have put it better.

Across the Channel in 1990 there were regional variations, but it was accepted in most European countries that pornography met a need. A day at Scala, a wholesale company in Amsterdam that supplied dealers throughout Europe, was instructive. Britons objecting to pornography would have found it worse than they expected; even those not objecting might have come away chastened. It was a long way from pin-up calendars, Page-Three girls or *Mayfair*.

The company was run without apology, selling videotapes, magazines, sex-aids, toys, novelties and leather 'glamourware'. A spring fair was in progress, and the concrete building that housed Gala had a tent set up outside where buyers, mostly middle-aged, could visit stalls. Screens showed videos of men and women having intercourse sometimes in such close-up that one might have been watching plastic instruments in action; now and then they *were* plastic instruments.

Wholesale customers stocking up for their neighbourhood sex shops walked slowly along the aisles with supermarket trolleys, as though buying Nescafé and cat food, selecting a *Girls Who Love Big Pricks* here, a *Little Miss Innocence* there. It was too rude for the British; the BBFC wouldn't issue licences, the Customs wouldn't let the videos in if it did. The box of a videotape in the 'Animals' section carried a picture of a girl and an elephant's trunk; a man in a leather hat looked thoughtful and put it in his trolley. A woman bought *The Beating of Rosie Keller*, advertised as 'New from the UK', apparently another export from the alleged home of juvenile flagellation; although the real Rosie Keller was a beggar, picked up by the Marquis de Sade in Paris one Easter Sunday two centuries ago and whipped by him for his pleasure, an act that was part of his downfall.

The core of Scala's business was in videotapes. Three catalogues listed thousands of titles in the broad categories of 'Sex' (straight heterosexual, though some of it wasn't), 'Gay' and 'SM', sado-masochism. These were further sub-classified, for example 'Teenager' (forty-two titles), 'Tits' (seventy-one), 'Anal' (fifty-three), 'Masturbation' (twenty), 'Hollywood Gold' (ninety-three), 'Bondage' (a hundred and six), 'Domination' (also a hundred and six), 'Animal' (twelve), 'Enema', 'Pregnant' and 'Fat Woman' (all six) and 'Nursing' (three). But categories overlapped or were obscure. *Girls Who Love Big Pricks* came under 'Ball Busters'. Anal sex and lesbians occurred under various headings. So did spanking, dwarfs, animals, urination and excrement, as well as hundreds of titles that sounded comparatively wholesome, *Girls of St Tropez* and *Velvet Edge* and *Exotic French Fantasies*.

About 60 per cent of Scala's video sales were 'straight', 20 per cent gay and another 20 per cent in SM, animals and other varieties. The company owned sex shops and was planning more in Eastern Europe. It sold leather skirts and boots and one-size lingerie, so that men buying it in sex shops didn't need to bother about measurements. The showrooms were stuffed with erotic trinkets, inflatable women, dolls that spoke obscenities, dollar bills depicting fellatio, condoms, creams, dildos, as well as the videotapes and crisp stacks of magazines by the thousand; the shelves with bondage had more than a hundred titles, mostly American.

The guide spoke about national characteristics. The French were not so keen on perversions. West Germany was 'very big on peeing, more than any other country in Europe. I don't insult the Germans, but that is the truth.' (Germany still had an odd reputation, though presumably no odder than Britain's. The guide's colleague said, 'You know, the Germans *discovered* SM.') The guide tapped a pile of shiny magazines from Britain. 'As you know, caning is a super-speciality with the English. In England, they say, fucking is not allowed, but spanking is. I think English magazines is a super example. They make the schoolgirls spanked without pubic hair.' The only speciality not to be seen was child pornography, which Charlie Geerts the proprietor (and Charlie Geerts' lawyer) said he had never touched, and would be crazy even to think about, there being so much money in the other kind.

Geerts was known to the police, having begun his career twenty years earlier, smuggling porn into the Netherlands from Scandinavia, and once finding himself arrested and briefly in prison in the United States on mail-order conspiracy charges. This was due to an unfortunate misunderstanding about a porn movie that starred a girl aged sixteen, legally of age in Europe but not in America. Geerts, large and affable behind his cigar, said sales were up and Eastern Europe was wide open. The mentality of people was changing, although 'even in this country many don't feel free to go to a counter and buy a videotape. If you are a bank manager, a school director, you prefer to buy it by mail order.' He added that women often bought or rented pornography without shame nowadays, videos having normalized it for them.

A new product was lying around in boxes, a harness with large plastic organ attached, described by an aide as 'not specifically for lesbians' but rather 'a fun thing for everyone.' Geerts said he had sold more than a hundred thousand pounds worth of them in a few days. He spoke lovingly of the workmanship. The literature said it was 'moulded direct from an actual erect penis,' with 'hand-coloured detail to capture every vein, bulge and crease.' He was anxious to give one to his visitor, but agreed that, in spite of Conegate, the Customs at Dover might be unhelpful.

In Britain an underground porn trade flourished and the above-ground trade relied on magazines and half-hearted videos. The videos have been described already. The magazines were perhaps less explicit than they had been for a while in the 1970s, but as long as they followed the unwritten laws to do with limbs and crevices, they could show women flaunting themselves with a high degree of abandon, though not women being abandoned *with men*. Why the latter was guaranteed to deprave and corrupt, while a woman contorting herself for the camera – perhaps accompanied by lewd text of stunning insensitivity – raised no eyebrows, was never clear.

Lawyers solemnly went through proof copies of the leading men's magazines, and there was a retailers' code of practice – no detailed close shots of organs, no suggestive objects nearby, no penetration, no erections, no rape, no flagellation, no incest, no Satanism, no necrophilia. Some of these activities were hardly mainstream subjects in men's soft-porn, but banning them presumably gave the magazines a defence to keep up their sleeve ('You see, we care about standards. We will not tolerate necrophilia'). Some smaller-circulation magazines ignored guidelines and existed in a zone between what was approved and what was frowned on, sold by newsagents in neglected streets where few policemen bothered.

Text, whether in books or magazines, was virtually immune from prosecution. Technically speaking, no one could now be corrupted by words, only by pictures, especially moving ones. Pornographic adventures of the kind that fill so many volumes in the British Library's 'private case' could be read (in prose that hadn't improved over the years), chopped up by magazines into readers' fantasies or sexual confessions. There was no such thing as an unwilling woman, except to lend an extra thrill. Women could be observed in many tawdry tales having their resistance overcome by a combination of persistent men and their own unquenchable randi-ness.

'Doreen,' a married woman of twenty-four, worked in an office with three men and the boss, and was determined to fend them off, until one day the boss pounced on her and called the others in. 'By now I was desperate for a good fucking,' etc. (*Fiesta*, Vol. 24, No. 2, 1990). Feminine availability was also emphasized in magazines – genuinely, in these cases – by the pictures of 'readers' wives' (and girl-friends) that filled pages cheaply with women-next-door, making up with their realistic ordinariness what they lacked in professionally lit glamour. If one breast was smaller than the other, or the flesh was mottled, at least their eyes were less glazed than the models', and they earned their fifty pounds or whatever with a self-assurance that their predecessors as 'Liberated Women' would have been appalled by, yet might have come to forgive with a grudging admiration for such brazenness.

By its nature the British approach to erotica, sly and underhand, encouraged commercial exploitation; the mail-order videos from British addresses offering 'steamy Scandinavian lovers going all the way' did not deliver what they promised. The oddest manifestation was the thriving industry of telephone sex-lines that grew up in the late eighties, offering the crudest fare in recorded messages as a means of satisfaction for the young, the lonely and the bored. Soft-porn magazines and Sullivan's *Sport* newspapers, among others, carried thousands of these dial-a-thrill advertisements, which became an important source of income for the publishers. Lines offering live conversation with underpaid women were available, but most of the business was done through recorded messages. 'Titty-Bum-Bum', 'Naked', 'Samantha's sticky knickers', 'Give me a hard one any day', 'Very wet and waiting', 'Do it to me **** fashion' for the more orthodox; 'Wanna watch me suck this little blonde lesbian off', 'Rubber klimax just feel it', 'My back door is open', 'I can't move in these shackles', 'Lick the heel you wimp!', 'All-girl jelly wrestling' for the adventurous.

A long non-erotic preamble to messages meant that the caller might pay forty pence just to hear bursts of tinny music interspersed with warnings to naughty boys under eighteen to 'put down the telephone before the totally explicit action begins. Do it *now*. Have you done it?' As often as not the explicit action consisted of a girl who couldn't read, let alone act, using a recording machine that was past its best, telling some tale about a husband who brings his mates in to watch her doing things to herself with a piece of fruit, or re-enacting events in the headmistress's study, or being pawed in a cinema by a stranger. The rudest words were 'enormous', 'soaking wet', 'panties', 'trousers' and 'Ooo!' Sometimes there were jokes. 'I love large portions of spotted dick,' moaned a woman. 'Ooo! The warm feeling I get inside when I've had it all.' Eventually the caller learned she was talking about steamed pudding.

Beyond pornography as shameful vice and crude expression were the gleaming new manifestations of porn-in-art, as in the classy photographs of Robert Mapplethorpe, or even the much-publicized Madonna package of picture-book and CD, *Sex*, laced with perverse fantasy that Havelock Ellis would happily have put in a volume with restricted circulation nearly a century earlier. The young, for better or worse regarding sex as a consumer product like any other, refused to draw the old distinctions between what was acceptable and what was not. Against that conviction, the tiny hands of the censors beat in vain.

14

'I Love You with All My Hart'
Forbidden Pleasures

'SEXUAL LIFE', wrote Auguste Forel in 1908, 'is beautiful as well as good. What there is in it which is shameful and infamous is the obscenity and ignominy caused by the coarse passions of egoism and folly, allied with ignorance, erotic curiosity and mystic superstition.'

This division of sex into two kinds, the permissible and the forbidden, has been an abiding theme throughout the twentieth century. The churches' dislike of sexual pleasure was evident for most of the time. When Harold Davidson, the entertaining Rector of Stiffkey, was on trial by a Church court for immorality in 1932 (he was defrocked for sexual misdemeanours, and died, still protesting his innocence, after a lion mauled him in its cage), his solicitor asked him questions that were designed to show how virtuous he was:

> –Have you ever in your life used preventatives?
> –No.
> –Have you ever had connection with your wife without having prayed first?
> –I do not think so.
> –Have you ever had it for any other purpose than for the sacred purpose of procreating children?
> –No.

Only the devoutest Christian took literally this idea of sex as a duty, though in public it took a long time to be admitted.

But it was not only the churches that divided sex into good varieties and bad. Almost everyone had categories of which they approved or disapproved. This was inevitable by the end of the First World War, when sex had ceased to be a secret subject. Its everyday relevance had to be acknowledged, and the only prudent way to do this was by inventing some ideal of disciplined, responsible behaviour, which could safely be approved of. 'Sex is a jolly good thing,' ran the popular prescription, 'as long as one recognizes that there are limits.' Sex within marriage was a wonderful experience, but sex outside it was unspeakably wrong. Without contraceptives it was natural and glorious, with them it was unnatural and dirty. There were always limits, underlined by popular moralists to show that it was not sex itself they were opposed to − not at all, they enjoyed sex as much as anyone − only its distortion or exploitation.

Mary Whitehouse, the schoolteacher who came to stand for 'morality' as no one had done in recent times, believed that before permissiveness burst forth, 'a healthy and open attitude towards sex had been developing gradually from the nineteen-twenties, in a way that individuals and society could assimilate.' The implication of such views was that had it not been for wickedness or greed or folly, the nation might have achieved the sexual contentment that still eludes it; as though sex was a prize for good behaviour.

Not only moralists had their lists of right and wrong sex. D.H. Lawrence, damned as a pervert in the twenties, held rigorous views on how sexual intercourse should be undertaken; those who didn't conform − which meant most of British manhood, badly in need of what he called 'cunt awareness' − were pathetic. Van de Velde, Europe's first liberated sexologist, told his readers that the genital kiss was in order, but strove to 'keep the Hell-gate of the Realm of Sexual Perversions firmly closed.' Fetishism, beatings, and the 'water sports' that attracted Havelock Ellis were on Velde's blacklist; he had serious doubts about masturbation, too.

By the nineteen-eighties a decisive part of the population had widened its ideas of what was permissible in sexual attitudes to an extent that would have spelt national depravity not many years earlier. Oral sex was now so unexceptional that even the fundamentalist CARE, asked to state its position on the matter, said the practice came into the category of 'some couples finding it helpful and fulfilling, and others not. Some Christians might rule it out completely, and others advise a cautious acceptance. We would suggest the guiding feature should be mutual love and respect.'

The change in perceptions was remarkable only to those who had seen it happen. Few people born before, say, 1945 failed to be surprised at times by a frankness in print and broadcasting that they weren't brought up to. Much of what had been forbidden had become unexceptional. They might approve of it afterwards, but when encountered it caught them unawares.

The 'coarse passions' and 'erotic curiosity' that Forel condemned were now grist to the agony column's mill. Magazines for girls and women made a virtue of explicitness, in a way that the old sex-educationists might have approved, once they had recovered from the shock. 'I'm 14 and two months' pregnant, but I don't know how to tell Mum' (*Mizz* magazine, 1990) was unexceptional. So was 'Recently I swallowed my boyfriend's sperm ... Can I get pregnant doing this?' (*Just Seventeen*, 1988). A practical question, it was rewarded with a practical answer (No; the writer adding that fellatio appealed to some but not to others). Magazines had become much bolder since the mid-seventies, when Anna Raeburn, who then edited the agony column in *Woman*, had to wait for a couple of years before the magazine would print letters about oral sex. She had 'a real battle over a boy of fifteen who was worried about an undescended testicle.' Like many of its contemporaries, *Woman* was aware of readers waiting to be shocked. 'Well, Sir,' a man wrote privately to the editor, 'I can see you are a good pupil of Satan, and God allows him to come on this earth for people like you.'

By 1988, when Virginia Ironside was the one offering to 'share your problem,' *Woman* could carry this, from a single parent worried about her teenage son:

> I often watch telly with him in my bra and pants and never lock the bathroom door. But recently I've noticed he gets an erection and he's masturbating in bed using a pair of my pants. What should I do?

(Stop flaunting yourself, said the magazine, and keep the doors locked.)

Inhibitions were easier to dispense with when a particular audience was being addressed. Interviews with rock musicians in the *New Musical Express* contained colourful sexual language that would never have done in most magazines (although the visual content of *NME* was tame beside, for example, the displays of penises to be seen in respectable women's magazines by the nineties). They were said to disturb IPC Magazines, who owned *NME*, but who had to tolerate the verbal horseplay that went with the genre. Asterisks were inserted to make a girl singer say, 'I was f****ing shitting myself,' but members of a group could rant away happily about real or imagined obscenities involving naked women and excrement (to mention the least unmentionable), hoping to find someone to shock. The rock scene and its videos used sex continually, but not all the explicit material was allowed on British television.

Television, which had to address the nation rather than a slice of it, had to be more reticent about sex. It was the medium where unreceptive audiences were most likely to find their ideas of what was permissible outraged, and a system of internal censorship existed to protect them, together with the Broadcasting Act of 1990. Lovemaking was allowed in carefully selected cases. Dennis Potter was able to incorporate a quick burst of heterosexual intercourse in *The Singing Detective* (1986). Lesbian love scenes with nude bodies artistically photographed featured in two BBC2 drama serials of 1990. Ten years earlier such things would have been impossible.

More often the daring, which appeared less daring as time went on, concerned sex without depicting it. 'I don't know what to do,' said one woman to another in a BBC serial (1988). 'You could have a little wank,' said the friend. A woman garage attendant who had been robbed told police (*The Bill*, 1987) that the villain was 'well hung'. How did she know? Well, he was naked except for his mask. Police officer: 'Straight up?' Woman: 'Nar, straight down, worse luck.' Bawdiness came and went; a few years later *The Bill* seemed to have been sanitized. But old British jokes were never far away. In *'Allo, 'Allo* (1987) a pretty girl fondled a German sausage as she hung it up, explaining to her boss, the café proprietor, 'I went into a day-dream – all zee 'appy times we 'ad.'

Lists existed of words that needed care. In ITV's film department, 'bollocks' was regarded as ruder in dialogue than 'balls'. Jeremy Isaacs, the Channel 4 controller, invented the 'Red Triangle' as a symbol to appear in a corner of the screen and warn viewers of impending eroticism. Whitehouse complained that given the nature of men ('and perhaps women as well') it served only to keep them glued to the set. Intended as a decent liberal compromise for a minority channel late at night, the Red Triangle became a joke for the wider audience of BBC 1, where an episode of Johnny Speight's *In Sickness and in Health* had Alf Garnett discussing it with his friend Arthur:

> ALF: Look for the red triangle.
> ARTHUR: Red triangle?
> ALF: That's what they say. Programmes with the red triangle, Channel Four, that's where you'll find the filth . . .
> ARTHUR: I've looked at Channel Four. I've never seen anything worth watching much.
> ALF: You've got to search for it, Arthur.
> ARTHUR: I'll give it another go, then.

The cinema was evidence of what millions now thought permissible.

Bouts of vigorous sexual intercourse in mainstream Hollywood movies became as commonplace as car chases. For television they had to be bowdlerized, but going to the cinema was not the same as letting sex into the living room. British films developed a humbler eroticism, at once comical and crude, as in *Wish You Were Here* (1987), about a girl (Emily Lloyd) growing up in the fifties; this was the film with echoes of Cynthia Payne's adolescence. Getting into bed with a bus conductor, who shows her an old-fashioned packet-of-three condoms, the girl sees that one packet is empty. 'That's because I'm wearing it,' he says.

By the standards that had prevailed for most of the lives of most of the population, such things were filth, tolerable in private, perhaps, but not in public. The ease with which the old filth became the new entertainment suggested a latent appetite for seeing sexual behaviour as it was, not as generations of moralists had wished to disguise it. The same was true of novels, where, unlike the cinema, which remained subject to a degree of censorship, there was in effect no limit to what a writer could describe, now that the DPP had given up on the printed word.

Most novelists used the freedom sparingly or not at all. Those who set out to write dirty often sounded as if they were caricaturing the genre, and perhaps were. One scene (from *Ambition*, 1989, by Julie Burchill, b. 1960), can stand for hundreds. Our heroine, who is drunk, stands on her head and has champagne poured into her vagina at the instigation of the lecherous villain, who has been watching black twins fornicate with her. 'Champagne,' he declares, 'tastes best out of cunt,' and the twins have to drink it.

The barriers between what was and wasn't permissible were further weakened by accounts of real lives. They contained nothing that would have surprised Havelock Ellis, but they made sexual eccentricities seem less strange by demonstrating how potent they were for people one had heard of. James Joyce's letters to his wife Nora (published 1975) had anal and masochistic preoccupations. Eric Gill's biography (1989) showed his enthusiasm for incest. Mrs Kenneth Tynan (1987) was forthcoming about her late husband's sado-masochistic interests. A biography of Percy Grainger, the composer (1976), described his obsession with canes and whips. Many more examples could be cited. Sexual idiosyncrasy in those long dead was well enough known – Swinburne, Rousseau, the Marquis de Sade. To read about it so frequently in modern times normalized it more thoroughly.

Tabloid newspapers did their bit by creating news items from private lives, usually of well-known figures, with details of their sexual habits. The captains of industry who made love five times a night, the police officers with curious tastes in dress, the soap-opera actresses with histories, the Members of Parliament who liked spanking, went past in a long procession. The information was often sold by mistresses or wives, acting out of pique, with greed as a secondary consideration. Moral vigilantes like Coote and his friends used to lay information about misdemeanours (a brothel, an indecent novel) in the interests of cleaning up society. Now the information was laid via bonking confessions and exposés, in the interests of amusing the readers and keeping up the circulation. The 'revelations' were likely to be presented with the same air of moral unction that had accompanied court-reports of indecencies, in the days when they were the nearest that newspapers could get to sex.

The popular 'surveys' that appeared regularly, usually commissioned by magazines, bristled with statistics but said little about the limits of behaviour that wasn't known already. They liked to look at love and happiness, leaning towards optimism; *Elle* magazine found 81 per cent of British women happy in their relationships in 1988. The surveys rarely asked indelicate questions, lacking both the resources and the hard-nosed persistence to be mentioned in the same breath as Kinsey. They offered glimpses of marginal truths – that nearly 16 per cent were still virgins when they reached twenty; that 56 per cent of sexually active girls aged sixteen had sex using condoms; that the average young man thought about sex every five minutes; that in the past year only 2 per cent of women had three sexual partners, as against 5 per cent of men between sixteen and twenty who had lost count; that 35 per cent of couples liked to have sex with the light on, sometimes.

For what it was worth, an academics' study in 1984 of a hundred London heterosexual men, aged between twenty and thirty-five and living with a partner, found that on average they had about four orgasms a week, three with the partner and one from masturbation. This was little if anything more than Kinsey's elderly subjects remembered from the start of the century. Perhaps they were better orgasms in 1984, or their partners enjoyed it more; perhaps less had changed in real lives in ninety years than we supposed. The survey was published in America, serious sex research in Britain being still frowned upon.

The acceptable limits of behaviour had edged towards 'perversion'. At a distance, the appetite for deviant sex of one kind or another was easy enough to acknowledge. The literature of pain, a central feature, went back to the Romans. Thomas Shadwell's Restoration satire, *The Virtuoso* (1676), had a brothel that provided floggings on demand. The young Revd Francis Kilvert, who immortalized his Victorian curacy on the Welsh border near Hay with diaries of rural life, had an eye for young girls and their punishment, dwelling fondly on what he saw or imagined, even volunteering on one occasion to attend to a culprit himself, 'if it would shame the girl and have a good effect.' Swinburne's novel about juvenile flagellation, *Lesbia Brandon*, wallows in pain.

The Victorian and Edwardian pornographers, operating at a different level, catered for this and every other kind of behaviour that someone, somewhere, might find sexually stimulating. Accounts of sex with children, homosexual sex and excremental sex were on offer (so were dildos with harnesses, artificial part-women, condoms with ticklers and rude banknotes; much as in any Continental sex shop eighty years later). Flagellation was the chief obsession in *The Pearl*, and the subject was heavily advertised in the Parisian English-language catalogues. The British Library's collection of erotica is dominated by books about sadism and masochism, two sides of the same coin.

The taste for sex involving pain and humiliation was supposed to be peculiarly English. It exists in all cultures, but Continental writers winked and pointed across the Channel, as they still do. Ivan Bloch, an influential German sexologist, said that English 'flagellation mania' began with the Anglo-Saxons and became both punishment and aphrodisiac. The public schools with their frequent beatings were blamed for encouraging it. Expensive brothels certainly catered for it. Twentieth-century folk-wisdom made flagellation a vice of the upper classes, where powerful men – judges, bankers – indulged their infantile memories of helplessness by submitting to ladies with rolled-up sleeves. Prostitutes liked to say their masochistic clients were top-drawer gents, though this was hardly surprising, since 'special services' were expensive.

With sexual emancipation, the appetite for deviant sex, both SM and other varieties, was seen to exist at all levels. 'Kinky sex' came in around the time of the Profumo affair, and 'perversion' passed decisively from the psychiatrist's case-notes to the columns of newspapers. The word 'perversion' continued to be used, part of the business of distancing normal, decent people, us, from the practitioners, them. Those who felt sympathetic talked of 'deviance', or fell back on Havelock Ellis' 'anomaly'.

The idea that deviants must be ill and in need of treatment was attractive; a narrow sympathy could be extended to them without risk of contamination. This was especially true of the deviants that society found most alarming, homosexuals, many of whom, when in trouble with the law, were for a long time enthusiastic, or pretended to be, about taking drugs or having psychotherapy that would make them like other men. After homosexual behaviour was more or less decriminalized in 1967, the 'illness' view was quickly eroded. The case of heterosexual deviants was not strictly comparable, but there, too, the idea spread that 'whatever turns you on' was a valid part of one's nature, not a demon to be exorcized.

Kinsey found that a fifth of men responded sexually to sado-masochistic stories. By the nineteen-seventies papers by academic research-ers were appearing in the United States which treated SM as a phenomenon, not a perversion. It became a cult. A 1985 study (by three researchers based in California, where the cult flourished) found a significant number of women among devotees of SM. In Germany, where SM clubs and videos developed quickly, a young woman made a name for herself in 1990 with a book about how she found sexual fulfilment by letting her lovers beat her. *Stern* magazine made her account of the 'terrible beauty' of pain its cover-story, 'I AM A MASOCHIST', complete with action photographs. This kind of thing was unwelcome to feminists, though acceptably explained in terms of women's conditioning by centuries of male aggression (male masochists, rather more numerous, were of course not to be explained by centuries of female aggression).

The SM scene (referred to by initiates as 'The Scene') generated a range of magazines, with America leading the field. The serious student of SM — with its division of roles in sex-games into dominant 'Tops' and submissive 'Bottoms' — looked for such publications as *The Sandmutopia Guardian & Dungeon Journal*, of San Francisco. An editorial note said it was published 'for the benefit of men and women who play together, for women who play with women and for men who play with men. We avoid, by our use of gender-neutral language, any suggestion that either Top or Bottom role is appropriate for persons of a particular gender.'

Articles in the *Dungeon Journal* carried safety warnings, which was just as well. A notice in No. 6 advised readers that a drawing of areas it was safe to whip, contained in No. 5, had one or two mistakes. A corrected version was given, with instructions to make a photocopy and 'carefully paste it over the rear view drawing.' An advertiser offered 'genital tormentor clips', described as 'actually tiny plastic clothes-pins that are perfect for nipping a bit of skin . . . just right for rows of clips up and down the cock shaft and all around the scrotum.' An article was headed 'Electrotorture/Electropleasure' and described how the electric-shock methods used by interrogators could be adapted for SM use.

Such things were not peculiar to California and Germany. The British dungeon scene was said to be well advanced, if not as well publicized. In 1972 the *People* named a Kent manufacturer of SM equipment who could supply nipple clips weighted with 6 oz. brass balls (£6), not to mention a whipping block (£28); a torture chamber was available (£15 for the weekend). Leather, rubber and shiny plastic all had powerful SM associations when used in clothing or accessories, and addicts used them to enhance and ritualize their activities.

The violent activities were too disturbing to be viewed calmly; it was easier for most of us to laugh or condemn. The journals of the British painter and illustrator Keith Vaughan, extensively quoted by his biographer (1990), would have been shown small mercy if some misdemeanour had brought them, and him, into the open. Vaughan, born 1912, had his work on show in public collections around the world. He was also a homosexual masochist who, among other things, felt impelled to inflict ingenious tortures on his genitals.

The journals record his sexual encounters with men and his increasing absorption in private self-punishment and masturbation. 'I really hate writing these things,' he noted (November 1970), 'yet feel I should . . . Because no one else — to my knowledge — reveals such things. They record only what they think will enhance their self-image.'

Vaughan pursued his obsessions with feverish energy — doing fearful things to himself with needles and mustard and weights, studying pornography (some of which he wrote and illustrated), self-flagellating with lead-tipped canes, using what he called his 'black box' or 'soft machine' to give his genitals electric shocks. He half envied straightforward heterosexuals their lives, compared with his 'inordinately complicated rituals.' Before he was fifty he was writing that three-quarters of his waking time was 'preoccupied with thoughts, ideas or sensations connected with sexual pleasure.' In 1977, aged sixty-five and suffering from cancer, he committed suicide.

Vaughan speculated endlessly on his nature. He wrote persuasively,

One could say that Catholicism is a moral or human perversion in the same way that sado-masochism is a sexual perversion. Both are private, personal ways of avoiding the issue, the difficult issue of living for a time on the earth with others.

However bizarre his tastes, presumably no one would have lost sleep over them at the *Sandmutopia Guardian & Dungeon Journal*. Vaughan wrote about how he feared his own sexuality as a young man, with 'no reassuring case-histories at hand then to show one was not alone.' But even in more enlightened times, those like Vaughan were still isolated. Maps of the sexual sub-cultures had not been drawn – perhaps were never to be drawn – and the shudder they evoked in those less haunted by their fantasies kept such cultures at a distance. And if a shudder was not the response to bizarre behaviour, it was laughter. Sexual deviants were said to lack a sense of humour. Considering what they got up to, this was not surprising.

'The Scene' in Britain could be glimpsed in its magazines. Much of it centred around fashion, pages of shiny women (sometimes shiny men) in leather and plastic, thonged dresses, rubber miniskirts. Watered-down versions of the same fetishistic styles appeared in the fashion features of conventional magazines. Those who took the thing seriously could buy specialist videos. 'The young lady,' promised one video-ad, 'takes her many rubber mackintoshes out into the beautiful countryside and enjoys the sensation of each slippery smooth rubber moment.' Some persons were excited by gas masks. Perhaps it was the war, friends said apologetically. A German video that circulated in the eighties had naked men and women wearing steamed-up gas masks as they made love; red plastic macs were also in evidence.

Enthusiasts met at clubs and parties. Ilustrated accounts were published. A nun in a shiny cape stands next to a blonde whose equally shiny dress leaves her buttocks exposed. A slave-figure in a tight leather corset has her hands manacled to her thighs; an apparatus of rods and nipple-rings extends from her breasts; her head is encased in a leather helmet. A mistress holds her on a velvet lead attached to a collar. 'The slave,' says the text, 'was breathing strongly through the two tiny nose holes and nearly swooned with pleasure as many of the guests were invited to take a picture.' Through perspexed lenses in the helmet, the eyes look slightly mad. All this was in a Surrey garden, one summer's evening.

Fantasies were less secret than they had been. Chris Gosselin, a clinical psychologist, wrote sympathetically about deviants, seeing them as 'script writers and actors in rather specialist plays, put on in the theatre of fantasy which every one of us possesses inside us.' He also noted 'the greater willingness of people to reveal to sympathetic investigators the intimacies of fact and fantasy in their sexual lives.'

In the past these were hard to come by. When Mass-Observation reporters were responding to questionnaires on sexual matters, they occasionally mentioned fantasy. The 'Little Kinsey' survey of 1949 included a question about erotic day dreams and touched a few nerves. A young man, a former soldier, fantasized about his only sexual experience: 'I dream of the girl (the only one),' he wrote, 'who I had intercourse with while I was in Burma. She was Burmese. I really loved her. She was killed by the Japs.' This was more a memory than a fantasy; but the line was hard to draw.

Similarly the line between a 'normal' and a 'deviant' fantasy was not always clear. A Mass-Observer aged twenty, a single man, had been elaborating the same fantasy for years. It revolved around a young woman who appeared in sex films. One was about rape in Germany; another, life in the Army. She was always in her underclothes, being made love to by men, among them her step-father and brother-in-law. Earlier in the century psychiatrists would have said the dreamer was ill and needed treatment. But what if millions had such fantasies? They weren't all ill. Even men with particular obsessions led otherwise normal lives. A schoolmaster in his thirties who answered the 'erotic dreams' question used flagellation fantasies. Since puberty the subject had fascinated him. He had never been beaten as a child, had no desire to punish boys, and felt no emotional satisfaction when he did. It was his wife he wanted to spank, and she wouldn't let him. So he fantasized instead.

Thirty years later the airing of personal fantasies about sex, frequently deviant sex, went on for all to see. Porn magazines and the letters columns of sleazier newspapers printed readers' fantasies of all kinds in the form of true stories; some were editorial fantasies that pretended to be letters, thus blurring the distinction between personal accounts and straightforward pornography, but others were written by addicts of some kind, and welcomed as free copy to fill a page. Because much of this was happening in the open, in widely read publications, it was not easy to dismiss it as unacceptable behaviour.

Forum, the magazine owned by the same firm as the British *Penthouse*, was one of the few publications with a claim to be taken seriously as an outlet for voices from the shadows. It had an air of sobriety, insisting that it never faked letters. At the same time it was unable to guarantee that letters sent to it always described real events. This was irrelevant, since if the letter was the work of a fantasist, then the fantasy was all that mattered.

True or false, those who found it appealing could then use it for private stimulation, and presumably be the better for it, as Mortimer's Circus had argued in the seventies. The fantasy might be something small. There is an entry in Harry's diary of 1952 where he recalls a remark made years earlier by a corporal cook at an RAF station, as a squad of airwomen marched past the mess: 'You can smell the burning hair.' Harry wrote, 'For weeks I could not rid my mind of the image it conjured up. But it was nothing at all! A crude joke!' As with Havelock Ellis' adolescent, who was stimulated by flies coupling and reports of girls saved from drowning, the *Forum* genre was all-embracing. A 'mackintosh fetishist of many years' wrote briefly about women who had appealed to him. His eye perceived what most would miss. He recalled his wife in a black rubber mac, a dance routine in a Billy Cotton show where they all wore macs, a television play where an actress kept her mac on throughout, a woman in a yellow rubber cape, and a rubber-mackintoshed female cyclist; he pedalled along behind her and had an orgasm.

Anything would do. A woman claimed that she found the statistics in a *Forum* survey of penises 'truly erotic', and obtained an orgasm 'as I tried to picture all those cubic capacities!' A wife, married twenty years, dressed up as a bride to re-enact in real life a wedding-day fantasy of making love to the best man as well as the bridegroom – according to her husband, who wrote the letter. Masochistic voyeurs watched their wives with other men. A woman recalled 'a scene I witnessed a long time ago,' viz, her parents making love on their twentieth wedding anniversary ('When he stood up I almost cried out, "Oh Daddy!"').

Respectable ladies smacked their hubbies' penises with rulers, locked them up in 'long-leg pantie girdles', manacled them to the banisters and violated them with dildos. Bathrooms were put to strange uses; punishment was dished out; men put on baby clothes, wore nappies, were pushed about in prams, and found (they claimed) 'security, love and happiness' – if this sounded too odd to be true, there is a psychiatric technique, 're-parenting', which treats patients by invoking infantile situations. A Channel 4 documentary of 1991 showed 'infantilism' in action. As Gosselin remarked, it didn't do to believe all the stories of deviants, or to disbelieve all of them, either.

A *Forum* correspondent kindly passed on his partner's dream, or his own fantasy, of being sold in a slave market to pigmies who violate her. This, too, was a not unknown scenario. One of the Scala catalogues from Amsterdam contained half a dozen dwarf videos, including *Caught by Dwarfs* and *Dwarfs Have More Fun*. The fantasy might have been supposed to excite men rather than women. Scala, however, reported no difficulty in finding women ('housewives, for example') who were eager to perform in both dwarf and animal videos. They were said to 'write letters asking not once but ten times to be in the movies. They do not even want payment.'

Mud sometimes featured in *Forum* fantasies (Caroline 'scooped up a couple of handfuls of very wet mud and slapped it firmly over my genitals'). From mud it was but a step to other kinds of messy, reasonably innocent horseplay. A magazine called *Splosh!* appeared in the late eighties, welcomed in issue No. 3 by an ecstatic letter, possibly genuine, saying 'At last, a real magazine for lovers of the wet and messy.' The letter continued,

> My current girlfriend will, every now and then, jump into the bath with me, and seems to enjoy it as a lead-up to a rampant session. However, I think mud would put her off, but I may be surprised.

A colour-feature titled 'Maid of Mud' was photographed on the shores of a muddy estuary at low tide. Mud and water were not the only erotic elements. There was food. A small-ad read, 'Male hippo seeks single ladies for mud pleasures or dinner – on each other.' Veronica described in an interview what she and Phil got up to. First he put custard down her blouse; she retaliated with Angel Delight inside his vest. More custard went into her underwear ('the sensation is indescribable'), before they anointed one another's heads with apple-pie filling and black treacle, finishing off with trifle in Phil's underpants. Veronica told readers her all-time favourite. It was Golden Syrup, which 'slowly creeps down your bum.' This kind of thing mattered to *Splosh*. It might even have argued that there were few ways a man could be more innocently employed than in pouring custard over his partner.

To publicize any bizarre activity was to go some way towards validating it, which was the objection of those who saw fantasy itself as dangerous, or at least unwholesome. The books of Nancy Friday, an

American writer who collected sexual fantasies and published them, were widely sold. Her first and best-known book, *My Secret Garden. Women's Sexual Fantasies*, published in America in 1973, appeared in Britain in 1975, and was in its fifteenth British paperback reprint by 1990. She used the fantasies that women, about half of them British, sent her as a result of newspaper advertisements. Detractors implied they must be exhibitionists, representative of no one but themselves. Friday had met similar sentiments when she was working on the book. Men whom she knew became truculent and nervous. Women were reticent and said things like, 'What's the matter with good old-fashioned sex?' (Nothing, wrote Friday. 'Nothing's the matter with asparagus, either. But why not have a hollandaise, too?').

About two hundred fantasies were collected, in letters and interviews. They included sex with strangers (one or several at a time), with animals (including an octopus), with a Rajah (for whom she was procured by her mother), with a doctor. Rape, sometimes ceremonial rape, was a dominant theme; beating and humiliation were not uncommon. Less frequently, men were visualized in inferior situations – tormented till they lost control of themselves, tied up naked after strip poker. Their appearance in tight trousers set off speculative thoughts, but in general the fantasies were not as physical as men's. One of Friday's later books was *Men in Love*, where she admitted that when she came to deal with male fantasies, 'many seemed outpourings from macho braggarts out to shock or trap me in filth.' In the end she braced herself and came to terms with what men were like. 'The thesis of this book is that men's love of women is filled with rage,' she wrote, adding hopefully, 'Observation shows that in the end love wins out over rage.'

Men were beasts and women were not much better: outpourings of fantasy either gave prominence to an unfortunate state of affairs, if it were true, or committed a gross libel on the human race, if it were not. The potential of fantasy had always been recognized. An article in the London *Referee* of 5 August 1906, declining to review (or even to identify) a novel thought to be indecent, remarked that 'Fantasy is nowhere in any civilized community allowed an unrestricted play. There is a point at which all modern people divide the endurably coarse from the intolerably indecent and abominable.' Eighty years later the demarcation line had moved but similar sentiments could be heard.

The connection between men's fantasies and rape might be unclear, but even those who declined to make pornography a culprit could hardly deny that fantasy had consequences, if only for the fantasist. Keith Vaughan, seeing himself as a victim of his nature, wrote that his auto-erotic practices led to 'a coarsening of the fibre of personality.' Vaughan was hardly typical. But the argument that sexual fantasy was the private prerogative of a hedonistic society and harmed nobody made some people, including fantasists, uneasy in its assumption that psychodrama behind the bedroom curtains, however extreme, was invariably a harmless entertainment, to be switched on and off at will. Such doubts may have been due to the doubters' own feelings of guilt. But whatever one's point of view, there was no such thing as an objective appraisal of sexual behaviour.

The effect of fantasies on real lives could rarely be observed; what one saw was the fantasy as the fantasist wanted it to be seen. The reality might be less amusing. The following story is from divorce-court papers of 1987. Identifying details have been changed.

Wendy and Tom were working-class children in the fifties, adolescents by the seventies, married in 1977. The marriage lasted nine years. Divorce proceedings were complicated by a dispute about custody of the two children. In long affidavits the parties did their best to blacken one another. According to them both, things the neighbours didn't know about had gone on at their semi-detached house in a suburb. Wendy said that on their wedding night Tom refused to sleep with her, saying he meant to have a sex-change operation. That was only the beginning.

He had fantasies about watching a man make love to her while he was tied up. He sent her out to buy a woman's wig and a pair of false breasts, and often dressed up in women's clothes. She had to burn off his pubic hair with lighted matches and indulge various other of his masochistic fantasies. These included being kept naked, 'like a dog', sometimes locked in the greenhouse, being beaten with a belt and daubed with paint. There was more *Splosh*-like behaviour when Wendy had to tie him to the bed and put rubbish from the rubbish-bin in the bed with him, following this with buckets of water. Once he said he wanted her to cut off his penis ('a good thing the knife he gave me was too blunt').

Tom said this was all lies. The sex-change idea was a passing aberration, soon forgotten. Wendy was the one who had sexual problems and needed to use fantasies; it was Wendy who wanted to be naked in the greenhouse. He had to behave like a dog, clean up the kitchen while naked and submit to being beaten in order to excite her sufficiently to make love. As for sitting in rubbish bins or having rubbish shovelled into bed with him, those were the inventions of a fertile and perverted mind. 'I love you with all my hart,' he had written to her, in an attempt at reconciliation. 'You don't have to be afraed of me. I have lernt my lesson.'

Who could tell what their life and its fantasies were really like? Jokes about 'kinky behaviour' and the fantasies that went with it were often heard from police officers in vice squads. But their cynical amusement at what the punters got up to was not to be confused with tolerance. Some were not even amused. They breathed distaste. 'I am an old-fashioned moralist,' said a senior officer, who had done his stint with Obscene Publications at Scotland Yard. 'The depravity is unfathomable.' He might have seen echoing Jeremiah, 'The heart is deceitful above all things, and desperately wicked.' Yet fifty years ago the same fantasy-worlds must have existed. Did people formerly lock up fantasies in their heads, while nowadays they let them out? If so, what were the consequences?

Many things about sex remained shameful. The polite view persisted that it should be a somehow hygienic activity, performed in a wholesome, therapeutic fashion. That view was common among reformers in the past, the argument being that a narrowly moralistic society made sex 'dirty' when it should be joyful. Bertrand Russell, addressing the Sexual Reform Congress in London in 1929, declared that nine-tenths of the appeal of pornography was 'due to the indecent feelings concerning sex which moralists inculcate in the young.'

Nearer the end of the century a counter-view was heard, suggesting that indecent feelings were exactly what was needed. Millions knew this already but (apart from the young, who were more hardboiled about sex) didn't like to say so. A young woman, discussing fantasies in the Channel 4 series *Sex Talk* (1990), said, 'You feel so bad and so dirty sometimes. But it's quite a nice feeling to feel these things.' The columnist Julie Burchill (of the novel *Ambition*) suggested, in writing about sex education, that after giving children 'a simple, unembarrassing leaflet,' adults 'should back off and children should be left to snigger in corners, for *there*, among all the misinformation and silliness, is a real germ of understanding of the mystery, surreality and sheer filthiness of sex, not on some bland blackboard or over a cosy cup of tea.' Woody Allen observed that 'sex shouldn't be dirty, but it is if you're doing it right.' Women could be read saying the same thing more earnestly in magazines.

What earlier generations would have found surprising was that as the boundaries of the permissible were extended, much of the new sex was concerned with masturbation. The 'self-abuse' that was once unspeakable had first become pardonable, then (by the seventies) was smilingly regarded as harmless 'wanking', only to be upgraded over the next twenty years and made to seem a positive virtue.

This was in part the result of HIV anxieties, since 'safer sex' propaganda emphasized the jolly things one could do that were less dangerous than letting the genitals make contact. More significantly it was connected with feminism, which made female masturbation part of the good news that women need not depend on men for sexual satisfaction. To an extremist like Andrea Dworkin, the anatomical necessities of intercourse meant degradation for women: '[Woman] is defined by how she is made, that hole, which is synonymous with entry.' For Dworkin and such militants, largely lesbian, '[Man's] thrusting into her is taken to be her capitulation to him as a conqueror.'

But even the milder breed of heterosexual feminists often tempered their enthusiasm for old-fashioned intercourse with talk of alternative, self-erotic pleasures. Shere Hite, another American, began her *Hite Report on Female Sexuality* (1976) with a chapter on masturbation, arguing that this was the best way to approach her subject. Intercourse, in the new sex, had to be re-examined and was often found wanting; the pushing and thrusting part seemed to bother Hite and some of her interviewees. Nancy Friday's re-investigation of women's fantasies in 1991, *Women on Top*, wrote ecstatically of the new breed of women who had found masturbation to be 'one of life's greatest sources of sexual pleasure, thrilling in itself, a release from tension, a sweet sedative before sleep, a beauty treatment that leaves us glowing, our countenance more tranquil, our smile more mysterious.'

Negative views about masturbation could still be found, but its detractors had to tread carefully. *Lessons in Love* (1990) was a British video for teenagers about sex and relationships, made by CARE. The sixth of seven sections, 'Behind Closed Doors,' dealt with masturbation. The casual young family man who did the talking (in jeans and leather jacket) said that not only did most people masturbate, but the Bible was silent on the matter. Since God didn't forget things, the only conclusion was that masturbation 'wasn't high on his agenda.' Scripture didn't classify it as a sin, so neither must Christians. The speaker added that it was not a good idea to be enslaved by the habit, which became positively sinful if sexual fantasy were employed. Still, this was hardly bringing down the wrath of God on the youthful masturbator.

Everyday usage made the subject less threatening. In 1990 the journalist Peregrine Worsthorne (b. 1923) was surprised to hear the best man begin his speech at 'a grand country house wedding' by saying, 'I met the bridegroom at school, on the day he first masturbated.' At the reception a young woman wondered what the fuss was about, suggesting that the best man was 'simply drawing attention to one happy sexual initiation as a good omen for the next.' The older guests, said Worsthorne, were struck dumb (So, possibly, were older readers of the *Daily Telegraph* to find the item in their newspaper). Nicholas Barker's *Vox* (1992) described itself as 'a novel about telephone sex' and consisted solely of a conversation between strangers which leads to mutual orgasm. Masturbation had become the sex without penalties that the sixties hedonists craved.*

'I know my 14-year-old daughter is masturbating because I can overhear her,' a woman wrote to the agony aunt of *People* magazine (1991). 'Being a single mother I regularly relieve my own frustrations in this way but I worry because she is so young.' The reply merely said that masturbation gave girls a chance to explore their bodies, and dropped a hint about respecting other people's privacy.

The new approach was grimly matter-of-fact. For women, masturbation had become a cause; or at least the cause was available for anyone who might otherwise have felt bad about auto-eroticism. A supplement to *Company* magazine sponsored by London Rubber, with the word 'Durex' liberally sprinkled throughout, gave masturbation a page (1990). 'It is hardly surprising,' it noted, 'that female masturbation should have been frowned on by a patriarchal society' — it being something that women could do by and for themselves. *My Secret Garden* was recommended as a good source of fantasies. For those who wanted to use an appliance that mimicked the male, two popular models were recommended. Or, if the new woman experiencing the new sex preferred, she could 'also use candles, carrots, cucumbers or bananas, covered' — since this was, after all, a Durex supplement — 'in a condom!'

---

* Auto-eroticism had an interesting future. 'Virtual Reality' — computer-based techniques that offer sensory contact between a suitably wired-up human being, and imaginary objects and events that are then experienced as real — was being explored; there would be money in it by the end of the century. Sexual applications were not hard to think of, as a 1992 film about VR, *The Lawnmower Man*, demonstrated. The novelist Aldous Huxley had thought of them sixty years earlier, when the indoctrinated citizens of *Brave New World* went to the 'feelies' instead of the cinema.

Operation Spanner

For a young heterosexual man or woman with a good carnal appetite, Forel's denunciation of 'coarse passions' would have meant little in late-century Britain. The law certainly had no interest in them. Even if they went in for deviant sex, the authorities were rarely interested. Acts in private between consenting couples were their own business. If they happened to be middle-aged homosexual men, however, interested in the extremes of SM behaviour, the case was different. Sex (a liberalized society agreed) was a good thing, even for men who were not as other men. But there might be limits, as was suggested, inconclusively, in the 'Operation Spanner' prosecution of 1990. This time it was not only moralists who were drawing the line. The law was suddenly hot under the collar.

Homosexual SM could not be casually dismissed as just another private deviation in life's rich sexual pattern. It may have been that, but it was also disturbing to those of other sexual persuasions. Pain, blood and suffering, in the interests of sexually exciting both those giving the punishment and receiving it, were involved. The case was sketchily reported because the behaviour it examined was so unpalatable. Much of it concerned beating, which at least was familiar ground for any British court or newspaper. Some of it went beyond that, dabbling in torture and mutilation, matters that had too many parallels in the real world of evil for their employment in some private world of re-enacted fantasy to be taken lightly.

Yet closed circles of SM behaviour existed in Britain, as they did in South California for readers of *The Sandmutopia Guardian & Journal*. Sado-masochism, it was said, more often went to extreme lengths in the hands of male homosexuals. Gay men in general, ran the argument, needed to experiment more than heterosexual couples, whose behaviour fell into obvious patterns, conditioned (at least on women's part) by romantic love. For gay men, their sexuality was central, and sado-masochistic relationships a useful ancillary. Apologists for SM activity always stressed its ritual and symbolic aspects. Everything was done by permission. The person on the receiving end of the punishment was ultimately in charge, able to stop whatever was going on, usually with a pre-arranged word. Thus 'Stop it, help me, police, murder!' would produce renewed activity, but 'Stop it, Bill!' would stay the hand.

That heterosexuals should find distasteful the spectacle of mature citizens doing things to one another and to younger men with whips, wires, spikes, scalpels, knives, sandpaper, matches and hot wax was hardly surprising. But distaste for other people's sexual habits had a long and equivocal history. For much of this century the subject of sexual relations between men was regarded as so filthy that judges could barely restrain themselves when they had to deal with it. Masturbation was almost universally denounced; so was contraception, which for years was illegal in the United States. Oral sex had once been disgusting for the majority, and remained so for some. Many heterosexuals still found anal sex between man and woman outrageous, as well as activities involving rubber sheets, or whips, or gas masks, or tickling with feathers, or anointing with golden syrup.

'Live and let live' had become a persuasive sexual dictum. It was not, however, to be applied in the case of the fifteen defendants who stood in the dock in December 1990 — three years after police began their inquiries. They included a forester, a care assistant for the mentally disabled, an ice-cream salesman, two restaurateurs (one of them a lay preacher), a lawyer, a former fire officer, a missile design engineer, a computer operator, a retired finance officer, an antiques restorer, a tattooist, a porter and an ex pig-breeder. Their average age was fifty. They belonged to a loose circle of friends and acquaintances living in many parts of the country, not all of whom knew everyone. This was the 'vice ring', so-called. It had no finite limits. The police could have extended their inquiries indefinitely to friends of friends, but had to draw the line somewhere. Men in their twenties and one or two mysterious figures of uncertain age were also involved as recipients of punishment, but were neither charged nor identified.

The case rested on home videotapes that were made by the participants, and circulated privately as pornography. Unluckily for the group, four tapes came into the hands of Greater Manchester police in 1987. They showed such things as the restaurateur using a scalpel to inflict wounds on the genitals of the antiques restorer, who at the time was hanging on a scaffold. Manchester was the wrong place for a dodgy videotape to turn up. Its chief constable, James Anderton, made sure his men kept a keen eye open for prosecutable immorality.

The tapes were undeniably gory. Police came across more of them, and hinted afterwards that they thought murder had been committed. 'Snuff movies', where filmed violence was supposed to lead to filmed death, had long been an obsession with anti-pornographers, sought-after but elusive. No investigator would have passed up the chance of finding one. Devotees of homosexual SM did sometimes get more than they bargained for. Two male masochists, members of the same gay sports club in London, died in separate incidents in 1988 and 1989; one, a clerk, asked to be beaten up by men on Hampstead Heath and was taken too literally; the other, a senior Bank of England official, was found floating in an East Anglian river, having been asphyxiated.

The 'Spanner' inquiry found no deaths. As evidenced by the charges that were eventually brought, it uncovered some mild drug abuse, a breath of child pornography, and one instance of a teenage minor who had been involved by two of the fifteen. Most of the evidence, taken from the videotapes that piled up as police identified participants and raided their houses, was of the fearful games they played. There were severe beatings, the finance officer being especially active in this department. Mr A, one of the ghostly participants, was branded with a hot wire to the sound of a Gregorian chant. Genital torture was practised, of the kind that Keith Vaughan wrote about in his journals. Sandpaper was used on the missile engineer. The computer operator did things with a nail. The fire officer carved his initials on the lawyer's buttocks with a Stanley knife. The forester did much the same to the ghostly Mr E. In some cases both the agent and the victim were charged with the same offence; thus the missile engineer was accused of torturing the fire officer's genitals, and the fire officer was accused of aiding and abetting him. In all cases the violence was mutually agreed to. Some of the charges related to 'keeping a disorderly house', which meant no more than providing the premises where activities took place. Most involved assault or bodily harm.

Because the activities were recorded on videotape, the only defence was to say that they were not criminal activities. If everyone consented, how could anyone be guilty? Before the trial began, defence counsel put that proposition to the judge, J. Rant. But he rejected it, saying that liberty was not to be confused with licence to commit acts that society saw as cruel. The leading case on the subject turned out to be something that happened in 1934, when a man took a willing girl of seventeen to a garage in south London and caned her. Later she changed her mind, and the man was charged with assault and given a prison sentence. The verdict was reversed on appeal, but because of misdirection by the judge, not because assaults could be condoned. An unlawful act, said the appeal court in 1934, could not be rendered lawful because the victim consented to it.

Faced with Judge Rant's decision, the defence advised their clients to plead guilty, which they did. No trial as such took place. Instead the prosecution stated its case, without fear of contradiction, and the lawyers made pleas in mitigation. The prisoners, who had thought they were safe because whatever they were doing was being done in private among friends, sat in a long unhappy row, listening to a recital of their misdeeds.

The judge was at pains to point out that 'this case is nothing to do with the homosexual nature of the accused.' That didn't stop the gay SM community feeling oppressed. They wanted tolerance for their games; a tall order.

As the pleas of mitigation unfolded there were occasional exchanges between counsel and judge where other issues than the ones in the charge-sheets glimmered for a moment. Anna Worrall QC (for the computer operator) spoke of acts that, however distasteful to those who viewed the videotapes, were enjoyable to the participants. The judge replied that he found it hard to accept that 'any sensible, intelligent, mature man' would feel he should indulge in such conduct. 'If something is plainly unacceptable, then surely, that is a matter that I am entitled to take into account, am I not?'

Worrall suggested that there might be things 'disgusting to those of us who have a normal sexual outlook' which society might condone when they were done in private. Criminal law, she said, was not concerned with moral standards.

> JUDGE RANT: It's not a question of morals, it is a question of sheer common sense . . . How can any intelligent, sensible man think that it is acceptable to nail the foreskin of another man's penis to a board, for example?

As often happens in courts of law, the case seemed to exist in a closed world of its own. Counsel made one or two references to ancient examples of SM activities. Ann Mallalieu QC (for the missile engineer) said that bondage, piercing and flagellation were portrayed in Pompeii and frescoes of the Renaissance. Lawrence Kershen (for the finance officer) quoted Havelock Ellis on pain and Kinsey on the widespread nature of SM interests (one-in-five men and one-in-eight women).

Within a mile of the court one could have bought books on the subject of erotic piercing, the process whereby nipples, sexual organs and perineum are pierced to take rings and studs; akin to some of the 'Spanner' activities. One might have found works by Dr Eric Dingwall, one-time assistant keeper of books at the British Library, which occasionally turn up in second-hand shops, his rare *Male Infibulation* (1925) or *The Girdle of Chastity* (1931), a historical study of the chastity belt; both of them books about strange practices.

But 'Operation Spanner' evoked a shiver, and the shiver was what mattered. Behind the detail of group sex and bloody deeds, and the court's view that injuries couldn't be condoned by the injured, lay a wider sense of abhorrence which emerged as traditional headlines in the tabloids. There had been 'VILE GAY SEX ORGIES' in which 'FIENDS' SICK THRILLS BLOTTED OUT AGONY' (*Sun*). The only tabloid to follow the story on a daily basis, David Sullivan's *Sport*, excelled itself. Its first report was headed 'SLAVES TO TORTURE' and 'NUDE PERV'S PAIN ORDEAL ON RACK'. Alongside it were blocks of advertisements for telephone sex lines. Many of these offered recorded messages about heterosexual SM − rubbish designed to part the caller from 44 pence a minute, aimed at exploiting men's taste for masochistic fantasies. Relevant titles included 'My Rod − Your Cheeks', 'Bend Over − No Trousers', 'Body Search Ordeal', 'Madam Spike Corrects', 'Madam Stern Restricts', 'Lick My Shoes'. Heterosexual fantasy was in order.

In passing sentence, Judge Rant re-emphasized his earlier remarks, saying that 'This is not a witch-hunt against homosexuals. The unlawful conduct before the court would result equally in the prosecution of heterosexuals or bisexuals . . . Nor is it a campaign to curtail the private sexual activities of citizens of this country.' The judge was less encouraging when he remarked that 'much has been said about individual liberties and the rights people have to do what they want with their own bodies, but the courts must draw the line between what is acceptable in a civilized society and what is not. In this case, the practices clearly lie on the wrong side of that line.' Judge Rant's certainty begged the question.

The forester and the care worker, who had lived together for years, and whose rural house was a popular venue, were each sent to prison for three and a half years. The computer operator and the ice-cream man, the two involved with the teenager, each got four and a half years. The missile engineer and the lay preacher were sentenced to three years; the finance officer, thirty-three months; the pig breeder, a year. Of the remaining seven, four were given suspended sentences, one was fined, one put on probation and one given a conditional discharge.

Even before the men were sentenced, the head of the Obscene Publications Squad, Supt Hames, was writing in the press about the 'most horrific porn ring [which it was not] ever to appear before a British court.' Few tears were shed for them outside the gay community. Few bothered to distinguish between society's view of what was winked at when men and women played games in private, and the way in which men doing things with men was regarded. Two years previously police had busied themselves with goings-on at a hotel in Cumbria, where heterosexuals went for 'weekends of bondage and torture', the latter in a cellar equipped as a dungeon, with hooks, chains and whips. The prosecution described naked women used as table decorations, games of forfeits with beatings as penalties, and a selection of videotapes recording the activities. For publishing the tapes the proprietor was given a short suspended sentence; for causing bodily harm to two women he was fined two hundred pounds.

The 'Spanner' case was an opportunity – as Dr Martin Cole remarked – for society to see how far it was prepared to go. There was uneasiness about its implications. For *The Times*, another activity had been criminalized, and

> Police forces will now make it their business to seek out perverse sexual activity to which they think a jury would take exception. Judge Rant, QC, unwisely remarked: 'The courts must draw the line between what is acceptable in a civilized society and what is not,' thus binding the police to enforce moral judgments and extending the always grey area between unpleasantness, immorality and statutory crime. The case . . . is an illiberal nonsense.

The *Independent* said much the same, expressing a 'mixture of horror and pity that human beings can deliberately inflict such extremes of degradation on themselves and others,' but again challenging Judge Rant's dictum about drawing the line. Where there was room for discretion by a judge,

> there should be a preference for interfering as little as possible in the private lives of citizens . . . Public sensibilities would not have been affected at all if the matter had not been brought to court. The appeal will provide an opportunity to clarify a case that could set disturbing precedents.

It took more than a year for the case to reach the appeal court, which upheld the convictions though it reduced most of the sentences. The Lord Chief Justice, Lord Lane (b. 1918 and on the verge of retirement), let it be known that 'the satisfying of the sado-masochistic libido does not come within the category of good reason.' So much for the 'English disease' and its mountainous literature.

A final appeal to the House of Lords had not been heard when this was written. Were the services of Miss Kane and Miss Birch now outside the law? Could the diaries of someone like Keith Vaughan have him sent to prison as evidence of attacks on his own person? Would there be no more phone calls to Madams Spike and Stern? Was the love-bite illicit? 'It would be distressing to learn,' said the *Independent*, 'that the Law Lords endorsed the view that penal sentences should be imposed as a mark of social disapprobation.' Once again the British had tied themselves in a knot.

Meanwhile consenting adults, gay and straight, continued to assault one another behind closed doors, being careful not to use video cameras. Their idea of what was permissible would remain the same, whatever the courts decided. One of the 'Spanner' survivors was certainly involved in the SM scene a year or two later. He was reasonably cheerful, all things considered. His neighbours still called 'Good morning' (not all of those convicted were so lucky). He said that a friend he was seeing a lot of had a T-shirt with a discreet logo that read, 'Sticks and stones may break my bones. But whips turn me on.' He was laughing as he said it.

15

'A Sex Life of Sorts'

Escaping the Past

IN AUTHORITARIAN TIMES it was easy to insist that sexual tastes and habits were subject to immutable moral laws. But they seemed more immutable than they were. A society that tolerated adulterers, fornicators, homosexuals (up to a point) and a wide range of idiosyncratic behaviour came into existence without disaster, though not without dissent. People forgot how recently it had happened, or grew up taking it for granted.

By the nineties there was little to be gained from moralizing about the young and their sexual experiences. Newspapers had stopped being shocked a decade earlier. Magazine articles about the new morality yellowed in the cuttings files. Fornication had been effectively separated from its natural consequence, the stigma of unwanted pregnancy, and with that separation, what had passed for a moral argument collapsed. Droves of unmarried women let themselves become pregnant, accidentally or on purpose; they knew they would not be condemned or penalised.

By the old standards, hundreds of thousands of children were corrupted. From sexual pleasures while they were at school, droves of them went on to set up home with one another, not using the apologetic language of the thirties, when 'trial marriage' was talked about and sometimes experimented with, but simply 'living together', and marrying if one day they felt like it. Over half the couples who married had lived together first, often for years, and had children. Parents smiled weakly when they told their friends, saying, 'Well — you know what they're like these days.'

The young spoke differently about sex. The jolly word 'bonking' appeared, making it possible for the first time in English to describe sexual intercourse without risk of offence. The new term was playful and friendly, coined by the young from the facetious word for a blow or a knock; 'bonking' described an activity you felt at ease with.

There were many opponents of all this, saying it had to stop. Towards the end of the eighties, social surveys were reporting a taste for the 'old values' that the decade of Thatcherism had been telling the nation was appropriate. A 'greater censoriousness' towards extra-marital sex, homosexuality and pornography was indicated; although the answers people gave, and the things they did, were not necessarily the same. At the beginning of the nineties, thirty years since the 'permissive society' was supposed to have started, voices were raised condemning the sixties, 'the root of all today's evils' (Lord Lewin, Admiral of the Fleet), the decade that 'undermined the moral fibre of the people' (Sir David Napley, solicitor). Beyond the overstatements was a real uneasiness, shared by millions, about the sexual consequences of what had happened, a feeling that new dangers and cruelties had come into ordinary life. Incest (now subsumed under 'child abuse') and rape claimed attention on a scale that made it hard to tell how much was new wickedness, how much merely the result of bringing into the open what was formerly hidden.

Yet whatever fears people (especially older people) had, and whatever answers they gave to the social surveys, the new sexual freedoms were evident. Whole areas of behaviour were accepted as inevitable by much of the nation because nothing could be done to change them. When the 'moral backlash' was making news, as early as the seventies, Freda Parker, by then the Family Planning Association's director of education, argued that it was already impossible to put the clock back:

> What would a counter-revolution mean? Go back to single-sex schools, ban contraceptives for the unmarried, stop girls going into men's rooms at university? We'd have to talk to women very seriously about their roles as wives and mothers. We'd have to go back to the double standard — it's all right for chaps but not for girls. Try to put things like *that* in a programme.

So the rough had to be taken with the smooth. The 'natural restraint' that Marie Stopes and others spoke of had turned out to be illusory, or at least not to operate at the simplistic level that they suggested. There were a hundred and twenty thousand teenage pregnancies in a year, of which forty thousand were terminated by legal abortion. Miss E was thirteen when she first had sex, in the early eighties:

> There was me and my friend, and her boyfriend and my boyfriend. It was very sort of basic, man on top of woman. She was in one room, I was in the other room, and we suddenly started calling out how many times we'd done it — 'Oh, I've done it three times,' or 'I've only done it

two,' you know? I think she beat me, though. I was expecting to feel pain and blood gushing everywhere, or something like bells, 'cos of these adverts and movies where it seems to be so romantic or sexy. It wasn't earth-shattering, put it that way. It was just basically something to do at the end of a party, I think.

I'd seen things like porno magazines and thought, 'They all look like they're enjoying that,' so I knew there must be something else to it. One bloke I went out with, I used to sing while he did it to me and wave to people, read a book. I think somebody did it to me in the end properly. Obviously as you grow older you realize there's much more to it, and there's more entangled with it, and it gets a bit more complicated then.

New standards had to be accepted, whatever reservations people had — moral, aesthetic or merely practical. An advertising agency suggested that a materialistic generation of super-brats was coming of age, its males swigging lager from the age of twelve and having sex at thirteen. Few were surprised to hear it. People were used to reading that more of the British got divorced than almost anywhere else in Europe. Older people came to terms with unmarried motherhood, and if it was in their own family, the same apologetic formula worked: 'Well — you know what they're like these days.' Three of every ten births were to single mothers, some of them to careless teenagers but many reflecting the existence of well over a million unmarried couples who chose to live together with the appearance of stability, and shared hundreds of thousands of dependent children. Most of them married eventually, but only when it suited them. There was, too, the rise of the lone-parent (usually lone-mother) family, which meant that one-sixth of all families with children were lone-parented — the highest figure in Europe, a distinction shared with Denmark. The practical argument that two guardians were likely to be better than one failed to deter them.

Britain had to live with the results of new freedoms. So did all Western countries, but the British had their peculiar history of sexual repression to haunt them. By making changes deep within its social structure, the nation was perhaps finding ways to escape its past.

No clear line was drawn between old standards and new. Miscellaneous prudery was unvanquished. A Church of England school sacked its matron, aged twenty-one, because she was pregnant and declined to marry her lover (1989). Thomas Hardy's character Tess of the d'Urbevilles was not permitted to appear on a postage stamp because the Palace disliked the idea of an unmarried mother next to the royal head (1990). A 'Captain Condom' campaign on the Isle of Wight to promote safe sex, consisting of pamphlets, badges and a cardboard cut-out of the Captain, was told it was not welcome at Cowes Week (1991).

Sterner issues to fight over included old favourites like sex education. The 1986 Education Act voiced the Conservative creed. It gave local governors the right to decide whether their school should have sex education, and what its nature should be. Lessons must encourage pupils 'to have due regard to moral considerations and the value of family life.' A year later a circular from the Education Department said the same thing in more detail, requiring emphasis on the benefits of a stable marriage.

Moralists saw this as the answer to twenty years of disgracefully explicit sex education. 'Schoolchildren are reported as saying they want to learn about contraception. That does not mean that they should be taught about it,' said a booklet sponsored by CARE (1988). Non-moralistic sex educators groaned and said it was impractical to pretend that children were susceptible to moralizing. 'Sex education,' wrote the Family Planning Association's director, Doreen Massey (1990), 'cannot be left to chance or paralysed by power games between adults persecuted by their own inadequacies, uncertainties or over-ripe moral judgements.'

Sex education was slowly becoming more explicit, accompanied by howls of rage from right-wing commentators who deplored the social benefits enjoyed by (for example) teenage mothers, and who secretly hankered after institutions, carbolic soap and discipline. Radical texts were still guaranteed to provoke thunder and lightning from those who believed that the innocence of children was being destroyed, rather than their questions answered. *Knowing Me, Knowing You* (1990), a guide for primary schoolteachers, with selective material for use by children, took in masturbation, contraception, sexual intercourse and Aids. Objectors to its publication included Mrs Victoria Gillick, who had campaigned some years earlier to stop doctors giving contraceptive advice to girls under sixteen without parental consent, taking legal action that would have succeeded but for a final ruling by the House of Lords. Gillick thought that sex education helped cause promiscuity. So did most moralists. It was the 'lambs aren't thinking about sex' syndrome. The other view was that in a highly sexed age, it was appropriate to treat children as sexual beings, who continually picked up carnal messages from the world around them. As Liz Swinden, co-author of *Knowing Me*, said, 'Children are not blank slates.'

Arguments about sex education went on above the heads of the children themselves, who had better things to think about. Perhaps it made little difference whether the lessons consisted of left-wing brutality, putting condoms on cucumbers, or right-wing brutality, stressing the perils of infidelity and abortion; or merely the more usual haphazard mixture of biology and social studies. Massey suggested (1991) that 'where we've made the mistake in sex education is in thinking that if we tell them, they'll do something about it.'

It was certainly no longer possible to see ignorance about the facts of life and contraception as a simple evil to be erased by knowledge. Tens of thousands of teenagers became pregnant every year because it suited them. The natural tendency of teenagers, and everyone else, to suit themselves was an aspect of sexual emancipation that upset many of those who had paid lip-service to reforming ideas. Not surprisingly, the privileged often disliked it. It was true that society could cope more easily with sexual licence enjoyed by the few (as it had always been) than by the majority. But that was not a moral objection.

Another old favourite was abortion, where attempts to overturn the Act of 1967 persisted. The way the law worked was less than perfect, since permission had to be negotiated with doctors, and facilities sought within the Health Service, which was unable or unwilling to meet more than about two-fifths of the demand; the 'private charity' clinics did most of the rest. The total was large, one hundred and seventy thousand abortions a year in England and Wales, one in five of all pregnancies. It was a routine procedure, physically safe though not without mental anguish for some. By 1991 an abortion drug, mifepristone, had been licensed, and was likely to make some terminations simpler.

Compared with the horrors and inequities of the old system, the service was decent and humanitarian. But opposing groups with Roman Catholic leanings couldn't bring themselves to accept that women knew what they wanted, as they had always known, and were entitled to have it. It was true that the 'worn-out mother' of the old propaganda was now barely a memory. Three-quarters of those treated were single; the majority, whether married or not, had no children, and few had more than one or two. They used abortion to cope with life-styles that the pioneering reformers of the thirties would have deplored, but which for them were appropriate to the times. Even the teenagers, one in three of all single women having abortions, were exercising some kind of right.

The interesting Miss E, who was on the pill, kept forgetting to take it as a teenager. She became pregnant twice, but there was a solution. Sixty years earlier she might have been one of the rough diamonds who was polished up in Homes. In a more accommodating age she had two abortions. Why not? If the alternative was the nineteen-twenties trick of turning fallen girls into drudges, crushing the life out of them in the process, abortion seemed the lesser evil.

Miss E was fifteen the first time:

> The thought of pregnancy put a shiver up my spine. I'd seen people who were quite close to me have children, and I knew their lives weren't made any better by it. Like a girl I used to know, same age as me – she's got three children [Miss E was now twenty] and she hasn't got any money. It doesn't appeal to me. I didn't have any skill in anything, so I wanted to get that, and I was in a bad relationship, so the thought of actually having a baby seemed a way of ruining my life. I couldn't see the bloke I was with letting me go out to college and him looking after the baby. Also, we'd been going out about one and a half years but I was starting not to like him, so I thought, 'That's not a brilliant way of bringing up a kid.'

The lesser evil admittedly left a lot to be desired. Radicals were as unhappy as conservatives about juvenile abortions; and as barren of practical solutions.

In the first dozen years after the Act there were seven unsuccessful attempts by individual MPs to weaken it with new legislation. Talk of action to stop 'late' abortions, say after the twentieth week, often concealed the real purpose of Bills, to narrow the medical criteria or cripple the abortion charities. Further attempts failed in the eighties.

In 1990 a Government Bill dealing more widely with fertility included proposals to shorten the term of pregnancy within which abortion was legal. As a Government measure it was not vulnerable in the way of private Members' Bills. The anti-abortionists badly needed a symbolic victory, which they could exploit later when renewing their assault on the Abortion Act. In an attempt to influence MPs, the Society for the Protection of Unborn Children sent them all plastic replicas of twenty-week foetuses costing £10 a time, without success. A series of free votes did more harm than good to the restrictionists' cause, and perhaps marked the end of attempts to dislodge the Act, after twenty-three years. It was said that an anti-abortion MP, a woman, was so grief-stricken that she vomited in the taxi on her way home after the voting. The subject retained its power to disturb.

Laxer moral standards gave the impression that people were more tolerant, but the changes they tolerated were usually those they approved of in their own lives. Unforgivingness was still in plentiful supply. AIDS, Acquired Immune Deficiency Syndrome, was identified in Los Angeles in 1981. Two years later the HIV virus, which is supposed to produce the condition, was described in France. The new disease (unless it was an old disease given a new lease of life) came to frighten us and provide a focus for examining our moral state. In 1988, when calls for a return to traditional morality because of the threat posed by AIDS were particularly loud, Wendy Cope responded with an ironic poem, 'The Monogamous Union', about the new targets of the Right, such as 'The deserted, the pooftahs, the difficult spinsters' who should 'get themselves lawfully wed'. It was 'poofters' who came in for the worst intolerance. Not only had a minority dared to make themselves highly visible since their lives were more or less decriminalized in the sixties, campaigning for 'gay rights' and flaunting their sexual habits in life and in fiction, but they were now identified as a threat to clean-living heterosexuals. In the West it was in homosexual communities that HIV first developed and was recognized; though it was also possible for heterosexual couples to infect one another through normal intercourse.

Millions of heterosexual men used the derisive word 'poofter' in private, and one or two tabloid newspapers did the same in public, arguing (when they bothered to argue at all) that it was a word their audience was familiar with. When the Press Council made an ill-advised attempt to outlaw such language, a leading article in the *Sun* (1990) said cheerfully that its readers 'KNOW and SPEAK and WRITE words like poof and poofter.' The *New Statesman*, interviewing a group of teenage heterosexuals in Surrey (1990), found them 'vigorously anti-gay ... two of them make a great point of saying that AIDS stands for "Anally Induced Death Sentence".' Radio phone-in programmes allowed glimpses of the popular prejudice that journalists were reluctant to quote in newspaper articles, though one could hear it in any saloon bar. If homosexuality could be justified by a loving relationship, a man from Hampshire said on Radio 4 (1988), why couldn't incest or sex with animals, 'or for that matter lying, stealing, violence and murder, which seems to come naturally to some?'

Distaste simmered for the sustained promiscuity that some gays went in for – before AIDS was identified, if less frequently afterwards. Two novels of 1988 dwelt on it in a literary sort of way, *The Beautiful Room is Empty* by an American, Edmund White, and *The Swimming-Pool Library* by an Englishman, Alan Hollinghurst. A reviewer wrote, 'The protagonists of these novels may spend their time grovelling around the damp floors of urinals, but goodness they're cultured.' A sentence from White's book gives the general picture: 'The businessman with the expensive briefcase has planted his face between the farmboy's buttocks in total disregard of his expensive trousers, which are getting damp and dirty on the floor, wet with backed-up sewage.'

It was distaste for the physical details that had always fed homophobia, back to the more genteel times when police said they could rarely obtain convictions for male indecency in Hyde Park because it was hard to convince juries that 'men exist capable of committing such filthy acts.' John Betjeman, when he was at school in the early twenties, was warned by his father about buggers, 'two men who work themselves up into such a state of mutual admiration that one puts his piss-pipe up the other man's arse' (Young Betjeman was 'absolutely sick and shattered,' as intended).

The association with lavatories didn't help. Along with parks and commons, public toilets ('cottages') were the places to make acquaintances and have sex with them, and 'cottaging' was a necessary part of the homosexual sub-culture before gay pubs and clubs began to emerge in the seventies. A Mass-Observer, a homosexual aged forty-five, who formerly haunted Britain's lavatories, boasted (1990) that 'I have probably had sex with as many as three thousand partners in the last twenty-five years.' Many were more discriminating and lived quietly with permanent partners, but it was the overtly promiscuous (or the politically committed) who got under the heterosexual skin.

Irritation was a common response, even among men who said they respected the rights of homosexuals, and may have wanted to. Gays could have the rights as long as they shut up and didn't flaunt themselves; the promiscuous homosexual and the thought of what he got up to was disturbing. So was much that heterosexuals did. Their promiscuous or deviant behaviour gave frequent offence to more upright citizens. But it was less unforgivable when it was men with women. The coarseness of heterosexual novels, not to mention pornography, could be well up to homosexual standards. The same distinction applied. What homosexuals did was disturbing in a special way. That was the perception of the majority. However regrettable, it was too deeply felt to be eliminated by a few decades of 'reform'.

If distaste was one powerful response to homosexuals, fear was another. Their role as vectors of the HIV virus was undeniable in the West. AIDS was first recognized as an epidemic among Californian homosexuals. It remained chiefly a disease of gay men, as well as of intravenous drug-users who spread the virus through infected needles, and haemophiliacs who had received infected blood. Apart from these two sub-categories, only a handful of heterosexuals in Britain developed AIDS, most of whom were probably infected abroad; in parts of Africa, women were as likely as men to have the virus, and visitors could be infected by prostitutes. The London borough of Islington, ever helpful in such matters, offered a free packet of three 'extra strong' contraceptives to residents who were going abroad (1990).

British Government health-education programmes harped on the risk to everyone, gay or straight, and would have been blameworthy had they not done so. Whether they over-emphasized the dangers was unlikely to be known before the end of the century. In the meantime the idea that AIDS was or might be a heterosexual disease was attacked by Right-wing politicians, newspapers and commentators for raising false alarms and deflecting attention from the real victims (and culprits), the homosexuals. It was said that the gay community was anxious to show that anyone could be stricken with AIDS, so as to avoid collecting all the blame, and to ensure that it received its fair share of funds and sympathy. If homosexuals did follow this strategy, it was hardly surprising, given the jaundiced view that society had of them; they would have been unwise not to protect themselves.

Just as people looked back to a Britain with less crime and rape in it, so they were nostalgic for a time when upsetting sexual habits were kept out of sight. 'Surely,' said a woman from Berkshire in a radio phone-in about AIDS 'it's better to have sex quietly and feel guilty about it, because you're less likely then to flaunt it everywhere.' Similar sentiments were heard within the Church of England, from both clergy and laity, as the issue of homosexuals in the priesthood stirred uneasily. The Church may have changed its mind about sexual pleasure, but the benefits of its conversion had been confined to heterosexuals. In a television programme the Bishop of Chester, Michael Baughen (b. 1930), suggested that

> In some ways it's better to be secret about it than open about it. It's been the coming-out that's caused the problem, hasn't it? To a large extent the policy of things like the gay and lesbian movement has been to push it and to say, this is an alternative lifestyle ... Whereas if people had acknowledged this as something which they kept totally private, then the problem wouldn't have raised its head so much in the Church.

But they didn't, and it had.

Men and women as sexual partners had a bad time, at least if one judged the modern heterosexual relationship by the books, articles and television programmes that examined feminism, post-feminism, the male backlash, the backlash against the male backlash, and all the permutations of discontent that arose from the disturbance of the old balance of power between the sexes. The redistribution of power being among the least tractable of human problems, the sexual kind proved no exception.

The rise of feminist aggression was duly noted. Not since the suffragettes had men been so upset. Writers like Dworkin steamed with rage; few men read her books, but even the thickest-skinned male was vaguely aware of threatening noises from radical womanhood, often expressed in a casual way, like the stripper who spoke on Channel 4 television (1990), explaining that as a lesbian she enjoyed feeling 'an incredible amount of power' over men who were desperate enough to pay to watch her take her clothes off. A proportion of women wanted to get their own back. The fact that this was understandable made it no less unsettling, as in *Dirty Weekend* (1991), a novel by a heterosexual writer, Helen Zahavi, in which Bella, a young woman in Brighton who is persecuted by a peeping tom and other male low-life, spends a weekend murdering them all. They have violated her space; they have to die. Dworkin called the book beautiful and true, enough to make a male reader hesitate, but it was an instructive insight into a realm of female fantasy in which Bella shrivels up men and their private parts on behalf of 'all her sisters'.

The predatory woman who frightened men by her directness and her overt sexuality was half a joke, half a cloud on the horizon. Women who 'saw their bodies as their own', who controlled their fertility if it suited them and earned their own living, could take a relaxed view of their partners. They were encouraged to see the funny side of them, as the sexually-aware glossy magazines for women (sometimes those for men as well) indicated to their substantial readerships.

'What Men Do Wrong in Bed' (*Cosmopolitan*, 1991) belonged to a genre of amiable revenge. 'Time and time again I've watched wearily, with shrinking libido, as his trousers crinkle down to the ankles, the tie is loosened and the socks remain stubbornly *in situ*.' Socks and underpants were good for a laugh; so were men's personal habits, like the delusion (quoting *Cosmopolitan* again) that in bed, 'passing wind is the ultimate in machismo.' The women's magazine *Company* (edited by a woman aged twenty-seven, selling two hundred thousand copies a month) included, in a Durex-sponsored supplement called 'Sex, Desire & Him' (1991), a two-page spread that displayed thirty-six sepia photographs of male genitalia, each captioned with a synonym of 'penis', from 'John Thomas' and 'Pecker' to 'Shagbatten' and 'Blue-veined Piccolo', not terms one hears every day. With its title, 'ROGUES' GALLERY. THE FULL-FRONTAL PICTURE GUIDE THAT PROVES THEY'RE NOT ALL THE SAME!', it was not difficult to suspect a sly turning of tables on men who enjoy seeing naked women; nothing could look more naked than thirty-six flaccid male organs. One could imagine a hint of revenge, too, in the male strip-shows and videos that found women audiences ready to laugh, screech, point and chant 'Off, off, off!' at the oiled bodies stripped down to G-strings, and give delighted giggles when the penises finally shook themselves free.

Feminist writers speculated about the historic suppression, by men, of women's sexual drive in the interests, firstly of not letting it interfere with maternal responsibilities, secondly of reassuring husbands that the wives' offspring were really theirs. Non-feminist writers who used to stress the virtues of such suppression were out of fashion by the 1990s. But fear of hypersexual wives and sweethearts had too long an ancestry to vanish overnight. Marie Stopes heard her books accused by 'Lord X' of making sex-mad vampires out of married women. D.H. Lawrence hated and feared the self-sufficient woman with a clitoris that he perceived as a beak.

After two or three decades of feminism, a proportion of men had certainly concluded that egalitarian women were not as erotic as the other kind. Much of this was a joke, but under the joke were suspicions. 'WHAT WOMEN WANT IN BED' (*GQ*, 1989), presented a dialogue between four women.

> STEPHANIE: Have you ever had the feeling that they don't know where it is?

RHODA: Oh God, yes.

DENISE: Oh, yeah.

STEPHANIE: Now, sometimes I show them. I say, 'This is where you put your cock in and where the babies come out. And *this* is the clitoris, up *here*.' Otherwise they fiddle away down there for ages, and you have to keep saying, 'Up a bit.' '*Oh*,' they say, '*up*?' And you say, 'Ye-es.' And they're clearly thinking, 'Very strange, all this "up a bit." It's like *The Golden Shot*.'

JULIA: At least at the end of that you got a toaster.

Serious evidence of neurotically anxious men may have been fragmentary. But few men would have failed to recognize a truth of sorts in tales about the flattening effect of superwoman.

The huge romanticism of marriage kept going, despite the divorce and adultery statistics nibbling away behind the cake and the congratulations. A wedding remained the most costly piece of ritual behaviour in the average person's life. The literature of modern marriage proliferated, both scholarly and informal, the latter dwelling on life-stories, as though the telling of endless tales about other marriages would bring comfort and enlightenment to those whose own marriages were too close for self-examination.

'Francesca', in south London, thirtyish, affluent, married to a professional man, worried about their relationship. The children were demanding, being able to 'scream louder than your husband.' They enjoyed 'a sex life of sorts, but on a daily basis it's impossible.' He thought she was a feminist; she thought she was a realist. Part of her believed that

> men and women are fundamentally incompatible. It seems very cruel, at a time when we should be much more realistic about what we expect from each other, that the media thrust it down our throats that we've somehow got to go on expecting love and romance and sexual compatibility. We were never meant to shut the front door and have one man and one woman inside, saying, 'We can give each other everything.' That's romantic rubbish.

Francesca said sternly that she didn't want him patting her bottom while she was standing at the sink in rubber gloves. At the same time – now sounding less stern – she didn't exclude romance. 'You certainly want him to *be* romantic. So maybe poor men are never, never going to get it right.'

It was the reality of a million husbands and wives: knowing there were escape routes, reluctant to take them; eating their hearts out.

Politicians, mainly Conservative, and other crusaders, among them the enduring Mary Whitehouse, continued to demand a return to old values that would re-institute the mythically stable family. My own parents' marriage (1923–1946) was a chaos of misunderstanding and sexual incompatibility from which divorce came as a happy release. Optimists thought they knew better. There were hints of coercion. The National Campaign for the Family's booklet about divorce reform (1988) suggested that the law should not be 'indifferent to the morality of the behaviour of spouses towards each other.' But the law no longer dictated morality. It had to adapt itself to the behaviour of people who knew that values changed, like everything else.

The 'sexual revolution' was attacked by those who regretted the anarchy that accompanied the new freedoms, and disbelieved in by those who insisted that too little had changed to justify the term. It remained a reality in terms of what life had been like for the first half of the century.

The results were undeniably mixed. Harry wrote in a jaundiced mood on his sixtieth birthday (1988), 'Would it honestly have mattered had we all continued to the bitter end with our marriages? Would it have mattered had I thought less about Sex and more about Conversation?' Lord Hailsham's question about happiness still hung in the air. Sexual fantasy, a game for those who like it, had its ominous side. Child molesting and sadism crept about on the edges of everyday life. What was it that waited, still, to be freed?

Sexual revolution turned out to be a more savage beast than the early reformers allowed for. But there was a convincing argument in its favour: the only practical alternative would have been to stay as we were.

Notes

The following abbreviations are used:

BL: British Library
BMJ: British Medical Journal
M-O: Mass-Observation Archive, University of Sussex
PRO: Public Record Office
VR: Vigilance Record

'In an interview' means an interview with the author

Chapter 1

1. *Reminiscences* — 1. *osteopath,* 2. *housewife,* 3. *teacher*: M-O. 1. and 3., 'Age Differences' directive replies, July 1979. 2., 'Little Kinsey', Box 13, File D, QQ 352.

2. *Tabitha John: Tabitha. The story of a Llanelli character,* privately published, 1979.

2. *Booth and Devon*: quoted in Abraham Flexner, *Prostitution in Europe,* New York, 1914.

2. *Letter to Marie Stopes*: her *Contraception. Its theory, history and practice,* 1925.

4. BMJ: February 8, 1902.

4ff. *Ellis, biographical information*: Vincent Brome, *Havelock Ellis, Philosopher of Sex,* 1979; A Calder-Marshall, *Havelock Ellis,* 1959.

5. *Inspector Arrow: VR,* April 1902.

6. *Blackpool nudes: VR,* August 1902.

6. *Edwardian catalogues*: the British Library's 'Private Case' has a collection, much of it thanks to the eccentric, occultist and bibliophile, Dr Eric Dingwall, who was an honorary assistant keeper in the department of printed books. See, eg., PC 16m 6.

6. *Havelock Ellis and* Gynecocracy: the speculation is by G. Legman, in his Introduction to Patrick J. Kearney, *The Private Case,* an annotated bibliography of the British Library's erotica, 1981.

7. *The Hon. Miss Vavasour*: From 'Miss Pokingham, or They All Do It', in *The Pearl. A Journal of Facetive and Voluptuous Reading.* Ballantine Books, New York, 1978.

7. *Glyn on marriage*: her autobiography, *Romantic Adventure,* 1936. Other biographical information: A. Glyn, *Elinor Glyn,* 1955.

7. *J.B. Priestley: The Edwardians*, 1970.

7–8. *Rosa Lewis*: see Anthony Masters, *Rosa Lewis. An Exceptional Edwardian*, 1977; Michael Harrison, *Rosa*; Daphne Fielding, *The Duchess of Jermyn Street*, 1964.

8. *'Tarts and backsides'*: Theodora FitzGibbon, *With Love*, 1982.

9. *Pinero's doll*: J. Johnston, *The Lord Chamberlain's Blue Pencil*, 1990.

9. *J.B. Watson: Formation of Character*, 1908.

10. *'The rose is red'*: *Llanelly Mercury*, 11.1.05.

10. *Packets of eight*: J. Peel, 'The Manufacture and Retailing of Contraceptives in England', in *Population Studies* XVII, 1963–64. One of the condoms was examined at the British Museum by Eric Dingwall. He said it was a generous 190mm long, its texture thinner than the modern article's.

11. *Diachylon*: A. McLaren, 'Abortion in England 1890–1914', *Victorian Studies*, summer 1977.

11. *The Chrimes brothers*: ibid.

12. *Times on Waste*: quoted in Norman St John-Stevas, *Obscenity and the Law*, 1956.

12ff. *Coote, the NVA and morality prosecutions*: VR, 1900–1910.

14. *Land of Pure Morals*: Russell Davies, 'In a Broken Dream: some aspects of sexual behaviour and the dilemmas of the unmarried mother in South West Wales, 1887–1914', *Llafur* III, 4, 1983.

14. *Welsh verse*: *Medieval Welsh Erotic Poetry*, edited and translated by Dafydd Johnston, 1991.

Chapter 2

16. *Ensor: England 1870–1914*, 1936.

18. *Bishop of Ripon*: VR, April 1904.

19. *Harmsworth's magazines*: Paul Ferris, *The House of Northcliffe*, 1971.

21ff. *H.G. Wells, biographical information*: Lovat Dickson, *H G Wells. His turbulent life and times*, New York, 1969; Norman and Jeanne Mackenzie, *The Time Traveller: The life of H G Wells*, 1973; Anthony West, *H.G. Wells: Aspects of a life*, 1984; G.P. Wells (ed.), *H.G. Wells in Love: Postscript to an experiment in autobiography*, 1984; David C. Smith, *H.G. Wells: Desperately mortal*, 1986.

24. *Beatrice Webb's diary*: *The Diary of Beatrice Webb*, ed. N. and J. Mackenzie, 1984.

28. *Madame Osborne Gray*: VR, December 1913.

29ff. *NVA, Coote and vice*: VR, passim.

31. *Mr George's catalogue*: Family Planning Association collection.

Chapter 3

Passim Feminists and Suffragettes: Susan Kingsley Kent, *Sex and Suffrage in Britain, 1860–1914*, Princeton; David Mitchell, *Queen Christabel: A biography of Christabel Pankhurst* and *The Fighting Pankhursts: A study in tenacity*; Antonia Raeburn, *The Militant Suffragettes*; R. Fulford, *Votes for Women: The story of a struggle*.

34. *Isaac Bashevis Singer*: 'Guests on a Winter Night', in *A Friend of Kafka*, 1972.

35. *Lewis and Levy: People*, 26.7.03.

35. *Disgusted, Alexandria: VR*, January 1909.

35. *Danks alias Stuart: VR*, February 1909.

35fn. *Mamie Stuart*: I investigated the story in the 1960s for an article that was never published. Her husband, George Shotton, was a violent man who probably found that his chorus girl was deceiving him. Police dug up the garden where they had lived on the Gower coast, hoping to find a body; newspapers spoke of 'Dark Secret of the House on the Bay'. But all they could do in the end was have him put away for bigamy. He died in his bed at the age of 77, three years before the skeleton was discovered. The inquest (1961) concluded that he murdered her.

36. *Liberal critic*: Frederick Handel Booth MP, a north-country iron master, opposing a second reading of the 'White Slave' Bill, 10.6.12.

37. *Four incorrigible rogues: News of the World*, 3.11.12; the case was heard at London Sessions.

37–8. *Davies alias Torriani: News of the World*, 28.7.12.

38. *Bullock interview*: 22.9.12.

39. *White Slave fever*: eg. *News of the World* 5.1.13, 'WHITE SLAVE TRAP. GIRLS WARNED AGAINST AGENTS' DEVICES'; Edward J. Bristow, *Vice and Vigilance: Purity movements in Britain since 1700* has useful insights.

39fn. *Northcliffe's children*: Ferris, op. cit.

41. *'Behave like a man'*: Robert Baden-Powell, *Rovering to Success: A book of life-sport for young men*, 1922.

43–4. *Discovering '606'*: Ferris, op. cit.

44–5. *William Acton*: see Alex Comfort, *The Anxiety Makers*, 1967.

45. *New Statesman*: 25.8.28, 'The Vulgarity of Lesbianism', a review of Compton Mackenzie's novel *Extraordinary Women*.

46. *Olive Schreiner*: see Ruth First and Ann Scott, *Olive Schreiner*, 1980; Joyce Avrech Berkman, *The Healing Imagination of Olive Schreiner*, 1989. Schreiner's relationship with 'a man who was a sadist' was described by Arthur Calder-Marshall in his life of Havelock Ellis.

47ff. *Queenie Gerald*: PRO, HO 45/24649; Hansard, 12.8.13, cols 2336–2342, . 2389–2396; 14.8.13, cols 2745–2752.

Chapter 4

56. *Church Army Homes: Church Army Review* files of the period. Article about the Frances Owen Home, August 1910, reprinted from the *Daily Chronicle*.

57. *'Outrageous insult'*: *Church Quarterly Review*, February 1915. Archbishop of Canterbury: *The Times*, 10.2.15.

57ff. *Women police and* (from p 58.) *Women's Patrols*: see David Mitchell, *Women on the Warpath: The story of the women of the First World War*; Mary S. Allen and

Julie Helen Heyneman, *The Pioneer Policewoman*, 1925; Allen and Heyneman, *Woman at the Cross Roads*, 1934.

58. *Home Office Advice*: quoted in *VR*, Christmas 1914.

58. *Deputation to Home Office*: PRO, HO 45/10806.
    Chief Constable of Bradford: PRO, HO 45/10806.

59. *Lancashire vicar*: *Daily Express*, 3.11.14.

59ff. *'Interfering toads' and subsequent quotations from reports*: PRO, HO 45/10806.

60. *Newspaper praises patrols*: *Weekly Despatch*, 26.11.16; police comments, PRO, Mepol 2/1710.

60. *Norwood and Blackheath*: Mepol 2/1710.

60. *Intercourse in Hyde Park*: PRO, Mepol 2/1708.

60. *Effects on Park Lane*: PRO, Mepol 2/1720, summary of superintendents' reports on 'whether there is any truth in the statement that members of the [women's patrols] have, by their moral influence, cleared the parks and open spaces of London in a way which men cannot do.' The answer was no.

60. *Gross indecency*: PRO, Mepol 2/1708.

61. *Mr Mead gives a lecture*: PRO, Mepol 2/1710.

61. *At the cinema*: PRO, Mepol 2/1691.

62. *Max Pemberton*: *Weekly Despatch*, 8.7.17.

62–3. *To the flappers*: ibid., 29.1.17, Mrs Alfred Praga.

64. *Marie Corelli*: *Daily Chronicle*, 20.4.16. Later in the war the patriotic Miss Corelli was fined £50 for hoarding sugar to use in making jam. She said the police had gone too far and forecast 'a revolution in England in less than a week.'

64. *Mrs Creighton*: *VR*, July 1917.

64. *Gen. Dorrien and the girls*: *VR*, September 1916, October 1916.

65. *Social-purity group*: Association for Moral and Social Hygiene, in its magazine *The Shield*; quoted in P.S. O'Connor, 'Venus and the Lonely Kiwi', *New Zealand Journal of History*, I, 1967.

66. *A WAAC on the knee*: quoted in David Mitchell, op. cit.

66. *Compton Mackenzie*: *Vestal Fires*, 1927.

66. *British soldiers, Indian women*: PRO, WO 32/11401, General Childs of the War Office at a conference on 'Temptations of overseas soldiers in London', part of the Imperial War Conference, p.197; W.N. Willis, *Western Men with Eastern Morals*, 1913.

67. *Kitchener's leaflet*: G. Arthur, *Life of Lord Kitchener*, 1920.

67. *Mary Scharlieb*: quoted in E.J. Bristow, op. cit.

68. *The Army order*: Richard Davenport-Hines, *Sex, Death and Punishment: Attitudes to sex and sexuality in Britain since the Renaissance*, 1990, an important account of its subject – the prejudice engendered by sexual disease and homosexuality.

68. *1917 conference*: WO 32/11401, op. cit.

69. *Unseemly differences*: see, eg., conflicting remarks by Sir Edward Henry, police commissioner in London, and General Childs at the 'Temptations of soldiers' conference, WO 32/11401, op. cit.

69. *Virile Australians*: PRO, WO 32/11404.

69. *Prostitutes with ladders*: Dr M.W. Adler, 'The terrible peril', *BMJ*, 19.7.80.

69. *Selling infection*: ibid.

70. *White flag and condom*: O'Connor, *New Zealand Journal of History*, I, 1967, op. cit.

70. *Massey and Borden*: WO 32/11401, op. cit.

70. *Shuffling around Whitehall*: the issues are examined in Suzann Buckley, 'The failure to resolve the problem of venereal disease among the troops in Britain during World War I', in *War and Society: A yearbook of military history*, Vol 2, 1977.

70. *Germans and chastity*: Magnus Hirschfeld, *The Sexual History of the World War*, New York, c. 1945. 'Intended for circulation among Mature Educated Persons only.'

71. *Dr Turner*: letter to *BMJ*, 8.10.22. 'I lectured on venereal disease to about 500,000 of our troops . . .'

71. *Four Army chaplains*: *A Corner-stone of Reconstruction*, 1919.

71. *The German Prisoner*: privately printed by the author. Introduction by Richard Aldington, who describes it as 'a terrible story, terrible in the reality it expresses.' In 1935 it was prosecuted for obscenity – it contains strong language but nothing remotely erotic – and twelve copies were destroyed.

71. *Ziegler's account*: *King Edward VIII: The official biography*, 1990.

72ff. *Brothels row*: PRO WO 32/5597 tells the story, notably in Salisbury to Derby, 21.1.18; Riddell to Derby, 25.1.18; Derby to Riddell, 26.1.18; Canterbury to Derby, 9.2.18; Derby to Canterbury, 22.2.18; Canterbury to Derby, 16.3.18; memo, Derby to War Cabinet, 15.3.18; Haig to War Office, 4.6.18.

74. *Murdered wife*: Four Chaplains, *A Corner-stone of Reconstruction*, op. cit.

74. *Soldiers' divorces*: *News of the World*, 24.3.18.

74–5. *Armistice scenes*: *Daily News*, 12.11.18.

Chapter 5

76. *Character in a walk*: Robert Baden-Powell, *Lessons from the Varsity of life*, 1933.

77. *American writer*: Alfred Kazin, Introduction to Thomas Burke, *Limehouse Nights*, New York, 1973.

77. *Savoy murder*: recounted in Andrew Rose, *Scandal at the Savoy*, 1991.

79. *'Kissing her fingers'*: *Married Love*.

79–80. *Hall's biography*: *Passionate Crusader*.

81. *Mr O*: *Enduring Passion*.

81. *The vital-fluid treatment*: Sir Arbuthnot Lane in *Guy's Hospital Gazette*, 30.11.18; speech by Dr W.H.B. Stoddart at a conference on birth control, reported in *BMJ*, 22.7.22.

82. *The long-married wife*: quoted by Janet Chance in *Proceedings* of 3rd congress, World League for Sexual Reform, 1930.

83. *A man's failing*: *Married Love*.

83. *Electrical currents*: *Enduring Passion*.

84. *American writer*: Dr W.F. Robie, according to Stopes 'the wisest and most helpful of American sexologists.'

84. *'Disgusting acts'*: quoted in Ruth Hall (ed.) *Dear Dr Stopes*, 1978.

85. *Letters to Stopes*: Most are at the Wellcome Institute for the History of Medicine and the British Library. As well as Ruth Hall's selection, op. cit., Lesley A. Hall quoted extensively from the letters in her *Hidden Anxieties: Male Sexuality, 1900–1950*, 1991.

86–7. *Professor Deaking*: *Llanelly Mercury*, 7.2.01.

87. *Strand litigation*: John Peel, 'The Manufacture and Retailing of Contraceptives in England', op. cit.

87. *First advertisement*: ibid.

88. *Lady Barrett*: *Conception Control and Its Effects on the Individual and the Nation*, 1922.

88. *Medical Women's Federation*: *BMJ*, 2.7.21.

88. *Scharlieb letter*: *BMJ*, 16.7.21.

88. *Dundee letter*: 27.8.21.

89. *Halliday Sutherland letter*: 30.7.21.

89. *Lane on doctors*: *BMJ*, 22.7.22, 'Conference on birth control'.

89. *Lane on constipation*: see Alex Comfort, op. cit.

90. *Turner speaks*: *Daily Express*, 12.10.21.

90. *Turner to* BMJ: 30.7.21.

92–3. *Chesser's survey*: *The Sexual, Marital and Family Relationships of the English Woman*, 1956.

93. *Freak parties; dancing craze*: Patrick Balfour, *Society Racket: A Critical Survey of Modern Social Life*, 1934.

93. Daily Mail *report*: ibid.

93. *Raid on the Cursitor*: *Daily Express*, 3.2.25.

94. *The Kit Kat*: Patrick Balfour, op. cit.

94. *Stephen Graham*: the title essay in *London Nights*.

94. Methodist Times: quoted in *VR*, February 1925.

96. *Magnus Hirschfeld*: Charlotte Wolff, *Magnus Hirschfeld: A Portrait of a Pioneer in Sexology*, 1986.

96. *Isherwood's description*: *Christopher and His Kind: 1929–1939*, 1977.

97. *Costler/Koestler*: Arthur Koestler, *The Invisible Writing* (autobiography), 1954.

Chapter 6

99ff. Ulysses *and the authorities*: PRO, HO 144/20071.

101. *Walter Gallichan*: in *A Text-book of Sex Education*.

101. *Manchester Stipendiary*: *VR*, August 1905.

102. *Balzac intercepted*: PRO, HO 45/24805.

104. *The English conscience*: Ivor Montagu, in *Proceedings* of 3rd congress, World League for Sexual Reform, op. cit. The film was *Nju*.

104. *Snails copulating*: ibid. Also forbidden was a scene depicting 'the injection of sperm into sea-water by an echinoderm.'

104. *The reviewer*: Bertram Higgin in the *Spectator*, quoted in *VR*, April 1923.

104. *Lawrence's paintings*: Norman St John-Stevas, *Obscenity and the Law*, 1956.

105. *French police and pubic hair*: *Report* of the Joint Select Committee on Lotteries and Indecent Advertisements, 1908.

105. *Surviving file*: HO 45/13944. The *Daily Telegraph* article was on 4.3.30. It also said, '[Lawrence's] later books and poems were rightly banned by the censor, like the unspeakable pictures which were brazenly exhibited in London last summer.' S.W. Harris minuted, 'If all the critics were to write as plainly and boldly . . . we should have no further cause for anxiety.'

105–6. Sleeveless Errand *prosecution*: *The Times*, 21, 22, 25, 28 February; 5 March. Eric Partridge (1894–1979), the philologist, founded the Scholartis Press in 1927 and ran it for four years

107. *Legal lesbianism*: see Susan S.M. Edwards, *Female Sexuality and the Law*.

107ff. *Radclyffe Hall*: biographical information, Lovat Dickson, *Radclyffe Hall at the Well of Loneliness: A Sapphic Chronicle*, 1975; Una, Lady Troubridge, *The Life and Death of Radclyffe Hall*, 1961; Claudia Stillman Franks, *Beyond the Well of Loneliness: The Fiction of Radclyffe Hall*, 1968.

108–9. *'The Sink of Solitude'*: reproduced in Donald Thomas, *A Long Time Burning: The History of Literary Censorship in England*, 1969.

109–110. *Printing history of* Well of Loneliness: Michael S. Howard, *Jonathan Cape, Publisher*, 1971.

109. *S.W. Harris draws attention*: PRO, HO 45/15727. This is primarily a file about an ephemeral novel of 1928, Compton Mackenzie's *Extraordinary Women*, but has incidental references to *Well of Loneliness*. It is odd that papers about the former should have been retained, while the latter's were pulped; the *Well* prosecution was the most notorious of a novel this century until the *Lady Chatterley* case thirty-odd years later, and the Home Office papers of that case have been destroyed, too. The Director of Public Prosecutions has a *Well of Loneliness* file but was unable to make it available (apart from a transcript of the magistrate's judgement) because 'other departments are involved.'

109. *Hicks, Bodkin, Hailsham and Biron consult*: HO 45/15727, op. cit.

110. *New Statesman*: 25.8.28, op. cit., p. 45.

111. *Harris and the BBFC*: John Trevelyan, *What the Censor Saw*, 1973.

114. Lancet *and Scharlieb on masturbation*: Peter Fryer, *The Birth Controllers*.

114. *Sutherland*: letter to *BMJ*, 30.7.21.

114ff. *The Heinous Sin*: E.H. Hare, 'Masturbatory Insanity: the History of an Idea', *Journal of Mental Science*, January 1962; Alex Comfort, *The Anxiety Makers*, op. cit.; Havelock Ellis, *Studies in the Psychology of Sex*, Vol. 1, 3rd ed., 1913.

116. *Sylvanus Stall*: Patricia J. Campbell, *Sex Education Books for Young Adults 1892–1979*, New York, 1979.

116. *A. Dennison Light*: in *Marriage: Before and After*, price one shilling.

116. *Havelock Ellis*: Vol. 1, op. cit.

117. *Leslie Weatherhead*: *The Mastery of Sex through Psychology and Religion*, 1931.
117. *1949 questionnaire*: the 'Little Kinsey' survey.
119. *Stopes*: *Enduring Passion*.
119. *Guilty letters*: Lesley A. Hall, op. cit.
119. *The vicar*: Ruth Hall, *Dear Dr Stopes*, op. cit.
120. *Exhibit 106*: Gary Cross (ed.), *Worktowners at Blackpool. Mass-Observation and Popular Leisure in the 1930s*, 1991.

Chapter 7

121. Woman's Own: quoted in Terry Jordan, *Agony Columns*, 1988.
122. Woman's Life: ibid.
122–3. Daily Mirror: 22.1.39.
123–4. *Isherwood on Berlin*: *Christopher and His Kind*, op. cit.
124. *Sun Ray case*: VR, October 1926.
124. *Postcard poem*: *Worktowners at Blackpool*, op. cit.
124. *Three million nudists*: Frances and Mason Merrill, *Among the Nudists*, 1931. The authors, a New York couple, were converted to nudism ('earthly paradise') while on holiday in Germany.
124–5. *Koestler's Germany*: *The Invisible Writing*, op. cit.
125. *Hirschfeld and the Nazis*: Charlotte Wolff, op. cit.; Isherwood, op. cit.
125–6. *Sex and the Nazis*: see Hans Peter Bleuel, *Strength through Joy: Sex and Society in Nazi Germany*, 1973.
126. Lebensborn: *Independent* magazine, 11.4.92, and *Forty Minutes*, BBC2, 21.4.92.
126. *Peter Nichols*: 'Naughty But Nice', *Listener*, 16.2.89.
127ff. M-O, 1939: 'Directive' on Age Differences.
128. *Ginger Rogers*: the film actress. Mrs Chamberlain was the Prime Minister's wife.
129ff. *Van de Velde*: see Edward M. Brecher, *The Sex Researchers*.
130. *A former employee*: in an interview, 1977.
132. *Greenwood's initials*: PRO, MH 55/289.
132–3. *Social Hygiene Council and the Ministry*: PRO, MH 55/1371.
133. Veribest *rubber goods*: PRO, HO 45/15753.
134. *Slot-machines*: ibid.
134. *Mrs Booth at the Ministry*: HO 45/24939.
135. *The Fun House*: M-O, 'Worktowners at Blackpool' typescripts.
135. *What the butler saw*: ibid.
136. *Propositions*: Cross, *Worktowners at Blackpool*, op. cit.
136. *Sex in streets, on sands*: ibid.
136–7. Boy: Anthony Burgess, introduction to reissue of the novel, 1990; interview with Mrs Pamela Morris, former Boriswood director, 1990.
137. The Sexual Impulse: Geoffrey Robertson, *Obscenity*, 1979.
138. *Novels left alone*: PRO, HO 45/24939.
138. *Eliot at Home Office*: PRO, HO 144/20071.
138. *Lane and* Ulysses: J.E. Morpurgo, *Allen Lane: King Penguin*, 1979.

138. *Leaving* Ulysses *alone*: HO 144/20071.

138. Men Only: early copies, obviously regarded as hot stuff in 1935, are in the British Library's private case, at Cup. 803.g.1.

139. *Lorant and* Lilliput: Stefan Lorant, *I was Hitler's Prisoner*, 1935; Tom Hopkinson, *Of this Our Time: A Journalist's Story, 1905–50*, 1982.

139. Lilliput: early copies of this, too, are in the private case, at Cup. 701.a.2.

Chapter 8

142. *LRC history*: LRC *Supervisor's Bulletin*, July 1951; interviews with anon.

142. *Latex*: Norman E. Himes, *Medical History of Contraception*, New York, 1936.

143. *Origin of 'Durex'*: interview with Ian Franks, 1990.

143. *Lord Chamberlain's conference*: John Johnston, op. cit.

144. *VD meeting*: M-O, typescript in 'Sexual Behaviour', Box 1.

144. *VD leaflet*: M-O, 'Sexual Behaviour', Box 1.

144. *Ulcers and organs*: Richard Davenport-Hines, op. cit.

145. *Ecclesiastical critics*: Paul Langford Adams, doctoral thesis, 'Health of the State: British and American Public Health Policies in the Depression and World War II', at Wellcome Institute of Medicine.

145. *Government propaganda*: ibid.

145. *VD myths*: M-O, replies to Directive on VD, December 1942.

145. *Little VD from prostitutes*: Paul Langford Adams, op. cit.

145. *1944 survey*: Typescript and reports for 'Sex, Morality and the Birth-rate' (issued 1945, FR 2205).

145–6. *Mrs A and other interviews*: M-O, replies to Directive, April 1944, 'Sexual morality and effects of recent developments'.

146–7. Learning about Sex: BBC Home Service, 16.3.44, No. 10 in 'To Start You Talking'. Script edited by Mary Somerville.

148ff. *Kinsey's life*: Wardell B. Pomeroy, *Dr Kinsey and the Institute for Sex Research*, 1972.

152–3. *M-O survey*: reports and typescripts in 'Little Kinsey' files.

153. *Five articles*: 3.7.49 to 31.7.49.

153. *Home Office papers*: PRO, HO 302/10.

155. *'Feelies for feelies'*: 'Close Relationships' Directive, 1990.

156. *Alan Turing*: Andrew Hodges, *Alan Turing: the Enigma*, 1983.

156. *Fyfe quoted*: Jeffrey Weeks, *Coming Out: Homosexual Politics in Britain, from the Nineteenth Century to the Present*, 1977.

157. *Kinsey in London*: Wardell B. Pomeroy, op. cit.

157. *The 1954 trial*: Peter Wildeblood, *Against the Law*, 1955.

157. *Wolfenden's memoirs*: *Turning Points*, 1976.

157. *1942 trial*: of Dr Eustace Chesser, at the central criminal court; the judge was the Common Serjeant, Cecil Whiteley, KC.

158. *Lord Snow*: quoted by Davenport-Hines, op. cit.

158. *Wolfenden explains*: eg. *American Journal of Psychiatry*, December 1968.

159. *Angus Wilson blackmailed*: 'Angus Wilson – Skating on Thin Ice', *Bookmark*, BBC2, 24.10.91.

159. *Wilson and* Monitor: Paul Ferris, *Sir Huge: The Life of Huw Wheldon,* 1990, where Wilson, then alive, was not identified.

160. *Lorry girls:* PRO, MH 55/1371.

160. *The madam of Streatham:* Paul Bailey, *An English Madam,* 1982.

161. *Bessie and others:* (ed.) C.H. Rolph, *Women of the Streets: A Sociological Study of the Common Prostitute,* 1955. Commissioned by the British Social Biology Council.

161–2. *1958 article:* 'Prostitution Notebook: So Many Varieties in "The Game"', *Observer,* 30.11.58.

162. *Duke Street brothel: Paddington News,* 14.5.38.

162. *Harrisson on prostitutes:* M-O, at FR 2465, typescript of 'Article for Polemic'.

163fn. *Geoffrey Robertson: Obscenity,* op. cit.

Chapter 9

166. *Wells Street magistrate:* in an interview.

167. *Identifying Ashbee:* G. Legman, Introduction to Patrick J. Kearney, op. cit.

167. *'The Pin-Up King':* BL, PC 16.m.18.

167. *Janson/Crawley:* Norman St John-Stevas, op. cit.

168. *Home Office list:* PRO, HO 45/24972.

168. Basinfuls of Fun: BL, Cup 701.b.19.

169. *Man in his thirties:* M-O, 'Sexual Behaviour, 1939–50', Box 15, File E.

170. *BBFC and nudity:* John Trevelyan, op. cit.

170. *American nudist films:* a 1990 episode of *The Incredibly Strange Film Show,* Channel 4, presented by Jonathan Ross.

172. *Amis quoted: Time Out,* 2.3.88.

173. Decameron *file:* PRO, HO 302/10.

173. *John Gale article: Observer,* 1.8.54.

175. *Lane and* Lady Chatterley: J.E. Morpurgo, op. cit.

175ff. *DPP letters and other* Lady Chatterley *papers:* Crown Prosecution Service, DPP 2/3077, parts 1–4.

176. *72 defence witnesses:* Michael Rubinstein, 'Not only Sex in the Jury Room', *The Author,* Winter 1990.

178. *Leavis quoted: Daily Mail,* 17.8.60.

178. *Three women jurors:* Geoffrey Robertson, op. cit.

179. *Connolly and Weidenfeld:* Barbara Skelton, *Weep No More,* 1989.

180. *C.H. Rolph:* in *The Trial of Lady Chatterley,* 1961, his editing of the transcript.

181. *Lord Hutchinson:* in a letter to the author, 31.12.90.

181. *Sole survivor:* PRO, HO 302/11.

Chapter 10

187. *Whitehouse on manipulation:* Paul Ferris, 'Mrs Whitehouse and the Great TV Plot', *Observer* magazine, 10.11.68; in an interview, 28.3.77.

187. *Television ruling:* Minute from Director of Television, Kenneth Adam, to Controller of Programmes, 20.11.65: 'This is just to confirm that DG has

ruled that we should lay off inviting Mrs Whitehouse and Mrs Fox on to our screen *for the time being*. They will of course continue to make the News on their merits, if any.' BBC Written Archives, T16/585. Mrs Avril Fox had started a group called 'Cosmo' to oppose the Clean-up TV Campaign.

188. *Boots and condoms*: John Peel, 'Manufacture and Retailing of Contraceptives', op. cit.

189ff. *The Abortion Wars*: I still have files of interviews and other material, collected in the 60s and 70s for articles and a book (*The Nameless: Abortion in Britain Today*, 1966), and use these throughout.

189. *McCardie*: Mr Justice McCardie at Leeds, 1931. Quoted in Hindell and Simms, *Abortion Law Reformed*, 1971.

190. *1938 case*: a surgeon, Aleck Bourne, aborted the pregnancy of a girl aged fourteen who had been raped by two soldiers. He was charged with criminal abortion but acquitted. Bourne became a reluctant hero of the reformers, and kept his distance from them.

192. *The picnic basket*: in an interview, June 1965.

192. *Elephant and Castle*: July 1965.

193. *Baird on trawlermen*: in an interview, July 1965.

194. *Diggory in public*: at an FPA conference, 'Abortion in Britain', April 1966.

194. *Chesser's childhood*: his son, Dr Edward Chesser, in an interview, December 1990.

195. *The expert witness*: see Geoffrey Robertson, op. cit., on *R v Gold*, pages 39–40.

198. *Abse's autobiography*: *Private Member*, 1973.

199–209. *Family planning in the 60s and 70s*: author's files of interviews and other material

200. *'We all looked at one another'*: Family Planning in the Sixties, report of an FPA working party, 1963.

200. *'When I worked in a branch'*: former FPA official, in an interview, October 1990.

202. Daily Mirror: 15.11.63.

202ff. *Developing the pill*: J.M. McGarry, 'The discovery of the contraceptive pill', *British Journal of Sexual Medicine*, January 1987; Kenneth S. Davis, 'The story of the pill', *American Heritage*, Aug/Sept 1978; M.C. Chang, 'Development of the oral contraceptives', *American Journal of Obstetrics and Gynaecology*, 15.9.78.

203. *Wells and Sanger*: Anthony West, op. cit.

204. *Greer*: Sex and Destiny.

204. *Helen Brook and the clinics*: Mrs Brook interviewed for *In the Club* (Channel 4, 1988), transcript at Television History Centre, London; also in an interview, 26.4.66.

210. *'The most profound change'*: Lawrence Stone, *Road to Divorce: England 1530–1987*, 1990.

211. *Catullus*: Carmina, lxiv, 11, 376–8.

211. *Arthur Thomson*: 'Problems Involved in the Congress of the Sexes in Man', *BMJ*, 7.1.22.

212. *Mills & Boon style-sheet*: quoted by Christina Koning, 'Labour of Love', *Time Out*, 20.4.88.

212. *Clerkenwell magistrate*: *Daily Mail*, 14.2.21. His name was Symmons.

213. *Stopes and Lord X*: *Enduring Passion*. op. cit.

214ff. *Divorce Bills*: see Peter G. Richards, *Parliament and Conscience*, 1970.

216. *Hailsham on divorce*: quoted in Lawrence Stone, op. cit.

Chapter 11

218ff. *Sixties radicals*: Anderson and Zinsser, *A History of Their Own*, Vol. II, 1990; Angela Neustatter, *Hyenas in Petticoats*, 1989; Margaret Walters (presenter), *Wake Up Sister!*, BBC Radio 4, February 1988.

220. *Rennie Macandrew*: *Encyclopaedia of Sex and Love Technique*.

221. *Bob and Tina*: the *News of the World* carried a feature, 'Sexperts who trade on misery', on 23.5.82, by Tina Dalgleish and Bob Strange. This reported the encounter with Cole under a subheading, 'Touching ways of Dr Cole', who was pictured with his third wife sitting on his lap. The article said that he touched Dalgleish to test the skin-response machine, 'then lay by her side. Later he asked her to remove her trousers. She refused.' Cole, described as 'Britain's best-known sexpert', was treated politely by tabloid standards. His charges were said to be 'by far the most reasonable at £10 per session.'

222. *Miller and Burroughs*: Calder in an interview, 7.9.90.

224. *'A blow for righteousness'*: in an interview, 30.10.90.

227–8. *The pig woman*: William Levy (ed.) *Wet Dreams*, 1973, magazine describing the 1971 *Suck* film festival, BL, P.C. 16.m.24.

228. *Mary Whitehouse*: in *Whatever Happened to Sex?*, 1977.

229. *'A taboo word'*: BBC Written Archives, television programme review board, 17.11.65.

229. *Ned Sherrin*: in 'Sex on Television', *Signals*, Channel 4, 2.11.88.

229. *Mortimer's opinion*: Kathleen Tynan, *The Life of Kenneth Tynan*, 1988.

229. *A.P. Herbert*: quoted in the Introduction to *Pornography: the Longford Report*, 1972.

231. People *exposé*: 6.2.72, 'Exposing the pornography scandal in Britain,' and subsequent issues.

231. *Police corruption*: Cox, Shirley and Short, *The Fall of Scotland Yard*, 1977; Ben Whitaker, 'The case of the bent policemen', *New Society*, 17.2.77.

232–3. *Lindsay on schoolgirls*: in an interview, 31.3.77.

233. *Lindsay on Ashworth*: ibid.

234. *The joke*: John Mortimer, *Clinging to the Wreckage*, 1982.

235. *'A lot of old rubbish'*: interview with Arabella and Colin, 1977.

Chapter 12

236. *Nurse Phyllis*: in an interview, 30.3.77.

237ff. Sex in Our Time: interviews with Udi Eichler and others at Thames Television, 1.3.77 and 15.3.77.

239–40. *Grapevine*: in various interviews, March 1977.

240. *Elaine*: in three interviews, March and April 1977.

242–3. *Valerie Riches*: in an interview, 29.3.77.

243. *Mrs Dallas; the Nuffield official*: in interviews, March 1977.

Chapter 13

248–9. *London prostitutes*: in interviews with police, 1990.

251. *David Sullivan*: in an interview, 21.2.90.

251. *Peter Kay*: in an interview, 16.2.90.

253. *Hames*: Daily Mail, 15.12.90.

254. *Rob Parsons*: in an interview, 26.11.90.

256. *Howarth*: Hansard, 3.4.87, col 1332.

258. *Customs instruction*: C4–34, Indecent articles, Amendment No. 10, June 1978.

258–9. *The inflatable dolls*: 'Indecency and obscenity: the view from Europe', *New Law Journal*, 19.1.90; a Customs official and David Sullivan, in interviews, 1990.

259ff. *Scala*: in interviews, March 1990.

Chapter 14

264. *Praying before intercourse*: quoted in Tom Cullen, *The Prostitutes' Padre: The story of the notorious Rector of Stiffkey*. Davidson was a first-class publicist who gave much pleasure to newspaper readers in the thirties. He argued his innocence at length and took to money-raising protests and stunts, exhibiting himself in a barrel on the front at Blackpool, then appearing in a lion's cage at Skegness for the 1937 summer season. A lion called Freddie pounced when the clergyman told him to get a move on. As the dying Davidson was carried to safety, he is said to have murmured, 'Phone the London papers, we still have time to make the first editions.'

265. *Whitehouse on gradualism*: in an interview, 28.3.77.

265. *CARE and oral sex*: letter to the author from Nigel Williams, campaigns director, 9.1.91.

266. *Waiting a couple of years*: in an interview with Anna Raeburn, 31.3.77.

266. *NME*: examples from 19.3.88 and 16.4.88.

267. *Lesbianism in TV serials*: Oranges Are Not the Only Fruit, from the novel by Jeanette Winterson; *Portrait of a Marriage*, from the book by Nigel Nicolson.

269. *1984 study*: Reading and Wiest, 'An analysis of self-reported sexual behavior in a sample of normal males', *Archives of Sexual Behavior* (USA), Vol. 13, No. 1.

270. *Bloch*: A History of English Sexual Morals, tr. W.H. Forstern, 1936.

271. *1985 study*: Breslow, Evans and Langley, 'On the prevalence and roles of females in the sadomasochistic subculture: report of an empirical study', *Archives of Sexual Behaviour*, Vol. 14, No. 4.

272. *Vaughan's journals*: in Malcolm Yorke, *Keith Vaughan: His life and work*, 1990.

273–4. *Gosselin*: Sexual Variations: Fetishism, sado-masochism and transvestism (with Glenn Wilson), 1980.

279. *Burchill*: 'Why we must keep all the sniggering in sex', *Mail on Sunday*, 10.4.88.
280. *Dworkin*: *Intercourse*, 1987.
284. *Leading case*: R v Donovan.

Chapter 15
290. *Freda Parker*: in an interview, 21.3.77.
290–91. *Miss E*: interviewed for *In the Club* (Channel 4, 1988), transcript at Television History Centre, London.
291. *Generation of brats*: *Spoilt Brats*, report by Gold Greenlees Trott, 1990.
292. *CARE booklet*: *Towards a New Sexual Revolution*, by Christians in Education and the Order of Christian Unity.
292. *Doreen Massey*: 'School Sex Education: Knitting without a Pattern?', *Health Education Journal*, Vol. 49, No. 3.
293. *'Not blank slates'*: in an interview, 17.4.91.
293. *'Where we've made the mistake'*: in an interview, 15.11.90.
295. New Statesman: 29.6.90, 'Dangerous Liaisons'.
295. *Man from Hampshire*: *Call Nick Ross*, 12.1.88.
296. Reviewer: Peter Parker, 'Beautiful uptown Firbank', *Listener*, 17.3.88.
296. *3000 partners*: M-O, 'Close Relationships' survey.
297. *AIDS phone-in*: BBC Radio 4, *Tuesday Call*, 3.12.91.
297–8. *Bishop of Chester*: BBC1, *Heart of the Matter*, 28.2.88.
298. *The stripper*: Channel 4, *Sex Talk*, 31.10.90.
300. *'Francesca'*: in an interview, 1991.

Select Bibliography

Abse, Leo, *Private Member* (Macdonald, 1973).

Addison, Paul, *Now the War is Over: A social history of Britain 1945–51* (BBC and Cape, 1985).

Anon, *Looks Can Kill: Pornographic Business* (I-Spy Productions, Leeds).

Anon, *The Pearl: A journal of facetive and voluptuous reading* (New York, Ballantine Books, 1978).

Allen, Mary S., *The Pioneer Policewoman*, edited and arranged by Julie Helen Heyneman, (Chatto, 1925).

Allen, Mary S., *Lady in Blue* (Stanley Paul, 1936).

Allen, Mary S. and Julie Helen Heyneman, *Woman at the Cross Roads* (Unicorn Press, 1934).

Allsop, Kenneth, *The Angry Decade: A survey of the cultural revolt of the nineteen-fifties* (Peter Owen, 1958).

Anderson, Bonnie S. and Judith P. Zinsser, *A History of Their Own: Women in Europe from prehistory to the present*, Vol. 2 (Penguin, 1990).

Baden-Powell, R., *Rovering to Success: A book of life-sport for young men* (Herbert Jenkins, 1922).

Baden-Powell, R., *Lessons from the Varsity of Life* (Pearson, 1933).

Bailey, Paul, *An English Madam: The life and work of Cynthia Payne* (Cape, 1982).

Balfour, Patrick, *Society Racket: A critical survey of modern social life* (Bernhard Tauchnitz, Leipzig, 1934).

Barrett, Florence E., *Conception Control and its effects on the individual and the nation* (John Murray, 1922).

Berman, Joyce Avrech, *The Healing Imagination of Olive Schreiner* (U. of Massachussetts, Amherst, 1989).

Bleuel, Hans Peter, *Strength through Joy: Sex and society in Nazi Germany* (Secker, 1973).

Bloch, Ivan, *A History of English Sexual Morals*, tr. by William H. Forstern (Francis Aldor, 1936).

Bond, Brian and Ian Roy, ed., *War and Society: A yearbook of military history*, Vol. 2 (Croom Helm, 1977).

Borden, Mary, *The Technique of Marriage* (Heinemann, 1933).

Brecher, Edward M., *The Sex Researchers* (Deutsch).

Brentford, Viscount (Joynson Hicks), *Do We Need a Censor?* (Faber, 1929).

Bristow, Edward J., *Vice and Vigilance: Purity Movements in Britain Since 1700* (Dublin, Gill and Macmillan, 1977).

Brome, Vincent, *Havelock Ellis, Philosopher of Sex* (Routledge, 1979).

Brown, Ivor, *I Commit to the Flames* (Hamish Hamilton, 1934).

Burchill, Julie, *Ambition* (Bodley Head, 1989).

Calder-Marshall, Arthur, *Havelock Ellis* (Rupert Hart-Davies, 1959).

Campbell, Patricia J., *Sex Education Books for Young Adults 1892–1979* (R.R. Bowker, New York and London).

Camp, William, *Prospects of Love* (Longman, 1957).

Camp, William, *The Ruling Passion* (MacGibbon & Kee, 1959).

Chance, Janet, *The Cost of English Morals* (Noel Douglas, 1931).

Chesser, Dr Eustace, *Love Without Fear: A guide to sex technique* (Arrow, 1970, first published 1941).

Chesser, Dr Eustace, *The Sexual, Marital and Family Relationships of the English Woman* (Hutchinson Medical, 1956).

Chesser, Dr Eustace, *Sex and the Married Woman* (W.H. Allen, 1968).

Cleland, John, *Fanny Hill: Memoirs of a woman of pleasure* (Mayflower, 1970).

Cole, Martin, and Wendy Dryden, ed., *Sex Therapy in Britain* (Open University, 1988).

Comfort, Alex, *The Anxiety Makers: Some curious preoccupations of the medical profession* (Nelson, 1967).

Comfort, Alex, *The Joy of Sex* (Quartet Books, first published 1972).

Costello, John, *Love, Sex and War: Changing values 1939–45* (Collins, 1985).

Creigton, Louise, *The Social Disease and How to Fight It: A Rejoinder* (Longman Green, 1914).

Cross, Gary, ed., *Worktowners at Blackpool: Mass-Observation and popular leisure in the 1930s* (Routledge, 1991).

Crozier, Brig-Gen. F.P., *A Brass Hat in No Man's Land* (Cape, 1930).

Cullen, Tom, *The Prostitutes' Padre: The story of the notorious Rector of Stiffkey* (Bodley Head).

Cumberbatch, Guy, and Dennis Howitt, *A Measure of Uncertainty: The effects of the mass media* (John Libby, 1989).

Davenport-Hines, Richard, *Sex, Death and Punishment: Attitudes to sex and sexuality in Britain since the Renaissance* (Collins, 1990).

Denning, Lord, *Lord Denning's Report* (HMSO, Cmnd 2152, 1963).

Dickson, Lovat, *H.G. Wells: His turbulent life and times* (New York, Atheneum, 1969).

Dickson, Lovat, *Radclyffe Hall at the Well of Loneliness: A Sapphic chronicle* (Collins, 1975).

Dworkin, Andrea, *Intercourse* (Secker, 1987).

Dworkin, Andrea, *Mercy* (Secker, 1990).

Edwards, Susan S.M., *Female Sexuality and the Law* (Oxford, Martin Robertson).

Ellis, Edith, *Seaweed: A Cornish Idyll* (University Press, Watford, 1898).

Ellis, Havelock, *Studies in the Psychology of Sex* (Philadelphia, F.A. Davis, Vols 1–6, 1900–1910; Vol. 7, 1928).

Ellmann, Richard ed., *Selected Letters of James Joyce* (Faber, 1975).

Enser, A.G.S., *A Subject Bibliography of the First World War: Books in English 1914–1978* (Deutsch, 1979).

Ensor, R.C.K., *England 1870–1914* (OUP, 1936).

Feminist Anti-Censorship Taskforce, *Caught Looking: Feminism, pornography & censorship* (Seattle, Real Comet Press, 1988).

Ferris, Paul, *The Nameless: Abortion in Britain Today* (Hutchinson, 1966).

Ferris, Paul, *The House of Northcliffe: The Harmsworths of Fleet Street* (Weidenfeld, 1971).

Ferris, Paul, *Sir Huge: The life of Huw Wheldon* (Michael Joseph, 1990).

Fielding, Daphne, *The Duchess of Jermyn Street: The life and good times of Rosa Lewis of the Cavendish Hotel* (Eyre & Spottiswoode, 1964).

Finch, B.E. and Hugh Green, *Contraception Through the Ages* (Peter Owen, 1963).

First, Ruth and Ann Scott, *Olive Schreiner* (Deutsch, 1980).

Fischer, H.C. and Dr E.X. Dubois, *Sexual Life During the World War* (Francis Aldor, 1937).

FitzGibbon, Theodora, *With Love*, autobiography (Pan, 1983).

Flexner, Abraham, *Prostitution in Europe* (New York, Century, 1914).

Forel, August, *The sexual question: A scientific, psychological, hygienic and sociological study for the cultured classes*. English adaptation by C.F. Marshall (Rebman Ltd, 1908).

'Four Chaplains to the Forces', *A Corner-stone of Reconstruction: A book on working for social purity among men* (SPCK, 1919).

Franks, Claudia Stillman, *Beyond the Well of Loneliness: The fiction of Radclyffe Hall* (Avebury, 1968).

Freeman, Gillian, *The Undergrowth of Literature* (Nelson, 1967).

Friday, Nancy, *My Secret Garden: Women's sexual fantasies* (Virago, 1975).

Friday, Nancy, *Men in Love: Men's sexual fantasies: the triumph of love over rage* (Hutchinson, 1980).

Friday, Nancy, *Women on Top* (Hutchinson, 1991).

Fryer, Peter, *Mrs Grundy: Studies in English prudery* (Dobson Books, 1963).

Fulford, Roger, *Votes for Women: The story of a struggle* (Faber).

Furlong, Monica, *With Love to the Church* (Hodder, 1965).

Gallichan, Walter M., *A Text-book of Sex Education: For parents and teachers* (T. Werner Laurie, 1919).

Gallichan, Walter M., *The Poison of Prudery: An historical survey* (1929).

Gillis, John R., *For Better, for Worse: British marriages 1600 to the present* (OUP, 1985).

Glyn, Anthony, *Elinor Glyn* (Hutchinson, 1955).

Glyn, Elinor, *Three Weeks* (Duckworth, 1907).

Glyn, Elinor, *Romantic Adventure*, autobiography (Nicholson and Watson, 1936).

Gosselin, Chris and Glenn Wilson, *Sexual Variations: Fetishism, sado-masochism and transvestism* (Faber, 1980).

Graham, Stephen, *London Nights* (Hurst and Blackett).

Graves, Robert and Alan Hodge, *The Long Weekend: A social history of Great Britain 1918–1939* (Faber, 1940).

Greer, Germaine, *Sex and Destiny: The politics of human fertility* (Secker, 1984).

Griffith, Edward F., *Modern Marriage* (Gollancz, 1935).

Haire, Norman, *Hymen, or The Future of Marriage* (Kegan Paul, Trench, Trubner, 1928).

Haire, Norman, ed., *Encyclopaedia of Sexual Knowledge* (Francis Aldor, 1934).

Hall, Lesley A., *Hidden Anxieties: Male sexuality, 1900–1950* (Polity Press, Cambridge, 1991).

Hall, Radclyffe, *The Well of Loneliness* (Cape, 1928).

Hall, Ruth, *Marie Stopes* (Deutsch)

Hall, Ruth, *Dear Dr Stopes: Sex in the 1920s* (Deutsch, 1978).

Hanley, James, *Boy* (Boriswood, 1931).

Harrison, Michael, *Rosa* (Peter Davies).

Hebditch, David and Nick Anning, *Porn Gold: Inside the pornography business* (Faber, 1988).

Herbert, Mrs S., *Sex-Lore: A primer on courtship, marriage and parenthood* (A & C Black, 1918).

Hillier, Bevis, *Young Betjeman* (John Murray, 1988).

Himes, Norman E., *Medical History of Contraception* (1936, reprinted by Gamut Press, New York, 1963).

Hindell, Keith and Madeleine Simms, *Abortion Law Reformed* (Peter Owen, 1971).

Hirschfeld, Magnus, *The Sexual History of the World War* (Cadillac Publishing, New York, c. 1945).

Hite, Shere, *The Hite Report on Female Sexuality* (Pandora Press, 1989).

Hite, Shere, *Women and Love: A cultural revolution in progress* (Penguin, 1989).

Hodges, Andrew, *Alan Turing: the Enigma* (Burnett Books, 1983).

Hopkinson, Tom, *Of This Our Time: A journalist's story, 1905–50* (Hutchinson, 1982).

Hopkirk, Mary, *Nobody Wanted Sam: The story of the unwelcomed child 1530–1948* (John Murray).

Howard, Michael S., *Jonathan Cape, Publisher* (Cape, 1971).

Humphries, Steve, *A Secret World of Sex: Forbidden fruit: the British experience 1900–1950* (Sidgwick & Jackson, 1988).

Hunter, T.A.A., ed., *Newnes Manual of Sex and Marriage* (Newnes, 1964).

Hutton, Isabel Emslie, *The Hygiene of Marriage* (Heinemann Medical, 1923; 8th edition, 1940).

Huxley, Aldous, *Brave New World* (Chatto, 1932).

Hyde, H. Montgomery, *A Tangled Web: Sex scandals in British politics and society* (Constable, 1986).

Irving, Clive, Ron Hall and Jeremy Wallington, *Scandal '63: A study of the Profumo affair* (Heinemann, 1963).

Isherwood, Christopher, *Christopher and His Kind 1929–1939* (Eyre Methuen, 1977).

James, Norah C., *Sleeveless Errand* (Paris, Henry Babou and Jack Kahane, 1929).

John, Tabitha, *Tabitha: The story of a Llanelli character* (Gwerin, Llanelli, 1979).

Johnston, Dafydd, ed. and tr. *Medieval Welsh Erotic Poetry* (Cardiff, Tafol, 1991).

Johnston, John, *The Lord Chamberlain's Blue Pencil* (Hodder, 1990).

Jordan, Terry, *Agony Columns* (Macdonald Optima, 1988).

Joyce, James, *Ulysses* (Bodley Head, 1937).

Kauffmann, Stanley, *The Philanderer* (Secker, 1953).

Kearney, Patrick J., *The Private Case: An annotated bibliography of the private case erotica collection in the British (Museum) Library*. Introduction by G. Legman (Jay Landesman, 1981).

Kennedy, Ludovic, *The Trial of Stephen Ward* (Gollancz, 1964).

Kent, Susan Kingsley, *Sex and Suffrage in Britain 1860–1914* (Princeton University Press).

Kinsey, A.C., and others, *Sexual Behaviour in the Human Male* (W.B. Saunders Co., Philadelphia and London, 1948).

Kinsey, A.C., *Sexual Behaviour in the Human Female* (1953).

Koestler, Arthur, *The Invisible Writing* (Collins with Hamish Hamilton, 1954).

Krafft-Ebing, Richard von, *Psychopathia Sexualis* (Mayflower-Dell, 1967).

Lawrence, D.H., *Pornography and Obscenity* (Criterion Miscellany – No. 5, Faber, 1928).

Lawrence, D.H., *Lady Chatterley's Lover* (Penguin, 1960).

Lawson, Annette, *Adultery: An analysis of love and betrayal* (OUP, 1990).

Lee, Carol, *The Ostrich Position: Sex, schooling and mystification* (Unwin Paperbacks).

Leonard, Diana, *Sex & Generation: A study of courtship and weddings* (Tavistock, 1980).

Light, A Dennison, *Marriage: Before and After* (Health & Vim Publishing Co.).

Longford, Lord, ed., *Pornography: The Longford Report* (Coronet, 1972).

Lorant, Stefan, *I Was Hitler's Prisoner* (Penguin, 1939).

Macandrew, Rennie, *Life-Long Love: Healthy sex and marriage* (Wales Publishing Co., 1938).

Macandrew, Rennie, *Encyclopaedia of Sex and Love Technique* (Wales Publishing Co., 1941).

McGregor, O.R., *Divorce in England: A centenary study* (Heinemann, 1957).

Mackenzie, Compton, *Extraordinary Women: Theme and variations* (Martin Secker, 1927).

Mackenzie, Compton, *Vestal Fires* (Chatto 1964, first published 1927).

Mackenzie, Norman and Jeanne, *The Time Traveller: The life of H.G. Wells* (Weidenfeld, 1973).

Mangan, J.A., and James Walvin, ed., *Manliness and Morality: Middle-class masculinity in Britain and America 1800–1940* (Manchester University Press, 1987).

Mansfield, Penny and Jean Collard, *The Beginning of the Rest of Your Life? A portrait of newly-wed marriage* (Macmillan, 1988).

March, Norah H., *Towards Racial Health* (George Routledge, 1915).

Masters, Anthony, *Rosa Lewis: An exceptional Edwardian* (Weidenfeld, 1977).

Merrill, Frances and Mason, *Among the Nudists* (Noel Douglas, 1931).

Mitchell, David, *The Fighting Pankhursts: A study in tenacity* (Cape).

Mitchell, David, *Queen Christabel: A biography of Christabel Pankhurst* (Macdonald and Jane's).

Mitchell, David, *Women on the Warpath: The story of the women of the First World War* (Cape).

Montgomery, John, *The Twenties: An informal social history* (Allen & Unwin).

Morpurgo, J.E., *Allen Lane: King Penguin* (Hutchinson, 1979).

Mort, Frank, *Dangerous Sexualities: Medico-moral politics in England since 1830* (Routledge).

Mortimer, John, *Clinging to the Wreckage* (Weidenfeld, 1982).

Neustatter, Angela, *Hyenas in Petticoats: A look at twenty years of feminism* (Harrap, 1989).

Pankhurst, Christabel, *The Great Scourge and How to End It* (London, E. Pankhurst, Lincoln's Inn House, 1913).

Pearsall, Ronald, *The Worm in the Bud: The world of Victorian sexuality* (Weidenfeld, 1969).

Pillay, A.P., and Albert Ellis, ed., *Sex, Society and the Individual* (selected papers from *Marriage Hygiene* and the *International Journal of Sexology* (Bombay, International Journal of Sexology).

Pomeroy, Wardell B., *Dr Kinsey and the Institute for Sex Research* (Nelson, 1972).

Priestley, J.B., *The Edwardians* (Heinemann, 1970).

Raeburn, Antonia, *The Militant Suffragettes* (Michael Joseph).

Raphael, Frederic, *Darling* (Fontana, 1965).

Richards, Peter G., *Parliament and Conscience* (Allen & Unwin, 1970).

Robertson, Geoffrey, *Obscenity: An account of censorship laws and their enforcement in England and Wales* (Weidenfeld, 1979).

Rolph, C.H., ed., *Women of the streets: A sociological study of the common prostitute* (Published for the British Social Biology Council, Secker, 1955).

Rolph, C.H., ed., *The Trial of Lady Chatterley: Regina v. Penguin Books Ltd* (Penguin, 1961).

Rolph, C.H., *Books in the Dock* (Deutsch, 1969).

Rose, Andrew, *Scandal at the Savoy* (Bloomsbury, 1991).

Rout, Ettie A., *The Morality of Birth Control* (John Lane, the Bodley Head, 1925).

Schofield, Michael, *The Sexual Behaviour of Young People* (Longman, 1964).

Schofield, Michael, *Promiscuity* (Gollancz, 1976).

St John Stevas, Norman, *Obscenity and the Law* (Secker, 1956).

Sanders, Pete and Liz Swinden, *Knowing Me, Knowing You* (Cambridge, Learning Development Aids, 1990).

Selby, Hubert, *Last Exit to Brooklyn* (John Calder, 1966).

Shapiro, Rose, *Contraception: A practical and political guide* (Virago, 1987).

Shilts, Randy, *And the Band Played On: Politics, People, and the AIDS epidemic* (Penguin, 1988).

Skelton, Barbara, *Weep No More* (Hamish Hamilton, 1989).

Smith, David C., *H.G. Wells: Desperately mortal* (Yale University Press, 1986).

Stone, Lawrence, *Road to Divorce: England 1530–1987* (OUP, 1990).

Stopes, Marie Carmichael, *Married Love: A new contribution to the solution of sex difficulties* (G.P. Putnam, 1918).

Stopes, Marie, *Wise Parenthood: The treatise on birth control for married people* (Putnam, 1918).

Stopes, Marie, *Contraception: Its theory, history and practice: A manual for the medical and legal professions* (John Bale, Sons & Danielsson, 1923).

Stopes, Marie, *Enduring Passion* (Putnam, 1928).

Szasz, Thomas, *Sex: Frauds, Facts and Follies* (Basil Blackwell, 1981).

Taylor, G. Rattray, *Sex in History* (Thames and Hudson, 1953).

Tenenbaum, Joseph, *The Riddle of sex: The medical and social aspects of sex, love and marriage*. Introduction by Vera Brittain. (Routledge, 1930).

Thomas, Donald, *A Long Time Burning: The history of literary censorship in England* (Routledge, 1969).

Thompson, Charles, *Manhood: The facts of life presented to men* (Health Promotion Ltd, revised edition, 1919).

Thompson, W. (of the Dept of Sociology, Reading University), J. Annetts and others, *Soft-Core: A content analysis of legally available pornography in Great Britain 1968–1990* (1990, no publisher shown; the report was funded by 'GJW Government Relations Ltd').

Trevelyan, John, *What the Censor Saw* (Michael Joseph, 1973).

Troubridge, Lady Una, *The Life and Death of Radclyffe Hall* (Hammond, Hammond & Co., 1961).

Tynan, Kathleen, *The Life of Kenneth Tynan* (Methuen, 1988).

Van de Velde, Th. H., *Ideal Marriage: Its physiology and technique* (Heinemann Medical, 1928, and subsequent editions).

Watson, Revd J.B.S., *Formation of Character* (H.R. Allenson, 1908).

Weatherhead, Leslie D., *The Mastery of Sex through psychology and religion* (Student Christian Movement, 1931).

Weeks, Jeffrey, *Coming Out: Homosexual politics in Britain, from the nineteenth century to the present* (Quartet, 1977).

Weeks, Jeffrey, *Sex, Politics and Society: The regulation of sexuality since 1800* (Longman, 1981).

Webb, Peter, *The Erotic Arts* (Secker, 1975).

Wells, G.P., ed., *H.G. Wells in Love: Postscript to an experiment in autobiography* (Faber, 1984).

Wells, H.G., *Anticipations* (Chapman & Hall, 1901).

Wells, H.G., *Ann Veronica* (Fisher Unwin, 1909).

West, Anthony, *H.G. Wells: Aspects of a life* (Hutchinson, 1984).

Whitehouse, Mary, *Whatever Happened to Sex?* (Wayland Publishers, Hove, 1977).

Wildeblood, Peter, *Against the Law* (Weidenfeld, 1955).

Williams, Bernard (chairman), *Report of the Committee on Obscenity and Film Censorship* (HMSO, Cmnd 7772, 1979).

Willis, W.N., *Western Men with Eastern Morals* (Stanley Paul, 1913).

Wilson, Colin, *The Misfits: A study of sexual outsiders* (Grafton, 1988).

Wolfenden, John, *Turning Points: The memoirs of Lord Wolfenden* (Bodley Head, 1976).

Wolff, Charlotte, *Magnus Hirschfeld: A portrait of a pioneer in sexology* (Quartet, 1986).

Yorke, Malcolm, *Keith Vaughan: His life and work* (Constable, 1990).

Zahavi, Helen, *Dirty Weekend* (Macmillan, 1991).

Ziegler, Philip, *King Edward VIII: The official biography* (Collins, 1990).

Index